Smoke Screen
Elin Barnes

This is a work of fiction. Names, characters, organizations, places, events, and incidents are either products of the author's imagination or are used fictitiously.

Published by Paperless Reads.

www.elinbarnes.com

ISBN 978-0-9899880-3-2

Cover design by Lisa Fitzpatrick.

Printed in the United States of America.

*To my mom, who sticks by me, supports me, loves me,
doesn't let me give up, and always tells me when I've whined
enough. I couldn't have done this without you.*

CHAPTER 1

Monday

Ethan Mitchell pulled the gas mask over his face and watched his crew do the same. The light rail came to a stop, and the sun reflected on the sliding doors as they opened. One passenger exited. The eight men came out of hiding and got in. As the doors closed, they grabbed the canisters hooked to their belts and yanked the pins.

It took just a second for the gas grenades to start spewing gray smoke inside the Silicon Valley train. Nobody had a chance to escape.

Most people fell forward or to their side. A few dropped on the floor. Ethan stepped over two bodies on his way toward the one person he cared about. His men held their positions by the doors. Ethan grabbed the tall black man who was passed out in the middle of the car, threw him over his shoulder and moved to the closest exit as the train started slowing down. When they reached the next station and the doors opened, nine men left as stealthily as the eight had come in just a few minutes earlier.

CHAPTER 2

Specialty's Café was quiet. The lunch crowd had dissipated a while ago. Darcy Lynch sat across the table from Saffron. He leaned over and put his hand on hers. She wrapped her long fingers around it. Her smile reached her eyes, and he felt a rush of warmth fill his chest.

"I'm very happy you finally decided to name your dog," she said. "Shelby suits her, even though it's also the name of your car."

"It's not the name of my car. It's the model." Darcy teased her.

"Well, excuse me." She stuck her tongue out.

He leaned back and scratched his left temple.

"Does it still hurt?" she asked, looking at his eye.

He blinked a few times. "It's more a reflex than anything else." He crossed his arms.

"Do you hate him? Kozlov, I mean," she asked.

"Every day. Not because he took my eye, but because he killed Gigi."

A few weeks earlier, he'd told her the story of his last undercover assignment in Seattle. His last job as a rising star in the SPD and how, feeling responsible for the death of his confidential informant, he'd left everything behind and secured a transfer to the Bay Area. Once here, he refused to do real police work and only dealt with low-profile cases nobody wanted. Those that didn't put anybody else in danger.

He thought about how they'd met and how incapable he'd felt of protecting her just a few weeks earlier. What started as a simple hit-and-run call turned into a mass murder case in which a killer was determined to get rid of her and a dozen other people.

He'd fallen for Saffron Meadows the moment he saw her. He'd fought to not take the case. He'd begged his captain to assign it to a real detective, because he'd felt unfit to protect her, and he needed her to live.

"But you saved me," she said.

He closed his eyes, pushing away the thought of almost losing her. When he opened them again, she was staring at him, a curious look on her face. Before he was forced to say anything, his phone rang.

"Lynch," he said.

"We have a situation. You need to come to the station right now," his partner, Erik Sorensen, said.

"On my way. Fill me in."

They both stood from the table.

"I love you," Saffron whispered in his other ear, and kissed his cheek. They walked to the parking lot, holding hands, and got into separate cars.

A few minutes later, at the Santa Clara Sheriff's Office, he and Sorensen stood behind their captain, staring at a grainy video flickering on a monitor. She was short and plump but didn't take much space in front of them.

When Captain Virago hit Play again, the three of them watched the split image come to life, showing the interior of two Santa Clara light-rail cars. Most of the passengers looked bored. Some were reading, while others played with their phones or stared out the window.

A man with dark skin and a turban got out of his seat, disengaged a bike from its stand and waited by the door. A few moments later, the light rail stopped. He was the only passenger who got out. Right before the doors closed, eight people got in. Two in each door, four in each car. They were dressed in black, hoods hid their heads, and gas masks covered their faces. As the doors closed, they reached for their belts.

Some of the people minding their own business looked up at the newcomers. Curiosity immediately turned to apprehension, then fear. The men in black dropped gas grenades on the floor, and gray smoke began to rise. A passenger stepped into the aisle, looked behind him, then toward the front as if he was trying to decide where the closest exit was. He took two steps forward, clasped his chest, gasping for air, and dropped to the floor. The gas soon reached the cameras, and the monitor went gray except for the digital time stamp, showing 2:38 p.m. and counting.

One more stop and three minutes and seventeen seconds later, the gas had dissipated enough for the detectives and captain to see inside the car again. The eight men had disappeared, and the passengers were on the floor, bent over the seats in front of them, or slumped against the windows. Seventeen people and five bicycles, still surrounded by dissipating gray gas, peppered the ghostly VTA cars.

"Jon needs to see this," Darcy said. He wanted to get the intern's perspective because he always thought outside of the box. Jon had been integral in cracking the case that saved Saffron and pushed Darcy to join the homicide unit. Since then, both he and Sorensen relied on his analytical capacity.

Sorensen dialed his extension from Virago's phone. "Come to the captain's office right now."

A few seconds later, Jon knocked on the door.

"Come in," they all said in unison.

"Check this out." Sorensen nodded for Virago to share the video.

They all watched as intently as they had the previous three times.

"Holy crap, is this real?" Jon asked as soon as it was over.

"Yes. We just got it about twelve minutes ago. The VTA conductor pressed the alarm and stopped as soon as he realized that the cars were filled with smoke. The Transportation Authority sent it to us right after." Virago pinched the bridge of her nose, probably fighting a nascent headache.

"Can I see it again?" Jon asked. His voice had risen, which it always did when he was excited, but his eyes were focused.

She clicked Play again and said, "CSU is on its way, and I'm about to send these two to the scene, but I'd like to know what you think."

When the man with the bicycle walked out of the car, Sorensen asked, "Do you think he's nodding back at the commando guys?"

"It doesn't look like that to me," Darcy said.

"Me neither," Virago agreed.

"Dammit. I was hoping for something," Sorensen admitted.

"Let me take a closer look on my computer in slow motion and see if I catch anything," Jon said.

"We'll head out to the scene," Darcy said.

Virago leaned back into her chair as she shooed them out of her office.

CHAPTER 3

Darcy stopped by his desk and opened the drawer. Sorensen let out a loud sigh and waited for him by the door, chugging the last few drops of his third can of Red Bull that day.

"You need to powder your nose too?" he asked while Darcy was rummaging for something.

Not finding what he was looking for, Darcy closed the drawer but didn't lock it. Catching up with Sorensen, he said, "Let's take the stairs. You need the exercise."

"Screw you." Sorensen pushed the elevator button while Darcy chose the stairs.

When the doors opened on the ground floor, Darcy asked, "Who's the slow one now?" Heading toward the front door of the precinct, he added, "My car."

"Did you put the top on?"

"It's still nice out," Darcy protested.

Sorensen stopped walking. "I'm not getting in that death trap."

"Fine."

The two detectives got into Sorensen's Jeep, and Darcy eyed his candy-apple-red 1965 Cobra parked opposite the old Cherokee. Before they were out of the parking lot, his phone rang.

"Lynch."

"It's Jon. You have to come back up. We've had another hit."

"What do you mean, 'another hit'?" Darcy put the phone on speaker and looked at Sorensen, who stopped the car in the middle of the lane.

"I was downloading the video when I got a text from a friend to check a link. I clicked on it, and it was an amateur video of a bunch of guys dressed in black gassing a coffee shop."

Before Jon had finished his sentence, Sorensen put the car in reverse and pulled back into the same parking spot.

"Is it a hoax?" Sorensen asked while they walked.

"Hard to tell at this point, but it's gone viral," Jon said.

"Send it to Virago. We're in the elevator."

A moment later they walked into the captain's office as if they'd never left.

"What the hell's going on?" she asked, rubbing her eyes and smudging mascara all over them.

Jon pressed Play, and they watched the images, which were obviously taken with a phone. The video was shaky, as if the person was walking while filming it. Darcy observed the six men with gas masks covering their faces coming from the south side of the street. The sidewalk was flanked by parked cars, including a large black SUV big enough to fit the perps. The men could have come from there or from any other place, Darcy thought.

The person filming walked across the sidewalk and hid behind the corner of a building. The red brick blocked the lower right portion of the frame. The only sounds were the person's breathing, traffic, and the beeping of a distant van backing up.

One of the six men opened the coffee shop door, while the others walked in. A white car passed in front of the phone, blocking the view for a moment. Seconds passed. The cameraman moved the phone from his right to his left hand, and the brick no longer blocked part of the image. After fifty-four seconds, the door of the coffee shop opened, and a mass of gray smoke spilled onto the sidewalk.

"Woah," the cameraman said, and moved from the side of the building to behind a light blue car.

When the smoke finally disappeared, the men and the black SUV were gone.

The video stopped, and the download count, indicated by the ticker, kept growing, now with over a hundred fifty thousand hits.

CHAPTER 4

"Go to the Red Bean first. CSU is in the middle of processing the VTA, so you may get more at the coffee shop crime scene," Virago instructed her two detectives. "And remember: be nice to SJPD. We're trying to make this pilot task force work."

Waiting for the elevator, Darcy said, "Are you sure we can't take my car?" He paused, not fully convinced he should say what he was thinking.

"Yes, I'm sure," Sorensen said.

"Your car smells like wet dog," Darcy mumbled.

"What? It's your fault. It smells like dog from when you rescued the mutt from that crazy cabin in the woods." The elevator doors opened, and they walked into the garage. "You still owe me a detailing, by the way," Sorensen said, getting in his jeep.

The office was not that far from downtown San Jose. Sorensen drove and double-parked on First Street right behind a couple SJPD patrol cars and three ambulances. Curious bystanders stood behind the orange tape, snapping photos as if everything was worth sharing on social media.

"I wonder if the city gets the orange tape because it's cheaper," Sorensen said as they approached the cordoned-off area.

"Uh?" Darcy was searching for familiar faces from SJPD.

15

"You know, like at the Sheriff's Office we have the crime scene yellow tape. At least it says 'crime scene.' But SJ only has this plain orange tape." Sorensen grabbed the tape and shoved it toward Darcy. "It looks more like decoration for a quinceañera party."

Darcy gave him a pleading look to not antagonize SJPD.

"What?" Sorensen raised his hands, faking innocence.

They showed their credentials to an officer, who jotted down their names and the time. Sorensen lifted the tape, and Darcy ducked underneath it. Before he was on the other side, the tape came loose on one end and fell limp onto the ground.

"Sorry." Sorensen handed it to the uniform and walked past him. Seeing the sergeant in charge by one of the ambulances, he yelled, "Hey, Marra, what's going on here?"

"Oh no. You?" Marra joked. "Causing trouble again?" he asked, looking back at the officer retaping the scene.

"Nah." Sorensen shook his hand.

"I just got here." Marra released the officer he'd been talking to and addressed the two detectives: "You saw the video? Six perps. Everybody passed out, but the gas doesn't seem to be lethal." He looked toward the door of the coffee shop, then to the paramedics loading the victims into the ambulances.

"You heard about the VTA, right?" Darcy asked.

"Yep." Sergeant Marra brushed a hand over his shaved head.

"Any connection?" Sorensen asked.

"You know as much as I do."

"Did they take any cash?" Darcy asked. "Something like this, I expect a bank or a jewelry store. But a coffee shop and a VTA train?"

Marra shrugged. An officer walked toward them.

"Sergeant, all the victims are heading to the hospital. They're stable, though they're rushing an older man with a possible heart attack."

"We're going to take a look around," Sorensen said. He pulled two pairs of latex gloves from his pocket and handed one of them to Darcy.

"Thanks. I couldn't find my box."

"I stole it," Sorensen said.

Darcy almost smiled. When Virago made them partner together, he'd expected some rough edges, but working with Sorensen was proving to be more interesting than he'd predicted.

They both walked into the store.

"It smells sweet. It could be halothane gas, but Marra said there were no casualties, right?" Sorensen said.

Darcy inhaled through his nose, trying to get any other nuances, but didn't. Gas was not his field of expertise. "Isn't that what they used in the Russian theater?"

"That's the theory."

The coffee shop was empty. There were half-filled coffee mugs and plates with uneaten food on several tables. The place looked eerie. As if aliens had come and snatched the patrons while they were going about their business. The shop was dark. The tainted windows kept most of the light out.

Darcy pulled out his Maglite and walked around, searching from left to right methodically.

"There's still money in the register," Sorensen said from behind the counter.

"Do SJPD and EMTs wear regulation boots?" Darcy asked, aiming the light at a partial boot print on the floor.

"Some do. Not all. Did you find something?"

"Maybe."

He took his phone out and, after placing a pen next to the boot print, took several shots. It was fairly obvious the man had stepped in some spilled coffee and then left a large mocha print against the gray floor.

Darcy emailed the photos to Lou, the head of CSU, and wrote, "From the coffee shop on First Street. Need info yesterday."

After a split second, his phone beeped with a reply. "Do you ever have realistic expectations?"

Darcy smiled and put the phone back in his jacket and continued to walk the scene.

"There's nothing here. A dropped gallon of milk on the floor, but it didn't even spill," Sorensen said.

Sergeant Marra walked in. "All the victims are going to Good Sam. The kid who shot the video is outside."

"Keep him there," Sorensen said. "When is CSU getting here?"

"As soon as they're done at the VTA."

"We only have one team or what? That's ridiculous," Sorensen protested.

Marra shrugged for the second time and headed toward the door.

"Sergeant," Darcy called after him. "Can you give me a list of every officer at the scene and include what shoes they're wearing and their size."

"You found something?" Marra retraced his steps and met the detective by the counter. Darcy pointed at the boot print a few feet away. The sergeant walked to it, bent over to get a closer look, and said, "It could be one of ours. I'll send you that list."

"Add the paramedics as well."

"You got it."

Darcy and Sorensen followed Marra out to the sidewalk.

"This is Jinkoo Song. He took the video."

Darcy introduced himself. The kid was tall and lanky, and even though he looked barely out of high school, he already had a strong handshake.

"What made you shoot the video?" Sorensen asked.

Jinkoo looked at him as if he were crazy. "Man, when you see something weird, you shoot it. I bet I'll be a number-one hit by the time I get out of here," he said without an accent.

"You live close by?"

"Yeah. I go to Santa Clara U. I hate the library there. It's too quiet, so I always come here to study." He moved his backpack from one shoulder to the other as if he'd just noticed how heavy it was.

"Can you tell us what happened?" Darcy asked.

"I saw these six dudes coming from the south. They were dressed in camo and wore gas masks." Looking from one man to the next, he raised his voice a couple notches when he added, "Weird, right? So, I pulled my phone and started shooting."

"Did you see them leave?" Darcy eyed the street, assessing the possible escape routes.

"No. Well, sort of. The moment the door opened, the smoke spilt into the sidewalk, so I assumed they were leaving but didn't actually see them walk out."

"The black SUV—did you notice if they came in it?"

"The black SUV?" Jinkoo asked.

"Yes, it was parked close to the coffee shop. It was there at the start of the video. When the gas dissipated, it wasn't there anymore."

Jinkoo looked in the direction Darcy was pointing at, as if trying to recall something, then shook his head. "No, sorry, didn't pay any attention to it."

"Anything else? Something about the guys maybe, or anything that might have caught your eye?" Sorensen added.

"Not really. I was just trying to record the whole thing and hoping they wouldn't see me. I wasn't paying attention to anything else."

They asked him a few more questions that got inconsequential answers and then got the closest officer to collect Jinkoo's contact info.

Darcy looked around, taking in the scene, watching the people standing there, curious about the crime. Then he focused on the street, trying to imagine the six men coming, gassing the coffee shop and leaving as fast as they'd come.

"Detective Lynch, what can you tell me?" Janet Hagen asked from the other side of the tape.

Darcy looked in her direction. The Channel 6 News anchor shoved a large microphone toward him as if a few inches would make a difference when they were so many feet apart.

"You know better than that, Miss Hagen. No comment."

He turned away from her, pulled out his phone and called Jon. "Can you tell me the time of the two videos?"

"The VTA happened at 2:38 p.m. The one at the coffee shop started at 2:56 p.m."

Darcy thanked Jon and hung up. "These two incidents happened almost fifteen minutes apart."

"You're brilliant, Sherlock. Any more insight the rest of us haven't figured out yet?"

"Could they have been done by the same perps?"

Sorensen thought for a few seconds. "No, unless they use teleportation. Given the distance between the two scenes, it would be impossible, even if they had motorcycles."

Before Darcy could reply, his phone rang again.

"Yes?" he answered, putting it on speaker.

"I know what they took at the VTA," Jon said, his voice singing with excitement.

CHAPTER 5

The bartender put a mojito in front of Blake Higgins and left. Blake took the straw out and took a sip. After nodding in approval, he rubbed his tongue over his teeth to make sure there was no mint stuck on them. He had a feeling he was going to get lucky tonight. It had been a shitty week, and he needed something petite and sweet to take his mind off of things.

Blake eyed the bar. The music was loud—too loud to have a meaningful conversation. But that was okay. He hadn't come here to talk. He took another sip, left a twenty on the counter and moved to one of the sofas by the open windows. The air was cool, but he had a much better view. He surveyed his surroundings again but still found nothing to pursue. Blake wasn't worried. The night was young.

After answering a few emails on his phone, he texted his CEO. "Meet me at Braseiro."

Martin Dunn responded that he couldn't. He was still reviewing the paperwork for the acquisition with Karsum Conglomerate.

"Do you need me there?" Blake texted him.

"No," the CEO responded.

He felt a pang of dejection but washed it off with his drink. He called the waitress over. The skinny blond in the short peacock dress that showed her lean legs took his order.

A sense of dread made his mouth dry. He had to find out if anybody else knew about the papers he'd been served a couple weeks ago. A few more people sat at the bar. He caught a petite Asian lick her lips as she made eye contact. Blake drank his second mojito and made up his mind. He needed to go back to the office a lot more than he wanted to get laid.

His car unlocked as he got within Bluetooth distance. Blake inhaled the smell of new car and revved his Jaguar XK convertible as he took each corner out of the parking lot a little faster than he needed to.

Even with traffic, he reached Mountain View in twenty minutes. He parked in his assigned spot and waved his badge by the security reader when he reached the door. The receptionist had left already, but there were still plenty of people plugging away in their cubes. He reached the executive conference room and entered without knocking.

Five faces turned toward him. He saw a shadow go over Martin's face but decided to ignore it.

"What did I miss?" he asked, settling by his CEO, who was sitting by himself on the left side of the large table.

Blake felt Martin tense beside him. Then his friend set both elbows on the table and said, "We'd just finished discussing Q1 and Q2's road map."

Martin pressed the remote, and the next slide appeared on the large screen to his right.

Blake saw the bullets listing the patents filed by the company through the four short years of its existence. The list filled the slide. Blake swallowed hard and wished he had stayed back at the bar.

"I thought we covered the patents yesterday," Blake said before he could stop himself. Blaming the alcohol, he swore to never drink again before a meeting with Karsum Conglomerate.

"We did. Just doing a quick run through everything to show we have all our t's crossed." Martin said.

Blake twirled between his fingers the thick Montblanc fountain pen his dad gave him and forced himself to look across the table at the three Karsum men. He met their eyes, one by one, and hoped that his jaw didn't show his muscles tensing. "Of course." Blake leaned closer to the table, mimicking Martin's posture.

"As we discussed yesterday, NanoQ has filed twenty-eight patents, and the approval dates are pending. We're very confident that all twenty-eight will pass."

The three men nodded. Blake watched them scrutinize the list as if it was the first time they'd seen it. He held his breath, hoping that the information he gave them yesterday had satiated their curiosity and they could move on to the next slide.

When nobody protested, he silently sighed, sure that his secret was still safe.

CHAPTER 6

Sorensen followed Lynch as he moved away from the crowd so they wouldn't hear what Jon had learned. "What did they take from the train?" he asked.

"A man." The intern took a deep breath, probably to calm himself down. "I watched the video at least ten times and finally realized that there was a passenger missing when the gas dissipated. They took a guy," he said, almost yelling, as if that would make his point stick.

"Is there anything particular about him? Could he be rich?" Sorensen asked.

"He's using the VTA. How rich can he be?" Lynch asked.

"This is Silicon Valley. When are you going to learn? People ride the VTA for environmental reasons. And to avoid rush hour."

"This was the middle of the afternoon."

"There's still the environment."

Lynch ignored him and spoke back to Jon: "Can you make out anything from the coffee shop?"

"No. Only the gray smoke."

Lynch hung up. Sorensen looked back to the coffee shop. "You think they took somebody here too?"

"They didn't take money," Darcy said.

"We need to go to the hospital. Maybe somebody will know."

About thirty minutes later, Officer Wilkes met them by the ER entrance at Good Sam. He informed them that none of the victims were going to die or suffer major side effects. They were going to keep them for a few more hours under supervision just in case, but they expected everybody to go back home before the day's end.

"How many are there?" Sorensen asked.

"Eight. Six were patrons. The other two worked there." Wilkes opened his notebook and said, "Actually, Jessica Molton's the owner. She was coming from the back, so she's the only one who's awake enough to talk."

"Where is she?" Sorensen asked, moving forward already, but he looked back to confirm he was going in the right direction.

"End of the hallway on the right."

When they reached the last curtain, Sorensen pushed through into the small space next to the gurney.

Lynch followed. "Best not to do that," he said to a pretty woman in her early thirties who was rubbing her eyes. A colorful bandanna held her huge Afro away from her face.

Jessica stopped, a little startled. She looked up while she slid both hands under her thighs.

"We understand you were in the storage room when this whole thing started," Sorensen said after he made the introductions.

Wilkes tried to step inside the cramped space, but Sorensen stopped him. "We need photos of each of the victims. Go take a few and bring them back here."

Wilkes looked disappointed but left them alone.

Jessica had a dreamy voice, as if she were recalling something long forgotten. "I went to get some more milk. When I came back, I wasn't even paying attention. Then I heard Matt . . ." She looked at the detectives and added, "He works for me at the store. I heard him curse, which he never does, so I looked up, and I saw three men wearing gas masks and black clothing. Then everything went gray, and I passed out."

"You only saw three men?" Lynch asked.

"Yes. I hadn't made it all the way to the counter, so I could only see half the store."

"Was there anything else remarkable about them?"

"Honestly, they looked like they were from one of those sci-fi movies."

"How about the patrons? Do you normally get pretty much the same clientele?"

"We have our fair amount of regulars. It's sort of like a neighborhood hangout. In the afternoon there're a lot of college kids."

"Was there anybody who looked suspicious or nervous or was acting in a way that seemed weird?"

She thought for a while. Started to rub her eyes again but stopped herself, probably remembering Lynch's admonishment.

She looked up at him and shook her head. "Not that I can think of."

Wilkes came back. He shoved the phone into Sorensen's hand. "Seven pictures. I assumed you didn't want me to take profile shots as well."

Sorensen almost responded but instead showed the first photo to Jessica. "Can you tell me who are your regulars?"

She scrolled through each picture and identified Matt, her employee, and three other people.

After a few more routine questions, they left her to interview the rest of the victims as they were waking up. The other stories were very similar to Jessica's, though most of the patrons had seen six men, not just three.

"Matt, any of these people looking suspicious or weird today?" Sorensen asked Jessica's employee, a kid of college age sporting sleeve tattoos and multiple piercings.

The barista checked the pictures several times. After the third pass, he said, "I don't see Seth."

"Who's Seth?" Sorensen asked.

"He's one of the regulars, and he was there today for sure. He's always there on Mondays. I had just made his large iced Americano, and he was settling by the wall, last table."

Matt looked from one detective to the other and then scrolled through the pictures as if he had missed the one showing Seth's mug shot.

"Could he have left before all this happened?" Lynch asked.

"No. As I said, he'd just picked up his coffee from the counter and pulled his computer out."

"Do you know his last name? Where he works or lives?"

Matt shook his head. "He's a decent guy. Always chats a little. He's working on a book, but that's all I know." He rubbed his eyes for a few seconds. "I think he's a Marine, or maybe air force. No, Marine, I think. Something like that."

The two detectives exchanged glances. While Lynch stayed and continued asking Matt questions, Sorensen stepped out and called Sergeant Marra.

"Sorensen here. Have your men collected all of the personal belongings in the coffee shop?"

"Yep. Wrapping up as we speak."

"We have a potential missing person. Did you see any governmental equipment—a Toughbook maybe?"

"Oh shit. Not sure. I'll take a look and let you know ASAP. Then I'll send everything to your office." Before he hung up, he asked, "Are you seriously thinking some national security shit's going on here?"

"As soon as you can find me that computer, I'll be able to tell you."

CHAPTER 7

Saffron Meadows shifted her weight from foot to foot while she stared at the blouses hanging in her walk-in closet. She hadn't seen her sister in a couple weeks and was looking forward to it.

She stepped on a pair of jeans already discarded on the floor and finally chose a black silk top with spaghetti straps. Her sister had the best clothes, and even though Saffron hated to admit it, she always felt like she had to compete a little.

She turned around in front of the mirror: fitted raspberry blazer, dark skinny jeans, and new Prada Mary Janes. Satisfied, Saffron grabbed her car keys and coat, scratched Cat behind the ears and left for Santana Row.

Twenty-five minutes later, she parked on the fourth floor of the parking garage in front of Best Buy. It had taken her longer to find an empty spot than to drive the ten miles to the Row. Five girls waited for the elevator. Three blonds, two Asians. High heels, tight tops, light coats too light for November. They talked fast in high-pitched voices and a little too loud. Saffron passed by them and took the stairs around the corner.

She checked her phone, but instead of seeing the time she saw a text: "At the Village. Braseiro was packed. And where are you? You're never late."

Saffron weaved her way through the crowd. Some people were going in and out of high-end stores and restaurants, but most seemed to just stand there, in endless conversations, blocking the sidewalk. Even on Monday, Santana Row was flooded with Valley businessmen and up-and-coming twentysomethings looking to hook up with somebody after a few too many drinks.

"I'm glad you changed restaurants," Saffron said a few minutes later, kissing her sister's cheek.

"I walked into Braseiro, and the bar was a sausage fest."

"I thought that's why you liked that place." Saffron said, laughing. She took off her coat and sat down next to her sister at the bar. "What are you drinking?"

"Merlot." She picked up the glass. "Want to try it?"

Saffron shook her head and opened the wine menu. "Nah, I feel more like a Petite Sirah."

After she ordered, Saffron leaned back in her chair.

"Long day?" Aislin asked.

"Long frigging month."

"I'm glad you're not dating that loser boss of yours anymore," Aislin said.

"He's not my boss," Saffron protested. "We're not even in the same organization."

"Whatever." Aislin smiled a perfect smile.

"Have you talked to Mom and Dad lately?" Saffron asked.

"Yep, just yesterday, and they're expecting both of us to come for Thanksgiving. Oh, and they want you to bring your hot detective boyfriend."

"What? You told them about Darcy?"

"What do you mean? We're all excited that you're finally dating somebody decent. And besides, he saved your life, so we all want to meet him." She winked.

"Oh, shut up. I've had plenty of nice boyfriends," Saffron said, avoiding the other topic. She shivered and worked hard to push the memories away. But every night when she closed her eyes, she felt the same cold she'd felt trapped in that basement with all of those people whose common fate was the most terrifying seppuku one could ever imagine. She shook her head, and focused on Aislin again.

"Right. Like the one who wanted to move in after dating you for a week because he hated to commute. Or the one who kept telling you how much he missed his ex-wife. Oh, no wait. My favorite was that lawyer who always had to be right and got into pissing contests with everybody—"

"Oh my God, look who's talking. What about Sean?"

"I was fifteen," Aislin protested.

"Yeah, and Dad had to pull all kinds of strings so you wouldn't be sent to juvie for shoplifting at Nordstrom."

"He was pissed." Aislin said, laughing.

"And who was the other one? Oliver?"

"Oscar. Yeah, Oscar was bad news, but you know I have a soft spot for bad boys."

"And that, girlie, is going to get you in real trouble one day."

"Okay, enough." Aislin raised her glass. They clinked.

"Changing subjects . . . I can't believe what you did to Aunt Jenny and Uncle George," Saffron said, recalling the prank and almost snorting her wine.

"Was that my best yet or what?" Aislin asked.

"How many people ended up showing up at their house?"

"At least twelve or thirteen. You should've seen their faces." Aislin cracked up. "I swear they were getting redder and redder the more people they had to turn away." She put the glass to her lips but didn't drink. "Can you imagine slinky-dressed couple after couple knocking on the door, expecting a swingers' party and finding Jenny and George opening the door with increasingly more horrified faces?"

"You should have videoed it." Saffron shook her head, wishing she could have been there to see it.

"I tried with my phone, but I was too far away. I didn't want them to spot me." She moved her long bangs away from her eyes and flashed a big rock on her middle finger.

"What's that?" Saffron asked, almost blinded by the gorgeous solitaire.

Aislin pulled her hand out of sight and looked away.

"Nothing. I have to return it tomorrow, but it was too beautiful to not enjoy it for a couple days."

"What do you mean you have to return . . . ?" Saffron stopped herself. She felt her face tighten as she started frowning.

They both looked away. Saffron breathed in and out slowly, trying to convince herself that it was better to drop the subject. The last time she'd seen her sister, it didn't end well for the same reason.

"Listen, Saffron, can we just not talk about it?" Aislin asked, holding her stemless glass of wine with the hand that had no jewelry.

"Fine. Whatever," Saffron said, but then she added, "But you promised."

"I know, and I will, okay? It's not the right time right now, but I will stop soon."

CHAPTER 8

Ethan Mitchell looked down at the inert body of Ben Walters. Two of his men undressed him less carefully than they could have. Ethan looked around. The basement had gray concrete walls and some wet marks on the uneven floor. It was humid, almost muggy. A couple men laughed, bringing Ethan back to what they were doing. Walters was now lying on the cold floor, fully naked.

"Hey, Bishop, he's ready for you," Toby yelled over his shoulder to summon them around the body.

Ethan watched the seven men look down at Gunnery Sergeant Ben Walters. A couple giggled, elbowing each other.

"Who's gonna do it?" Toby asked.

"You signed up for it." Bishop slapped his neighbor and started cracking up.

"No fucking way. I'm not touching that thing. Have you seen how huge it is?" Toby took a step back, as if that would get him off the hook.

A few others made similar comments, all laughing like teenagers.

Finally Ethan left the group, walked to the table and grabbed the sharp shaving razor that was lying there. "Fine, you fucking pussies. I'll do it, but somebody has to hold his dick for me."

Bishop knelt down and grabbed it, extending the penis as far as it would go. The razor flashed under the light as Ethan drove it down to Walter's crotch.

CHAPTER 9

After pulling into the station's parking lot, Sorensen headed up to the office, leaving Lynch behind. Sorensen got to his desk and started going through the evidence Sergeant Marra's men had dropped off. Backpacks, laptops, wallets, phones, notebooks, a couple textbooks. There was nothing special.

Jon appeared in the bullpen.

"Hey, is this all the evidence from the coffee shop?" Sorensen asked.

The intern looked at the table. "I don't know."

Sorensen huffed and picked up the phone. Dialing Marra, he asked, "I don't see any Panasonic Toughbook in the evidence you gave me. Are you still collecting things?"

"Nope. What you have is all there was."

"Are you sure?" Sorensen pressed.

Marra didn't respond.

"Okay, okay. We may have a situation."

"Marine's computer missing?"

"Possibly." Sorensen sat down and rubbed a beefy hand over his sweaty forehead while he cradled the phone between his ear and shoulder. "Let me make a couple calls before we start panicking. I'll keep you posted."

Sorensen searched his contacts until he found the number he was looking for. He dialed one more time.

"First Sergeant Loren, how's life?"

"Sorensen? Son of a bitch. What the hell do you want?" There was no humor in his voice.

"Hey, hey, what kind of greeting is that?"

"I'm hanging up now."

But the line didn't go dead.

"I can't believe you're still mad at me for something that happened when we were in college," Sorensen said, only slightly surprised.

"I got suspended, and it took me another year to get into the Marines. And I had to do a full year of community service because you made me take the fall for the bar fight."

"But I'm sure the streets looked a lot cleaner." He had a hard time picturing Loren picking up garbage.

"You're an asshole, and I'm hanging up now."

"Wait, wait," Sorensen said, knowing he'd gone too far. "We may have a situation that involves a Marine."

Loren sighed but remained on the line. "What's going on?" he finally asked.

"You heard about the gas incident at the coffee shop? We think a Marine was abducted from there."

"Who?"

"We only have a first name: Seth," Sorensen said without looking at his notes. "We also know he used to go there with his computer, but we can't find any Toughbooks among the evidence we recovered."

"Let me find out if he's one of our guys. I'll call you back as soon as I have something."

"And First Sergeant, please keep it quiet for now. We don't want to start a panic."

"Understood."

CHAPTER 10

Darcy Lynch reached out to CSU to see if they were done collecting evidence at the VTA stop. Mauricio confirmed that they'd wrapped up and he was going back to the lab to process what they had, which wasn't much. The other techs were heading to the coffee shop. Darcy got into his car and drove to the light-rail station to take in the crime scene on his own.

The orange SJPD tape still protected the area, which was flanked by a uniform standing at each end, keeping curious civilians out. Four high-powered halogen lights, almost brighter than daylight, illuminated the site.

Darcy flashed his badge and stepped into the perimeter. He looked at the platform, the benches, and the rail tracks. The LED panel announced that the next train to Alum Rock would arrive in less than a minute. He walked slowly to the other end of the platform. There was nothing. No gum wrappers, no discarded cans or empty plastic bottles. He knew CSU would have collected whatever was there, just in case it led somewhere. Darcy peeked into a trash can and saw that it was also empty.

"That's a lot of pointless work," he said out loud, shaking his head. He'd watched the video enough times to know that these guys were professionals and hadn't left any evidence on the platform or in the cars.

The train came. Two wagons. It didn't stop. Darcy saw a man by one of the doors. His face showed surprise when he realized the VTA wouldn't be stopping. The train disappeared, foliage twirling in its wake, leaving Darcy alone, in silence.

His phone vibrated in his pocket. It was a message from Officer Wilkins: "First VTA victim just woke up. Coming back to interview her?"

"OMW," Darcy texted back. He checked the time. Just after 7:00 p.m. Wow, they must have used a lot more gas in this one, he thought, surprised that it had taken so long for the first victim to wake up.

Before leaving, Darcy turned his back to the rails. It took a bit of time for his eyes to adjust to the darkness. He scanned the empty lot. He imagined the field in front of him to be dry, the tan earth dusty behind the wire fence. He wondered when they would start construction on another Silicon Valley office building.

Darcy walked to the edge of the platform. There was a ditch. He couldn't see the bottom of it. He turned on his flashlight and checked. It was about four feet deep. The men must have hidden there until the train came. There were no cameras pointing to that side of the platform, so there was no way to know. He jumped down and almost slipped.

I really need to start wearing shoes with better treads, he thought. He walked back and forth, every once in a while looking back at the platform to figure out where the men must have been to enter the train so effortlessly. When he got to the middle of the platform, he figured he was close—close to where the first set of doors would have been.

Darcy took one more step, trying to get aligned, and then pointed the flash back toward the ground. Right before he was about to plant his foot, he saw it. Almost losing his balance, he managed to step to the right of the boot print. He bent down and looked at it. It was very similar—if not the same—as the one he had found at the coffee shop. He took a couple photos and sent them to Lou.

After he'd walked the entire ditch a couple times, finding nothing more than a few other blurred boot prints, he knew it was time to go. He headed back to where he had come from and said good-bye to the officer before he drove to Good Sam.

A few minutes later Wilkins met with him by the ER entrance.

"Feels like déjà vu," the officer said.

Darcy nodded, patting him on the shoulder.

Wilkins started talking, this time checking his notes. "There are seventeen victims. They had to double-bunk them, since they're running out of space. Most of them are still passed out, but alive. The first one who woke up is Mrs. Ramirez. She doesn't speak a lot of English unfortunately."

As they got closer, Darcy saw that the curtain was already open. A full-figured woman in her fifties huffed and puffed and waved a hand in front of her face, trying to fan herself. Before they reached Mrs. Ramirez, Darcy turned around and walked back to the front desk.

Almost startling the nurse behind the counter, he asked, "Can I have a manila folder?"

She stared at him for a minute but didn't move or say anything.

Darcy pulled his badge out and said, "Sheriff's Office."

The nurse nodded and turned around, opened a drawer behind her and gave him an empty yellow folder.

"Thank you," Darcy said, and walked back to his witness.

When he got there, he opened the curtain all the way, and after introducing himself he said, "Buenas tardes, Sra. Ramirez. Cómo se encuentra?"

"Ay, Dios mío, que calor."

"Quizá ésto le ayude." Darcy offered her the manila folder, which she took and immediately started fanning herself with.

A faint smile lit her face, and she closed her eyes for a few seconds.

Darcy asked her in Spanish to tell him what happened at the VTA. The woman explained what she remembered and got more agitated with each word, until she reached the part where she passed out. With a long sigh, she ended, "Y lo siguiente, es que me desperté aquí."

She locked eyes with Darcy and crossed herself twice, blinked a few times and passed the folder to the other hand. The black permed curls around her head moved back and forth as the folder did its job.

"Gracias. Le agradezco mucho su ayuda."

Darcy shook her hand and left her, taking Wilkins with him.

"That's some serious Spanish. Please tell me you learnt that from Rosetta Stone."

Darcy laughed. "No. I lived in Spain for a couple of semesters when I was in college. Then I took salsa lessons when I lived in Seattle."

"I never liked dancing."

"Me neither, but it kept me in shape and my Spanish fresh." Darcy translated what Mrs. Ramirez had told him. "She basically corroborated what we saw on the video. A bunch of men came in, gassed the train and then she woke up at the hospital."

"Anything about the missing man?" Wilkins asked.

"Nope. She doesn't remember anything about him. Can't even say whether she saw him or not."

They visited the rest of the victims as they woke up. All had a similar story. Nobody remembered the man who had disappeared, not even those sitting around him.

CHAPTER 11

Sorensen was glued to his computer. From the corner of his eye, he saw his partner enter the bullpen and walk straight toward him. Lynch didn't say anything. Instead, he grabbed one of the three open Red Bull cans off of Sorensen's desk and shook it, weighing the contents.

"What are you doing?" Sorensen asked, wondering why Lynch had to touch his stuff.

"I bet these are all half-full."

Lynch reached down to check another one. Before he could touch it, Sorensen snatched it and gulped the rest of the liquid. It was warm and gross.

"I bet they aren't." He crumpled the can and dumped it in his recycle bin.

"I can't believe you have your own recycling," Lynch said. "You know, it wouldn't hurt to get off your ass occasionally and use the one in the kitchen."

Sorensen flipped him the bird and said, "I'm not fat, I'm big boned."

Darcy laughed and went to his desk. Powering up his computer, he asked, "What have I missed?"

Sorensen told him about the possible missing Marine equipment.

"Do you think we have a national security threat case?"

"I don't know. I'm waiting for my buddy to confirm that the guy's actually a Marine and that he had his gear with him."

The phone rang. He picked it up.

"Sorensen."

It was his wife.

"I just wanted to let you know that I left your dinner in the microwave. Macaroni and cheese."

"Oh, yum. I wish I'd been there for dinner," he lied. They were only in the first week of his mother-in-law's month-long visit, and she was already driving him crazy. He was thankful for the long work hours.

"We all missed you. Maybe this weekend it will be warm enough to fire up the BBQ."

"That's a great idea. We may even invite Lynch," he said, glancing over at his partner, who looked up, arching the eyebrow of his good eye. It often amazed him how undetectable Lynch's fake eye was. "Okay, honey, I have to go. Don't wait up."

"Love you."

"Love you too."

As soon as he hung up, the phone rang again.

"Did you forget something?" he asked.

"First Sergeant Loren."

"Oh, sorry. I thought you were somebody else. What do you have for me?" He put the phone on speaker.

"I got good news and bad news."

Sorensen and Lynch exchanged glances.

"Your missing guy, Seth, is definitely one of ours. Seth McAuley. He was last seen this morning. He was supposed to have reported back at the 4th LSG, the Logistics Support Group, at 1700 hours, but he didn't, and nobody can reach him."

"What's the good news?" Lynch asked.

Sorensen shook his head, but it was too late.

"Who's that?"

"My partner. I have you on speaker."

"I gathered that. Next time let me know before you do that." His voice was strained. "Anyway, I'm not done with the bad news." He paused, probably for effect. "We've been experimenting with a prototype of halothane gas. It's nonlethal and has no side effects. A case of grenades has gone missing in transit."

"Is there a way to test if the gas used at the VTA and Red Bean came from that case?" Darcy asked.

"I don't know, but I will find out."

"So what is the good news?" Sorensen asked.

"All McAuley's equipment is in his bunker."

Sorensen let out a long breath, releasing the air he'd been holding in since he picked up the phone. He saw Lynch do the same thing.

"Has McAuley ever disappeared before?" Sorensen asked.

"No. He has a stellar record: two tours in Afghanistan and about to be deployed again in a few weeks." First Sergeant Loren paused before he continued. "Sorensen, you have to find my man."

"I will. We're on it," he said before he hung up.

"I'm sure NCIS is on this too," Darcy said.

"Yep." Sorensen rubbed his face with his beefy hand and looked at Lynch. "Tell me you got something."

"A few boot prints at the VTA station. They were definitely hiding on the other side of the platform before the train showed up." Lynch slouched in his chair. "What I would like to know is if they targeted those guys on purpose, or if they just took somebody at random."

"This is not random. Two incidents, almost identical, in two different places, and they take somebody random? I doubt it. They were targeting whomever they took."

Lynch nodded in agreement.

"What we need to figure out is who's the guy they took in the VTA. Is he also a Marine?" Sorensen asked.

Lynch didn't reply.

While watching his partner get up and document the updates on the whiteboard, Sorensen tried to figure out how much longer he could stay at the station without making his wife mad.

CHAPTER 12

Ethan Mitchell washed his hands. The discarded razor rested in the sink, now clean from the running water. His shoulders were stiff. He rubbed his hands under the lukewarm water a couple more times and forced his body to loosen up a little, releasing the tension.

"We need to get out of here," Bishop announced from the bathroom door.

"I know," Ethan said. "Did you grab the rest of the halothane grenades?"

"Already hidden in the van."

Ethan grabbed a few paper towels and, after drying his hands, made a ball and threw it toward the garbage can, missing it. He walked past the paper towels without picking them up.

The body of Gunnery Sergeant Ben Walters was nowhere to be seen. He figured they'd moved him already to the back of the van. He went up the stairs two at a time and saw that everybody was waiting for him. Ethan locked the door and jumped into the passenger seat.

There was no more giggling or laughing. Back on the job, they were watchful, staring out the windows, holding their breath each time they stopped at a red light. It was late, and the streets were fairly empty. They'd planned the route to avoid the more trafficked areas.

"Fuck. PD at six o'clock," Bishop said, breaking the silence, fixing his eyes on the rearview mirror.

A San Jose patrol car pulled up behind them. Nobody breathed.

"Nice and easy," Ethan said.

"This is not the first time I've done this, compadre," Bishop replied.

The light turned green. Bishop tapped the accelerator, and the van rolled forward.

"Turn left," Toby said.

Bishop hit the turn signal, and when he reached the next intersection he turned left. The patrol car followed. They drove straight through the next street, only passing a few cars. Then Bishop turned right, after signaling. The patrol car trailed right behind them.

"What the hell's up with this guy?" Bishop shifted in his seat.

Before they had reached the middle of the next block, the cop turned the spinners on.

Bishop stopped the van and rolled the window down. Ethan checked his seat belt was on. It was. Toby tucked the corner of the blanket, ensuring that the body was completely hidden.

"Good evening, sir," the police officer said when he reached the window. He looked inside and nodded at the men. "License and registration, please." While Bishop fetched both documents, the officer asked, "Do you know why I stopped you?"

CHAPTER 13

Darcy had his feet on the table and was engrossed in a heated discussion with Sorensen about all the possible ways this case could go.

Virago got out of her office and headed toward them. "Feel like calling it a day? It's almost 11:00 p.m. My treat for a beer."

"I could definitely use a break," Sorensen said. "This guy's driving me crazy."

"Nobody's forcing you to stay. Oh, wait. Yeah, your mother-in-law is," Darcy joked.

Sorensen rubbed the bridge of his nose with his middle finger.

"Ladies, please," Virago said, already walking toward the exit.

"How's the pilot task force with SJPD going?" she asked as soon as they got out in the street.

"Okay," Sorensen said, not looking at Darcy for confirmation.

They remained silent the rest of the way. Virago led, and the two detectives walked half a step behind her. A few minutes later, Sorensen opened the door of Fibar McGee's for her but went in before Darcy. She picked a booth at the very end and sat facing the door. Sorensen sat across from her but didn't scoot. Darcy stood looking from one to the other. When neither moved to share the booth space, he pulled a chair from the table behind him and sat facing the wall.

"Captain, it's been a while," the owner said when he appeared from the back.

"Too long, Bernie, too long." Her smile was wide and looked authentic.

They ordered beers. Bernie brought them to the table and left them alone.

Virago looked over the back of the booth, checking out the mostly empty bar, and said, "Carmen, SJPD's Bureau of Investigation's deputy chief, approached me with a proposition shortly after we formed the task force."

Darcy hadn't heard anything from his sister, so Carmen must have gone directly to Virago, not vetting the proposition with the sheriff first. This should be interesting, Darcy thought.

"As you both know, everybody is trying to make their departments mean and lean—"

"Don't say it. Don't even tell me that we're going to have furloughs," Sorensen interrupted.

Virago raised her hand to make him stop. "Detective, do you jump to conclusions in your investigations too?"

Sorensen looked as if he'd just eaten a live frog.

"As I was saying," she started again, and paused to make sure she had their attention. When they both looked at her, she continued: "Carmen wants me to transfer over to the SJPD to lead a squad of detectives focusing on special cases."

"You're leaving the Sheriff's Office?" they both asked.

"Jesus, keep it down, you two," she said. "I didn't want to talk in the office, because I didn't want everybody to know. If you keep yelling, we may as well have stayed there."

"Crap, I never would have figured you would leave," Sorensen said almost in a whisper.

"It's not a done deal. They want to see how the current task force is working out first. The Special Cases Unit will eventually be multidepartment, so what we're doing now is like a mini pilot."

"But then why do you have to go? Doesn't it make more sense to keep things the way they are, so all the departments contribute their part?" Darcy asked.

"That's what I thought at first. My take is that they want to ensure that this unit is successful with SJPD personnel, so if more departments want to join or get out of it later, it wouldn't really affect the unit."

"What about Captain McKenna? I thought she was leading the task force from the SJPD side."

"She's retiring. And that's not public knowledge, so don't share it."

"Oh," Sorensen said, and took a sip of his beer.

Darcy thought he looked defeated, as if he knew he was going to lose his captain.

"Part of the agreement is that I can bring three people with me," she said.

Sorensen looked up.

Darcy was watching the interactions more than he was paying attention to the implications of what Virago was telling them. He knew Virago and Sorensen were close, but he now started to realize that there was a friendship between them he hadn't understood before.

"I know you have history here and a lot of years, so I'm not sure it's fair to ask you, but I would like you to come with me."

"What?" Sorensen asked, faking surprise, but his eyes shined.

Darcy leaned back in his chair, wondering why he was there.

"I don't exactly know what the conditions would be, and I'm not sure you can carry over your pension."

"Ouch," Sorensen said, slouching in the booth. "That's fifteen years."

"I know."

She looked at Darcy, as if she wanted to let Sorensen think in peace. "I would also want you to come with me," she said.

"What?" the two detectives asked.

Darcy looked at Sorensen. It annoyed him that his partner couldn't keep his mouth shut, even if it was just out of courtesy.

The left side of Virago's mouth rose a little, and her crow's-feet deepened, as if she'd been planning for a long time a way to shock them both at the same time. And now she was pleased because she'd succeeded.

"I know you have a strong tie to the Sheriff's Office through your sister, so I don't want to cause any hard feelings there, but I think you could do well at the SJPD." She paused for a second. She looked like she was trying to figure out whether or not to say more.

"It could be nice to get the job for merits and not cronyism," Darcy said, and when she nodded slightly, he knew that was exactly what she'd been thinking.

"Who's the third?" Sorensen asked.

She looked from one to the other and smiled. "The best researcher we have, of course: Jon."

CHAPTER 14

The cool air came into the van from the open window. Ethan let out a very long and silent sigh while he locked eyes with the officer. He put on a curious, non-daring face and hoped Bishop was doing the same.

"No, sir, I don't know why you stopped me." Bishop's voice was affable and genuine.

The officer took the license and the registration, and before walking away said, "Your right brake light is broken, and you shouldn't drive without a side mirror." He pointed with his pen at the place where the mirror should have been.

Bishop nodded.

The officer took a few steps back to call in the information.

Bishop turned, his eyes darting between the men. "You motherfuckers didn't check the state of the van. What the hell's wrong with you?"

"Keep it down," Ethan said, moving his hand up and down.

"I know, but this . . ."

The police radio crackled, and they all looked toward the noise as if summoned by an order. Ethan watched the officer lean his head toward the microphone clipped to his shoulder, then press a button and talk into it. He couldn't hear the actual words, but a few seconds later the officer hurried to the van and almost shoved the driving license and registration into Bishop's chest.

"Get that fixed. Consider this a warning." He ran back to his car and sped away with the siren on and the spinners flashing.

"I wonder what that was about," Toby said from the backseat.

"Who knows? This is East San Jose. Probably some gang shooting or something." Bishop put the car in gear.

Ethan checked his watch and said, "Okay, let's move. We don't have all night."

Bishop started to drive, trying to use the brakes as little as possible. The men were quiet. The police stop had sobered their mood even more.

After what seemed like hours but was only minutes, Ethan broke the silence, pointing: "Here, take this spot here. I'll go in."

Bishop parked.

Ethan walked away from the van. The night felt crisp. He pulled up his jacket collar and quickened his pace. He turned left on Bascom Avenue and walked through the first door that would open.

The bus station was spacious. Even though it was not very busy, he found it noisy, especially after being outside in the quiet night. There were only a few ticket windows open. Ethan picked the one with an older man who looked half-asleep. After buying his pass, he checked the time and realized they would have to move quickly.

He searched for the right gate. Of course, it was toward the other end. He accelerated his pace, but not enough to call attention to himself. When he finally reached it, he went through the door and found bus 27.

There was nobody inside the coach. Good, he thought. He walked around and found the driver inspecting the cargo area.

"Alberto, my man. How you doing?" Ethan asked when he got closer.

Ethan watched the stocky old man push himself out of the hull with what seemed to be a lot of effort. Once he was standing, he looked up at Ethan and opened his arms. A warm smile framed his mouth with wrinkles.

"All good, all good." Alberto took a step back and said, "You look bigger. The Marines are treating you well."

Ethan smiled. "I wouldn't have gone in if it wasn't for you."

The men hugged.

"It's good to see you. You'll come for Thanksgiving, right?"

"Yes, yes. I'll drop in with Mom," Ethan said.

"Perfect. You know Gladys will make food for your full regiment if you want to bring them."

"Be careful what you wish for," Ethan said, patting Alberto's shoulder.

"Okay, we don't have a lot of time. You bought the ticket?"

Ethan took it out of his pocket and handed it to him.

"Perfect." Alberto looked around. The place was deserted. "Do you see that door at the end?" He pointed to the south side of the building. There was a sign that said "Emergency Exit."

"Yep."

"Okay, I'll prop it open, and you need to come back through that door. Make sure nobody sees you. I'll meet you back here."

"Won't it start an alarm when you open it?"

"No, I checked. We're good."

Ethan pulled out an envelope and handed it to him. Alberto didn't take it. "Make sure you get a decent turkey this year."

The man still didn't take the money.

Ethan placed the envelope in Alberto's jacket pocket and said, "Big turkey, okay? I want the biggest turkey in the neighborhood. See you in a couple weeks."

Ethan patted Alberto on the back again and left to get the body.

As he walked, he checked his watch. He had less than eight hours until his next move.

CHAPTER 15

Tuesday

At 0700 hours Ethan was fully dressed and ready to go. He was glad the day was gloomy and there was a 60 percent chance of showers. Maybe in the rain, fewer people would pay attention to his night-camouflage clothing.

He left his condo in Mountain View and headed over to pick up Bishop. Ethan had been hesitant about bringing Bishop into his side business, but after what happened to Gomez in their last mission in Afghanistan, he wanted another fellow Marine, and Bishop was someone he could control.

Bishop lived close to Japantown in San Jose. It only took him fifteen minutes to get there because traffic was light this early in the morning. Just as Ethan was pulling up outside the apartment building, Bishop came out wearing a matching uniform.

"No coffee?" Bishop shut the car door but didn't buckle his seat belt.

"I don't want my girls needing pee breaks in the middle of the operation," Ethan said, only barely joking.

Both men rode in silence for a few minutes.

"Do you think this is going to work?" Bishop turned to look out the side window.

"One hundred percent. We've been planning this for a long time. Every detail has been carefully addressed." Ethan eyed him.

"But this one's the real deal."

"There's no difference." Ethan showed a little frustration in his voice. "Are you chickening out?"

"No, man. You know that."

"Then stop asking stupid questions."

"Somebody needs to get laid . . . I was just making conversation." Bishop crossed his arms and stared out the side window again.

When they reached the rendezvous point, Curtis, Mac, and Barr were already there.

"How did it go?" Curtis asked Ethan referring to the VTA kidnapping.

"Perfect, of course," Bishop responded. "We're Marines."

Ethan saw Curtis roll his eyes. Bishop's need to establish the Marines' superiority over the other special forces was borderline amusing. But Bishop was the new kid, and Ethan had a long history with the other guys, so he understood why he was overcompensating.

The others had wanted to participate in the VTA job, but Ethan told them that it had to be done strictly by Marines. That's why he and Bishop did the job with their platoon guys.

He thought about Bishop again: he didn't measure up to the others. After this mission, I may have to fire you, he thought, looking at him.

"All ready?" he asked.

They nodded and, leaving Ethan's car behind, got into the black van they'd used the night before.

"I double-checked the license plates. Muddy as hell," Mac said. "And I fixed the brake lights," he added.

"Great." Ethan almost asked if they had inspected the equipment, but didn't. He didn't have to.

Bishop took the Taylor exit off of Highway 87. When he reached Coleman Avenue, he turned left and then right into the shopping center. Ethan had done enough recon to not be surprised by the number of cars parked there even though most stores were still closed.

Bishop parked in the third row, facing south, just far enough away from the cameras. They all watched the bank while they donned their equipment. Ethan heard clothing swishing and belts clicking, but his eyes were glued to the entrance.

An employee came to unlock the glass doors. A few minutes later a couple went in, then a man. A woman in her fifties came and left.

"Busy morning," Bishop said. A tinge of anxiety marked his voice.

"He's here," Barr said, watching a car pull into the parking lot.

"Gas masks on. Everybody ready?" Ethan looked at the dashboard clock. It was 0807 hours.

"Yessir!" they all yelled in unison, their voices muffled by the masks.

"On my mark."

Ethan watched the Mercedes E350 park at their one o'clock. A man in his mid-thirties got out and pressed the fob to lock the car. He was wearing a white polo shirt underneath a black windbreaker, khakis—a bit too baggy—and navy tennis shoes with a big N in dark brown.

Before he entered the bank, he turned and clicked the key fob again and watched the lights of his car flash. No sound followed. Satisfied that the car was securely locked, he walked into the bank.

"Now," Ethan said.

Bishop stayed in the van. The other four men jumped out of the vehicle and walked swiftly into the bank. Mac stopped just past the first set of doors. The others walked through the second double doors, took the gas canisters from their belts and yanked the pins as the doors closed behind them. Ethan walked straight ahead. Barr and Curtis flanked him from behind.

The gas filled the ample room, and Ethan hoped the tellers didn't have time to press the alarm button, but even if they did, they would be long gone before the police arrived.

Suresh Malik hadn't reached the counter yet. He had fallen to the floor, facing down, already passed out. Ethan grabbed his hair and pulled to check his face. Once he'd verified he was kidnapping the right man, he picked him up and threw him over his shoulder. He turned and saw two of his men already holding the door open. A second later they were on the street.

An older Asian man was on the sidewalk, en route to the bank. Mac stopped a few feet away and put his gloved finger against his gas mask, where his mouth would be. The man's eyes widened, and he stopped walking.

Ethan entered the van from the side and dumped Malik's body on the floor. Bishop started driving, while Curtis sat on the passenger seat. Mac and Barr got in back next to Ethan. Before all the doors were closed, the van pulled out.

As they turned left into Coleman, Ethan heard the first police sirens.

CHAPTER 16

Darcy zipped his jacket all the way up. He'd been too lazy to put the top on the Cobra and was freezing his ass off. It was early morning, and the temperature was just shy of 50 degrees. He hadn't been this cold since he moved from Seattle.

He checked the directions on his phone to make sure he'd arrived at the right place. Before he'd time to put the phone away, Jon came running out of the front door.

"Nice place," Darcy said, looking up at a skyscraper primarily made of bluish glass.

"I just moved in a few months ago." Jon pointed behind him, as if he needed to make sure he was addressing the right building. "It's a bit far from campus, but it's quieter."

Darcy was struck again by how much of an old soul Jon was. One of the smartest guys he'd ever met and yet charmingly naïve sometimes.

"Thanks for picking me up. I could have taken the VTA, but there're still delays due to the kidnapping," Jon said.

"No worries. It's on my way."

Darcy was driving north on Almaden when his phone buzzed. As soon as he saw the 211 code, he handed the phone to Jon and said, "Armed robbery. Where's it at?"

"Holy crap, armed robbery?" Jon looked at Darcy, his face a mixture of excitement and apprehension.

Darcy nudged him to give him the address.

"Ah, sorry. On Coleman. Close by," Jon said.

"Up for some action?" Darcy sped up. "Can you dig under your seat and grab the spinners?"

Jon put the lights up and turned them on. The blare of the siren muffled all the other noises on the street.

"Call out the intersections. I want to make sure we don't get T-boned."

Darcy saw Jon tug at his seat belt while looking right to spot incoming traffic.

"Clear," Jon said.

Darcy sped through a red light, turned left on Market and raced up toward Julian, passing by two police cars already setting up the perimeter.

"Clear," Jon said again when they were driving through another red light.

Now on Coleman, Darcy reached 65 mph while darting between the growing rush-hour traffic. He saw Jon grip the armrest and the seat. He wondered if the intern was more scared because of Darcy's handicap or the speed. It was probably the former. He felt that since Kozlov took his eye out, everybody thought he couldn't quite measure up. He decided to show Jon he had nothing to worry about and accelerated.

"New update. It looks like the perps left in a black van. No license plates yet," Jon said, looking at the phone.

"Make and model?"

Darcy decided to skip the crime scene and keep driving north.

"We just passed the bank." Jon pointed behind them, sounding disappointed that the ride hadn't come to and end.

"Did you see any black vans coming our way?"

"No."

"Exactly. Me neither. That means they must have gone north on Coleman, not south."

Jon nodded.

"I hope they didn't take the 880 exit," Darcy said, reaching 70 mph. The air was so cold, he felt his cheeks harden.

As they weaved between cars, Darcy honked when others didn't move out of their way. He thought through all the possible routes the van could have gone. He figured that unless they hid in one of the warehouses in the area, they would probably have continued going north.

Darcy wished he'd put on the top. His hands were so cold he could barely feel them.

"Can you turn the heater on?"

Jon did and immediately clung again to the armrest.

Two police cars came from one of the side streets and then veered off in different directions as soon as they reached the next cross street, leaving them alone.

Not even a minute later, Darcy shouted, "There it is," when he spotted a black van about a block in front of them. The traffic had worsened, and it was harder for him to weave between cars, even with the sirens. "Call the location in," he told Jon, but saw that the intern didn't loosen his death grip.

Darcy got closer. The van sped away, probably having spotted them.

There were only five cars between them now. Darcy swerved to the right lane and passed a car. The van took a left on Martin Avenue. Darcy slammed on the brakes and shot between two cars, almost scraping the one in front of him.

"Don't worry, I love this car," Darcy said, trying to humor Jon, who now looked green.

The intern tried to smile but didn't really succeed.

The wheels squealed as Darcy took the turn. The van was several yards ahead of them, but now there weren't any other cars between them.

"Jon, you've got to call it in."

Darcy slammed his foot on the pedal, and the Cobra roared as it accelerated to 80 mph. Before they got close, a rain of bullets hit the side of his car.

"Duck!" Darcy shouted as he thumped on the brakes and veered to his left, almost crashing into a parked car.

Shots hit the side of the car, the passenger door, and the windshield, cracking the glass, making it difficult for Darcy to see.

"Tell Dispatch we're being shot at," he yelled as he swerved, trying to avoid being hit by the spray of bullets sprouting more holes in the windshield. Then the police lights exploded, killing the siren, leaving them alone with the roaring engine and the crack of the bullets.

The van turned right, and the gunfire stopped. Darcy followed behind them, and the shots started up again.

"Please stop," Jon pleaded.

"We need to catch these guys. Just stay low." He pushed the car closer. "We need to get right behind them so they don't have an angle to shoot at us. You have to call it in—now."

The shots kept coming, but not enough to stop the Cobra.

The van turned left. Darcy followed. The van's back door opened a few inches and a muzzle appeared. Fuck, Darcy thought, and started swinging from side to side as new shots rained on them. A bullet clipped his right shoulder. Darcy felt it burn his skin. A few other bullets flew past him. He kept the target in sight but let the distance between them lengthen.

"Tell Dispatch we're losing them," Darcy yelled.

The only things he heard were the thunk of impacting bullets and the dying roar of the Cobra.

"Jon, I know you're scared, but you need to tell Dispatch we're about to lose them!"

But he still didn't hear Jon's voice.

Darcy diverted his eyes for a split second from the incoming fire to look at his passenger. The intern's eyes were wide open, and both of his hands were holding his neck. Blood sputtered out in between his fingers as he mouthed, "Please stop."

Darcy slammed on the brakes and stopped the car by the sidewalk. Dust rolled up behind them. The shots ceased as soon as the van took another left.

There was enough blood spewing through Jon's fingers for Darcy to know it was not a nick. He grabbed his dog's blanket from the backseat and pressed it right above Jon's collarbone. Then he saw the intern was bleeding from several other wounds.

"You're going to be okay, buddy. Hold on," he said as he reached between Jon's feet to pick up the dropped phone.

"Officer down. Code 30, code 30. I need an ambulance. I need a bus now!"

CHAPTER 17

As soon as the red Cobra stopped following them, Curtis told Bishop to take a left on Glade Drive and then a left on Monroe Street. Halfway through the block, he turned into a parking lot, and Curtis got out to open the warehouse door.

"We can't stay here long. My uncle comes by probably once a day. But at least we can wait for the noise to die down," Curtis said once the van was safely parked inside.

"Shooting at the police?" Bishop put both hands on his head and paced back and forth along the crates of paper. "Are you serious? We've shot at a police officer?" he yelled.

"I was just trying to scare them off," Mac said.

"What the fuck, man?" Bishop went on.

"If I'd wanted them dead, they would be."

"Oh, yeah. That's why you were shooting at the windshield."

"Bishop, stop it," Ethan said.

"What the hell have you gotten me into? We're fucked." His pace quickened, then he stopped and covered his face with both hands.

"Bishop, stop it," Ethan said.

They fell quiet. Curtis was barely five foot seven, but he was almost as wide as he was tall. When he leaned against the crates, he looked even shorter next to Mac, who was tall and wiry.

Mac walked around the car to check the status of the van. "At least the mud didn't come off the plates. How many black vans can there be in San Jose?"

Ethan wondered if the question was rhetorical. He didn't answer.

He checked Malik's vitals and said, "We need to move him before he wakes up. Unless you guys have something else to give him to keep him quiet." He pushed himself out of the van and faced his men. "It'll be easier to transport him if he's still out."

"But we can't use this van. I'll bet they'll be stopping every single black van they run into.

"For sure," Barr said. The right side of his face had a birthmark that looked like a falling star. He massaged it as he waited for instructions.

"Well, we can't stay here, as I said—" Curtis's voice was less deep than normal.

"We know. Your uncle will come soon," Mac cut him off.

"How attached are you to your van?" Ethan pulled out the thirty-two-ounce can of Kingsford lighter fluid he'd stashed in the van earlier.

"Are you kidding me?" Mac asked.

"You have a better idea?"

"And how the hell are we going to get out of here?"

Curtis walked out of the room. A few seconds later they heard the unmistakable rumble of a Harley. He rode it slowly into the room, his feet barely touching the floor. With a wide smile he said, "Meet my uncle's baby. He hides it here because his wife would kick his ass if she knew he had a hog."

The mood lifted a little.

"I can ride it to my house and pick up my car," Curtis offered.

Ethan nodded.

"We'll still need to figure out how to transfer the package," Curtis added.

"It won't fit in your car?" Bishop asked, as if he was afraid to be the one left behind.

"No, man. I got a Fiat. I can probably fit four of us max."

"You have a Fiat? What a pussy," Barr said.

"I got nothing to prove." He grabbed his crotch and shoved it forward. "You have a better plan?"

Since nobody did, Curtis left on the Harley, and Ethan asked Mac to stay in the van and keep an eye on Malik. If he woke up, they would have to knock him back into unconsciousness.

Ethan motioned for Bishop to follow him to the warehouse's office. The place was small but tidy. Several manila folders were piled on top of each other, competing for space with the phone and computer. Three gray filing cabinets occupied most of the back wall. There was only one chair, on the other side of the desk.

Both men stood facing each other. Ethan put a hand on Bishop's shoulder and waited until his colleague looked up at him. When their eyes met, Ethan hit him with a right cross. Before Bishop had time to react, Ethan punched him in the gut. Bishop doubled over, and Ethan hit him again with an uppercut that caught his lip and split it.

Stepping away, trying to avoid getting bathed in blood, Ethan crossed his arms and waited for the Marine to regain his composure. Bishop covered his mouth with his hand, and when it was drenched with blood he took off his sweater and pressed it against his face.

Ethan waited until their eyes met again, but this time he didn't hit him.

After a few seconds, when he was sure he had Bishop's attention, he said, "Do not ever embarrass me like that in front of the others." Ethan's voice was grave but low, just above a whisper. "I vouched for you. I brought you into this team because I thought you were a man. Your behavior today has been shameful, and I don't ever want to see this shit again. There were complications in this mission, and that's all it was. We have a job to do, and we're expected to do it." He waited until Bishop showed a sign of acknowledgement. When he nodded, Ethan ordered, "Go wash yourself."

CHAPTER 18

O'Connor Hospital was on the smaller side. The emergency room entrance was located on Forest Avenue, and though only one ambulance was stationed there, the parking lot was overflowing with patrol cars.

Saffron circled the lot until she found a spot, toward the west side of the complex. She ran toward the door, and as soon as she stepped inside she saw the mass presence of Santa Clara Sheriff's and San Jose PD personnel. She debated asking somebody for Darcy but decided to find him herself.

She walked down the hallway and weaved between people, noticing her breathing getting faster with each step. She spotted Captain Virago behind a group of broad-shouldered men. As she got closer, she heard her say, "Lynch is being treated."

"Darcy? Is Darcy okay?" she asked much louder than she intended. "He texted me about Jon but didn't say he was hurt."

Her eyes darted from Virago to the men, searching for answers in their faces. Virago was the only one who looked back at her. That's when she saw a trace of disdain in her eyes.

"Just a scratch. He should be here any minute."

"What do you mean, just a scratch?"

She saw one of the men nod to the captain, excusing himself. The other two followed.

When they were alone, Captain Virago said, "A bullet grazed his shoulder. He's fine."

Before Saffron had time to think about a bullet going through Darcy's body, he called her name. She turned and ran to him.

"Are you okay? You took a bullet?" she asked while checking his body for holes.

"No, not like that."

He turned and showed her the rip on his shirt where the bullet had gone through. It was bloody.

"Oh my God!"

"It's fine. See, they gave me a couple stitches and bandaged it," he said, turning his shoulder toward her face. "It looks worse than it is."

She hugged him and squeezed his freshly treated wound. He grunted.

"I'm sorry." She pulled away but kept her hand on his forearm. "How's Jon?"

"In surgery." Darcy's voice was grave. Saffron saw a few furtive glances from others when he said that. "He's very critical but was still alive when we got here."

She didn't know what to say. She'd only known Jon for a few weeks, but she was very fond of him.

They walked together toward Captain Virago.

"Any news?" Darcy asked.

"No." She turned and walked away from them.

Saffron looked at Darcy. His face said it all.

CHAPTER 19

Blake sat across from Martin Dunn in his minimalist office. The CEO had no paintings on the wall, no family photos on the desk, and no signed sports paraphernalia. There was a tall ponytail palm in a corner, but Blake didn't know if it was real. Martin had a 55-inch monitor mounted on the wall, an L-shape two-piece desk, and a five-hundred-dollar chair that stood empty behind it. Two nice leather sofas faced a coffee table on the other side of the room.

"Sometimes I wish we hadn't grown so big." Martin held a ceramic cup with the NanoQ logo in his hands. He was drinking designer green tea.

"Really?" Blake asked, not terribly surprised. He looked at the undisturbed cappuccino foam before he put it to his lips.

"Well . . . It was fun when we started. We had a dream, a vision, and we were all too naïve to think about the future. Remember when it was just the three of us?" Martin put the cup close to his face and inhaled, closing his eyes.

Blake nodded. He remembered the endless nights at their dorm, theorizing, drunk on beer and dreams. Then he remembered moving to the Bay Area and renting that awful house in Sunnyvale to "do the start-up thing in a garage" as Martin had put it. He was sure he didn't have the same fond memories his friend had.

"Blake, I really want to sell this thing so we can start something new. I'm tired of it."

"You tire easily. It hasn't been five years since we started it."

"What I'm saying is that I want to sell NanoQ for a profit. I don't want to start from scratch again," Martin said, ignoring Blake's remark.

"We're about to sell for a hundred sixty-eight million dollars. We have a few more days of due diligence, and the papers will be on your desk way before Thanksgiving. What are you worried about?"

The small and beady eyes of the twenty-seven-year-old CEO settled on his. Blake was unable to read his best friend's expression, so he didn't say anything more.

"You sure about that?" Martin asked.

The cappuccino Blake had just made in the fancy espresso machine suddenly tasted bitter. He rested the cup on the sofa's armrest and sighed. "Yep," he responded.

"So there's nothing about an impending lawsuit for patent infringement that I need to worry about?" His words came out slowly but deliberately, as if he was trying to hold back the betrayal he felt.

Blake combed a hand through his blond hair. It was thinning even though he wasn't thirty yet. "It's not a lawsuit. We just got notified. Besides, it's bogus. That's why I didn't tell you."

"We're in the middle of an M&A, and you don't think you need to tell me about a potential lawsuit for patent infringement of our core technology?"

"Martin, this happens all the time. The patent trolls hit companies like ours to get patents cheaply and see if they will get lucky making millions suing the giants." He took another deep breath. "I got this. I know our patents are fine.

They're just trying to scare us." He paused for a second, as if a new idea had just popped in his head. "Or maybe your buddies are doing this to get us to drop the price."

Blake saw Martin's jaw clench. He knew he'd just pushed a hot button. They'd had too many arguments about selling to Karsum Conglomerate, but Martin was ready to move on, so there was nothing more to discuss.

"That's ridiculous," Martin finally said, but his voice quivered a little.

Blake could see that the brilliant computer scientist was working his brain. He had managed to plant the seed, and now his friend was calculating the actual mathematical possibility that their buyer was playing dirty tricks on them. Blake knew Martin would ultimately decide that it was ridiculous and let the idea go, but at least he'd be distracted for a day or two.

And by then the problem would be solved.

"I don't think so either. You said they were good people." Blake made sure there was a hint of accusation in his voice.

Still thinking, Martin asked, "So, then, what do you think is going on?"

"I'm digging into it. You go on with your schmoozing and let me figure this out." He took the mug and got up. "Don't worry about it, okay? Let's sell this thing and start our next venture."

Blake walked toward the door, but before he left, Martin said, "You know if this gets out, the deal will be off the table."

Blake turned around, locked eyes with Martin and responded, "That's why I'm taking care of it."

CHAPTER 20

Darcy leaned against the wall, too antsy to sit. Saffron stood by his side. He didn't know what to say. He checked his watch. Jon was still in surgery. Darcy figured that as long as he was there, he was still alive.

He sensed Saffron looking at him, but couldn't meet her eyes. He pushed himself off the wall. She reached out and grabbed his hand. For the first time since he'd got to the hospital, he felt himself exhale.

"What the fuck's wrong with you?" Sorensen yelled from the entrance of the hallway.

Darcy turned to face him, releasing Saffron's hand. He felt everybody's attention turn first to the huge detective and then back to him, probably waiting to see how he would respond. But he didn't reply. He didn't know what was wrong with him, so he couldn't answer his partner's question.

"Sorensen . . ." Captain Virago started saying.

Sorensen reached Darcy and threw a punch that propelled him a few feet backward. Saffron tried to get in between, but Sorensen was faster. He got in Darcy's face, his left hand pressed against Darcy's chest, pinning him against the wall, his right fist raised up high, ready to punch his partner again if he didn't like what he had to say.

"I asked you a question," Sorensen hissed, pushing him harder against the wall.

"Enough!" Virago yelled, stepping beside them. "This is not appropriate," she said to Sorensen, who backed away but huffed while he did.

Darcy wanted to feel ashamed that the captain had to come to his rescue, but the only thing he felt was an overwhelming guilt.

A phone rang somewhere close by. Virago, standing in front of Darcy but looking at Sorensen, fished her phone out of her purse.

"What?" she barked.

Darcy couldn't hear the voice on the other end. Virago nodded while she listened. Her face was stern, every muscle tensed. When she finally hung up, she turned to Darcy and said, "Go back to the office."

"What? I'm not leaving until I know Jon's okay."

"It's not a request, Lynch. I'll keep you posted."

He didn't move. Her dark brown eyes looked onyx black under the fluorescent hospital lights.

"If you really want to help, find out who's behind this." Her voice was a little softer.

Darcy exchanged glances with Saffron, and they both started walking away.

"And Detective . . ."

Darcy looked back over his shoulder. He felt every officer and detective watching him.

"Yes?"

"Put on a jacket or something."

He nodded and touched his shoulder. He met Saffron's stare and grinned, trying to defuse her worried look.

Once they were out of earshot, Saffron said, "Loads of love in there."

"You've got no idea."

He was walking fast. Saffron's long legs allowed her to keep pace with him.

"Can I borrow your car?" Darcy asked.

"I thought that's why I was coming with you."

She put her arm inside his, and he realized how much he appreciated her warmth. Once they were outside of the hospital, Darcy stopped and hugged her. She kissed his cheek and squeezed him harder.

She let him go and handed him the keys. "Jon's going to be okay. He's a strong kid."

"I hope so." He kissed her and got in the Mini.

"Go get the bad guys, Darcy. I'll wait here until Jon's out of danger."

He nodded and started the car. "Keep me posted."

"You know it." She blew a kiss in his direction.

Darcy drove out of the parking lot, but before he was gone he looked back toward the hospital entrance. He saw Saffron stop and turn back. She saw him and waved.

Before he'd reached the light, he checked his phone and flinched. It was speckled with Jon's blood, silently accusing him of recklessness. He wiped it against his pants, but the blood was already dry. Darcy debated for a second whether to use the phone anyway but then put it back into his pocket.

CHAPTER 21

After Darcy left, Sorensen walked to the hospital's waiting area and searched the vending machine for a Red Bull. There weren't any, so he settled for a Diet Dr Pepper. He went back to talk to Virago.

"What do you have?" she asked.

"Not much. The van disappeared somewhere around Central Expressway. They're canvasing all the warehouses in the area, but no luck so far. Lynch never called in the license plates, so we can't dig through that angle."

"Traffic cams?"

"The assholes didn't run any red lights. Don't ask me how, or the stupid things weren't working. Who knows? But Traffic hasn't found anything yet."

"And the bank?"

"Same gig as the coffee shop and the VTA. But this time there were only four men. The ATM and the bank cameras caught that much. All in black, masks, threw the gas grenades, and then all you can see is gray."

"Did they take money this time?"

"It doesn't look like it either."

"Kidnapping?" Virago sounded as exasperated as Sorensen felt.

"We haven't verified that yet, but I have a gut feeling there'll be somebody missing."

"Witnesses?"

"Nobody awake, and nobody else has come forward."

Virago fell silent for a while. Her eyes were lost somewhere, but Sorensen knew she was thinking hard.

"It's up to you, Detective, but if you're up for it, I would rather have you out there solving this case . . ."

Sorensen hesitated. He cared about Jon as if he were his own kid.

"You'll keep me posted?" he asked.

"Play by play."

He nodded and followed Darcy's path out of the hospital. But instead of going back to the office, he went to the shooting crime scene. When he got there, he walked over to Sergeant Marra.

"What can you tell me?"

"We've found thirty-four shell casings. 5.56 mm, so these guys weren't kidding around. I'm surprised there wasn't more damage. How's your guy, by the way?"

"Still in surgery."

Marra nodded and started walking toward the end of the street. Sorensen followed him. The orange tape cordoned off an area flanked by light posts. Several yellow cones with numbers pinpointed the evidence within the perimeter. A burly man was hitching the Cobra to the tow truck. A tech knelt on the ground taking photos of a tire tread. Sorensen wondered how the scientist knew that that tread was more significant than the dozens of others on the street. He made a mental note to ask Lou one day.

When they reached the end of the street, Marra stopped. "From here, if they took a left we have no camera coverage for a couple miles, if they were smart enough to stick to side streets. If they took a right, they may have gone up to Central Expressway, and we may get lucky with a pic or two." Marra didn't sound very confident.

"Traffic hasn't found anything yet."

"Yeah, I heard." Marra looked toward the area behind them. "Maybe we'll get something here."

"No witnesses?" Sorensen did a 360, taking in the entire crime scene.

"I got a bunch of officers canvasing the area, but there are no storefronts; these are all warehouses. Most people probably thought it was safer to stay inside once the fireworks started."

"A man can always hope." Sorensen checked his phone in case he'd received any other leads. There was nothing. "Okay, thank you. I'm heading out to the station to see if I can dig up any connections with the other two incidents." He dreaded having to be in the same room with Lynch, but solving this case was more important than having to breathe the same air as the asshole who'd put Jon in the hospital.

"I'll let you know if I find anything here."

Sorensen shook hands with Marra and walked back to his car. As he drove, he wondered how long it would take the Feds to come knocking at this door, asking about the missing Marine.

CHAPTER 22

Ethan's place wasn't very big, but it was modern, clean, and it had an amazing view of Moffett Field. Ethan pulled cold beers from the fridge for everybody, even though it was barely noon. They all opened them and sat in the living room.

"We have to blow up the van," Ethan said.

He watched Mac's face show a pang of regret, but instead of saying anything, he emptied half his beer. Good boy, Ethan thought.

"Semtex?" Barr asked.

"That's some heavy-duty stuff," Curtis said. "They'll trace it."

"Maybe, but we need to completely destroy it. It's the only way to make sure there's no evidence." Ethan looked around to let the gravity of the statement sink in. "There're only two things that went well today: one is that we got the target. The other is that we didn't get caught. But it was a close call, and we shot at the police. They'll even have the janitor looking for us." He finished his beer. "What we need to do is get this job done ASAP so we can get paid and take a well-deserved vacation."

Mac got up and checked on Suresh Malik. He was still unconscious from the blow to the head Barr gave him when he started waking up at the warehouse.

Mac looked back at the group and asked, "Should we start then? I can't wait to go to Maui."

They toasted to hot beaches and finished their beers.

Then Ethan got up to begin the torture session.

CHAPTER 23

Sorensen was glad Lynch wasn't in the bullpen when he arrived. He looked at the boards and read the information his partner had added about the bank case, the van, and the shootout. He filled in a few blanks with what he'd learned from Marra. But his mind was on Jon. The last update from Virago told him that he made it out of surgery. At least he was still alive.

Sorensen sat in his chair and chugged the last few drops of an old Red Bull. The station was almost empty. It felt eerie, but he knew they were all gone, trying to find who'd shot Jon.

And he was here.

He looked up at the boards covered with crime scene photos of the VTA, the coffee shop, the bank, and the streets where Lynch pursued the van. The last check of the traffic cams still showed no leads. Some officers were canvasing the warehouses, asking people if they recognized, or had seen, the black van. So far, nothing. It had vanished. Just like that.

He went to the vending machine and got a bag of potato chips and another Red Bull. On the way back he heard his desk phone. He picked it up on the last ring.

"Sorensen."

"I'm not really sure how to tell you this," First Sergeant Loren said. There was dread in his voice, and Sorensen felt his neck hairs stand on end.

"National security threat?" the detective asked, sitting down.

"I never thought I would say this, but today I kind of wish it was."

"What the hell are you talking about? What could be worse?" He rubbed his eyes with his thick knuckles, then opened the can.

"Seth McAuley just called me."

"He's alive? That's good."

"From Seattle."

"Why? He deserted?"

"What? No. Why would you think so?"

"I don't know. You said this was worse than a national security threat. Can you get to the point? What the hell's going on?" Sorensen asked, losing his patience.

There was silence on the other side, and finally he heard an audible sigh that lasted forever. Sorensen imagined his long-lost friend bracing himself before giving him the worst news he'd probably ever given.

"We just put McAuley on a plane back to the Bay Area. He doesn't remember anything after the gas started spreading inside the coffee shop."

"Okay . . ." Sorensen said, encouraging him to continue.

"He woke up on a bus heading to Vancouver, BC." Loren swallowed. "He was dressed in a kilt—"

"He was what?"

"He was dressed in a kilt, and his eyebrows were missing."

Silence overtook both men.

Sorensen didn't know what to say. Finally he rose from the chair and yelled, "This is not fucking funny, Loren. I have three cases with the same MO, and one of my guy's in the hospital shot multiple times, his life hanging by a thread, and you're making jokes?" He started pacing by the side of his desk. "Grow up and get over what happened in college," he shouted, and hung up.

Still holding the receiver, now in the cradle, he looked up at the board and saw Jon's smiling face from the DMV photo. Sorensen lifted the receiver and slammed it three times against the desk, each time with increasing force, making a point to the world. But there was nobody around to see it.

The phone rang again.

"What?" he snarled, not caring who was on the other end.

"Sorensen, I'm serious," Loren said. "What I'm trying to say is that in McAuley's case, it doesn't seem to be a national security case or even a crime at all. I'm embarrassed to say that it looks like some shitbirds on my side of the fence wanted to make a statement. This was a prank."

"You can't know that after talking to a guy who doesn't remember anything." Sorensen paced again. "Make sure he comes straight here from the airport. I have a lot of questions for him."

"We'll have to debrief him first."

"No. You listen to me. I got a man in the hospital and dozens of shots fired from a van in a public street. That's no prank. If you want to debrief your man, you better do it in the car on the way to my station." He realized he was still yelling. "If you don't, I'll arrest you for obstruction," he said in a lower but equally firm voice.

"Very well. He'll land at 1330 hours. We should be in your office by 1400 hours."

Sorensen checked his watch. He had a little less than an hour to prepare.

CHAPTER 24

Ethan didn't really like to punch people. But it seemed that today he'd been forced to do it a few times. He looked down at Suresh Malik, tied to the chair and already bloody.

"How much do you want to live?" Ethan asked him again.

Malik's left eye was swollen shut and already the size of an egg. He was bleeding from his nose, and the front of his white polo shirt was soaked red. But still the only thing Malik did was beg.

Ethan turned around and walked to the table just a few feet away. He could sense Malik watching him.

"You can stop this at any time. I've told you that already," Ethan said, ogling his tools.

He picked a pair of pliers and faced his victim. Ethan swung the device from side to side as he approached Malik. The man retreated against the back of the chair he was tied to and gripped the ends of the armrests, as if that would protect his nails from being pulled out. Ethan got closer. When he was only a few feet apart, Malik started shaking his head and whimpered harder. Ethan stopped and just watched.

"You have to tell me what you want from me," Malik wailed. "I just don't know what you want. I'll say anything."

Now Ethan got closer still. Malik's eyes widened, and before he could get in another word he started heaving, as if he had a hard time breathing. He looked at Ethan in desperation.

He was trying to speak, but his mouth opened and closed like a fish out of water's.

Ethan hesitated, wondering if it was an act. "Curtis, get in here now!"

Curtis walked in, followed by the others. They stopped by Ethan, who had now taken a few steps away from Malik.

"He's having a heart attack," Curtis said, pushing everybody aside.

He cut the man's restraints and pulled him onto the floor. Everybody else watched their victim struggle for breath. Malik started clasping his chest, and he looked back at Curtis with bulging eyes strained with terror.

"We need to take him to a hospital," Curtis yelled, watching as the man faded fast.

"No can do, brother," Ethan said.

Curtis looked up at him for a second and started giving Malik CPR when he went into cardiac arrest.

"You're going to let him die?" Bishop asked.

"No, I expect the paramedic to save him," Ethan said, watching Curtis.

"I'm just an 18D. I can't work miracles. We need to take him to the emergency room now." Life was draining from Malik's body with each chest compression.

Everybody stood still except Curtis, who continued working on Malik. Barr and Mac exchanged furtive glances with Bishop, but nobody said anything.

Finally, Bishop turned around and, passing by Ethan, slightly hitting his shoulder, said, "I don't know you anymore, man." And left the room.

Ethan looked at the others, but the three men made themselves busy. "You better make sure he lives," he told Curtis, and followed Bishop out of the room.

CHAPTER 25

When Seth McAuley walked into the station, Sorensen almost spilled his drink. The Marine had discarded the kilt and was now in his class C uniform, but Loren hadn't lied: his eyebrows were gone.

Sorensen extended his hand and introduced himself, then said, "Thank you for coming by."

First Sergeant Loren stayed behind and just nodded, animosity radiating from his entire being.

"Really?" Sorensen shook his head.

Loren kept his hands interlaced behind him and didn't reply. McAuley looked from one to the other.

"Any coffee?" the detective asked, moving on.

When they both declined, he led them to an interview room.

"Can you run me through what happened to you?" Sorensen had the case file in front of him but didn't open it.

"Not much to tell, sir. I went to the coffee shop to get some writing done. I do this every week." He looked down at his hands and picked at a hangnail on his thumb. "I'd just ordered coffee and went back to my table. As I sat down, the doors opened, and a bunch of guys walked in, dressed in night camouflage and gas masks. I heard a pop, then saw gray smoke. Next thing I remember, I'm waking up on a bus in Seattle, en route to friggin' Canada."

"What are you writing?"

McAuley chewed on his thumb. Then, without fully removing his finger, he said, "A sci-fi opera."

"A what?" both Sorensen and Loren asked.

"It's like an epic. A lot of characters and different worlds set a couple hundred years from now."

"Anything confidential?"

"No. Of course not. It's futuristic fiction."

Sorensen eyed him. He'd read enough sci-fi books to know that even if there was anything nonfiction in it, it would be disguised enough for the information to not be a threat.

"Any idea who these men were?"

McAuley looked at Loren.

Sorensen leaned back against his chair, observing both. Loren finally nodded, and McAuley started talking.

"A couple weeks ago we had a football match against the guys from the 23rd Regiment, from San Bruno. One of their guys got injured, and it got pretty ugly very fast. I think they did this."

"Why would they target you?"

"I'm the captain of the team." He was sitting straight, not touching the back of his chair.

Sorensen remained quiet for a while. He was trying to process how preposterous this scenario was.

"I'll be right back," he said, and left the room.

He grabbed one of the tablets lying around the office and went back into the room. He tapped a few screens and finally pressed Play on the YouTube video of the kidnapping at the coffee shop.

"I'm sure you've seen this already," he said as the video started.

McAuley hadn't. His expression was a mixture of disbelief and anger. He traced his missing eyebrows but didn't say anything.

When the video ended, Sorensen said, "Some heavy-duty stuff."

McAuley nodded.

"Do you really think a group of Marines would do this as a payback for a stupid game?"

Neither Marine said anything, but Sorensen could see they both believed they would.

"Remember the prototype halothane gas I told you about?" Loren asked.

"Yes. You found the missing case?"

"No. But I think you should know that we've had a few reports that some Marines have been horsing around with it."

"And you waited until now to tell me this?" Sorensen yelled.

"It didn't seem relevant to your investigation."

"I'm the only judge of that." He wanted to punch him but instead pounded on the desk.

Sorensen stared at Loren for a long time.

Loren finally broke eye contact and, as a truce, offered the names of a few Marines from the 23rd Regiment who were at the game.

Sorensen walked them to the elevator, and before it arrived he asked, "Did they do anything else to you? It seems like a lot of trouble for just a pair of shaved eyebrows, a kilt, and a ticket to Canada."

McAuley looked back at Loren, then opened his shirt and pulled up his white T-shirt. On his right pectoral he had a brand-new tattoo. It looked like an action hero.

Sorensen laughed. "Man, I'm sorry," he said, almost choking. "That's mean."

"And it's not true," McAuley said.

The detective looked at him, not comprehending. "What's not true?" he asked.

Loren interjected: "That's a blue falcon, slang in the Marines for 'buddy fucker'—someone who doesn't take care of his troops."

"Oh," Sorensen said. "Why would the 23rd Regiment think that about you?"

"Exactly. It's baseless," the Marine protested, rebuttoning his shirt.

Sorensen decided to look more into McAuley. It seemed strange that the guys would have gotten him the tattoo if the accusation was completely unfounded.

The detective ran back to this desk to a ringing phone. It was Sergeant Marra. He said a couple officers had gone to investigate a loud disturbance, followed by dark smoke. They found a black van burning at the Alviso Boat Dock. They first thought it was vandalism, but when the scorchers finished putting the fire out, they found a body inside.

CHAPTER 26

"There've been some complications," Blake heard Ethan say as soon as he picked up the phone.

"We can't afford any complications." He got up and closed his office door. "I have less than a week to make this go away."

"Suresh Malik is dead."

Blake felt as if he'd been punched in the gut. When he was able to breathe again, he asked, "What happened?"

"Heart attack."

"Fuck." Blake felt cold sweat wetting the collar of his shirt.

"'Fuck's right. We need to talk."

"Meet me in Washington Park in a half hour."

"Okay, but not by the play area. I don't want some mom calling the cops because two creeps are hanging out there," Ethan said.

Blake laughed against his will. "I'll see you by the tennis courts."

About thirty minutes later, Blake arrived at the park. He zipped his leather jacket. The air was crisp. Nobody was playing tennis. He saw Ethan coming toward him. His pace was fast and determined.

"The way I see it," Ethan said when he got close enough to not have to yell, "is that we can walk away right now and hope to God we don't get caught."

Blake shook his head but didn't interrupt him.

"Or you find somebody else."

"Malik was the right person. I don't even know who else you can go after." Blake bent over as if he was going to puke, but instead rubbed his thighs. He was thinking, but he couldn't come up with what to do next.

"I say we go for the big guy," Ethan suggested.

"That's crazy."

"Why?"

"We don't know anything about him," Blake said. "We'd need to do a bunch of research to figure out how to do this and not fuck up again."

"I got all that."

Blake looked at him. "How? Why?"

"Because I knew you wouldn't come up with a plan B, partner, so I did," Ethan said, but there wasn't a hint of humor in his voice. "How fast do you really need this done?"

"As I said, this nightmare needs to go away in the next couple days. A week tops, and that's really pushing it."

"Well, if you don't want the top guy, you can find another target. Up to you."

Ethan started walking away.

"Wait," Blake called after him.

Ethan turned and smiled. "I'll call you in an hour with instructions."

For a second, Blake wished he'd never met this man.

CHAPTER 27

There was nothing Sorensen could add to the new crime scene. CSU was all over the burnt van, and the ME had already taken the corpse to the morgue. So he decided to go back to the station.

While he cruised down the highway, he thought about his cases. Maybe what they did to Seth McAuley really was just a prank, but what about the other cases? The dead guy in the van—an accident? Unlikely. And nobody shoots at the police for a lark. That was absurd.

As soon as he got to his desk, he called the main contact number for the 23rd Marine Regiment and asked for the commanding officer of the guys McAuley had given him.

"This is Sergeant Major Williams. Colonel Francis is in Washington and won't be back until next Monday. How can I help you?" The woman's voice was high pitched and sounded more like a teenage cheerleader's than that of a high-ranking officer in the Marines.

Sorensen introduced himself and jumped right into it. "I wanted to know if you've heard about a prank done to Gunny Seth McAuley, from the 4th LSG."

"I heard about it," she said.

Sorensen remained silent for a long time. She did too.

"Were your guys involved?" he finally asked, feeling as if he had just lost at a staring contest.

"You think that was retaliation because of the game?" she asked, not giving anything else away.

"You tell me."

She was quiet again.

"Sergeant Major, Seth McAuley was kidnapped in a coffee shop in San Jose yesterday. Six men gassed the place and took him. They shaved his eyebrows and tattooed a blue falcon on his chest while he was passed out. Then they put him on a bus to Canada wearing a kilt. He woke up in Seattle with no recollection of any of it."

"I don't know anything about this," she said after another long pause. Her voice didn't even try to conceal her amusement.

"I'm glad you find all of this funny," he tried to admonish her, but he also had to shake off a laugh, remembering McAuley with no eyebrows. "Do you know if any of your men might have any information?"

"Seriously, no," she offered.

"We've invested a lot of manpower in trying to figure out what went on at the coffee shop. The same MO was used at a kidnapping at the VTA. And as I'm sure you've heard, again at a bank this morning." He waited, but still nothing. "The one this morning resulted in a high-speed chase and shootout that critically injured one of my best guys. So, as funny as a prank can be—and trust me, the tattoo was priceless—I need to understand what's going on here ASAP, or a lot of heads are going to be rolling."

"I'm sorry to hear about your man, Detective. Let me do some digging, and I'll call you right back," she said, her tone matching the gravity of the situation for the first time.

CHAPTER 28

Darcy Lynch spent more time than was needed at the scene of the shootout. He always went back to crime scenes after CSU had left. He rarely found something the techs had missed, but what he was looking for was something different. He wanted to connect to the place, become almost intimate with it so he could understand why the perp had decided to use that site and not another.

This time he got nothing, especially because the shooters hadn't chosen the place. Darcy had offered it on a silver platter by pushing the pursuit way too far. So he finally left the crime scene because he couldn't justify being there any longer. Dread weighed on him more than he wished to admit.

He drove Saffron's Mini with his left hand. His right shoulder throbbed, but he didn't care. The pain was a reminder of what he'd done. He looked over at the passenger seat, half expecting to find Jon there. He thought about the intern's pleas to stop the pursuit, and his unwillingness to do so. Darcy then shut his eyes for a second and saw Jon's wounds spewing out, blood tainting his hands in dark red.

He was responsible for what had happened to Jon. He had to find out who'd done this to him.

As soon as Darcy entered the bullpen, Sorensen looked up at him, and his face changed, making Darcy feel worse than when he had punched him earlier. Darcy wondered if he should say something, but nothing came to mind. He went to his desk and powered up his computer.

Darcy sensed Sorensen's eyes on him and looked up. He would have to face him sooner or later, so he said, "I'm sorry, okay?"

"You're sorry?" Sorensen got up from his desk and stared down at Lynch. "What the hell were you thinking?"

"We were in pursuit. The license plate was covered with mud, and I didn't want to lose them. They didn't start shooting until we were on the side streets. I wanted to get close enough so they would lose the line of sight, and we could give the location to the other units."

"Jon's just an intern. He didn't even have a gun to defend himself!" Sorensen yelled.

The few people in the bullpen left like rats abandoning a sinking ship.

"I know." It was all Darcy could say. He knew. But he was just trying to do his job. He wondered who in that office would have done anything differently. But he didn't say it.

Sorensen shook his head and turned around to view the evidence, as if the sight of Darcy disgusted him. Darcy stood and walked to the boards too. He needed to work. He needed to make sure the shooting wasn't in vain.

Sorensen moved a few inches away when Darcy got close.

"They were shooting at us with an assault rifle. It could have been an M4. The military uses them," Darcy said when he saw the note below McAuley's name about being a Marine.

"Yeah, and a lot of other forces," Sorensen spat, "including some law enforcement around the Bay, and the East San Jose gangs."

"What do you have so far?" Darcy asked.

"I'm not wasting my time getting you up to speed. You just managed to get yourself pulled off the case this morning."

"I'm not off the case." Darcy shook his head. "We can either work this together, or we can work it separately—your choice—but I'm not off the fucking case."

His patience was running out.

Sorensen acquiesced and sat down. He told Darcy everything about the kilt prank, the call to the Sergeant Major, and the dead body in the burnt van.

"Do you have a pic of the van?" Lynch asked.

Sorensen pulled out his phone and showed him the few he had. "CSU will have more."

"That's the same van as in the shootout."

"How do you know?"

"Same color, make, and model, and the side mirror is missing."

Sorensen picked up the photos from the printer and pinned them on the board.

"Are you sure?"

"Absolutely."

Sorensen called Mauricio from his desk phone. "Hey, are you still with the van?"

"Yep."

"We're pretty sure this is the van the perps used to kidnap the guy at the bank and to shoot Jon, so go through every inch."

"You got it," Mauricio said.

"And tell Madison we need to know ASAP who's the crispy inside."

When he hung up, Darcy said, "I bet it's the guy they took at the bank."

"Why on earth would they kidnap somebody and then set him on fire?"

"I have no clue. But I bet it is."

Darcy went to the kitchen and came back with a fresh cup of coffee. Sorensen was talking on the phone. When he saw Darcy, he pressed the speaker button.

"Sergeant Major, you're on speaker. Detective Lynch is with me."

"Very well. As I was saying, none of my guys are fessing up to the prank. However, my gunny, Ben Walters, is missing."

"Your gunnery sergeant?" Sorensen asked.

"Yes."

Darcy looked up to the whiteboard and saw that McAuley was also a gunnery sergeant.

"Thank you, Sergeant Major. Let me know if you hear from Walters."

"Will do."

CHAPTER 29

As soon as Sorensen hung up the phone, Virago poked her head out of her office and summoned him over. The detective explained how Lynch had identified the burnt van as the one from the bank kidnapping and subsequent shootout. He also told her about the prank on McAuley and the missing gunny from the 23rd.

"I'm planning to meet with all of the guys who played at that match later today."

Virago checked her watch and arched an eyebrow.

"I know it's a lot, but maybe he can help," Sorensen said, looking over at Lynch, sitting alone at his desk. "If the kidnappings are just a prank gone bad, I'd rather know right away."

"I hope they don't start another fight." Virago pushed her glasses onto her head.

"I'll beat those punks' asses if they do."

The phone rang. Virago picked it up and, after listening for a few seconds, said, "A Sergeant Major Williams is trying to reach you."

"I'll take it at my desk. Give me a sec."

He excused himself and walked out. "What's up?" he asked before he had the receiver all the way to his ear.

"We found Gunny Ben Walters."

"Is he dead?"

"No. He's in Mexico."

"What's he doing in Mexico?"

"He doesn't know. The last thing he remembers was riding the VTA yesterday." She swallowed. "Looks similar to the gunny in Seattle you were telling me about. Border patrol woke him up. He was also wearing a kilt."

"Yep, just like the other guy." Sorensen shook his head. "Did he at least keep his eyebrows?"

The sergeant major didn't respond. "I'm very sorry, Detective. It seems that the Marines have wasted a bunch of law enforcement resources."

"You need to get in touch with First Sergeant Loren at the 4th LSG. I expect the appropriate level of disciplinary action," Sorensen said. "I still want to talk to your boys today."

"Today?"

Sorensen imagined Williams checking the time.

"As I explained earlier, we have a third incident, a burnt body and somebody in critical condition. They may have gone from prank to murder, and if so, I want to find that out today."

After she grudgingly agreed to send them over, Sorensen went back to Virago's office to give her the update. He closed the door behind him, even though there weren't a lot of people in the office. She was shutting down her computer and gathering her coat and purse. Sorensen didn't sit, letting her know he wasn't going to keep her there long.

"It looks like we may have closed the VTA and the coffee shop cases."

She looked up, took her coat off and put her purse back in the drawer.

CHAPTER 30

Darcy was only mildly surprised when Sorensen asked for help to interview the Marines. He knew it was only because it was late, they didn't have a lot of manpower, and it would probably lead to dead ends anyway. *Just a bunch of guys being stupid*, he thought. The bank was something different. Related, yes, but different. That was the main reason he hadn't refused his partner's request. He was going to find out what that connection was.

"Were you in a fight recently?" Darcy asked the fourth Marine on his list.

He had a split lip and a sizeable mauve bruise on his left temple. He kept adjusting his collar, as if it was itchy and was irritating his neck. Darcy had seen this behavior before and knew it didn't always mean the person was nervous, but it often did.

"No." The Marine licked his lip, but when he saw Darcy staring at him, he stopped and averted his eyes.

"How did you get the bruises then?"

"Playing football."

"Don't you wear a helmet?"

"It fell off."

Darcy pulled out a couple photos from a folder and spread them across the table. Without pointing at any one in particular, he asked, "Do you know who these people are?"

The Marine didn't say anything.

"Bishop, what started out as a funny prank has now turned into homicide."

The Marine slouched further in his chair and crossed his arms over his square chest.

Darcy pulled out the photo of the burnt van. "Do you recognize this van?"

"No." Bishop didn't even look at it.

"Let me see the bottom of your boots," Darcy said.

"What? Why?" The Marine craned his neck and fiddled with his collar again.

"I have a boot print. I want to see what yours looks like," Darcy explained.

Bishop placed his right boot on top of the table that separated them. "I got nothing to hide."

"What size are you, a twelve?" Darcy asked.

"Something like that," he said, showing no emotion.

"Okay, show me your other boot."

The Marine's left temple started twitching. He moved his right foot down, pushed the chair sideways and brought up the other boot.

Darcy looked at it for a long time. "Your left foot is quite a bit smaller than your right one."

Bishop stared at him while he lowered his foot to the floor.

Darcy looked down, still taking in the different-sized feet. "How did you get in the Marines?" he asked, genuinely curious.

"I'm that good," Bishop bragged. This was the first time he didn't show defiance.

Darcy opened the VTA file and searched through a set of photos until he found the ones he was looking for.

"At first I thought they belonged to two different people," he said, showing him two different sets of prints. One was of a right boot; the other was a partial of the left one, but it had enough detail to determine the shoe size. "But now I can see I was mistaken."

Bishop watched him.

"You were there." It wasn't a question.

"So what? You already know we did the prank on that prick Walters." He spat the words at Lynch.

"Yes. But what I really want to know is what kind of prank was this one." He opened the third file and showed him a photo of the entrance of the bank, where four men in dark clothing and gas masks were walking in.

Darcy watched Bishop.

"I got nothing to do with that," Bishop finally said. "Both our gunnys are dicks. We decided to fuck with them a little. We never thought it would become this big a deal."

Darcy pushed his chair away from the table and stood. He walked toward the one-sided mirror and, placing both hands on his head, shouted, "You go inside a public establishment wearing masks, gas the place up, kidnap somebody and you don't think it will become a big deal? Are you a fucking moron?"

"Listen, it was stupid, but it was a prank." Bishop looked at the picture from the bank and, stabbing it with his index finger, said, "I don't know anything about that one. It wasn't us. I've been at the 4th LSG until you called us here."

Darcy sat back down, crossed his arms and slouched in his chair, mirroring Bishop's pose.

Staring at the Marine, he said, "You know they do incredible things with forensic science these days."

He leaned forward, getting as close to Bishop's personal space as the table allowed him. The Marine didn't move an inch. Darcy pulled the picture from underneath Bishop's finger and studied it. He didn't find what he was looking for but didn't let his face show it.

"I can't tell which one of these guys is you. But CSU can take the video footage we have courtesy of the bank, and measure everybody's feet. When we find one pair that doesn't match, I'll have more than probable cause to arrest you. So if I were you, I would start talking now, and maybe I can help you."

Bishop closed the distance between them. He was so close, Darcy could smell oranges on his breath.

"Until you do, Detective, either bring me my lawyer, or let me go." He maintained eye contact with Darcy as he spoke.

CHAPTER 31

After escorting Bishop to the elevator, Darcy went to the kitchen to refill his coffee mug. He regretted not being able to get more out of the guy, but once Bishop invoked his right to a lawyer, Darcy knew he needed more to hold him. On his way back into the bullpen, he looked around and saw a few more Marines still waiting to be interviewed. He sighed and walked back to his desk to leave his jacket.

Sorensen's cell phone rang. Darcy looked around, but his partner wasn't in the bullpen. He saw Madison's name on the caller ID. He hesitated for a moment, knowing that Sorensen wouldn't be happy if he answered his phone.

"Madison, Lynch here. What's up?"

There was a pause. Darcy was about to say something when the soft voice of the ME said, "I was trying to reach Detective Sorensen."

"He's interviewing a witness. Do you have something?"

"I've finished the autopsy of the burnt victim."

"I'm coming over."

He hung up before the ME could protest. Darcy knew he was technically off the case and that the ME would be unhappy to see him, but he couldn't wait for Sorensen to be finished.

Darcy sprinted down the block, and when he got to the morgue he found Madison working on an unrelated body.

"Detective," the ME said. There was some contempt in his voice, but Darcy ignored it.

Madison moved away from the new body and located the file on the burnt corpse. He glanced over his report and then, facing Darcy, said, "I thought you were off this case."

"Our top priority is to find these guys. Sorensen is tied up. No reason why I can't help move things along."

Madison didn't look convinced, but after a long, audible sigh he started talking. "The victim had a hip replacement. I'm waiting to get the match to the serial number, then we'll know who he is." He lifted the sheet that covered the man's upper body and continued: "He was already dead when the van caught on fire."

Darcy thought about what he'd just heard. "So they didn't burn him to kill him. They burned him to get rid of the body or his identity," he pondered while he looked at the corpse. The man was charred black, but yellow adipose tissue was visible through the cracks. There was still a hint of the burnt chicken smell emanating from the body. "They probably didn't know he had the fake hip." Looking up at Madison, he asked, "Cause of death?"

"Heart attack."

"Heart attack?"

"That's what I said, Detective."

Darcy ignored him. "Any signs of assault?"

"That's really hard to establish with burns, unless the victims have broken bones." Madison thought for a second, probably trying to figure out how to explain something really difficult to somebody really stupid. "With burned skin, you can't see hematomas. Also, if there's broken skin, like a wound or ligature marks, for example, many times the heat alters the skin in so many different ways that these lesions are impossible to identify."

"So he could have been assaulted."

"I'm not prepared to say that. All I can say is that assault cannot be established or discarded with these levels of burns."

Darcy looked at him. He wanted more from the ME—maybe an educated guess perhaps, even if it wasn't a corroborated fact. "Doctor, this man was kidnapped and died of a heart attack. Do you think it may be plausible that he died of fear because he was being assaulted or tortured?"

"Detective, this man was kidnapped. It is plausible that he died before anybody had the chance to lay a finger on him." The ME turned his back to Darcy and started working on the other body. Emphasizing each word, Madison continued: "I provide you with the medical findings: the facts. It is your job to explore the theories."

He was right, and Darcy didn't have a clever comeback, so he left. His cell rang while he was on his way back to the station. He was surprised to see the ME's number.

"The serial number came back. Your victim's name is Suresh Malik. He had the hip replacement done in India in 2003."

Darcy thanked Madison and rushed back to the office. He hoped Sorensen was still interviewing so he could get a lead before his partner found out he'd been answering his phone.

He exhaled a sigh of relief when he got to the bullpen and saw there were no Marines left waiting to be interviewed. Without realizing it, Darcy looked over to Jon's desk and felt his gut wrench. I'm going to find the assholes who did this to you. I swear it.

ViCAP didn't turn up anything on Malik, but that didn't surprise him. The Internet did, however. Just as he was finishing reading the victim's profile on LinkedIn, Sorensen came into the room, rubbing his eyes as if he'd just woken up from a bad dream.

"Man, what a waste of time," he said, and collapsed into his chair. "Did you get anything?"

"Get up. We have somewhere to be." Darcy put on his jacket.

"You have a lead?" Sorensen asked, perking up.

Darcy told him about the visit to the morgue, avoiding how he'd learned that the autopsy was done. "Once Madison told me his name, I was able to find that he's a middle manager at a law firm."

"I don't like lawyers either, but burning him seems a bit extreme," Sorensen said. "What type of law firm?"

"From what I could gather, patent law."

"Patent law?" Sorensen asked. "I know there are millions at stake in that, but this seems like a very weird way to get rid of a body. And why burn him if he was already dead?"

"Let's say this guy gets kidnapped in the bank for some reason—ransom probably—but has a weak heart and dies. Now the perps have two problems. They have a hot van the police are after as a top priority, and the person they were after for money is dead, probably before he could give them what they wanted."

"So they burn the body and the van," Sorensen concluded.

"Exactly."

"But if they didn't get what they wanted from Malik . . ." Sorensen said, stopping before stating the obvious.

"They're going to do it again."

CHAPTER 32

Darcy managed to avoid the subject of how he came to learn about Malik from Madison the whole drive to Mountain View, but he could feel Sorensen was starting to deduce it. So he rushed out of the car before his partner could admonish him about this too.

The law firm was in one of the few high-rises in Mountain View. They walked in silence into the building. The reception area was spacious and modern, and several exotic plants decorated the room. Two gorgeous receptionists answered phones, which were ringing nonstop even though it was almost six o'clock.

"How is it that these companies always have models for receptionists? Where do they get these women?" Sorensen asked, probably a little too loud, since the redhead smiled at them.

"How can I help you, gentlemen?" she asked as soon as her call ended.

"We're looking for Suresh Malik's manager." Sorensen parked his elbow on the tall, shiny desk.

"That would be Mr. Leon Brantley. Who may I say is looking for him?"

"Detectives Sorensen and Lynch," he said.

She pecked at a few keys on the phone, whispered something to somebody on the other end, nodded a few times and hung up. "Please take a seat. Somebody will come and meet you shortly."

Just as Sorensen sat down, a man came into the reception area and said, "Detectives, I'm Carlo Buenavente. Let me take you to Mr. Brantley."

He looked very young, barely past college age. He was well shaven, his hair was short and shiny. His suit was probably more expensive than a week's paycheck.

The long hallway was flanked by offices with glass walls. Inside, people were busy, typing on their computers, going through files or discussing cases in small groups. Darcy had to check his watch to confirm that it was indeed early evening.

Carlo stopped by the kitchen's entrance. "Can I get you anything to eat or drink? We have specialty drinks, vegetarian sandwiches, quinoa salad . . . Pretty much anything you want, we probably have it."

Darcy looked at Sorensen. The big man's expression said it all. Darcy almost laughed, then said, "Coffee would be great. Black. Thank you."

"I would love a vanilla cappuccino with a splash of cinnamon," Sorensen quipped.

"My kind of drink." Carlo's face lit up.

He walked into the kitchen to start working on the seven-thousand-dollar espresso machine.

Sorensen rolled his eyes at Darcy and said, "I'm joking. Do you have a Red Bull?"

"Oh." Carlo stopped pouring the grounds into the portafilter and dumped it into the garbage. "I think we do." His voice was flat. He pointed to the fridge with glass doors that occupied the entire back wall of the kitchen.

There were so many different drinks there that Darcy felt he was in the minimart of a Los Gatos gas station.

Sorensen moved from one side of the fridge to the other, probably overwhelmed with the choices. He opened the left door, reached in, then decided he wanted something else from the other side of the fridge. After he had done this a couple times, Darcy said, "Detective . . ."

"Right, right," he replied without looking back.

He finally picked a strange-looking power drink that was very long and skinny, with a green neon label. When he opened it, Darcy heard it fizz.

Brantley's office was the second-to-last one on the right side of the long hallway. His door was closed, and Carlo knocked. The lawyer waved them in as he was finishing his conversation and hung up the phone.

"What can I do for you, Detectives?"

He walked around his massive desk and shook their hands.

Carlo excused himself and closed the door behind him.

"We understand that you're Malik's manager," Darcy started.

"That's correct." He looked from one to the other. His face didn't say anything at all. "He's not here today."

"Was that scheduled?" Darcy asked.

"No. And he's extremely reliable."

"Mr. Malik is dead," Sorensen said.

"What? How?" Brantley said, for the first time showing emotion on his face. He walked back around his desk and slowly descended into his chair.

"We're still investigating. What was he working on?" Sorensen sat across from Brantley and took a sip from his drink. He then set the can on the desk. Darcy saw the lawyer disapprove, but he didn't say or do anything. The can's condensation left a ring when Sorensen picked it up again.

"Are you suggesting that there is foul play?" Brantley asked, now looking into Sorensen's eyes.

"What makes you ask that?" Sorensen leaned forward. The leather chair made a farting noise.

"Detective, I'm a lawyer. You wouldn't be here if he'd died of natural causes or a simple car accident."

Darcy smirked. "A van was set on fire this morning in Alviso. He was in it. The van didn't belong to him, nor had he rented it. We're trying to figure out why he may have been in it."

Leon Brantley looked down to his desk for a long minute.

"What was his job exactly?" Sorensen asked, wanting to move the questioning forward.

"He was leading the ad coelum team."

Darcy offered him a blank stare.

"All our teams have names that are somewhat related to what they are doing but are a bit obscure. Sort of like an inside joke that only we understand."

Sorensen joined Darcy on the blank stare.

"Ad coelum is short for Cuius est solum, eius est usque ad coelum et ad inferos. It's typically a term used for property law, meaning that whoever owns the soil, he owns it up to heaven and down to hell."

More blank stares. Brantley looked smug, as if happy that their inside joke really was so clever that it went over the detectives' heads.

"English, please," Sorensen said.

"Malik was a senior reviewer."

"Mr. Brantley, in layman's terms can you tell us what Malik was working on?" Sorensen asked, now making a point of twisting the sweating can on top of the wooden desk.

"Suresh Malik led a team of engineers and lawyers working on a major lawsuit we are about to file. The team name is an inside joke, because when a company owns a patent they think they own it from heaven to hell, but in reality you only own it, if you can prove it's really yours."

"This is a patent troll law firm?" Sorensen asked.

"We don't really appreciate that term . . ."

Darcy looked at Sorensen, hoping for an explanation. There were so many things he still didn't get about Silicon Valley.

"These guys find smart start-ups and sue them for patent infringement in hopes that they will fold or go bankrupt. Then they acquire the patents for next to nothing and sue bigger firms for millions. They are leeches and, surprisingly enough, legal."

Darcy saw Brantley's face twist, so he moved on. "What was the lawsuit about?"

"Patent infringement."

"Yeah, we get that," Sorensen said. "What can you tell us about the case?"

"Not much without a subpoena unfortunately."

"Can you tell us who you were suing?"

Sorensen finished his drink.

"I can't tell you that either until we file."

"What does a senior reviewer do?" Darcy asked.

"They look at the patents at play, then validate if the case is well founded."

"Have you received any threats?" Darcy added.

"What do you think, Detective?"

"Do you have them?"

Brantley picked up the phone and made the request to have them brought over.

"Has anybody acted on the threats as far as you know?"

"A few people got their cars keyed. Our lead counsel was egged in the street a couple months ago, but nothing more serious than that."

The door opened, and both detectives looked back. Carlo and two other people brought in six boxes full of threats.

CHAPTER 33

The first thing they did when they got back to the station was to separate the threats that were directly made to Malik from those made to others. They were still going through them when the captain came out of her office.

"Please tell me this is not a total waste of time," she begged.

Both detectives remained silent.

"Nice." She shook her head and walked to the kitchen. When she came back, she was nibbling on a peanut butter and jelly sandwich.

"That looks good," Sorensen said.

"It is. My six-year-old daughter made it this morning."

"She'll be a famous chef one day," Sorensen said, stretching his back.

"You really have nothing?" Virago asked.

"We need to interview one more Marine, who didn't come with the others," Sorensen said.

Darcy scratched his temple. "I also think that Bishop's not saying all he knows. He got pretty defensive early on, even invoked his right to a lawyer. I'll check his alibi tomorrow morning." He stopped the rubbing when he noticed his colleagues were looking at him. "Oh, and his feet are dramatically different in size. Maybe CSU can check for this in the bank video."

Sorensen and Virago looked at each other.

"How different?" Virago asked.

"Two sizes."

"How did you figure that out?" Sorensen threw all his empty cans in the recycle bin.

"I asked him to show me the tread of his boots. I found a couple interesting prints at the VTA and the coffee shop crime scenes, so I wanted to check if his were a match to either."

Sorensen shrugged. "Those cases are now closed."

"If we can put him at the scene of the bank, we would have the connection between the VTA prank and the bank," Darcy said. "That would explain how the MO was identical."

Sorensen leaned back against his chair, pondering this.

"Did he leak the MO or lead the bank group through it?" Virago asked, and sat on the edge of the desk.

Darcy got up and pinned Bishop's DMV photo on the whiteboard. "I don't think this guy's smart enough to lead anybody."

Virago picked the phone up and called Rachel. She answered after the third ring.

"Rachel, I'm with Sorensen and Lynch. Do you have any prelim info on the video footage or photos from the bank?"

"Have you found anything specific about the two different-size feet?" Darcy added.

"No. Unfortunately none of the angles gave sufficient data to be able to calculate that, sorry." She shuffled through some papers. "I meant to call you earlier to let you know, but I got sidetracked."

"Shit." Darcy had hoped to have something on Bishop.

"Thanks, Rachel." Virago hung up. "How sure are you this guy's involved?" she asked Darcy.

"My gut tells me he has something to do with all of this. But I have nothing to prove it."

"He doesn't know that, though," Sorensen offered.

Virago looked at Darcy.

"If he calls my bluff, we're screwed."

"Is there any other evidence you're waiting for to nail this guy?"

"If they were as careful at the bank as they were at the VTA, I doubt we'll find anything."

"So you have nothing to lose, then." Virago finished the last bite of her sandwich and, licking peanut butter from her finger, she walked back to her office. Before closing her door, she said, "Oh, and Lynch, when you get done bluffing, don't forget to set up a time to meet with Internal Affairs to go over the shooting."

CHAPTER 34

Darcy looked at the remaining box of threats. He put the lid on it and cajoled Sorensen into finishing in the morning by offering the much more attractive option of going to visit Bishop.

Sorensen drove, and Darcy called Saffron.

"Hey, it's me. Long day at the office. Not sure when I'll be done, but if you don't mind, can you drop by my place and let Shelby out?" He kept his voice low and his body turned to the side window as he finished the voice mail. "It would be nice if you stayed over tonight."

"You're so cute," Sorensen mocked him.

Darcy regretted not having texted instead.

"At least I let her know."

"Oh, trust me, my family doesn't want to know. The less they hear from me, the happier they are." He laughed first, but then a shadow covered his face. "Let's make a stop at the hospital," he said.

The rest of the ride was quiet. Darcy thought of several new apologies to give about putting Jon in danger but opted to keep silent instead.

In the hospital they ran into several people they knew. They shook hands with each but moved on quickly. They were there to check on Jon, not socialize.

When they got to Jon's room, the door opened, and Jonathan, his dad, came out.

"Detectives, thank you for coming," he said, but his voice was dry. He crossed his arms rather than offering a handshake.

"How's he doing?" Darcy asked.

The intensity of Jonathan's eyes when he looked at him burned his soul. Darcy knew this man wanted to hit him. And he knew he deserved his ire.

The image of Kozlov laughing and his CI, Gigi, bleeding on the floor of the empty warehouse back in Seattle flashed through Darcy's mind. She was dead because of him. Jon may die because of him. He rubbed his left temple, trying to soothe his sense of guilt.

Jonathan looked at Sorensen as he replied, "He's sleeping." He briefly looked at Darcy again, then said, "Excuse me, I'm going to get some coffee for my wife."

He walked away from them, his steps heavy on the floor, and shoved his hands in his pockets before he turned the corner. Darcy looked at Sorensen, knowing that he would get more hatred from his partner, but instead Sorensen patted his shoulder once and nodded, then opened the door. Darcy went through, shaken by the unexpected sympathy his partner had just shown him.

A few minutes later they got back into the car and headed for Bishop's home. Darcy still felt cold from the hate that emanated from Jon's father.

Bishop's apartment complex was on North First Street. The VTA line ran by it, and there was no place to park. Sorensen circled the block and found a spot on a side street.

"We're looking for 207," Darcy said.

The concrete stairs were rough against their shoes. The building was a dirty gray and had zero personality. Somebody living in Unit 204 had tried to spice up the place by putting a colorful mat that said "Wipe Your Paws" in front of their door and hanging a garland from it, but it was brown and looked dead, making the place even more somber.

Darcy knocked on the door of 207. They could hear music through the thin walls.

"Coming," a female voice said. "Oh. I was expecting a friend," she said, retreating from the door as soon as she'd opened it.

"Detectives Lynch and Sorensen. We would like to speak to Rory Bishop," Darcy said, flashing his badge.

"He's not here."

Darcy studied her. She wasn't cold or despondent, but also didn't seem too surprised that two detectives would want to talk to him. She didn't ask why.

"Where can we find him?" Sorensen asked, probably realizing she wasn't going to volunteer the information either.

"He's at Trials. A few blocks down on First." She pointed south.

"I know the bar," Sorensen told Darcy.

They thanked her and went back to the car.

"You think she'll call him?" Darcy asked.

"I doubt it. She didn't look that shocked to see us there."

"Yeah, I noticed that too," Darcy said.

Sorensen parked on Julian, and they walked around the corner. Bishop was sitting outside with another man. Sorensen pulled his phone and checked something.

"Bishop's with Ethan Mitchell, the Marine who didn't care to show up earlier to talk to us."

"Are you sure?"

Sorensen showed the photo Sergeant Major Williams had sent him earlier. "Unless he has a twin, yes, I'm sure."

CHAPTER 35

Blake sat at the bar of the Z Lounge, from where he could have a view of the entrance. He was nursing a vodka martini. He watched some people come in, a few businessmen followed by a couple of women. He pondered how many of them would get lucky that night.

The door opened again, and a woman walked in sucking the air out of the place. Blake's mouth watered as he saw every man in the room look her way. She swung her hips when she walked in a more exaggerated way than she needed to. Her soft blond curls bounced as she took each step, and her silk dress flowed behind her.

"Hello, Blake, I'm Belle." She extended her hand. Her wide smile showed perfectly shaped pink lips. A little gap separated her front teeth, just enough to make her different and perhaps even sexier. His chest puffed. All eyes were on him.

She ordered a glass of 2005 J. Schram. She took the flute, smelled the bubbly and wrinkled her nose when the bubbles prickled it.

"To an unforgettable evening." Blake raised his glass for a toast. "Tell me about this event."

She took another sip of her sparkling wine, as if she needed time to think. "It won't be too big. Probably ten or twelve people at most. Some of them might be couples, but there will be a few who bring guests, like you."

He nodded. Her voice was soft. She looked at him while she spoke. He could feel himself beginning to get aroused. It is going to be an unforgettable night indeed, he thought.

"You've really never been to one of these parties?" she asked before she went on.

"No. Besides, I like to hear you talk." Her smile was contagious.

Blake realized she made him feel like the most desirable man on the planet. He was dumbfounded. He'd been with beautiful women before, and he had expected somebody gorgeous, since he was paying for it, but there was something special about this girl. At that moment he decided he would switch his regular for Belle. He shifted in his seat and waited for her to continue.

She placed a hand softly on his thigh—not too close to his crotch to be obvious, but not too far away to make the gesture simply friendly.

"Once we get in, we'll socialize a little first. Then the men and the women will separate and go into different rooms. We will get dolled up, and you will get comfortable. Then we'll all meet again, and the fun will begin."

She said the last part leaning toward him, almost whispering in his ear. He felt his entire body flush.

Blake checked his watch and said, "Let's go then. No reason to wait any longer."

He paid and took her hand to help her off the stool.

The drive from the Z Lounge to the mansion in Los Altos did not take very long. Belle kept the conversation light, and he felt even more drawn to her.

When they got to their destination, he pressed the intercom and said, "Emerald."

The gates swung open without disturbing the quiet night.

CHAPTER 36

Darcy stood beside Sorensen, who towered over the tiny table where Bishop and Mitchell were sitting. A group of young men were drinking beers next to them.

"We would like to speak with you for a few minutes," Sorensen said to Bishop, even though it had been Darcy who'd interviewed him back at the station.

Bishop locked eyes with Mitchell, who said, "Take a seat, Detective," and pointed to one of the empty chairs next to him.

Darcy and Sorensen exchanged a glance that said, Now we know who calls the shots.

"You're Ethan Mitchell, right?" Sorensen asked. Without waiting for confirmation, he added, "We need to talk to you too. Why didn't you come to the station with the other Marines?"

"I was busy."

"That, or you have something to hide."

Darcy cringed. Always alienating people, he thought.

Ethan didn't respond. He finished his nonalcoholic beer and stared back at Sorensen.

"Let's take a walk," Darcy said to Bishop, hoping to get something out of him before Sorensen pissed both off completely.

At first Bishop didn't move. He was being more defiant than arrogant. Like a little kid who doesn't want to eat the broccoli, even if that means he doesn't get to play after dinner.

Sorensen sat on the opposite chair to where Mitchell had pointed.

"Come on." Darcy moved a step backward, giving Bishop space to leave the table. "We'll just go around the block. By the time we're back, my partner and I will leave."

Bishop chugged the rest of his bottled water and stood. Darcy saw Mitchell lick his lower lip, and then he watched as Bishop did the same. He figured they'd just exchanged some kind of message.

They headed south and took a right on Divine Street, walking by a few Harleys parked on the corner. One hog was red, with the logo painted in shiny gold. The others were black. Darcy didn't speak until they were halfway down the block. He wanted to make Bishop wonder for a bit. Finally, he said, "We're getting the photos and the video from the bank kidnapping analyzed as we speak."

Bishop didn't skip a beat.

"You know I'm going to find you there. So help me now so I can help you."

Bishop scoffed and turned. "I'm going back now. You're wasting my time."

"Bishop, wait," Darcy said as the Marine walked away from him. "You're right. I can't put you on the scene of the bank. But let me tell you what I know."

He walked to where Bishop had stopped, then they headed toward Market Street and turned south. When he didn't complain, Darcy knew he was at least curious about what he had to say.

"You were at the VTA prank. The MO is exactly the same as the bank kidnapping. There weren't enough details released to the press for the bank kidnappers to have been able to match the job exactly. So somebody from the VTA prank took Suresh Malik." Darcy watched Bishop, but the Marine didn't even flinch at the mention of the victim's name.

"There were a lot of guys involved in the pranks. Why don't you go after them and stop bothering me?"

Bishop was not as gullible as Darcy had hoped. "How did you get roughed up?"

"I fell down the stairs."

"I thought you got it playing football." Darcy paused. "I think Mitchell hit you."

For the first time, Bishop twitched. It was subtle, but Darcy saw it.

"And I think you got into a fight because of what happened to Malik."

Bishop started walking faster.

Darcy was onto something. He couldn't afford to lose him now.

"I think you were trying to do the right thing, but Mitchell calls all the shots, and he wouldn't let you."

Bishop tucked his head down. Darcy was getting closer, but Bishop was clamming up. Damn.

"You're fishing. You're making this up, and it's all bullshit," the Marine finally said.

When they reached Saint James Street, Darcy started to cross, but Bishop turned left.

"Bishop, one man is dead and another critically injured in a shootout with the police. The pranks were fun, whatever, but now you're involved in kidnapping, felony murder, and attempted murder of a police officer."

"I got nothing to do with that." Bishop licked his broken lip.

"I think you do. I think Mitchell led the kidnapping, and he recruited a few guys to help him. He picked you, and now you're going away for good."

Darcy let his words settle for a few moments.

"You know that even if you didn't do it yourself, you're an accessory now. You'll get the death penalty, or at best life."

"I know nothing about all that. I was at the regiment. How many times do I have to tell you that? So, as I said back at the station, you either arrest me or you leave me alone."

Darcy tried a couple more tactics, but Bishop gave him nothing more. When they got back to Trials, Sorensen's face told him that he'd been as successful in his quest.

CHAPTER 37

As Blake went through the gates, he thought about the code word. Emerald. What kind of stupid-ass password was that? He drove up a few yards and parked behind the other cars already lining the driveway. Blake killed the engine of his Jaguar XK and went around it to help Belle out. They strolled toward the house, and he took in the grandiosity of the place. He wondered how many millions it cost. He decided to buy a bigger one as soon as the sale of NanoQ went through.

Before they reached the front door, it opened. A man dressed in a black suit and a black shirt but no tie blocked the entrance.

"Name please."

He waited until Blake introduced himself. The man nodded, probably having memorized the guest list, and invited them to walk in.

"Welcome. I'll be happy to take your coats," a middle-aged woman greeted them.

Blake helped Belle take hers off and handed it to the woman. Then he took off his sports jacket.

"I will need your cell phones as well."

She was affable and sweet, but her extended hand told them there was no negotiating.

Blake shrugged and pulled his out of his pocket. Belle raised both hands, indicating that she didn't have one.

"Enjoy." The woman pointed toward the direction where they needed to go.

Blake took Belle's hand and wondered if he would have time to play with her before the whole thing went down. He was enjoying himself and wanted to get a taste of his new girl.

He looked around the room. There were a few people already there. Most of the men were middle age; only one looked fit. He was not looking forward to seeing them naked. He counted five women. Two were Asian, both petite and almost fragile. They could have been sisters. Another had skin the color of caffe latte and was very tall, especially with her platform shoes.

The last two women were about ten to fifteen years older than the other girls. They were probably the only ones who weren't pros. One had had too many encounters with plastic surgery, and yet she seemed to be losing the battle against time. The other one was even older but had an aura of dignity. She reminded him of some famous actress he couldn't remember the name of.

The host came to meet them. "I'm so glad you could make it, Blake," he said, even though they'd never met.

When they shook hands, Blake grimaced at his host's sweaty palms.

Carlos de la Rosa moved to Belle and held her hand in his. "I'm very pleased that you brought such a lovely lady," he said to Blake, never moving his hungry eyes away from her.

Blake pushed away a pang of jealousy and thwarted his instinct to hit the man for ogling his woman. He was at an orgy after all; the whole point was to share.

The fake blond with too much Botox and collagen implants came to greet them. "Oh, what do we have here?" she asked Carlos as if she were opening a Christmas present. "I'm Hope. Welcome to our house."

She air-kissed Blake and led Belle away to introduce her to the other women.

"I assume this is not your first time, is it?" Carlos asked.

"I trust you got my test results," Blake said, more as a statement than a question.

"You wouldn't have made it this far if I hadn't."

"Yes, this is my first time," Blake said.

"Very well. You will have a fantastic time."

Carlos looked at Belle, and his lascivious stare made Blake cringe again, but he had come here to do a job and had to play nice until it was done.

The short Hispanic man led Blake toward the other side of the room and introduced him to the other four men. There were two lawyers and two venture capitalists. Exactly the type of crowd he wanted to be associated with but not necessarily see naked. And unfortunately that was going to happen sooner than he would ever be prepared for.

Carlos invited the men to follow him into yet another room, and there Blake saw six black silk robes neatly folded and placed equidistant from each other on top of a California king bed. He felt as if he were at a spa rather than a bacchanalia. It almost made him laugh.

He went into one of the bathrooms to change. It was extravagant, covered in marble, and the mirror had a broad, golden baroque frame. He undressed, checked his fit body in the mirror and caressed his pecs. He needed to schedule another wax session soon. He tied his belt tight around the robe and stepped back into the room where the other men were.

The host headed to the door but turned before going through it and said, "Let the fun begin."

He extended his arms wide, and the robe opened, showcasing an ample, hairy stomach, and a bush that almost hid his flaccid penis. Blake wished he'd never seen that.

They followed Carlos to the living room where they had originally met. It was now empty. Blake checked his watch—ten minutes to go. He needed things to start accelerating, or they may run into complications.

"We're ready," Hope sang from somewhere in the house.

Carlos rubbed his hands in anticipation and said, "Come on down." Then he led his entourage to the bottom of the wide, curling stairs to welcome the women.

Hope appeared and started descending. She was tall and very tight, thanks to hours at the gym and many tummy tucks. She wore high-heel glittery mules, nude thigh highs, and a black see-through baby-doll. If Blake hadn't seen her from up close, he would've been hard already.

The rest of the women followed her. One by one they came down, measuring each step, smiling at the men, but probably secretly wondering how much choice they would have.

Blake locked eyes with Belle. She was still the hottest one. He then checked his watch. Only five minutes to go. Fuck, he thought. I won't get to play.

Once the women were downstairs, Carlos and Hope led everybody back into the living room.

Carlos took a flute of champagne and encouraged everybody to do the same. When everybody had a glass, he clinked his with his wedding band to summon their attention.

Three minutes.

"All areas of the house are open. Be curious, be courteous, share, and have fun!" He raised his glass, made eye contact with his guests and drained the bubbly in one gulp.

Blake grabbed Belle by her waist and turned to kiss her. Before he had a chance to touch her shiny pink lips, Carlos pulled her away from him.

"You surpassed all my expectations, Blake. Thank you for such a delectable present," he said.

Belle smiled at their host, and as Carlos pulled her away she looked back at Blake and playfully blew him a kiss.

Blake wondered if she actually dreaded being with the sweaty man or she just considered that part of her job. He checked his watch. He would probably never know.

It was time.

CHAPTER 38

Darcy and Sorensen left the two Marines behind and headed to the Jeep. Darcy looked at his shoes as they walked and wondered how it would feel to have one foot much larger than the other.

"I think you're losing your charm," Sorensen said as soon as they were in the car.

"I don't think you did that well either."

"But I've never had any charm."

Darcy smiled in spite of being disappointed about not getting anything from Bishop. "I didn't even rile him up a little." He shook his head. "Maybe you're right. Maybe I'm losing my charm."

"Why are you so sure he's involved?" Sorensen asked, heading north on First.

"He's a follower, and something happened to him he doesn't want to talk about. He didn't get black and blue playing football or falling down the stairs. Besides, somebody from the pranks has to be involved." He thought for a second. "Or they shared with the bank perps every single detail and the gas grenades too, since they were all the same chemical composition."

Sorensen sped through a yellow light.

"What did you get from Mitchell?"

133

"A lot of laughs."

Darcy looked at him.

"No, seriously. Apparently the asshole found everything I had to say hilarious. And his laugh sounded genuine. I swear I felt I was in an episode of The Twilight Zone or something, like we were speaking different languages."

"That guy's weird. I wish he'd come to the station with the others."

"Yeah, me too. It's much easier to gauge somebody on our own turf." Sorensen combed his blond curls.

"You really got nothing from him?" Darcy asked.

"Literally."

"We're both losing our charm."

Sorensen nodded. "But I can tell you something: my gut feels about Mitchell the same way yours is bent out of shape by Bishop."

After they parked and walked into the station, they said hello to the officer at the reception area and got into the elevator. The bullpen was empty.

"We got no evidence, we got no solid motive, we don't have a single witness, and the alibis check out. We literally have nothing." Sorensen sat on his chair and covered his face with both hands.

"I heard that," Virago said, coming out of her office. She walked over to them and, standing between Darcy and the whiteboards, she asked, "Why do people kill?"

"Money, love, fear . . ." Sorensen said.

"Revenge," Darcy added.

"So what do we know about Mr. Malik?"

"Thirty-seven, single, workaholic, patent reviewer, PhD in computer science from Stanford."

"Law school?"

"Nope. Apparently the reviewers are the technical guys. They study the patents, compare them with others already filed and then submit their reports for the lawyers to do the rest."

"The threats that you reviewed—anything there?"

"We still have a box, but no. Mostly empty threats about the lawsuits not being valid and all that. They are mostly made against the lawyers, not the reviewers. The reviewer job is pretty private. No limelight or anything."

"You checked his place—anything there?"

"No. A lot of takeout in the garbage," Sorensen said. "Speedway Stout in the fridge, though, so the guy wasn't kidding around about his beer."

"Isn't that brewed in San Diego?" Darcy asked.

"Yep. One of the best beers in the world."

"Can we focus?" Virago knocked on the desk a couple times.

"Yeah. Right. He didn't have a landline, but he had a bunch of fancy computers and a kick-ass playroom with every single game console you can imagine. No photos with anybody, not even his parents."

"So, back to basics. If he's single and there's no love interest, maybe we can rule out love as a motive. What about money?"

"I went through all of his financials. Fat, steady paycheck. Nothing that jumps out in any way. Healthy savings account, very decent 401(k). Every year he goes skiing in Tahoe and treats himself to the Ritz-Carlton hotel. Yearly trip to India. Always one ticket. No offshore accounts."

"Okay, so maybe somebody was after his money." Her eyes darted over the whiteboard. She was probably trying to figure out what the missing connections were.

"There's really not that much for such a huge job," Sorensen said. "Maybe a total of $200K . . ."

135

"I wouldn't mind having that chunk of change," Virago said. "Revenge, fear?" she asked.

Sorensen raised both palms up in the air.

CHAPTER 39

One of the coolest things about being a Marine was that climbing a wall was as easy as walking through an open door. But Blake convinced him that it was better not to risk it, not to call attention, just in case. So Ethan drove his rented Porsche SUV up to the gate and pushed the speaker button.

"Hello?" said the voice on the other side.

"Emerald," Ethan said.

After a long couple of seconds, the gates opened and they were in.

He was the only one visible in the car. The others were hiding behind tinted windows in the backseat and for extra precaution covered by a black blanket. Ethan drove up the driveway and made sure he parked in a way that allowed him to drive back out fast.

He got out of the car and walked to the open door. A bouncer wannabe was eyeing him. This time Ethan was wearing a black suit instead of the night camouflage clothing he'd been wearing the last couple days.

"This is a couples-only event," the bouncer said, probably wary that somebody had the password but was not on the guest list.

"Oh, she's coming," he said, looking back as if he were expecting a beautiful woman to emerge from the car at any moment.

He sensed the bouncer look past him. Ethan turned around and punched his Adam's apple so hard the man toppled backward and then fell forward on his knees while grabbing his neck. He was coughing and gasping for air when Ethan kicked his head, making him fall flat on his back. Ethan checked his vitals. He was still alive. He looked up to his parked car and signaled for his men to come over.

Bishop handed him his Beretta, and Ethan shot the bouncer in the head. He felt the kickback, but the suppressor masked the shot noise. Before they entered the living room, an older woman came out of the entry closet. Curtis moved behind her and covered her mouth with his hand, then subdued her with a chokehold until she passed out. Ethan looked at her lying on the floor. He pointed the gun and fired, piercing her forehead. Mac stepped over her body but made sure he didn't touch the spreading blood.

Ethan sent Bishop and Mac upstairs to recon the house. He went into the living room, followed by Curtis and Barr. What he saw made him stop in his tracks, but only for a second. There were four men, naked, sweaty, and already hard with desire. The women wore the same black see-through baby-dolls. They looked hot, even the older ones. As soon as they saw him, they all stopped playing with each other and stared at him. Blake walked in from the opposite door and acted as surprised to see them as Ethan had prepared him to.

"What the . . . ?" A scrawny guy with a shaved head and a salt and pepper goatee started saying.

Ethan raised his Beretta, and the man stopped talking.

"This could go easy, or it could go hard," he said.

The women recoiled, instinctively trying to find protection behind the naked men. But Ethan saw that they looked just as scared as the women were. The expectation that a man is the protector creates a lot of anxiety in moments of truth. He knew. He'd been there many times. Those were the moments where only real men shone.

"You. Come here," Ethan said to Blake.

Blake hesitated for a second, then walked toward him.

"I want you to use this to tape everybody's ankles together." He was pointing at the thick roll of duct tape Barr was holding in his hand.

Blake passed him and took the tape.

"I want all of you to form a line. I want boy, girl, boy, girl. Understood?"

Nobody moved.

"What are you waiting for?" Ethan didn't have to raise the volume of his commanding voice that high to make everybody sprint into action.

The guests moved around, trying to figure out who should stand next to whom. Once they were all set in the right order, Ethan motioned for Blake to start working.

"You can take anything you want," Hope said.

"You don't know what I want," Ethan taunted the woman he knew to be the hostess.

"Anything you want. We have money in the safe and more in the bank. Or jewelry. We have jewelry too." She looked around. "We're all rich. We can give you anything you want."

Ethan ignored her. The fat guy next to Hope started crying.

Blake was taping the third person when Ethan observed one of the women scan the room.

"Don't even think about it," he said to her, but the tall woman with the bristly Afro was already running toward the opposite side of the living room.

Curtis followed her. Before she reached the door Blake had come from, he tried to grab her, but his hands didn't get a grip on the slippery material of the baby-doll. She bolted into the other room, and a second later they were both out of sight.

Ethan heard a scream, followed by a thud. Blake had stopped taping, and all heads were turned toward the direction in which they had disappeared. Several women gasped when Curtis walked back into the room with the girl over his shoulder.

"Is she dead?" Ethan asked.

"Not yet," Curtis said.

Ethan smiled. Curtis knew how to play the game.

"People, we are prepared to go all the way. If you try to run, we'll catch you. So please don't be stupid," Ethan said, getting everybody's attention back. "You, go on. We don't have all night," he urged Blake.

Curtis laid the woman down on the love seat. Ethan nodded for Barr to cover the door she had just tried to escape through.

Mac and Bishop came into the room pushing de la Rosa and a blond pro. The tall man whispered something in his ear that he knew he would have to act on after they took care of the main mission.

"If I have to tell you again to keep taping, you'll end up like her," Ethan told Blake, pointing at the woman on the love seat. When he was done restraining everybody, Ethan said, "Pick one."

Blake stared at him, but all he did was tie his robe tighter around his body.

"I said pick one," Ethan repeated.

"What do you mean?" Blake asked.

Everybody turned from one to the other, looking as lost as Blake felt.

"You're going to pick the first person who's going to die tonight."

The women gasped and recoiled as much as their restraints would let them. Blake took a step away from Ethan. Two of the men started to cry.

"Why are you doing this?" Carlos asked, choking on the words.

Ethan pointed the Beretta at Blake's head and waited. His men closed in around him, ready to act. Blake looked at Ethan, then at the other guests. Then back at Ethan. He's enjoying his act a little too much, Ethan thought. Everybody was silent. He wondered how long it would be before they realized they were holding their breath.

Blake scanned the room as if he was considering his options. Ethan saw him study each victim. They all looked away, probably hoping that would save them from being picked. Finally Blake turned toward the woman who had tried to escape. She was still unconscious, lying on the sofa as if asleep.

Blake pointed a shaky finger at her.

Ethan could see the relief in the other guests' faces. He then motioned for Mac to take the sleeping beauty away from the living room. The house was so quiet he could hear every step moving away and fading down the hallway. He heard a door open, a much softer thud, and then the metallic sound of a Sig P226 firing once.

CHAPTER 40

Wednesday

Saffron woke up and felt Darcy's hand resting on her hip. She smiled and rolled over to face him. His eyes were closed, but she knew he was faking being asleep. She inched toward him and kissed the tip of his nose. He opened his eyes and kissed her lips. His mouth was soft, inviting. Only the tip of his tongue teased her first. Then his kisses became hungrier. He held her neck as he pulled her closer to him. Their bodies touched, and she melted into his embrace.

Darcy pulled her camisole over her head. It got stuck on her elbow and they laughed. She caressed his tight chest. He watched her as she took him in: his tanned torso, his scars, his defined muscles. His body made her quiver. He leaned back. She kissed him and pulled herself toward him. He slid his hand underneath her lower back and pulled her even closer. She exhaled. He licked her neck.

The phone rang. He grunted but ignored it. Five rings later it stopped. Darcy flipped Saffron so now she was on top of him. He watched as the sun shone through her auburn hair.

The phone rang again. Three rings. As soon as it stopped, it rang again.

Saffron leaned over, picked it up and, seeing the name on the display, said, "It's your captain."

"I need to quit this job. The calls always come at the most inopportune times."

Saffron winked.

After tapping the green button, Darcy said, "This better be good."

The room was very quiet, and Saffron heard Virago say, "Detective, every time you get a call from me, it's a good call. No need for you to ever question that."

Darcy didn't reply. Saffron leaned backward on his lap, pushing her hips toward him, waiting to see if he would need to rush off to some crime scene but hoping he wouldn't.

He did.

Thirty minutes later, Saffron looked over at Darcy and thought about how natural it felt to see him driving her car. She wondered if he felt the same way, or if the Mini was way too small for a man of his height.

He pulled into the hospital's parking lot and drove all the way up to the front door.

"Are you sure you'll be okay without your car?" he asked.

"Absolutely. It's much more important that you can get around."

He leaned over and kissed her on the lips. He lingered there a little longer than a simple "thank you" kiss required. She opened her eyes as soon as he pulled away. She still got butterflies in her stomach when he kissed her. He looked at her, and his smile filled her heart.

"I'll try to rent one sometime today," he promised. "And I'll make it up to you for this morning."

"You better." She caressed the shoulder with the bullet graze and blew him a kiss before she left the car. "Don't stress about the car—really. I'll keep you posted on Jon's progress."

"I was just going to ask you that."

"I know," she said, looking back at him.

She smiled and walked into the hospital. She turned one more time and saw him wave before he disappeared into the street.

She'd told her boss that she wasn't going to go to the office but would try to work remotely. As she walked down the hospital hall to Jon's room, she checked email on her phone. Nothing interesting. She really needed a new project soon or she would die of boredom.

Before Saffron put the phone away, she noticed she had a voice mail she hadn't yet seen.

The call had come at just past eleven the previous night. She had been watching a movie curled up against Darcy. She thought about that morning, his embrace, his kisses. How strong he was, and how crazy she was for him. She focused back on the call. It was a blocked number. That was weird. The only blocked calls she ever got were the ones Darcy made from his office phone.

She entered the passcode. The recording went on for what seemed like minutes, with all kinds of information she didn't care about, before the message played. As soon as the actual voice mail started, she stopped walking. It was her sister Aislin.

"Saffron, help." Her voice was muffled, as if she was talking so close to the handset that her own lips were making the words hard to understand. "They're going to kill—" And the line went dead.

Saffron pulled the phone away from her ear and looked at it, as if the screen would tell her the end of the message. A distant digital voice asked her to press seven to delete the message or nine to save it. Saffron pressed four to listen to it again.

She did—three more times—but the voice mail didn't get any clearer the more she listened to it. Could this be one of her jokes? she thought. Saffron listened to it again and decided that the urgency in Aislin's voice was real. She recognized the fear in her voice. It sounded just like her own voice had a few weeks earlier when she was stuck in a basement about to be burned alive.

Saffron called her sister. The phone rang, but Aislin didn't pick up. Her chirpy voice told the caller to leave a message or not to expect a call back. Saffron almost smiled, but a sense of dread overwhelmed her.

"Aislin, are you okay? What was that message you left me last night about? Call me ASAP. Oh, and it better not be a joke, or I'll beat the crap out of you."

She hung up, but before putting the phone away, she left another message, and then called their parents. They hadn't heard from her either. Saffron checked her purse and saw that she still had the extra set of keys Aislin had given her.

Jon's room was only a few feet away. She couldn't leave without seeing him. She reached the door and knocked lightly. Only Miranda, Jon's mom, was there. She looked up, and her eyes lit up a little. They hugged.

"How is he?" Saffron asked.

"He's doing much better. Woke up for a bit but fell back asleep." She looked hopeful. "The doctor thinks the worst has passed."

"That's great news. How are you holding up?"

Miranda shrugged her shoulders. "Probably better than my husband."

Saffron could tell she was just saying that. She looked down at Jon. A little pool of drool made a round stain on the pillow. She squeezed his arm and told Miranda, "I'll be back soon."

She left the hospital, grabbing the first cab that pulled up by the main entrance, and texted Darcy to let him know Jon's good news.

CHAPTER 41

Detective Lynch gave his full name to the officer guarding the entrance and ducked under the yellow tape. It was just past nine thirty in the morning. The house was gated. There was a wide lawn split in two by a short, paved path leading to the house. The front door was open. The foyer was bright and warm, with a large, curling staircase that led to the second floor. He'd only seen something this ostentatious in movies. There were several officers inside as well as CSU, already collecting evidence.

He nodded hello, but before talking to anybody Darcy wanted to take in the scene. There were two bodies by the door. The first one looked like a club bouncer. The other was a middle-aged woman dressed in a slightly tight burgundy suit and beige patent leather pumps. They were both shot in the head. The blood had spread out and away from the bodies, mixing at some point on the white marble floor.

Darcy walked around the man's body, away from the head so he wouldn't spoil the evidence. When he reached the living room, he stopped, astounded. Five people had been tied to each other with duct tape and shot in the forehead. Some of them had their eyes open. There was blood and brain matter spattered behind them. The entry wounds were of a decent size. All the men were naked except one, who was wearing a black silk robe. It was open, showcasing a torso that had seen better days. The women were wearing the very same negligees and glittery shoes. Only a few pumps were still on.

All of the victims were Caucasian, except for one man, who was African American, and two women, who looked Asian. The white leather sofa behind the bodies was sprayed red, and the Persian rug below them was still damp with blood.

The room was spacious and cool. The sun streamed through the white drawn curtains. There were several glasses of champagne on the tables and a few on the floor, but only one was broken.

"Madison, what's your take on all this?" Darcy asked the ME, who was concentrating on the body farthest from Darcy.

"They were all killed by the same caliber gun. I found eight .40 shell casings. You'll have to confirm ballistics, but they probably all came from the same gun." The tall man stood and pulled his latex gloves off. "They died between ten and one in the morning."

Darcy looked at the bodies. "There are only seven bodies."

"That's my count too, Detective."

"A warning shot?" Darcy asked, more to himself than to the medical examiner.

The ME shrugged his shoulders but pointed at the opposite wall. "There's a hole on that wall. They've already retrieved the bullet."

Darcy looked over to where Madison was pointing, but instead of going there he leaned over the closest body and inspected the entry wound, then looked up at the other bodies.

"This is definitely not done by an amateur."

Madison nodded and turned to leave. Halfway to the door, he asked over his shoulder, "You'll be at the autopsies?"

"Yes, I'll come by as soon as I'm done here."

Darcy saw the ME exchange pleasantries with Rachel as she came in but couldn't quite hear the conversation.

"I think this was an orgy," Rachel said matter-of-factly when she reached him.

"What on earth could have given you that idea?" Darcy teased her, looking down at the mostly naked bodies.

She waved her arthritic hand in dismissal. "And I think they were just getting started. Only one room shows signs of play."

She walked toward Darcy and stopped about a foot away. They both stared down.

"There were more people here," she said.

"We have witnesses?"

She looked up at him. "I didn't say that." She eyed the door she'd come in from. "There's another body in a room across the hall. But I still think there were more people here last night."

"Why?" Darcy asked.

"There's a coat room at the entrance. I think we'll be able to match the DNA to the victims and see if there were others."

She motioned for him to follow her there. She was small but had an imposing presence wherever she was.

The two bodies Darcy saw when he came in were already gone. The blood, however, was still there. An officer was sitting on a chair, cataloging something, and had several evidence bags on the floor by his feet.

"We found eight cell phones. We're assuming they belonged to the guests, but we'll have to confirm that." She faced him. "All of the phones are password protected, so it'll take a while to figure out who they belong to. Hopefully, we'll be able to determine if we have some witnesses out there."

"Do they leave the phones behind to ensure privacy?"

"Very good, Detective." She patted his forearm. "Based on the size of this house and the neighborhood, I'm going to bet your victims are all very rich and possibly influential people."

After they discussed the rest of the preliminary evidence, which wasn't much, she urged him to go upstairs to get acquainted with the fringes of the sex world.

Each of the five bedrooms was decorated differently. Diverse styles, not always complementary: one was rococo, another Japanese, a third had many African motifs. The largest room, however, was the most interesting. It was red. All the track lights pointed to the huge round bed that occupied the center of the room. It was surrounded by a canopy with sheer curtains that secluded it from the rest of the world. Darcy wondered if the point was for others to watch. Then he realized that was exactly it when he saw the love seats facing the bed. The sheets were barely rumpled. This was the only room that looked used and might give CSU some fluid samples to match to possible perps.

He went downstairs again, looking for Rachel. He found her across the hall from where they'd been earlier, where the other body was.

"Are all these women pros, or is this more like a swingers' thing?" Darcy asked, studying the body of a very tall woman with an Afro covered in blood.

"You probably have both. Normally each person invited brings a guest of the opposite sex. Some people have open relationships where they do this. Some don't or are single, so it's not uncommon for them to bring a call girl," Rachel explained.

"Rachel, you know this first hand, or you just read a lot?"

The senior crime scene investigator winked at him but didn't answer.

Darcy blushed, feeling he'd crossed an invisible line "Have we been able to identify any of the victims yet?" he asked, changing the subject.

"No, but I doubt we'll have a lot of problems with that. It looks to me that whoever did this didn't really care about us finding out who these people were. We'll break into the phones soon enough, and even though we haven't found any wallets, there are a bunch of cars parked at the end of the driveway."

"I'm going to check that out."

Darcy left the house through the front door and walked around the perimeter. There were four high-end cars parked in two rows. Two were silver, the other two black. The garage was detached from the house and was as big as a shopping mall. He opened the side door and stopped.

"Who the hell cleared the garage?" he yelled.

Nobody answered, but he heard a few people run toward him. As soon as he got two deputies behind him, he walked inside. There was another man. He looked to be in his midforties, and was naked, very thin, and toned. He had a salt-and-pepper goatee, and his head was shaved, probably to offset the balding. He had a gun in his inert hand, and a dark splatter of almost-dried blood tainted the wall he was leaning against.

Darcy walked to him, and after kicking the gun away he checked his vitals even though he knew the man was dead.

"I got another one here," he shouted out the door while the two other deputies inspected the rest of the garage.

He pulled his phone out and took pictures of all the cars and their license plates. He was about to send them to Jon to get them run through the system when he realized Jon wouldn't be getting the message. He put the phone back in his pocket and touched his shoulder. It was still sore from the stitches.

CHAPTER 42

Blake hadn't been able to sleep all night. He took sleeping pills, chased with enough scotch to knock out a regiment, and still no shut-eye. The party hadn't gone at all the way he'd expected, the way they'd planned it.

He'd been very tempted to not come to work, but he knew he had to keep an eye on Martin. He needed to act as if everything were normal. Blake took a deep breath; it didn't help. Then he saw the stress ball by his keyboard and grabbed it. He squeezed it, harder and harder each time, but that didn't seem to help either. After a final crunch, he threw it across the room. It hit the wall with a thud and fell on the floor.

Staring at the spot where the ball had hit, Blake felt sweat moisten his body. He looked for a tissue but couldn't find one. He wiped his neck with his hand and dried it on his designer jeans.

"Do you know where Pete is?" Martin asked, peeking through the open door.

"No." He felt the sweat return as soon as he'd wiped it off.

"Hummm," Martin said. "Can you try reaching him? I need to talk to him."

"I'll try," Blake responded to an already-closed door.

Pete had taken the day off to go to the Redwoods and do whatever nature thing he liked to do when he was there.

Pete asked Blake to not tell anybody, for whatever weird reason, so now Blake had to lie to his best friend. Then he remembered the party, and he wished the worst thing he had to do in life was cover for a coworker.

"Dammit, Ethan," he whispered through clenched teeth, and punched the table.

He grabbed his burner cell and walked out of the office. When he reached the parking lot, he called Ethan.

"Meet me now. The usual place."

"I'm a little busy at the moment cleaning up your mess," Ethan said.

"My mess?" He paced along the line of cars. "My mess? Fuck you. None of this would have happened if you hadn't killed Malik."

Ethan didn't respond, but Blake could hear noises in the background.

"He was the perfect target. This whole mess should have been over by now," Blake insisted.

"You should have done better research. I would have told you it was a no-go if I'd known Malik had hypertrophic cardiomyopathy." More clinks and clanks came through the phone. "People with abnormally thick hearts don't do well in stressful situations, especially if it involves the threat of losing body parts."

"You only needed to threaten him." Blake started walking between cars again, now faster.

"Your instructions were to make him agree to your proposal. 'By whatever means necessary' was the expression you used." His voice was cold and had a hint of arrogance.

Blake had used that phrase. But he never thought it would get that far. He'd expected Malik to fold relatively easily, but Blake wanted to make sure he would never even consider backing out. So he asked Ethan to make sure to scare Malik so much that noncompliance would never be an option. I guess Ethan accomplished that goal all right, he thought.

"Anything else? Because as I said, I'm rather busy right now," Ethan said, breaking the long silence.

"I don't understand what happened last night," Blake finally said. We had a plan."

"No, Blake. You had a plan. I had a different one."

CHAPTER 43

On the way to Campbell, Saffron listened to the message again. She should tell Darcy. *Kill?* She should definitely tell Darcy, but kill what? Animals? People? Aislin? What if it really was a bad joke? Leaving that kind of message in the middle of the night was a joke in very bad taste but not unlike something Aislin would do. And the alternative was much worse.

Aislin's apartment building had two stories, a courtyard, and a small pool. It was high-end and well groomed. Saffron used a fob to get into the complex, then walked up the stairs to the second floor.

The apartment was bright and bathed in the morning sun. The open kitchen was to the left, and the bay windows faced the pool. The velvet sofa was a dark eggplant color that complemented the rich peach walls. Saffron checked the mail. There were several unopened letters, mostly advertisements from high-end stores.

She walked into the kitchen and saw the monthly dry-erase calendar stuck to the fridge. Aislin coded all of her events as "party," followed by a dash and the time. Saffron understood what it meant.

Focusing on yesterday's activities, she learned that Aislin had been busy. The party started at 9:00 p.m. Before that she had a haircut appointment, yoga, and one class at Stanford at 10:00 a.m. Saffron looked at the other dates and saw that there were only a few Stanford references here and there. She frowned. Aislin had told her she was enrolled full-time.

Saffron went to the closet and found many designer clothes. She was starting to realize that Aislin was a full-time call girl and a part-time student, not the other way around.

Listening to the voice mail again, now on speaker, the urgency in Aislin's voice seemed more vivid, more real. Saffron spotted a laptop on the coffee table and opened it, hoping she could access the calendar with details of the event Aislin went to last night. The password screen came up. She entered the name of their childhood dog and she was in.

"Oh, Aislin, haven't I taught you better?" she said, sighing.

The online calendar had a lot more detail than what was on the fridge. The party was at a house in Los Altos. But she was meeting a "B" at the Z Lounge beforehand. She wrote down the address of the house and called another cab as she walked out, locking the door behind her.

While she waited, she texted her sister just in case she wasn't listening to her voice mails. "Aislin, I'm freaking out. Call me back ASAP if you're okay. Otherwise, I'm going to look for you." She followed with another one: "And if you're okay, you better tell me now, or I'm seriously going to kill you myself!"

The taxi ride was long—it took over forty-five minutes— and when they got a few streets away, they found a police car blocking the entrance to the street. Saffron's heart jumped, and all the hairs on her neck stood on end.

"Do you live in this street?" an officer asked Saffron when she rolled the window down.

"No, but—"

"Please move on then," he said, and turned away.

Saffron asked the driver to let her out a few streets ahead and almost choked when he asked her for $135. That was just plain robbery.

She walked a couple blocks toward the address she had. Another police car with the lights on also blocked the street leading to the house she was trying to get to. She decided to try her luck anyway. As she walked closer, she saw a young and beautiful officer blocking her path. She was frowning, making her look menacing.

"I need to get through," Saffron said.

"Do you live here?" the officer asked.

"No." She didn't want to talk about her sister. She looked up, trying to come up with something, when she saw her car. "I need to pick up my car. It's that Mini over there."

The officer turned to check in the direction Saffron was pointing at, and with an exaggerated expression of disbelief she asked, "What's the license plate?"

"I don't remember. But you can check the registration." When the officer didn't move, she added, "Please, I need my car."

"Why is your car here?" The policewoman pushed her aviator glasses up her nose.

Saffron was numb. She didn't want to tell her.

"Please check the registration." She felt the young woman's piercing eyes, even though they were behind mirrored glasses.

"Okay, give me the keys."

She extended her hand, palm up.

Shifting from one foot to another, Saffron said, "I don't have them, but..."

The officer puffed and turned away from her.

Saffron pushed a loose strand of hair behind her ear. Why didn't I give Darcy my spare keys? she cursed, wishing she could shove her car keys into the officer's hand as proof of ownership. She looked back at her car. She could tell the officer she was with Darcy, but she didn't want him to know she was there—and especially not why she was there.

CHAPTER 44

Ethan felt disgusting driving his M3 to the VA hospital. He had thought about renting a less flashy car for his weekly visits, but that would have made him feel even worse. Like a phony. Like an asshole.

He took the Summer Road exit off of Highway 280 and then pulled into the farthest parking spot he could find. Ethan left his leather jacket in the car, even though it was cold out. He exhaled and waited to see his breath, but it wasn't quite that cold.

The building was gray, the windows were small, and the front entrance was drab. It felt like a second-class facility. Ethan thought about the Palo Alto and Menlo Park hospitals, which were much better. As he walked in, he wondered whether vets would be happier there if the place had more color. Maybe it needed a woman's touch.

This made him think of Belle, the high-end hooker in his hiding place. He hadn't expected to bring a present home from the mission, but as the saying went, "No plan survives first contact." So when he saw her he adjusted, as he always did, and brought her home, making her a great addition to his playground.

She was so beautiful. He normally liked them a bit feistier, but her looks made up for it. He wasn't quite sure what he wanted to do with her. Every time he thought of a toy to use, it felt somehow inadequate, making him move on to another one. Except for his favorite. Yes, the welding torch had been perfect: little tiny blisters decorated her back and thighs in symmetrical patterns. But aside from that, she was still a blank canvas.

The fat receptionist with the hairy mole on her cheek brought him back to the present. She had a nice smile, but he didn't seem to be able to pull his eyes away from the mole. It repulsed him. He'd often thought of asking her why on earth wouldn't she pluck the hair, or better yet, remove the mole? But he never did.

"Ethan Mitchell, here to see—" he said in lieu of a salutation.

"Manuel Gomez. I remember you," she said, waving her index finger at him.

He leaned back as if her long red nail could burn him. Was she flirting with him? A rush of nausea reached his throat. He swallowed hard.

"I know the way," he said, already walking away.

Shaking his head, he told himself to be nicer to her next time. He may need a friend at the VA one of these days.

Ethan had been coming here every week for almost eighteen months. The only exceptions had been when he was out of town on a job or deployed. He knew the place well, especially the smell of decay and disinfectant. He walked by the playroom. As always it was full of people playing games or watching TV. He'd tried bringing Gomez there a few times, but he'd refused. After a while, he'd stopped insisting.

When Ethan reached his friend's room, he paused and looked at him before going in. The only man he'd ever been afraid of competing against had now withered to almost nothing.

"Hey, buddy, how are you doing today?" he asked after he walked in.

The Marine was lying on his back. Only his head moved to greet him. "Peachy. I'm going to start training for the marathon next week," Gomez said. There wasn't a hint of a smile on his face.

"I brought you a beer," Ethan said, pulling a sweating bottle from his backpack. He twisted the top open and headed toward the bed.

Gomez shook his head.

"Come on, don't be a prick. You know you want it," Ethan said. "Even if it's only to piss the doctors off."

This brought a tiny smirk on Gomez's face, and he relented. Ethan put the bottle in the man's mouth and tilted it until the liquid started pouring in. After a few swallows, he stopped and dried a drop that was rolling down his friend's cheek.

"Fucking A, man. Why do you keep coming?" Gomez faced the wall, as if that would push Ethan away.

"Because you're my friend, and I like spending time with you."

"I'm not your friend. When you saved my life in Kandahar, you stopped being my friend. You need to leave me alone, like you should have left me there."

"Don't start with this all over again. We never leave anybody behind—you know that. That's who we are."

"Well, you should have left me. If you were really my friend, you should have killed me. Ended my misery. I would have been much happier that way. So fuck you. Take your beer and go fuck yourself. Leave me alone."

Gomez shut his eyes so hard his forehead furrowed.

Ethan didn't move. Gomez had this ritual of trying to make him feel like shit before he calmed down enough to have a good time. At first Ethan had wondered if Gomez was right, if he should have let him die there with a bunch of holes in his chest and a bullet lodged between his C2 and C3 vertebrae. He wondered every time he came to see Gomez if it would have been better to end his life instead of letting him live in this hell. But he did what he had to. What his code demanded. So Ethan saved him, and now Gomez hated him for it.

CHAPTER 45

While Darcy waited for Madison to come to the garage, he kneeled down and checked the body.

"Is this exactly how you found him?" the ME asked from the door.

"I removed the gun, but otherwise, yes."

Darcy watched while the doctor worked. His movements were slow, as if he were perpetually immersed in a mud bath.

"Which hand had the gun?" the ME asked.

"The right one."

"Interesting," he said, checking the palms of both hands.

"Why?"

Madison checked the liver temperature, then the exit wound. The bullet had taken off most of the back of the victim's head.

"What is it?" Darcy insisted.

"I will have to verify this when I get to the morgue, but my preliminary assessment is that the entry wound is not consistent with suicide."

"How so?"

Madison extended his index and thumb fingers, then opened his mouth as if he were going to shoot himself.

Darcy nodded, indicating that he was following.

"When you shoot yourself, the barrel is typically angled slightly upward, so normally the upper part of the head is what gets blown off. When it's another person pulling the trigger, the angle is much smaller. The bullet travels more horizontal to the ground." After taking a short breath, he added, "Also, depending on whether you are left-handed or right-handed, there is a slight angle toward the opposite side. Furthermore, this man was left-handed, and yet the gun was in his right hand."

Darcy thought about this and looked at the vic on the floor. "The watch is on his right wrist . . ."

"Yes. Though this is not always an indication, he also has a smidge of ink on his left index finger, probably from a fountain pen."

Darcy looked at him. The ME didn't even look smug while he talked.

"Of course," the doctor went on, picking up where he'd left of, "if the shooter is shorter or taller, or if the victim is sitting or standing, that will make a difference in the angle of the bullet trajectory. That's why I need to get the body to the morgue and perform some tests."

Darcy nodded. He was disappointed. For a second he hoped this might be a murder-suicide that could be closed fast so he could go back to the bank case. He was responsible for what had happened to Jon, and he wanted to be the one bringing the assholes who almost killed him to justice.

He watched as Madison placed the Sig P226 in an evidence bag. "This may have been the gun used on the African American woman found in the other room," he said as he was sealing it.

Rachel came in and started taking pictures.

Besides the spatter from the shot, the rest of the blood had accumulated in a pool around the body. The vic had been sitting on the floor when he was killed, with his back against the wall.

When she was done taking photos of the body, she moved on to photograph everything else in the garage.

"I don't get it." Darcy was sweeping the floor with his Maglite on the opposite side of the garage.

"This is the eleventh victim. There may be more," Rachel said.

"I don't buy this staging. Somebody came in and did a number here and then tried to frame this guy but was so sloppy about it that it took Madison about thirty seconds to determine that it was not a suicide?" Darcy kneeled down to reach for the shell casing underneath the car. "Maybe the perp did this on purpose. Or maybe—"

Rachel stopped taking pictures for a second and turned to face him. "Do you always theorize out loud?"

Darcy laughed. "Sometimes. It helps me think. By the way, I found a shell casing. It's another .40, so that's consistent with all of the other casings. The triaging will have to tell if there are more guns."

"We found a Beretta too," she said.

"Was it tossed?"

"Not really. They found it under a side table in the living room," she said, shrugging her shoulders.

After they had gone through the entire garage, Darcy said good-bye and headed out. He wanted to check with the officers to see if the canvas had turned up anything at all.

Outside the house's fence, he spotted Diaz, the sergeant in charge. "Anything?"

"I never know if these rich people don't talk because they really don't know anything or because they all keep each other's secrets."

"That good?"

"Yeah, that good." Diaz did a sweep, looking for someone. "Brier," he called out. When the young officer came over, he asked, "You got something?"

"I don't know, maybe. The people in the house over there." He pointed to an even bigger house hidden by tall trees and a brick fence. "Mrs. Hollister is not very fond of the neighbors. She told me that they host these parties every couple months. That normally they are frequented by influential people from the Valley."

"Influential as in politicians, or influential as in venture capitalists?"

"Both, from what she was saying. But she had nothing more."

Darcy wrote down her contact information and thanked both. "Email me the yellow sheets when you're done," he told Diaz before he walked away.

"You got it. I'll collect the interview notes from everybody else."

Darcy pulled out his phone. "Sis, I have a question for you."

"Is it about the big case on Almond Avenue?"

"News travel fast." Having a sister married to the Santa Clara sheriff had its perks. Sometimes. "Do you know anything about a Carlos de la Rosa and his parties?"

There was silence. After what seemed too long for her to be swallowing, he asked, "You still there?"

"Yes, I know about them."

"Have you participated in these parties?" he teased her. Then hoped her answer was no.

"No. But I have friends who have."

"'No' as in 'no, never,' or as in 'I don't want to tell you'?"

165

"Don't be cute. 'No' as in never. But there are prominent people in the Valley who do attend."

"So I heard. De la Rosa's gone. You think he could have done this?"

"I don't know him personally."

"Anything helpful you can actually offer?"

There was silence again.

"Darcy, this is going to be really big. There're a lot of eyes on this already, and I'm not talking about the media." She sighed audibly for a long time. "Don't screw up."

"Jesus, really?" he asked.

"I'm sorry that's not what I meant."

"Oh, no? Then what did you mean? I'm more than a little tired of your husband's constant worry that I'm going to give him a bad name."

He hung up. Darcy put the phone in his jacket and felt it vibrate with an incoming call. He ignored it. He walked to Saffron's car and when he was within a few feet clicked the fob to unlock the door.

"Darcy."

He heard his name from behind and turned. Saffron was waving at him from the other side of the yellow tape. His gut wrenched, and he fought an overwhelming need to throw up.

"Is Jon okay?" He reached her and lifted the tape for his girlfriend to duck under.

"He was resting when I got there, but his mom says the doctors think the worst is over. It seems that because the bullets went through the car door first, the impact to his body was much less than it could have been."

"That's great news." He exhaled a breath of relief. "How come you're here?"

"I needed my computer. I heard about this on the news and figured this is where Virago sent you this morning. I thought I would just come and get my laptop, but they wouldn't let me go through."

"I'm done here. If you can drop me off at the station, you can have your car back." He put his arm around her waist and pulled her toward him.

When they reached the car, she took the keys from him and jumped in the Mini. He sat in the passenger seat.

"Bad case?" she asked.

"Eleven dead. This is going to make the news big-time," he said, looking over at the news vans, cameramen, and overly coiffed anchors trying to get the scoop.

"Men and women?"

"Yep, six women, five men."

CHAPTER 46

When Darcy got to the station, Sorensen was gone. He wondered if his partner was pursuing a hot lead on the bank case and hadn't told him. He dismissed the idea and decided to go talk to Mauricio at the lab. On the way there he thought about the multiple homicide case he'd just landed. He hoped Virago hadn't assigned it to him to keep him from working on Jon's shooting.

Mary wasn't in the reception area. Instead, a young guy who could have been Jon's brother manned the entrance to the CSU Lab.

"Detective Darcy Lynch," he said, showing his badge. "I need to talk to Mauricio."

The receptionist punched a few numbers on the phone and waited, then left a voice mail after nobody answered. "I don't seem to be able to reach him. Would you like to wait in the lobby until he comes to meet you?" It was more a statement than a question.

Darcy looked at him, surprised. "I'd rather just go in and look for him myself."

"Nobody's supposed to go in unescorted."

Before Darcy could argue, the doors to the lab opened, and a broad black man with a pockmarked face came out.

"Detective Lynch, what brings you to my kingdom?"

They shook hands.

168

Darcy told him and then asked, "So, Lou, I can't go in unescorted?"

"Ah, new staff. They're so cute." Lou walked over to the receptionist and leaning over the counter, said, "Detectives can go in whenever they want. This allows our scientists to keep working instead of wasting their time having to come all the way to the front to meet them."

"Understood." The young man fidgeted with the phone's cord.

"Okay then. Open the damn door for the detective."

The buzzer reverberated in the otherwise quiet room, and Darcy opened the door.

Before he went in, Lou said, "Some nasty case, this new one. Good luck."

That didn't sound like a good omen. Darcy headed toward the last room. He knew Mauricio and Rachel always fought for it because it was the largest one. While he walked, Darcy checked his phone to see if his sister had sent him any information, but he had nothing.

Mauricio's head bobbed as he listened to music. Darcy opened the door, and the tech pulled out his earbuds. Darcy heard faint dance music until Mauricio paused it.

"Hello, Detective." His smile was wide and genuine. "You only bring coffees for Rachel? I feel no love." His smiled turned into a fake pout that made him look ten years younger.

"My bad. We should go and get one now."

Mauricio checked his watch and then looked over at the full table. "Too much to do. Next time. Anyway, what brings you here?"

"I was wondering if you had anything new on the van."

"We went through it with a fine-tooth comb as Sorensen requested, and I'm telling you, these guys were either really good, or they were wearing head-to-toe moon suits."

Darcy was silent. Nothing? he thought. His stomach tightened in a knot. "There was no way to get any identifiers in the car?"

"No. We've tried everything." Mauricio stretched his back. "I'm sorry, Detective. I know you really want to catch these guys."

CHAPTER 47

Saffron decided to go back to her sister's apartment. Maybe Aislin was back already, or maybe she would find a clue to where she was. On the way there, Saffron ran through what she'd learned from Darcy.

He normally shared some basic information about his cases, but he'd been pretty quiet about this one. Darcy hadn't met anybody from her family yet, and Saffron and Aislin looked different enough that he probably wouldn't have made the connection. Since he didn't volunteer much, she had to ask him questions.

She learned that two of the six dead women were Asians, one was an African American, and three were older Caucasians. Saffron was pretty sure that if Aislin had been in that house at all, she wasn't one of the dead victims. Aislin could be dead somewhere else, but at least she survived that massacre.

The apartment was exactly the same way she'd left it a few hours earlier. The laptop was open but asleep. She moved the mouse and saw the IM window flicker. Somebody with the alias of Madam X had sent Aislin a message.

"Aislin, are you okay? I heard about what happened at de la Rosa's house."

Another message followed: "Dammit, Aislin, I've called you a million times. I know you're angry with me for sending you to that party, but at least tell me you're okay."

The last message Madam X had sent said, "Fine. Have it your way."

The icon next to her screen name was green; Madam X was still online. Saffron sat on the chair and rested her fingers on the keyboard. She didn't know what to say.

She started typing, then deleted it. Wrote something else. Stopped. Then entered, "Why on earth did you send me there?" She read it out loud, deleted it and finally wrote, "What the fuck's wrong with you?" and hit Send without rereading.

She crossed her fingers and waited. A whole minute passed, and she thought she'd blown it. Then rolling dots appeared on the IM screen. Madam X was typing.

"Yes," she said out loud and punched the air with her fists.

"I'm sorry. There's no way I could have known that something like that was going to happen." Madam X paused and then started writing again. "They're old clients. Group stuff, nothing super-kinky . . . Exactly what I told you."

Saffron pulled her hands away from the keyboard as if it were on fire. "Oh God, Aislin," Saffron said to an empty room.

"So what happened?" Madam X asked. "Are the others okay?"

Who were these people? What had they got Aislin into? Could she be involved in murder? No, that was ridiculous. But could she? Saffron would have never thought her little sister would become a prostitute, and here she was going to group parties where nothing super-kinky was expected. And she definitely had a thing for bad boys. Oh God.

"Not over IM. Let's meet."

Saffron knew she couldn't play her sister for much longer. She needed to get this Madam X in a place where she couldn't run away from her too easily.

"Regular place?" Madam X asked.

"Crap," Saffron said, but didn't type anything.

Before she could come up with a clever way to ask exactly where the "regular place" was, Madam X started typing again.

"Never mind. Let's go to the Cotto Lounge. I could use a mojito. It's already past noon."

Saffron checked her watch. "I'll meet you there in an hour," she typed, and after getting confirmation she closed the computer and rushed off.

On the way to the hotel's bar, she stopped by her condo to pick up the can of mace Darcy had gotten her when they first met. He'd told her to carry it in her purse at all times, but she always forgot to transfer it whenever she changed handbags.

There was an accident on 280 right before the exit to Sand Hill Road, and traffic was backed up for miles. When it finally cleared, Saffron had to drive like a maniac to get there on time. She pulled up and gave the keys to the valet. He called after her to hand her the ticket.

The hotel was spacious, luxurious, and the restaurant was airy and warm. She walked past it into the bar, which was much smaller. It was not very crowded, but there were enough people for Saffron to wonder who Madam X was. After a careful sweep without finding any likely candidates, she settled at the bar and asked for a drink.

The bartender's name was David. His hair was messy and styled with product, every lock a different length, as if the stylist was having a seizure while cutting it. Oddly enough it suited him, making him look cool. Over the collar of his black shirt she saw the edge of a cyborg tattoo.

"That's some interesting artwork." Saffron pointed at her own neck when he set the glass of Shiraz in front of her.

"You should see the one on my back." He winked.

Saffron wondered how many times he'd said that since he got the tattoo. She took a sip. The wine warmed her mouth.

She turned around and scanned the room. A few more people had walked in, but nobody fit her preconceived idea of what a high-scale madam should look like.

When David came by to squeeze a lime around the rim of a glass, she decided to risk it.

"Do you know anybody named Madam X?" she asked.

David eyed her for a minute. "Are you a cop?"

"No. No, of course not." Saffron blushed, thinking a cop would say exactly that.

David looked past her toward the opposite wall. She turned around and saw a massive print of John Singer Sargent's Madame X. Saffron almost laughed. Underneath it, sitting in a plush sofa, was a handsome black man in a steel-gray suit, purple shirt, and matching tie.

It couldn't have been more cliché.

"Seriously?" she asked David.

He nodded. She left a twenty-dollar bill and went to get some answers.

Madam X sat straight. He almost looked statuesque. His eyes were slivers, and only his thumb moved, drumming against his knee. As Saffron got closer, she could see that even if his head was not moving, his eyes darted across the room. He loosened his tie a smidge, then adjusted his collar.

Saffron reached him and sat in the chair across from him. He looked at her and started to say something, but Saffron put her palm up a foot away from his face.

"I'm Aislin's sister. You're going to tell me what the hell you got her into."

Madam X looked toward the door. Saffron wondered if he was weighing his chances of running. But then she saw two goons and swallowed hard. Madam X was communicating with his bodyguards.

"Don't even think about it." She put both hands on her knees and leaned toward him. "My boyfriend's a cop, and he's here. He'll have you arrested before your boys can touch me."

Madam X sighed audibly and drank the rest of his mojito. "So, you don't know where she is either," he said.

CHAPTER 48

Ethan summoned everybody to his house but refused to talk until they were all there. When Mac finally arrived, he gave him a beer from the fridge and said, "The police came to talk to Bishop and me." He left out the fact that it had been yesterday, before the job.

The room was quiet, but Ethan felt the anxiety building in the air. They all looked back at him without a hint of defiance. Bishop may still not get it, but everybody else did. In the eighteen jobs they'd done together, Ethan had proven that he always had their backs. Not only was he fattening their pockets fast, but every one of his missions had been successful.

"Two detectives came to see us. One talked with me, the other took Bishop for a little stroll."

He saw a few furtive glances at the new member. Everybody knew he was the weakest link. Bishop picked at the scab on his lip.

"We agreed to talk to them to gather information. It was the easiest way to find out how much they know. At this point"—he paused to make sure everybody was hanging on his every word—"they have nothing. It was a fishing expedition. They were claiming that they could put Bishop at the bank scene, but we know he was in the car. We got more out of that visit than the police did."

Bishop looked more composed. Ethan thought that the visit from the detectives had actually made him feel better.

"The van is a different story. They've been able to identify Malik as the corpse from the burnt van, so it's only a matter of time until they tie him to the bank." Looking at Curtis, Ethan asked, "All identifiers were removed from the vehicle, right?"

Ethan was sure they had been but knew that some confirmation would reassure the others, because they trusted Curtis.

"Absolutely. Pulled the VIN number off the dash, firewall, the driver's door, and trunk. I removed all the registration papers and made sure to wipe every inch of the van. Just like the Austin job."

Ethan nodded. "Mac, did anybody see you when you torched the van?"

"No worry if they did. I was in full disguise, so any witness would lead them to look for a fat black dude with dreadlocks wearing sweats and a dirty hoodie."

Ethan smiled. This was why he'd kept this crew together for five years.

"I think we are as covered as we can be. Now we need to finish the job and go on a long vacation."

"We should get paid more," Barr said.

Ethan's black eyes honed in on him. "Has there ever been a time when I didn't pay you what you were worth?"

Barr got up and walked to the fridge, as if the scrutiny from the other men had suddenly made him thirsty.

Ethan waited for his answer. He knew everybody was thinking the same thing, so he was curious about what they would do.

"You always pay me what I'm worth."

"Then I suggest you worry about getting the job done and leave the rest to me."

"I didn't mean—"

"I know. I also know that when things get ugly, people start questioning things. We have a job to do. When the job's done, we'll all get what we deserve. And then some," he promised, and raised his beer bottle.

They all toasted, smiling for the first time that day.

CHAPTER 49

Madam X asked for another mojito. Saffron thought he was just buying time, to figure out what he wanted to tell her, or how much he wished to share.

"I know about the prostitution," Saffron said.

X looked behind Saffron, probably searching for the cop boyfriend she'd mentioned. Finally, nodding slightly, he said, "Very well." He took a sip of his brand-new drink and leaned back against the swanky sofa.

"I got a call from one of my regulars yesterday. He said he wanted to get into this particular private party he'd heard about."

"Why?"

"Honey, in my line of work, when somebody hands you a really large sum of money, you don't ask why." His tone was a bit condescending.

"Whose party was it?" she asked.

"Did you watch the news today?"

Saffron thought about the huge house she'd met Darcy at, surrounded by police cars and flanked by news vans. The same address she found in Aislin's computer calendar. She thought about the dead, and wrapped both arms around her chest.

"Go on." Her brain was racing, but she was unable to formulate any questions that made sense. She didn't even know where to start, and she wished Darcy were doing this with her, but knew better.

"That's all I know. I was hoping Belle could tell me what the hell happened at that place."

"Belle?"

"Your sister's working name."

"Right." Saffron looked around. "How did you know about the party?"

"You don't know how this works, do you?" Madam X asked.

Saffron shook her head. The bar was getting crowded, and she started to feel suffocated. She wished they could go outside, but it was too cold.

"These adult parties work one of two ways. Either people know each other and they just get together—sort of like a Fourth of July barbeque but with a lot more exposed skin and a lot less potato salad—or they know a few people but not enough to make it a party, so they hire professionals. When they go through a third party, the agency not only provides the mavens but may also bring in others who are curious to participate but don't have the connections yet."

X stared at Saffron, probably checking if she was following.

"How many people did you hook up?"

"I set the client up with Belle, and I provided dates for two other gentlemen."

"Have you heard from anybody?"

"No," X said.

"There were six dead women in that house and five men," Saffron said. Her voice was more accusatory than she had intended. "Do you know everybody who was there?"

He plucked a mint leaf from his tall glass and chewed on it for a moment. His face looked ashen under his dark skin.

180

"I've known the host and his wife forever. They were two of my first clients. Three of the girls were mine, including Belle, and I know their dates fairly well. I don't know who else was there." He finished his drink. "That's another thing I wanted to talk to Belle about. Under regular circumstances, we would have done a debrief after the party. I'm always looking to find ways to expand the business."

"Of course you are," Saffron spat.

X fixed his eyes on her. "You said you wanted to know how this worked."

"Do you know if the guy you sent Aislin with is alive?"

"I haven't heard any names on the news, but he's not picking up my calls. Is your sister one of the six . . . ?"

"Worried about your investment?"

"I'm not that cold." His voice had lost its edge for the first time since they'd started talking. "I actually care for Belle. She's a good girl."

Saffron tasted bile in her mouth. She wanted to get up and punch him in the face. He didn't care about her sister. It made her feel sick that he was trying to convince her that he did.

"What's his name, the guy you set her up with? What do you know about him? Where does he live?" she asked, pushing her rage away.

"His name's Blake. He's been a client for a year or so. He's one of those hotshots from Silicon Valley. I have no clue where he lives."

Blake, Saffron thought. That matched the B on Aislin's calendar.

"What company?"

"I'm on a strict need-to-know basis. And where he works is something I don't need to know. He has a lot of money to burn, though. Old money, if you know what I mean."

"Are all your girls college students?"

"No. Some of them have very successful careers and they do this for fun, earning a nice bonus on the side."

Madam X puffed his chest a little. He was proud of his brood.

"So if you don't know where your clients work, how do you ensure you don't send a career woman to somebody she may know professionally?"

X paused. He raised his almost empty mojito to Saffron. "Smart. You sure you don't want a side job?"

"What I want is to know where this Blake guy works."

"He's some VP or something at a company called NanoQ."

Saffron knew the name. It was a fairly big company. "And you're sure you don't have his last name?"

"I'm sure."

"He pays with cash?"

"Oh, sweetie, nobody pays with cash these days. We do exchange of goods. It's like a very expensive white-elephant gift party."

I knew that. Saffron remembered the huge rock shining on Aislin's middle finger when they met for drinks the other day.

"I want you to do something for me."

X looked more curious than annoyed.

"You know, in exchange for me not going to the police," Saffron added.

"Right," he said. "What is it that you want?"

"Call Blake and tell him you need to meet him."

"Oh, no. He would never believe that."

"Make up something believable."

"Don't be stupid. Instead of being so pushy and antagonistic—which, by the way, doesn't suit you—you could try to be nicer. You'll probably get further in life." After a wink, X said, "You know, the bees, honey, vinegar and all that."

Saffron tucked a long strand of hair behind her ear. "Okay . . ." she conceded.

"Blake has his regular appointment tonight. He hasn't called to cancel, and he's normally very good about that." He paused, probably curious to find out how his proposal would settle with Saffron. "Mind you, I don't know if he's still alive, so he'll either show up or he won't." X eyed Saffron before he continued: "You can go instead of his regular girl and try to get some answers."

Saffron's eyes opened wide. She'd never expected this.

"Why would he talk to me?" she asked.

"I'm sure you'll find a way." He leaned against the back of the velvet sofa.

Saffron thought about it. It was crazy, but what else could she do?

"I care about Aislin. I hope she's okay. If anybody can find her besides the police, that person is you," X said.

Saffron nodded. "She's my little sister."

"I also have a little sister. She's a pain in the ass," he shared.

They smiled at each other. For the first time since they'd started talking, Saffron felt that she was not fighting this fight alone anymore.

Saffron stood to leave.

"Can I ask you a question?" Madam X asked.

Saffron nodded.

"Do you really have a cop boyfriend?"

Saffron smiled. "Yes."

"Why isn't he looking for Aislin?"

"Because I don't want him to know what she does for a living."

Madam X nodded.

Saffron started walking away, but before she got too far she turned. "What's your real name?"

"Constantine."

"Madam X suits you better," she teased.

He lifted his glass and smiled.

Saffron walked by the two goons and nodded good-bye.

CHAPTER 50

Saffron went to the hospital to see Jon before heading over to Darcy's place. She crossed paths with several officers who had come to show their support.

As she walked in the room, her phone rang. She pressed her purse against her body, trying to muffle the sound. She mouthed, "I'm sorry," to Jon's parents and walked back out into the hallway.

"Yes?"

It was Madam X. A mixture of hope and fear made her stomach churn.

"You're on for tonight," X said.

"Did you ask him what happened?"

"I tried."

"And?"

"He changed the subject. So I didn't push it. I didn't want him to cancel."

"Yeah, that would have been worse."

"Saffron . . ." X said.

"Yeah?"

"You know that once you've gone through that door, there's no coming back."

Saffron remained silent. She'd asked herself what the hell she was doing, but forced herself to stop because she didn't want to get even more scared. She had to find her sister, and that was all there was to it.

"I don't have a choice."

"Don't you have a cop boyfriend?"

"And tell him my sister's a prostitute? He would have to arrest her."

"Only if he catches her in the act. But the point is that he would have to find her first."

Saffron paused. She'd thought about that too. "I know. Let me try this. If it doesn't work, I'll tell Darcy."

"I would've never pegged you for a lesbian." He sounded genuinely surprised. "You sure you don't want a side job? The market for girl-on-girl is skyrocketing."

"Darcy's a man."

"Oh, right. I guess I can't be that surprised."

"Exactly, Constantine, a.k.a. Madam X."

Saffron could feel his smile at the other end of the phone. There was nothing else to be said, but neither wanted to hang up.

"I'll see you there," X finally said.

"What? Why? As my chaperone?" Saffron asked. "Won't he be weirded out if he sees you there?"

"I'll make the intros. I'll feed him some bullshit about wanting to ensure he's happy with the new girl, since his regular couldn't make it at the last minute." After a moment, he added, "This guy's bad news. I want to see his face when he shows up."

"And what? Threaten him with a mojito straw if he looks at you the wrong way?" Saffron asked.

"Very funny, missy. Don't let the five-thousand-dollar suit fool you. I come from a rough neighborhood."

"Then why do you need those goons?" She thought about the two guys she saw earlier watching X's every move.

"Honey, because now I can afford to pay somebody else to do the dirty work."

Saffron smiled. The perfect manicured hands, the slightly gay mannerisms, and the gorgeous clothes hid the rough edges well.

"Okay, meet me at Belle's. We need to pick your outfit," he said, and before she could protest, the line went dead.

CHAPTER 51

Darcy had been trying to reach Saffron for the past couple hours. When the beep ended, he left another message: "Hey, babe, not sure if you're coming tonight, but I still have a few more hours here." He paused for a second. He wanted to say something else but finally settled for, "It would be good to see you."

He looked over and saw Sorensen pecking at his keyboard. Darcy sat on his chair and started organizing his thoughts about the multiple homicide case. He knew he would have to start producing some results fast, or everybody would jump on his back.

The files of the victims made a neat pile on the left side of his desk. He grabbed the first one. The victim's name was Eva Yung. She was twenty-four, a part-time student at Santa Clara University, majoring in art history. Apparently she didn't have a job, but she was able to afford a two-thousand-dollar-a-month apartment. He looked at the crime scene photos. He read the ME's report. Cause of death: exsanguination caused by a single gunshot wound to the head.

The second file was for Oscar Summers. He was forty-nine. Overweight. Was married to Joslyn Summers, another victim. Cause of death: exsanguination caused by a single gunshot wound to the head. He had no children. His financials looked in order. He was a very successful venture capitalist. Prima facie, there was nothing fishy with his money.

He wrote down all the information on the board and moved to the next one.

Sandra Howell—the one found alone in the other room. She was another beautiful young woman, also a student, but she was going to Berkeley. No job, so probably paying the tuition by being an escort. Same cause of death, different gun, confirmed by Rachel.

The rest were carbon copies of these reports. Different name, man or woman, either escort or highly successful businessman killed by a bullet through the brain. The last two were the bouncer and the older woman in the suit. They were neither rich nor successful. Darcy made a mental note to dig a bit deeper into their known associates in case there was something fishy, but he was pretty sure they were just collateral damage.

Darcy pinned DMV photos on the board and wrote out the details of each victim. As soon as he was done, he started working on the owner of the house. Mr. Carlos de la Rosa was MIA. He was forty-three, a multimillionaire, and one of the founders of McKenzie & Shaw LLP.

What? Darcy stood and walked to Sorensen's desk.

"What was the name of the law firm Suresh Malik worked for?" he asked, already knowing the answer.

"McKenzie & Shaw," Sorensen said, not looking up at him.

"Is his file here?" Darcy asked, leafing through his partner's papers.

"What're you looking for?" Sorensen planted a brawny hand on top of the files, halting Darcy's riffling.

"It's the company the host of my multiple homicide founded. Who, by the way, is missing."

"Are you sure?"

"That's what I was trying to find out," he said, looking down at Sorensen's hand, still safeguarding the pile.

Sorensen removed it, and Darcy grabbed all the files. He picked Malik's and opened it on Sorensen's desk, next to the keyboard.

"Yep," Darcy said, tapping at the company's name in his own file.

Sorensen looked at Darcy's board, then back at his partner and asked, "What the hell's going on here?"

CHAPTER 52

Saffron pulled down the red dress. It was too tight and too short. Aislin was a size or two smaller than her, so she felt stuffed in the outfit Madam X had picked out for her.

"This is not attractive," she protested.

X covered his ears and said, "I can't hear you," for the nth time.

"No, seriously. I don't look like a high-class call girl. I look like a sausage." Saffron pulled the dress down again.

"You need to stop doing that. You need to quit the whining, and you need to straighten your back." He waited until Saffron complied. "Now you need to put one foot in front of the other so your hips sway when you walk."

"What?" Saffron stopped walking.

"Yes, sweetie, walk as if you were on a rope, one foot in front of the other." X patted her butt as if to encourage her to try.

Saffron visualized a white rope. After a couple steps, her hips did sway. She felt ridiculous. At first she looked clunky, but the more she did it, the easier it seemed.

By the time they walked into the Vortex, the bar at the top of the Zenix Hotel, she had mastered the move.

Several men turned to look at her. Saffron's first reaction was to grab the hem of the dress and pull it down one more time. Before she had a chance X whispered, "Don't you dare."

Saffron almost laughed. This helped her relax a little. She flipped her hair and followed the host to a table in the corner.

"I specifically requested this one so we can watch the whole place." X said sitting next to her with his back to the wall.

They ordered two flutes of brut and waited.

The bench was covered by a cushion that matched the backrest on the wall. Saffron leaned against it and noticed that her skirt did not slide with the rest of her legs when she slouched. She straightened her posture and pulled the skirt down. It barely came to midthigh.

X checked her out and said, "Leave it where it is, or he'll think I sent a nun."

Saffron forced her hands away from her bare legs and scanned the restaurant. They had a panoramic view of the entire place but were far enough away from others to be able to talk freely.

"He's not here yet," X said.

Saffron tasted the bubbly. It was citrusy and light. "How many of these men are here to meet pros?" she asked.

X scanned the room. "At least four are clients of mine."

"No shit."

"Yep."

"How many girls do you have?"

Madam X eyed her as if gauging whether Saffron was fishing for information or genuinely curious. "I have eleven regulars. And another three who do sporadic jobs."

"So how does this really work?"

"Are you interested in an interview?" X teased her.

"Does it pay well?"

"You've seen your sister's closet."

"What if I don't want clothes?"

"Let me rephrase. The Guccis, Valentinos, Pradas, Armanis, et cetera, are gifts on top of the payment."

"Damn," Saffron said. "There's real money in this business."

"Well, you have to make it all when you are young and beautiful. If not, you'll end up in a corner hailing johns driving by."

"Nice image."

"Indeed."

A tall, blondish man with an angular face and a dimple on his chin walked toward them.

X stood to greet him, but before he could speak, Blake said, "Constantine, I didn't expect to see you here." His eyes never left Saffron.

"Blake, it's always a pleasure to see you. Please meet Cassandra."

He kissed Saffron's hand and left a moist spot. She had to fight the urge to wipe it off.

"Jaz got food poisoning, so I thought you might enjoy the company of somebody new," X explained, and then fed him the bullshit line "I wanted to personally ensure Cassandra exceeds your expectations."

Blake nodded very slowly after he gave Saffron a once-over. She worried he would think she was too old for him. It had never occurred to her to even ask, but he was probably five years younger than she was. He started smiling. Saffron shivered, wondering again what the hell she was getting herself into.

"Cassandra does," he finally said as if she weren't there.

X excused himself and left them alone. Blake sat next to her and ordered a dry vodka martini.

"So, Cassandra, tell me: What's your favorite color?"

What? she thought. Out of a million questions she'd prepared for, this wasn't one of them. She took a sip of her bubbly, faked the same smile she had for posing on photos and said, "Royal blue of course."

"I would have said red." He looked her up and down again.

"I only wear red to throw people off when they ask me that question." She interlaced her fingers on top of the table to avoid covering her exposed décolletage with her hands.

"How's that working for you?"

"Flawlessly."

Blake raised his cocktail to her. She toasted and finished her drink.

"Another one?" he asked, already summoning the bartender.

"I'm okay for now. Thank you."

He asked for the tab and finished his drink in two gulps. Once he'd paid, he said, "Shall we?"

Saffron nodded and swallowed hard. She stood but didn't trust herself to move yet. Blake put his arm around her waist as they walked through the bar. It took all she had to not squirm away from his touch.

He called the elevator and they got in. It was empty. Saffron looked up to see if she could spot the camera. She wasn't sure there was one, but she hoped there was and it was recording.

The doors opened on the fifteenth floor, and a floor-to-ceiling mirror greeted them with their own reflections. Saffron saw she looked scared. She tried to relax her facial muscles by forcing a smile. She realized he'd been watching her the entire time.

The hallway was empty.

"First time?" he asked.

She could use the truth to her advantage instead of trying to conceal it and failing miserably. "Yes," she said, no longer trying to hide her fear.

He opened the door and let her go in first. The room was dark, but through the window she could see the blanket of lights of the beautiful valley at night. Saffron heard the door close and the switch of the light. The view outside disappeared, and she winced. Saffron turned to face Blake and realized he was standing between her and the door. Not the way she wanted it. She sat on the bed, hoping to lead him away from her exit route.

"Anything to drink?" he asked, walking past her and opening the minibar.

"I'll have whatever you're having," she said, standing up as soon as he'd gone past her.

He kneeled down, inspecting the contents of the little fridge.

The path to the door was now clear.

Holding two tiny bottles of rum, he said, "I guess rum and Coke it is."

He decanted the contents in two glasses and then grabbed the red can.

She took a deep breath. She needed to confront him or run out the door.

"What have you done with my sister?" Her voice was merely a whisper.

"What did you just say?" He stopped pouring and turned toward her.

"Aislin. Belle. What have you done to her?"

He placed the Coke on the table, right next to the tiny bottles. His movements were slow, deliberate. Saffron knew he was assessing her. He looked up, past her, toward the door, probably calculating her chances of escaping. Saffron froze in place. This was a really, really bad idea, she cursed.

She squared her shoulders and said, "The party last night. You took her there. How did all of those people end up dead but you're alive and my sister's missing?"

"I'm lucky to be alive. All I did was bring a whore to a party. I don't know what happened to your sister."

"Why are you still alive? What happened in there?"

"A bunch of men came into the house and terrorized us."

"And yet you're here on your regular appointment, while eleven people from the party last night are dead, and my sister's missing."

"I needed to blow off some steam."

"Right."

"I don't have to explain myself to you. Now get naked or get the fuck out of my hotel room."

"I'm not leaving until you tell me what happened to my sister."

She took a couple steps toward him. Her hands were on her hips, accentuating each movement.

Saffron saw his jaw tighten, and his eyes were locked on hers. They were empty, like little black holes. Against her better judgment, she flinched and moved back. Her heart was beating so hard she was sure he could hear it.

"Get naked or get the fuck out, I said."

"Tell me what happened to her." Her voice was strong, loud. By now she was more angry than scared.

Blake moved fast toward her. She lost her balance and stumbled. He closed the distance and pushed her onto the bed. Before she could get up, he was on top of her.

"Get off me," she yelled with gritted teeth, trying to push him off.

He slapped her with so much force she was stunned for a few seconds.

"Tell Madam X he's fired." He pushed himself off of her and walked out of the room.

Saffron started crying. Her face burned, but mostly she was both relieved it was over and frustrated she got nothing out of him.

She stood and was pulling her dress down when she heard the hotel key unlocking the door. Her heart sank. She looked around for anything she could use to protect herself. She grabbed the tiny bottle of rum.

The door flung open, and Madam X's two goons propelled Blake back into the room. X followed and closed the door behind him.

"Sorry we took so long," he said to Saffron, who was now standing next to the small love seat by the window.

Blake was on the floor. X walked to him and kicked him in the gut. The goons moved to block the exit. Blake wailed and retreated until his back hit the TV stand.

"Two of my girls are dead and one's missing," X said, standing at kicking distance from Blake. "We all want to know what the hell happened at that party and where Belle is."

Blake hugged his stomach and, after taking a deep breath, said, "I don't know what happened. Five men came into the house and crashed the party. They put us all in the same room. One of the girls tried to escape, and they shot her."

Saffron wanted to interrupt but bit her tongue instead.

"I tried to take down one of them, and he hit me in the head so hard I passed out." He touched his head right above the left ear, as if to emphasize the spot. "When I woke up, a bunch of people were dead around me, so I bolted."

"That's the most preposterous story I've ever heard," X said, taking a step closer to him.

"Why not go to the police?" Saffron asked, still glued to the window.

197

"I can't. My company is about to be bought. If I get linked in any way to that party and what happened there, our buyers will pull out of the deal. We can't afford that."

"You care more about your stupid company than all of those dead people?" she asked.

He didn't answer.

"Were there any survivors?" X asked.

"I don't know. I didn't stay to check. I saw bodies and a lot of blood, so I ran."

"Did you see Belle?" Saffron walked toward them and stopped next to X.

"No. She might have been in another room, or maybe she managed to escape. I seriously don't know where she is."

"Why are you still alive?" X asked.

Blake scurried toward the window. "They probably thought I was dead."

"That must have been some blow if they thought that," X scoffed.

"I'm as much a victim of what happened in that house as everybody else." His voice was hollow.

Saffron stared down at him. "No. You're still alive."

X looked at his goons. One stayed by the door, still blocking the exit, and the other picked Blake up from the floor and pinned him against the wall. He grunted but was man enough to refrain from whining. X sat on the bed, crossed his legs and interlaced his fingers, resting his elbows on the top knee.

Saffron wanted to sit next to him, but he looked commanding and almost scary, so she stood by the side of the bed instead.

"Let me tell you how you're going to make this right," X said.

CHAPTER 53

Darcy's stomach protested. It felt hollow. He scratched Shelby behind the ears before he walked to the kitchen to find something to eat. The pantry was almost empty, but at the very end, forgotten in a corner, was a can of soup. He grabbed it and as an afterthought checked the expiration date.

"Damn, this must have been there from the previous owners," he told his dog, and threw the old can into the garbage.

He took a beer from the fridge. Shelby was blocking his exit, sitting in front of him, raising a paw, expecting to get a treat just because she was cute. He gave in after making her shake with the other paw. He took a sip of the cold beer and walked to the living room. The leather sofa felt cold. Shelby climbed next to him, and after circling a few times she finally lay down.

The night was chilly and very dark. He thought about putting a log in the fireplace. He got up and realized he didn't have any wood to burn. Lola swam in her tank on top of the mantel. He fed her and went back to sit next to Shelby.

He looked out the window. The steam lingered right above the lit pool, inviting him to jump in. But instead of going for a swim he checked his phone. Still nothing from Saffron. "Where are you?" he wanted to ask her. He didn't want to be pushy or possessive, but he really wished she were there with him right now. He missed her presence, her scent, how she looked at him over the rim of her mug when she drank coffee, and how she pushed the loose strands of hair behind her ear.

Mostly, he missed talking to her. She was bright and funny, always lifting his mood no matter what horrors the day had brought. But she wasn't here, and he had already left enough voice mails and texts that went unreturned. Darcy pushed away the fleeting thought that maybe she'd gone back to her ex-boyfriend. Ranjan. The douche bag who only realized how amazing she was once he'd lost her.

Pushing away the thoughts of Saffron only brought forward the guilt he felt for what happened to Jon. He believed he was justified in the pursuit, but looking back, he knew he'd gone too far. "What is wrong with you?" Sorensen had asked him. Darcy didn't have an answer then, and he still didn't. He thought he was doing the right thing going after the van. He needed to show his colleagues that he was as good as them, or better. He had balls. That having only one eye didn't mean he wasn't as good as the rest of them. And then he stopped. A chill ran through his body, and nausea churned his gut. There was nothing worse than becoming a bad cop because you had a chip on your shoulder.

CHAPTER 54

Thursday

The next day, Sorensen went to pick Lynch up, since the Cobra wasn't ready yet. He was getting tired of being Lynch's taxi driver and had told him several times to get a rental. He despised working with the guy after what he'd done to Jon, but Virago had made it very clear that he needed to put his resentment aside and focus on solving the case. And though he hated to admit it, they did work better together than apart.

They stopped at Starbucks, but Sorensen refused to get out of the car and opted for the drive-through. It wasn't even eight in the morning, and the line of cars already wrapped around the building.

"You know it would be much faster if we just went inside, right?" Lynch checked his watch.

"Next time you drive, you get to decide. Okay, sport?"

"I just wanted to be there before the guy shows up."

"They go fast here. Besides, we don't have a subpoena yet. And remember: they're lawyers, so we can't even con them." Sorensen lifted his foot from the brake, and the car moved ahead a few inches.

After about ten minutes, they got their orders and Sorensen sped through traffic, not touching his drink the entire ride.

When they arrived at McKenzie & Shaw, he took the first visitor spot he found, and they both bolted out of the car.

One of the receptionists informed them that Leon Brantley hadn't arrived yet.

"And you were so worried about going through the drive-through. I told you we wouldn't miss him." Sorensen sat down on the uncomfortable-looking sofa and combed his curls with open fingers.

Lynch checked his notes. Sorensen thought about Jon and how much he missed him. Not only his research skills and how he so often thought outside the box, but also his personality. He had this naïve side, which was very refreshing, especially around the station.

He pulled out his phone and called the hospital.

"This is Detective Sorensen. I wanted to check how Jon Evans is doing," he told the head nurse.

"Much better. He just had breakfast."

Her voice was low but singsongy. The way she spoke made him feel happy. Or maybe it was the news.

"Breakfast? That's great. Can I talk to him?"

She transferred him, and while he was on hold he looked at Lynch, who was staring back at him, expecting the update. Sorensen mouthed, "Jon."

"Yeah, I guessed. He ate?"

Before Sorensen could reply, Jon said, "Detective." His voice was barely a whisper. He coughed, and Sorensen heard him drink. "Please give me something to do," he begged. "I'm bored out of my mind."

"You need to rest." His fatherly instincts flared up.

"My Dad won't stop lecturing me, and my Mom won't stop babying me. One more day of this and I think I'll force myself into an induced coma."

202

Sorensen laughed. The elevator opened, and Brantley came out.

"Okay, buddy, let me see what I can do. I got to run, but I'll come by and see you later today."

Hanging up, he followed Lynch toward the manager.

"We need a few more minutes of your time," Lynch said.

Brantley checked his watch, then frowned but finally motioned them to follow him to his office. When they got there, he closed the door behind them.

"What can I do for you?" he asked.

Lynch took the lead. "Do you know Carlos de la Rosa?"

"Yes, of course. He founded this law firm, and he's my boss." His eyes were wide open, and he looked from one detective to another.

"He founded it?" Sorensen asked. "His name is not on the door."

"On purpose. When he founded the law firm, he didn't think he would get the high-end clients he wanted with a Hispanic name."

"We think he's missing."

"Missing? I just saw him yesterday."

"Yesterday?"

"No, wait, we were supposed to have a meeting, but he didn't show up. I guess I haven't seen him since the day before."

"Do you watch the news?" Sorensen asked.

Brantley looked at him as if he had spoken in a different language.

"Yeah, do you watch the local news? Did you hear about the multiple homicide in Los Altos?"

Brantley turned white and covered his mouth with both hands. "I didn't make the connection. They didn't mention any names." After he swallowed a couple times, he asked, "Is he hurt?"

Sorensen looked at Lynch. "He's missing. As in, we can't find him, so we don't really know if he's dead or alive . . ." He spoke each word as if he were talking to a four-year-old.

"Mr. Brantley, we need to know what he and Malik were working on," Lynch cut in.

"Do you think somebody's targeting us?"

"Why do you say 'us'? Have you had any specific threats lately?" Sorensen asked.

"Well, no," he said, looking from one detective to the other again.

"What cases were they both involved in?" Lynch pushed.

"It's going to take some time . . . De la Rosa oversees everything we do." Still ping-ponging from one to the other, he added, "And you know I will need a subpoena."

"Is there anything you can actually help us out with? All we're trying to do is find him at this point. We don't really care about all this patent stuff or any company secrets."

"I'm afraid it doesn't work like that."

"Fine. We'll be back in an hour, but you better have everything ready by then," Sorensen said, already heading out the door.

Both detectives walked back to the elevator in silence.

Once they got inside, Sorensen said, "You know, I don't get these guys. We're trying to help them, and they stall us for some frigging paperwork. What do they think we're going to do with all that stuff anyway? Bet on the stock market?"

A few minutes later they arrived at the station. While Sorensen went in to talk to Virago, Lynch typed up the subpoena.

"Give it to Judge Yu." Virago told Sorensen while she checked her watch. "He should be going on break soon. You better hurry before he gets stuck for another couple hours."

Sorensen met Darcy and they headed to the elevator. Before they reached it, Sorensen said, "Wait a sec. I forgot something."

He went back into the bullpen and grabbed Jon's laptop and power cord. He sensed Virago watching him.

"He said he was bored," he yelled over his shoulder, and left before she could stop him.

CHAPTER 55

Saffron woke up feeling like she needed to throw up. She opened her eyes and remembered Blake pinning her to the bed at the hotel room. She extended her arm, wanting to find Darcy by her side, but touched a hairy ball instead. Cat meowed, stretched and walked onto Saffron's chest, where she curled into a new ball.

She checked the time on her phone. It was just past eight thirty. She saw Darcy's unanswered text and voice mails, and her heart sank. Just give me a little longer, she thought, and hid the phone under the pillow. She didn't like keeping things from Darcy and knew she would have to tell him about Aislin soon.

She touched her face. It felt sore. She wondered if she had a bruise. Maybe. If she did, she would have a hard time explaining that one to Darcy. Cat purred on her chest. The cell rang, she grabbed it, and Cat jumped off the bed, expressing her discontent.

"Hello?" she answered.

"Are you going to join us?" her boss asked.

She'd totally forgotten about her conference call with the offshore team. "I'm sorry, I'm still on PTO," she said. "Personal stuff I have to take care of."

"I think you're running out of vacation days," he said, and hung up.

He was probably right. She made a mental note to check her vacation balance as soon as she got back to work . . . one of these days.

Shoving the covers away, she got out of bed. She took her tank top off and caught a glimpse of her face in the mirror. There was a shadow of a fist-size bruise on the left side of her face. Shit, she thought.

She took a long shower and thought about the encounter with Blake. After they let him go, Madam X told her to meet him in the morning for breakfast to talk about what else they could do to find Aislin. X said he had a few contacts in the underworld that might be able to help.

Without giving her clothes too much thought, she got dressed, fed Cat and searched for X's address in her phone. By the time Saffron got out of the house, the rush-hour traffic was dying. A block away from X's address, she saw two police cars and an ambulance. A terrible sense of déjà vu clenched her heart.

She walked toward the orange tape that kept the curious away from the crime scene. Two paramedics were wheeling Madam X into the ambulance. Saffron reached an officer with a clipboard. At the last second she decided to ask for forgiveness instead of permission, ducked below the tape and ran to X.

"Hey, lady, come back here," the officer yelled.

That caught the attention of two cops standing by the ambulance. "Miss Meadows?" she heard somebody say.

She stopped running. It was Officer Bush. He was one of the SJPD officers who had been assigned to protect her when that maniac was trying to kill her several weeks ago.

"Officer Bush." She walked toward him but pointed at Madam X. "He's my friend. What happened to him?" she asked.

He walked with her toward the ambulance. "He was assaulted by two men. They did a real number on him."

"But he's going to be okay?" she asked.

X's eyes were shut and swollen. He had a gash on his cheek, as if it had been slashed with a sharp knife. He was also bleeding from a few other wounds around his torso. Saffron noticed that his knuckles were bloody and raw. He must have put up a good fight.

One of the paramedics looked at her. "We need to get him to the hospital right now."

"You can go with him if you want," Bush said to her.

"Thank you."

She jumped in and sat on the small pull-down seat. She reached out to touch Madam X's arm but, not wanting to interfere with the paramedic's work, Saffron sat on her hands. Constantine, where were your goons when you really needed them? she thought.

They started moving, with the sirens blasting. The paramedic was trying to control the bleeding as they sped through the streets.

CHAPTER 56

"Are you sure it's a good idea?" Darcy asked, looking at Jon's computer in Sorensen's hand.

"He said he's bored and needs something to do. I think he'll be happier working"

"But you know he can't work on his own case."

"Oh, and you can?" Sorensen punched the G for garage, and the elevator started descending.

"It's not the same," Darcy said.

Sorensen didn't bother to reply.

When they got to the hospital, Sorensen was surprised to find it fairly empty. There were probably less people around because Jon was no longer in a critical condition. He was relieved to find that not even Jon's parents were in the room.

"Ah, thank you for saving me from a day of utter boredom," Jon said when he saw them walking in.

"Don't tell anybody." Sorensen handed him the laptop.

"What are we looking for?" he asked while he lifted the lid and powered it on.

"How are you feeling?" Darcy interrupted.

"Much better." He pointed at his bandaged shoulder. "No broken bones, and my blood levels are back to normal. I should be good to go in a few days. They just want to make sure nothing gets infected."

"I'm so sorry, Jon. I never—"

"I know. We were pursuing bad guys. It was actually kind of cool until I got shot."

He smiled that infectious smile of his, and the two detectives returned it. Sorensen brought him up to speed.

"We just got the subpoena signed, so we'll get more details, but anything you can find on McKenzie & Shaw and what they're all about would be great."

"You got it."

"Thanks, kid," Sorensen said.

"We've missed you," Darcy added.

Once they were back on the road, Sorensen took surface streets to get to the law firm.

Darcy's phone rang.

"Officer Bush, what's going on?"

"Detective, I wanted to let you know that we've just had a pretty bad assault case, and the victim seems to be a friend of Miss Meadows. I thought you would want to know."

"Who is it?"

"A Constantine Howard."

The name didn't ring a bell. "Who is he?"

"I don't have any information. We haven't run him through the system yet."

"Thanks, Bush, I appreciate the call. Where was he taken to?"

"Good Sam."

"Is he going to make it?"

"Not sure."

After he hung up, Darcy said to Sorensen, "We need to do a quick detour."

"Why?" Sorensen looked at him, then asked, "Where to?"

Darcy shared what little he knew.

"I think I know that name," Sorensen said.

"From where?"

"I'm not sure. He just sounds familiar. It'll come back to me."

They drove in silence the rest of the way until Sorensen pulled into the hospital's garage. After they went into the emergency room, Darcy flashed his badge, and the receptionist told him Mr. Constantine Howard was in surgery.

They went to the waiting room and found Saffron sitting by herself. She was nursing a cup of coffee in her hands, with both elbows resting on her knees, her hair loose and long covering part of her face.

"What happened?" Darcy asked her from the entrance.

She jumped, almost dropping the coffee.

"What are you doing here?" she asked.

"I heard. Bush called me."

"Ah," she said. She didn't pull her hair back; it still covered part of her face, shading the skin.

"Who is he? How do you know him? You've known him for long?"

"What is this, twenty questions?" she spat.

He was taken aback, hurt by her reaction. She avoided his gaze and looked past him at Sorensen.

"I'm getting some coffee. Need a refill?" Sorensen asked her.

"I'm okay, thanks."

When they were alone, Darcy just stood there.

"I'm sorry," she said.

He remained silent, waiting for answers, not apologies. She couldn't even look at him. He started to leave when nothing else came from her. "Okay, then. If you need anything, let me know."

"Darcy, please," she said, grabbing his arm.

He stopped but didn't turn.

"It's complicated."

"I'm sure it is," he said, and walked out, running into Sorensen in the hallway. "We're done here," Darcy said, walking past him.

Sorensen turned and followed him in silence. Darcy waited for a snarky comment that never came.

CHAPTER 57

When they got back to McKenzie & Shaw, Sorensen didn't wait for the receptionist to page Brantley; he barged right in. Lynch followed him until they reached his office. Through the glass they could see the lawyer was inside.

Sorensen knocked, but without an invitation, opened the door and walked inside. "Here's the subpoena you wanted," he said, and threw it on the desk.

Brantley skimmed through it. "I think I have everything you need here." He pointed to a couple boxes on the floor.

"Are you going to send us on another wild-goose chase, like you did with the threats?" Sorensen looked at the boxes but didn't make a move to pick them up.

"I'm sorry?" Brantley asked.

"Have one of your minions take these to my car," Sorensen said. "I hope whoever is targeting your company is not going to go after you next. Because with all the help you've given us, we may not catch him in time," he said, then walked out of the spacious office.

Before they reached the reception area, a clerk caught up with them, pushing a dolly with the two boxes.

After the kid loaded the car, Sorensen said to Lynch, "I want to go back to see Jon, we could sure use his help."

The hospital was busier than earlier, and Jon's parents were in the room. Lynch paused for a second before going in.

"Good afternoon," Sorensen said when he entered, and shook Jonathan's hand.

Miranda got out of the chair, as if she was offering it to the large detective, but he didn't take it. Sorensen saw Jonathan take Lynch's hand for the first time. His resentment had probably subsided a little since it became clear Jon was going to make it.

"How are you feeling?" Lynch asked Jon.

"Better now that I'll have something to do." He smiled, checking out the boxes they'd set on the floor.

"You expect him to work?" Jonathan said, blocking Sorensen from getting closer to his son's bed.

"Dad, stop. I asked for it."

"But you need to get your strength back," his mom said with a voice somewhere between a shriek and a whisper.

"Mom, seriously. I'm going to go crazy if I don't have anything to do." Looking back at Sorensen, he asked, "What do you need?"

Sorensen didn't say anything, but, looking at Jon, he tilted his head toward his parents.

"Oh, right," the intern said. "Mom, Dad, can you go and get me something to drink?"

"For God's sakes," the father said, and stormed out, followed by his wife.

"Well, we need two things." Sorensen set one of the boxes at the feet of the bed. "Apparently our bank and Los Altos MIA victims were working on a bunch of cases together. We want to know if there's anything that stands out. Anything big enough to get them hurt or killed."

Jon looked at the other box, the one Darcy was holding.

"Two boxes of cases . . . Do you think I can get the digital files instead?"

214

Sorensen looked back at Lynch. "Why didn't we think of that?" he asked.

"We did, but you wanted Brantley's minion to carry the boxes to your car just to make a point."

"Oh, right." Sorensen looked back at Jon, who was now smiling. "Damn, it's good to have you back, kid."

The warmth in Sorensen's voice made Jon blush a little.

"We'll get them to send you the digital files," Lynch said.

"Thanks. That way I can cross-reference much faster."

Sorensen took the box off the bed.

"What's the other thing you need help with?" Jon asked.

"We need to find a connection between the Marines' pranks, the crispy in the van, and the missing guy."

"All those cases are related?"

"We think so, but we can't prove it. That's why we need you," Sorensen said.

"Sorensen and I believe that Bishop knows at least something about the bank kidnapping. It's also too much of a coincidence that Malik gets killed, and the same day the founder of this law firm disappears."

CHAPTER 58

Saffron fumed the entire time she was waiting for X to come out of surgery. She knew she had to talk to Darcy, to tell him everything, but she needed to find the right time, the right way to do it. *How do you tell your cop boyfriend that your sister is a prostitute?* she wondered.

The worst thing about all of it was that she wasn't any closer to finding her sister. It had been way too long since she got the message from Aislin and the bodies were discovered. She thought about Blake. He knew something. Maybe he was the one who had killed them. She really needed to tell Darcy everything.

She rubbed her eyes. They were dry, sandy. Saffron pulled her phone out of her purse and called Darcy. It went to voice mail.

"It's me. Please call me back. I need to tell you something."

She sighed and looked around. There was an old magazine on one of the side tables. She grabbed it and leafed through it. Gossip. Nothing juicy. She thought about Darcy and how much she needed him. She didn't really understand why she hadn't confided in him earlier. Probably because she was embarrassed. Probably because she wanted to fix this so dirty family secrets stayed secret.

"Miss Meadows?"

"Yes." Saffron stood and walked toward the surgeon, who was waiting by the door.

"Mr. Howard is out of surgery. He's still unconscious, but we expect he'll make a full recovery as long as there aren't any unexpected complications."

"Oh, thank God," she said, breathing deeply for the first time in what felt like hours.

"You can go and see him now, but he'll be out for a while."

She thanked the doctor and walked to X's room. He looked so different. He was pale, even under that dark chocolate skin of his. Both of his eyes were still swollen and closed, but the gash on his cheek was now bandaged. A cast on his left arm covered everything from the shoulder to the fingertips.

Saffron pulled up a chair close to the bed and sat by him. "I'm so sorry, Constantine."

He didn't move. Saffron started to cry. She felt so hopeless, so vulnerable. But most of all, she felt guilty. She got him into this mess, and not even his goons were able to protect him. The salty tears started to roll down her cheeks. She wiped them away and made herself stop. She had to talk to Darcy. She needed him to help her.

Saffron left the room and looked for Constantine's doctor. When she couldn't find her, she asked the receptionist to page her. After a few moments the woman in the white lab coat and the green scrubs came back to meet her.

"Do you think he'll wake up today?"

"He's still under sedation, but he should wake up later today."

Saffron checked her watch. "When do you think that'll be?"

"A couple hours," the doctor said.

Saffron thanked her and decided she had enough time to go see Darcy at the station. She took the elevator and left through the Emergency entrance. Searching the parking lot, she tried to recall where she'd parked, then remembered that she came in the ambulance.

She grabbed a taxi and asked the cabdriver to take her to Madam X's house, where she'd left her car. It wasn't too far, and traffic was light. After she paid the cabbie, the taxi drove off.

She unzipped her purse, but before she could fetch the keys, she heard steps and looked behind her. A closed fist hit her left eye so hard she felt as if it had popped. She was thrown backward by the impact and hit the side of her car. She looked up and saw a man, his face covered by a ski mask.

She ducked, avoiding another punch, then stomped on his boot as hard as she could. His boots had steel toes, so she was the only one who felt the impact.

"What are you doing?" she screamed at him.

"You need to let things go, or you'll end up worse than your friend this morning."

He punched her in the stomach.

The intense pain made her double over. Fighting a huge urge to throw up, Saffron dug into her purse and pulled out the can of pepper spray. Before he could hit her again, she aimed and pushed the button as hard and as long as she could. The spray got into her assailant's eyes, and he started screaming. She pushed him. He stumbled a few feet back. She unlocked the car and opened the door. Before she could get in, he came behind her and wrapped his arm around her neck. Saffron tried to get away, but he was too strong. She managed to reach his head and pull off the ski mask. He let go, then shoved her against the car and ran away.

By the time Saffron managed to get on her feet, all she was able to see was her assailant's back as he ran away. He had short black hair in a military-style buzz cut.

CHAPTER 59

Saffron was shaking so bad she felt as if the whole world vibrated around her. She gripped the steering wheel and only let go to wipe the tears of fear away. After she calmed down a little, she noticed that driving with one eye swollen shut was harder than she'd thought. She'd always assumed it wasn't that bad, since Darcy did it so well. The hardest thing was judging distances, so she drove slowly. The tail of cars grew by the minute, and Saffron pulled over to let everybody pass her.

Once she got to the police station, she turned into the parking lot and killed the engine. She was curious but also didn't want to look. Finally, she lowered the visor and checked her eye. It didn't look as bad as X's, but it was still pretty swollen. She fetched her sunglasses from her purse and put them on.

The officer at the reception area paged Darcy, but he wasn't at his desk. She tried calling him, but it went to voice mail again.

"Do you want to wait inside?" the officer asked.

Saffron thought about it. She had no idea where Darcy was or how long he'd be gone. She also wanted to avoid a scene at the station. He was mad at her and would probably freak out as soon as he saw her eye.

"No, that's okay. I'll see him later," she said, and turned away.

Her place was only a few blocks from the station. She pulled into the garage and made sure the gates closed behind her. When she got home, Cat greeted her with happy meows. Saffron sat on the sofa and powered up her laptop. She opened the browser and looked for NanoQ. She checked the company's website, clicking through the different tabs, looking for an "About Us" or something similar. Sometimes Silicon Valley companies that began as tiny start-ups still had pictures of their founders on their websites. She hoped NanoQ was one of them.

Saffron finally saw it, buried on the footer with a lot of other innocuous links. She clicked it. The CEO's photo and bio appeared. She scrolled down, and a new picture appeared on the screen. A professional headshot of Blake stared back at her. His full name was Blake Higgins. He was the CTO. This should be interesting, she thought.

The other piece of valuable information in the "About Us" section was the contact number. She fished her phone out of her purse and dialed.

"NanoQ, this is Marissa. How may I direct your call?"

"I need to talk to Blake Higgins." Saffron scratched Cat behind the ears, and the purring became so loud she wondered if Marissa could hear it.

"Who may I say is calling?"

She hadn't thought about what to say. Blake didn't know her real name and probably wouldn't take a call from Cassandra, Belle, or Madam X either. In a moment of brilliance, she came up with the perfect caller. One Blake would never refuse to talk to.

"Jane Porter, on behalf of Jonah Boyer."

She felt pleased with herself. Boyer was the hottest venture capitalist in the Valley.

"Jane, what a pleasure," Blake said a few seconds later.

"Listen, asshole, you missed your chance to turn yourself in to the police."

"Excuse me?" He sounded genuinely confused.

"X was very clear in his instructions: you were going to turn yourself in to the police. But no. Instead you sent a bunch of thugs to beat the shit out of Constantine and me. So now I'm going to tell my boyfriend everything I know about you, and he's going to take you down, because he's a homicide detective."

She hung up. The exhilaration almost felt like a hot flash. She opened the balcony window and fanned herself. Her stomach still hurt, and her eye was getting worse, but the relief of knowing that very soon she was going to tell Darcy everything and he would help her was so great, nothing else mattered.

Saffron went back inside, fed Cat and decided to go back to the station and wait for Darcy there. But first she was going to take a long shower and change her clothes.

CHAPTER 60

Anurse came into Jon's room without knocking on the door. Darcy watched her check his vitals, cross out a few things in his file and make some notes. After she left, they finished discussing the case.

"Are you sure you're up for this?" Darcy surveyed the boxes they needed to exchange for digital files.

"Yep, I'm okay, I swear. I'll go crazy if I do nothing all day. Besides, I need an excuse to send my parents away for a minute or two." He smiled.

"Has Virago come to talk to you yet?" Sorensen asked him.

"She came earlier to say hello."

"So she didn't tell you anything?"

Jon stopped tapping on the laptop and looked at him. "About . . . ?"

"This and that." Sorensen avoided his eyes and picked up the box from the bed.

"The captain has a proposition," Darcy shared.

"She's going to pay me?" His eyes shined.

"Yeah, something like that," Sorensen said. "Well, don't want to ruin the surprise, so don't tell her we mentioned anything."

"But you haven't told me anything," Jon protested.

"Better if she tells you." Sorensen was already halfway out the door.

"I can't believe you just did that," Darcy said loud enough for Jon to hear.

"What?" Sorensen walked faster still.

"Really? 'What?'"

"Sorry. I thought she would have told him already."

"Tell me what?" Jon yelled from the room.

"Oh, for God's sakes." Sorensen turned around and walked back into the room. "The captain has an offer to lead a task force for the San Jose PD."

"She's leaving?" Jon asked.

"No. Well, yes. But she asked us to go with her."

"You're leaving?" His voice was a shriek, and his vitals spiked.

Darcy took a step forward, closer to the bed. "She wants the three of us to go with her."

"Me too?" Jon's vitals rose up even more.

The same nurse popped her head into the room and asked, "Everything okay here?"

"Yeah, all good," Jon waved a hand at her. "She wants the three of us to work for the SJPD on a task force? How cool is that?" he said to Sorensen, almost jumping out of the bed.

Darcy smiled. He hadn't seen Jon so happy in a while.

"When?"

"Not sure. We're still thinking about it," Sorensen said.

"You're not coming?" Jon asked, blinking several times.

"I didn't say that. It's complicated," Sorensen said.

"Are you coming?" Jon asked Darcy.

"Haven't thought about it too much yet."

"Oh." Jon looked down at his computer screen.

"Anyway, act surprised when Virago tells you, okay?" Sorensen said.

"Sure." Looking up at them again, he added, "Don't forget to get me the soft copies of all this. I'll call you with whatever I find."

Sorensen pulled his phone and called Brantley. A moment later he said, "You'll have them in less than five minutes."

They drove back to the station. Darcy felt agitated. There was something that was bothering him, but he couldn't put his finger on it. He agreed with Sorensen that there was something fishy about Bishop and Mitchell, but they didn't have any hard evidence against them to break the case. He couldn't find the connection between the Marines and Malik or de la Rosa, but there had to be one.

"Is there any way we can hack into these guys' bank records or something?" Sorensen asked when they walked into the bullpen. It sounded more like a rhetorical question than anything else.

"Bishop and Mitchell?" Darcy asked.

Sorensen nodded.

"I was just thinking the same thing. I have a feeling they're moonlighting."

"I'm leaning in the same direction. Nothing else makes sense."

They both looked at their boards.

Darcy picked up a black marker and stared at the information pinned there. "Let's say they are. For the sake of argument," he said.

"Who hired them? What did they want from Malik?" Sorensen asked, thinking out loud.

"Wait, let's start from the beginning."

"Okay." Sorensen got out of his chair. "This sounds like it's going to take a while. I need a Red Bull. You want one?"

"No, I'll get coffee."

When they were back in the bullpen, Darcy stood in front of the board, and Sorensen leaned against his desk.

Darcy started talking: "We have two Marine pranks with identical MOs. The two teams dared each other to kidnap their gunnies and ship them off, shaven and tattooed, to a foreign land."

Sorensen nodded and said, "Then we get another case, carbon copy of the pranks, but it's not a prank. They take a regular Joe."

"The media didn't release enough details for a copycat this perfect."

"Somebody who participated in the pranks, or knew somebody who did, shared enough information or participated in the kidnapping." Sorensen finished his first can and opened the second one.

"What if the first two were just a smoke screen? Something to take us on a wild-goose chase and make us waste our time investigating while they took Malik? Maybe we weren't supposed to find the gunnys so fast." Darcy sipped some coffee and went on: "And then, something went wrong."

"Or they realized he wasn't who they needed," Sorensen said.

"They made a mistake? No. These guys are too good. Everything was meticulously planned. Think about it: they haven't left a single piece of evidence anywhere. They knew exactly who they were taking."

"Okay, let's go with your theory. So, if Malik died before he gave them what they wanted, they had to go get somebody else. But why not do it the same way?"

"Because we were already on their trail," Darcy said.

"Yeah, shooting at the police is never a smart move. I bet the whole kidnapping with the gas and all that took a lot of planning."

They both paused. Darcy left to refill his coffee.

From the kitchen he started talking: "Okay, so they had to come up with plan B. De la Rosa goes MIA, and eleven people are dead at his home. Either he did this, or somebody kidnapped him too. We have no witnesses and still no clues." He paused. "Oh, wait." Darcy picked up the phone and dialed.

"Detective Lynch, how can I help you?" Rachel asked.

"I saw security cameras. Were there any tapes?" Darcy asked.

Rachel chuckled, and he saw Sorensen sneer.

"Detective, this is Silicon Valley. The security cameras were state of the art, and we haven't figured out where the footage is being stored."

"That's what I meant," Darcy joked.

"The perps severed the network cable anyway, so I'm not sure what you'll find once you get the records." Her phone beeped. "I'm getting another call. Anything else?"

"No, thank you, Rachel." Darcy hung up. Looking back at the board, he said, "Okay, so de la Rosa goes MIA."

"Maybe dead, maybe kidnapped, maybe in Mexico having margaritas."

"It can't be coincidence that Malik worked for de la Rosa. I hope Jon finds something."

Darcy's desk phone rang. It was Rachel. He put her on speaker again.

"I talked to Michelle and she confirmed that there were no prints. I mean, like no prints at all—as in the equipment and cables had been wiped clean."

They thanked her before she hung up.

"There's no reason for de la Rosa to get rid of the prints. It's his house." Sorensen opened a bag of potato chips and put three in his mouth. "We're no closer."

The phone rang again, but this time it was Sorensen's. He picked it up.

"Done already?" he asked.

Jon was now on speaker.

"Well, it's a lot easier with the digital files." Jon swallowed on the other end. "I found seven cases where there was a specific connection between Malik and de la Rosa. Four are cases that have been settled out of court already. Three were start-ups that grew to some decent size. The last one was a much more mature company. Not too big, but it had just started being profitable when they were hit with the lawsuit. It went bankrupt fighting the patent infringement in court."

"Jon, you sure you are doing okay?" Sorensen asked.

"Yes . . . Why?"

"I thought your math was better than that . . . that's eight."

"Oh. Yes. Eight. That's what I meant."

Darcy imagined the intern fidgeting as he blushed.

"Losing your company seems good enough cause for a grudge. What's the name of the company?" he asked to give Jon a break.

"ZoneTech."

Sorensen wrote it on the board.

"What's up with the other three?"

"There are two currently in litigation. One, HyperDyne, is in negotiations. The other, Rattle, is actually in court. The third one, NanoQ, apparently was served papers two weeks ago, but there's no court filing yet. No indication of whether they're thinking of settling or fighting."

Sorensen wrote everything down on the board. "Okay, can you dig more into the one that went bankrupt first and the three active cases?"

"Will do. I'll also start working on the connection between Malik, de la Rosa, Bishop, and Mitchell, and see if I can find something."

CHAPTER 61

Blake was unable to move for a long time after the woman hung up. He recognized the voice, of course. It was that bitch from last night. Belle's sister. He got out of his chair and closed the blinds. He needed privacy and time to think. He sat back down in his chair, then swiveled to look out the window. The parking lot was full.

He felt his torso. He was sure Madam X had bruised at least a couple ribs. He'd told them the truth: he didn't know where Belle was. All he knew was that Ethan had taken her with him.

He fetched his disposable cell and dialed. He didn't expect Ethan to answer. Blake had left him at least a dozen messages describing in detail what he went through the previous night and how it was all Ethan's fault. His desperation had increased with each call, culminating in the last one, where he'd threatened not to pay Ethan for the job. That should have got Ethan's attention, but he still hadn't called back.

When Ethan picked up, Blake's apprehension subsided. The threat had worked after all.

"You told me you fixed that little problem we had," Blake said.

"I did say that."

"Then why did she just call me at my office to tell me she's going to go to the police to rat me out?" Blake felt his heartbeat quicken. He took a deep breath. "Ethan, she called me at my office." Gritting his teeth, he added, "Why the fuck did you have to take Belle? If you'd killed the hooker like all the rest, none of this would have happened."

There was silence on the other end. It lasted so long, Blake wondered if Ethan had hung up. "You there?"

"You want me to eliminate the sister?" Ethan finally asked.

"No, no! Why would you ask that?"

"Well, I'm having a hard time understanding what you want." Ethan paused again for an eternity. "First you tell me you want this problem to go away. I offer you the only solution that can ensure that, and you tell me you don't like it." He exhaled with a low whistle that hurt Blake's ear. "I'm kind of confused about what it is that you really want."

Blake pushed himself against the back of his chair and wiped his face with his hand. "I want all this to be over," he said more to himself than to Ethan.

"Okay, well, I'm kind of busy here, so call me back when you've decided how you want me to handle this situation."

"Wait," Blake said. "How are things with de la Rosa?"

"That problem will disappear before your next exec meeting."

"Thank God," Blake said. Before Ethan could hang up, he added, "So what do we do about this woman?"

"Are you asking for my opinion?" Ethan's voice sounded sarcastic.

"Yes."

"The pimp should be out of commission for a few days. The girl . . . Very different than her sister. She put up a decent fight earlier and ended up pepper-spraying one of my guys, and after all that she still had the balls to call you at the office and threaten you. I would say this ticking bomb is about to go off."

230

Blake exhaled slowly. He knew Ethan was right. "This would have never happened if you hadn't taken the hooker. Why the hell did you have to do that?"

Ethan hung up.

CHAPTER 62

Darcy checked the emails Jon was sending as they came in in. "It's going to take a long time to check out all of these leads," he said to Sorensen.

"I know. We have to be smart about it."

"Can we get more people?"

"Why don't you ask the captain?" Sorensen snickered.

Darcy got up to get more coffee. Coming back with an empty cup, he said, "Why is it so fucking hard for people to brew a new pot of coffee when they take the last cup?"

"I have no idea." Sorensen wasn't paying attention. "How many people do you think went missing in your multiple homicide?"

"No way to know without the security feed. But if Rachel is right, it looks like they found twelve coats by the entrance that don't belong to de la Rosa or his wife, and four visitor cars, matched to some of the victims. Eleven bodies, so considering they probably went in as couples, I would say maybe three people missing."

"Let's say these are the same guys who did the bank job. You take three hostages and fit an additional five guys in your vehicle . . . What were they driving? A school bus?"

Darcy left the kitchen and came back to the bullpen, forgetting the brewing coffee. "Yeah, that seems a bit surreal. Maybe two getaway cars?"

"Assuming they had an even number of girls and boys at this party, if they took three people . . ." Sorensen checked Darcy's board. "That means they probably took two guys and a woman."

"They took the host. But why not take his wife?" Darcy stood and tapped at the picture of a woman with too much cosmetic surgery. "He was married to this woman."

"Was she in it?"

"She's dead," Darcy protested.

"Well, some jobs don't go as planned." Sorensen chewed the end of his pen. "If they kidnapped somebody else, they could get additional ransom . . . Have you got anything from your sister about a possible guest list?"

"No. She said that an acquaintance told her that she and a friend were supposed to go to the party, but something came up, and they had to cancel at the last minute. That may explain why there were so many pros."

"And no way we could get some names of possible guests?"

"She told me she was working on that."

"Can you tell her to work faster?"

"I'll get right on that," Darcy said as if he hadn't thought about it himself. "Any luck with prints?"

"No, it seems that we have no matches in the system, which is not surprising given the social status of the known guests."

I'm hungry. Let's order Chinese," Darcy said.

"Not again. Can we get pizza?"

"Fine, whatever."

They ordered, and Sorensen asked for it to be delivered. "Screw that. We'll come and get it." Sorensen hung up the phone. "Can you believe that, an hour to deliver?" he said as if somebody had committed a deadly sin.

He got up and started putting on his jacket.

"No, I'll go. I need some fresh air," Darcy said.

"Suit yourself."

Darcy stood by Sorensen's desk and extended his hand, palm facing up.

"What?"

"Keys."

"Oh, for God's sakes, you're always driving my car. Can you get your own?" he asked, but planted the keys on Darcy's hand.

"It should be ready tomorrow. I'll be back in a second."

CHAPTER 63

Ethan was getting fed up with the Rich Boy. He was whiny, needy, and not as smart as he claimed to be. Ethan was always a few steps ahead of Blake and he liked that, but still, the mission was getting old.

He put the phone on the table and looked into his special room. "Where were we?" he asked out loud.

He'd sent everybody home. Ethan thought about all their missions together. Most of them had included the elimination of some target. They'd been simple, straightforward. He never felt pity or remorse.

There was always a reason why the world was a better place without somebody.

Ethan thought about Blake's question. He usually didn't take or keep souvenirs from the missions, but this time he'd taken the hooker. It'd been a much more spontaneous action than was typical of him, and he had to admit that it had complicated things quite a bit. But there was nothing he could do about it now except get the most out of it. Ethan figured his crew were curious about his extracurricular activities, but they knew better than to say anything to him.

Carlos de la Rosa was naked, lying on a wooden table. His entire body was strapped to it, a la Dexter, but with medical restraints rather than saran wrap. The table was tilted about five degrees, so de la Rosa could see what Ethan was doing.

The fat man had attempted to free himself, fight, and even tried to bite Ethan once. He then gave up and switched to crying, without making too much of a sound. He was gagged. The chest that had been coated in hair not even twenty-four hours earlier now was covered in second-degree burns. Ethan had set the hair on fire and only extinguished it when de la Rosa had passed out from the pain. He didn't want another heart attack, or the job would never end. And he wanted to get paid.

De la Rosa had several other wounds. Looking at the bleeding feet, Ethan thought back to when he was pulling the toenails out. One by one. He'd heated the pliers, then touched the skin right below the nail. Grabbing the end of the nail with the hot metal, he pushed up hard every time, ripping the nail from the nail bed to the matrix in one fast movement. De la Rosa's screams were so loud, even through the gag, that at one point Ethan actually worried the soundproof room might not be as soundproof as he needed it to be. But nobody had come knocking on the door to ask what was going on, so he continued.

After all the nails were gone and the chest hair nicely removed, Ethan had pulled the man's mouth open and drilled tiny holes, not even that deep, in every receding gum he'd found. He'd read something similar in a book when he was a teenager. It was supposed to cause intense pain, and he'd wanted to do it to somebody ever since.

Ethan stood next to the table with his toys. He wasn't sure what he wanted to do next. He was bored with de la Rosa and knew the man had been ready to do whatever he'd ask of him long ago.

He faced the woman.

She wasn't lying down on a table or sitting. She was standing; her feet couldn't quite plant fully on the floor. Only the balls of her feet reached it. Her arms were raised, forming a wide V, and held away from her body by two metal cuffs that wrapped around her wrists with quarter-inch spikes turned inwards. Drops of blood descended down her arms, curving around her armpits and continuing their journey down her sides, hips, and long legs. Ethan found gravity fascinating. He could watch the red droplets fall all day.

She had beautiful blond hair that cascaded down her back. Her eyes were hazel. She had cried originally; the mascara had marred her rosy cheeks. With the care of a mother bathing her newborn, Ethan had soaked a washcloth in warm water and dabbed the makeup off her face.

She'd spat at him. He hadn't expected that, though he had to admit that it hadn't surprised him either. After he cleaned the spit off, he walked behind her and wrapped his hand around her hair. When he had it all in a tight ponytail, he twisted and yanked it, making her lose her balance, which pulled her against the metal spikes, cutting her wrists for the first time. "If you do that again, I will kill you so slowly you will wish you'd never been born," he promised her.

She'd been much more cooperative after that.

He watched her from his tool cart. Her breasts were perky, a solid B cup. Her stomach was tight, and she had no pubic hair. She waxed. He caressed the soft skin.

She had a small tattoo on her inner thigh. He was fascinated by it. It was a multicolored origami bird. He'd burned her twelve times with a torch others used for welding metal. He didn't brand her, though. Ethan had enhanced her tattoo by adding a circle of equidistant tiny burns around it. His favorite spot was her ass, though. He had burned a V shape following the curve of her lower back.

Ethan hadn't touched her face. She was beautiful, and he wanted to save that for last. "What to do, what to do?" he asked out loud. He shuffled through some of the tools and, bored again, looked at his new creation. The big metal box, covered in barbed and razor wire, was not quite ready yet.

He was planning on electrifying it with a high enough voltage to hurt, but not quite enough to kill.. The corner of his mouth tilted upward with the thought of experiences to come. "Not yet, though," he murmured, and went back to the table with toys.

CHAPTER 64

In Northern California it got dark around five in the afternoon in November. The night was crisp, and Darcy could see the stars. He headed west on Younger Street, then turned left on San Pedro. A few blocks south he saw Saffron coming in the opposite direction in her Mini. She hadn't recognized him driving Sorensen's Jeep.

He decided to go after her. A woman with a stroller and a dog started crossing the street in front of him. After she'd moved out of the way, Darcy sped toward the station, hoping to catch Saffron before she went inside.

A minute later he reached Younger and saw Saffron walking on the opposite side of the street. He then noticed a black SUV starting to roll in front of him. Darcy looked at Saffron. She hung her large purse on her shoulder and pushed a strand of hair behind her ear, revealing the white earbuds. She was looking at the phone in her hand as she headed toward the Sheriff's Office's front door. It was dark and he couldn't quite make out her face.

Darcy looked at the car. It was now speeding. It crossed the double yellow lines and screeched toward the opposite side of the street.

"Saffron!" he yelled, but his voice didn't travel far—all the windows in the Jeep were up. He jumped out of the still-moving car and ran toward the SUV.

Saffron disappeared from sight. Darcy heard a loud thump. The vehicle then veered off right before it hit the building. Darcy emptied his Glock at the SUV while he ran to Saffron. As the last bullet left the barrel, he reached her. She was on the ground.

The SUV accelerated toward the end of the street. Before it reached the light, its horn started blaring. The vehicle sped through North First, then crashed into the front of the bank on the other side of the street.

Darcy kneeled down next to Saffron.

"Call a bus!" he yelled at the first officer who came out of the station.

Her right leg was bent under her body at an unnatural angle. She had several welts on her face and probably other places hidden by her clothes. Darcy checked his girlfriend's vitals. They were faint but still there. As he checked for broken bones, he lifted her sweater and saw a purple stain grow under her skin.

"She has internal bleeding. We need to get her to the hospital now!" he shouted at the four other officers coming down the stairs.

Sorensen appeared behind them as the ambulance turned onto the street. The paramedics jumped out and ran toward them.

"Sir, please," an older medic with a full mustache told him.

Darcy let go and told them what had happened. He stood and watched them work.

They secured a neck brace, then lifted her onto the gurney. As soon as she was inside, Darcy heard the mustached paramedic urge the driver to move fast by announcing, "She needs a laparotomy."

"Go with her," Sorensen urged.

"Black SUV. License plate 4-N-H-5-5-2," Darcy told him before he jumped into the ambulance. "Never saw the guy. But he crashed into the bank. He may still be there."

CHAPTER 65

The moment Curtis walked into the room, Ethan knew something had gone wrong. De la Rosa and the call girl were nicely tucked away in the soundproof room.

"What's up?" Ethan asked.

Curtis took off his canvas jacket and removed his beanie. His dark hair was wet with sweat. Thick sideburns came down to his lower jaw.

"Beer?" Ethan opened the fridge and offered him one.

Curtis took it, twisted the top off and took a long gulp, downing half of it. He finally sat, but then stood again. "Barr's dead."

Ethan took a long breath and slouched onto the sofa. "What happened?"

Curtis explained how they followed the woman but had not had an opportunity to take her down until she was on foot on her way to the Sheriff's Office. They knew that would be the last chance before she talked, so they went for it and ran her over. A cop started shooting at them. One of the bullets blew half of Barr's head off, and then they crashed into the bank.

"I got the hell out and came here." He finished his beer. "This thing . . . This mission is blowing up in our faces."

Ethan squeezed the neck of his own beer bottle but didn't say anything. His eyes found Curtis's.

"I get that our first target died unexpectedly and we had to finish the mission some other way. But, man, all those people at the party, the beatings, the woman tonight . . . Are you sure we're not going too far?" Curtis threw the bottle into the blue recycle bin and took another one from the fridge.

"What's a successful mission?" Ethan asked. His voice was calm. His tone was firm and self-assured.

Curtis looked at him. When he finally sat down, he said, "A successful mission is when we've destroyed the high-value target as defined in the mission objective."

"And besides destroying the value target as defined, what's the most important thing?"

"Come out of it alive and in one piece."

Ethan let the words linger in the air. They both took a gulp of their beers.

Then Ethan leaned forward. "You've been with me for over five years."

Curtis nodded.

"I think we can safely say we've never had a more fucked-up mission," Ethan said.

Curtis laughed for the first time. "I think that's probably the understatement of the year."

Ethan nodded. "We need to see this through. I know it doesn't seem right, but many of the things we're doing we wouldn't have had to do if things had gone well from the start. But since Malik died while we had him in our hands, there are only two paths forward: one, we complete the mission successfully, no matter what the collateral damage. Or two, we give up, get nothing and have to look over our shoulders for the rest of our lives." Ethan's eyes met Curtis's again, and to ensure that the gravity of his words would sink in, he hammered the point home: "This many loose ends might get us the needle."

CHAPTER 66

Inside the ambulance, the paramedic cut though Saffron's top and got to work. Darcy held her hand, stroking it softly as her blood pressure dropped.

"Please don't die," Darcy whispered almost to himself. All he could think about was her expression when he'd walked out on her at Good Sam. He wished he'd stayed. He wished he'd been supportive and understanding instead of getting mad and leaving.

"She can't die. Please don't let her die," he told the paramedic.

The man looked at him for a second, sadness in his eyes.

When they arrived at the hospital, the emergency team was already waiting for them outside. They got the gurney out of the ambulance and rushed her through. Darcy followed, still holding her hand.

"You can't go in there," a doctor said. "We'll take it from here."

He held on to her hand for a second longer, then let her go. Two doctors and two nurses ran down the rest of the hallway, rushing through the swinging doors. After they went through, the doors swung closed, then open, then closed again, leaving him alone.

Darcy stood for a long time staring at the now-empty hallway. He leaned forward and put both hands on his knees, trying to center himself. When he stood up straight, he saw his hands were red with Saffron's blood.

A couple minutes later his phone rang. It was Sorensen.

"The van belongs to a Michael Johnston. He reported it stolen this morning. We have some units going to his house right now."

"Dead end," Darcy said.

"I know. That's why I'm not going with them. But we may learn something."

"What else do you have?"

"Lynch, I have to ask, do you think this was targeted?"

"Why? I don't know. What are you thinking?"

"I checked the assault victim she was visiting at Good Sam."

"And?"

"He was roughed up pretty badly. I wonder if there's a connection between the two hits."

"What do you know about him?"

Sorensen exhaled, probably buying time.

"What? Spill it." Darcy was losing his patience and realized he was rubbing his left temple again. He stopped and wondered if Saffron was having an affair. "Can you just say it?"

"Constantine Howard has been associated with high-end prostitution. Never charged, though. He's known in certain circles as Madam X."

"What? Are you saying Saffron . . . ?" He couldn't make himself finish.

"I'm not saying that. I'm just asking if you think there might be an explanation for why she was visiting him at the hospital and for the two assaults to be connected."

"I don't know what the fuck you're insinuating, but Saffron's not a prostitute."

"Jesus, man, that's not what I'm saying. You need to pull your head out of your ass and help me think who did this to her and why."

Darcy paced up and down the hallway. Then made up his mind and went to the reception area. Pulling the phone away from his ear, he said, "Saffron Meadows, hit-and-run. She just went in with internal bleeding and broken bones." His throat was dry, and he almost choked trying to finish the sentence.

The nurse looked at him without saying anything.

"I'm on the job." He showed his badge. "I want to know as soon as she's out of surgery."

"Okay."

She gave him a Post-it for him to write down his contact information.

To Sorensen, he said, "I'll be there in five minutes."

"Lynch, we got it. You need to be there for her."

"It's going to be hours. We can get a lot done in that time."

CHAPTER 67

Darcy was still wiping his hands off when he walked into the bullpen.

"Don't get comfy. You're going back out," Sorensen told him as soon as Darcy reached his desk. "Good Sam just called. The pimp woke up."

Darcy cringed at the mention of the hustler but shook it off when he realized Sorensen saw it.

"Sorry, man, I didn't mean—"

"It's okay. Let's go."

In a way, he wished Constantine Howard was in the same hospital as Saffron, so he wouldn't have to go so far to see the pimp. But until he knew what their relationship was, he also felt better knowing they were not collocated.

"How is she?" Virago asked, coming out of her office.

"In surgery. They told me she's with the best ER surgeon they have."

"If I hear anything from the hospital, I'll let you know," she said. "Detective," she called before he had gotten too far. "Tomorrow you'll need to talk to Internal Affairs about this and Jon's shooting."

"Tomorrow."

"Tomorrow," she said, and shooed them off with her hand.

They reached Sorensen's car, which had come to a stop by bumping into a parked car after Darcy jumped out to shoot at the SUV. It was inside the area marked by the yellow "Do Not Cross" tape.

Sorensen didn't bother to inspect the damage. Luckily, it wasn't much, and Darcy was grateful his partner didn't make a big deal out of it.

"We have too many cases going on. I think we need to divide and conquer once we get back," Sorensen said, breaking the silence.

"Not sure how we're going to do that. The bank and the multiple are connected—we both know that. And this one is about my girlfriend. How do you propose we divide and conquer?" Darcy's voice was ice cold.

"You know as well as I do that when you're too close, sometimes you don't have the best judgment. All I'm saying is that we're not closer to cracking this nut, and the bodies are piling."

"Don't you think I know that?" Darcy spat. "Everybody keeps reminding me every minute of every fucking day," he said, and looked out the window. He forced himself to calm down and added in a much lower voice, "But at least now Jon's back."

"He is." Sorensen took the exit for Highway 85. "I should have hit you harder," he said.

"I always knew you punch like a girl." Lynch shook his head but had a smirk.

"I saw you rubbing your jaw. I know it still hurts."

"If that makes you feel better . . . Sure," Darcy added.

When they got to the hospital, they showed their credentials and were told where Mr. Constantine Howard was.

Sorensen knocked on the door, but Darcy barged right in. "Mr. Howard, Detectives Lynch and Sorensen. How are you feeling?"

X twisted his head in a few different directions to try to see them better with his swollen eyes. "I've had better days," he said.

"Do you know who did this to you?" Darcy asked.

"No. A couple big dudes dressed in black with ski masks." The detectives exchanged glances.

"Do you know why they did this to you?" Sorensen asked.

"Are you saying I deserve it because I'm gay?"

"That's not what I'm saying." He hesitated. "I'm wondering if it may have something to so with your line of work . . ."

The vitals quickened on the monitors. X shifted on the bed.

"And what line would that be, Detective?"

"Mr. Howard, we're not vice," Darcy interjected. "We just want to find out who did this to you."

X didn't look convinced.

"How do you know Saffron Meadows?" Darcy asked, not wanting to waste any more time.

"The name doesn't sound familiar."

"That's odd, because she was here with you when you came out of surgery," Sorensen said.

"She was?" He seemed genuinely surprised.

"So?" Darcy pushed.

X took his sippy cup and shoved it at Sorensen. He looked inside and filled it, then handed it back. X drank half of it and shoved it toward Sorensen again. Sorensen sighed and re-filled it.

"I met her yesterday."

"For the first time?" Darcy asked, feeling a huge weight lifting off his shoulders.

"Yes. Her sister works for me. She couldn't get ahold of her, so she tricked me into meeting her, and we chatted."

"Which sister?" Darcy asked.

"I only know one. Aislin. She goes by Belle in some circles."

"So, where's the sister?"

"I don't know. I set her up to accompany a nice gentleman to a party two days ago."

"What party?" Darcy's neck hairs stood on end. The image of Saffron showing up unexpectedly at the Los Altos crime scene flashed in his mind.

"You know, the one in the news."

"Did you send any more guests to that party?"

"I had three girls there. Two are dead. Aislin is nowhere to be found."

"How did you know about the party?"

"How do we always know about these parties, Detective?" X sighed.

"Who called you to request your services?" Sorensen asked.

"Carlos de la Rosa called me first. He needed two girls. Interestingly enough, another one of my regulars called me because he'd heard about the party and wanted to go."

"Was that unusual?"

"It happens sometimes, specially when the party's really hot. This one wasn't so much, so I was a bit surprised, because this regular is a pretty big hotshot."

"Hotshot how?" Sorensen asked.

"He's rich, good looking, and young. He could have his own parties, and everybody would line up to go, if you know what I mean. Anyway, I told him I knew about the party and I could set him up. He asked if he could bring his regular, but she was already booked, so I sent him Belle."

"Which ones were your girls?" Lynch asked, thinking about the three young women at the crime scene.

"Eva Yung and Sandra Howell." After another sip of water, he added, "I believe there was another girl, but she wasn't one of mine."

"And you haven't heard from Aislin since then?"

"No. I haven't. But Aislin left Saffron a cryptic and pretty scary message the night of the party."

"What kind of message?"

"It didn't make any sense. It sounded as if it got cut off in the middle, but she said something about killing."

"Killing?"

"Yeah, something like, 'They're going to kill . . .'" X took another sip of water and added, "Saffron was pretty freaked out when she couldn't get ahold of Aislin and went to her place. That's where she saw my IM and lured me into the Cotto Lounge to meet her. I thought I was meeting Aislin, but Saffron was the one who showed up demanding answers."

Darcy felt cold and empty. He thought Saffron felt comfortable enough with him to share anything, and yet she'd turned to a total stranger for help rather than come to him. Pushing the feeling away, he changed gears.

"Who's the guy who wanted to go?"

"Blake Higgins."

"Did he say why?"

"I don't ask questions, Detective. I just hook them up."

"What happened when you met Saffron?"

X told them about their plan to meet with Blake later.

"You did what?" Darcy asked. He paced back and forth and combed his hair with his hand. "Are you crazy?"

Sorensen positioned himself between Darcy and Constantine.

"I don't know if you know that woman well, Detective, but she's very persuasive."

Darcy caught Sorensen chuckle before he said, "Just a little."

"Exactly," X said.

"So what happened next?" Darcy asked, still pacing behind Sorensen.

"We didn't get anything out of Blake. I thought I had persuaded him to go talk to you guys, but the next thing I knew, I'm getting into my car and two massive thugs beat the crap out of me."

"Do you think it's related?"

"You don't?" He wiggled to find a better position. The big cast on his arm didn't give him a lot of extra room on the bed. "I don't claim to know anything about your job, but I would bet my 401(k) that this is all related."

Nobody said anything for a few seconds. Then X added, "Why aren't you asking Saffron all of these questions?" There was a hint of suspicion in his voice.

"She was in a hit-and-run tonight. Less than an hour ago."

"No," Constantine said, covering his mouth with his well-manicured hand. "Is she . . . ?"

"In surgery right now," Sorensen said.

"We were supposed to meet for brunch, but I never saw her." He shook his head. "You need to talk to Blake Higgins. He knows something."

They got Blake's contact information from the pimp and left, promising to let him know how Saffron was doing.

On the way to the car, Darcy called the hospital. Saffron was still in surgery.

CHAPTER 68

Sorensen drove toward O'Connor Hospital. Traffic was pretty bad even though it was almost seven.

"Call Jon. See if he has any updates," he told Lynch.

As soon as the intern picked up, Lynch told him what they'd learned from Madam X and asked, "Have you come across Blake Higgins in your research?"

"Sounds familiar. Give me a sec to run a few queries."

Lynch set the phone on speaker and held it between them so they could both hear.

Jon came back on: "Yeah, he's the CTO of NanoQ, one of the companies that's being sued for patent infringement by McKenzie & Shaw."

"That's the first link we've had," Lynch said.

"Any connection with Bishop or Mitchell?"

"Haven't found any yet, but I'll look closer now that we have a name. I'll call you if I find something."

Before he hung up, Sorensen asked, "How are you feeling, kid?"

"Pretty good. And my mom's bringing me her pumpkin cream cheesecake later."

Sorensen felt his mouth start to water. He realized he hadn't eaten much all day. "Don't eat it all in one sitting." He checked the time and, turning to Lynch, said, "It's barely seven. I say we go to his office first and see if he's there. If not, we'll try to catch him at home."

"I'll text you the address," Jon said.

"And save us some pie," Lynch said before hanging up.

Sorensen sped up and took the Stevens Creek exit for the hospital.

"Where are you going?" Lynch asked him.

"I'm dropping you off at the hospital. Saffron's been in surgery now for almost two hours. She's going to get out soon, and you need to be there when she does."

"I can do more good getting the asshole who did this to her," Lynch protested.

"And you will. Let me go on and talk to this guy. I'll keep you posted. If something comes up, I'll come and get you. Mountain View is only a hop, skip, and a jump away." He felt his partner was not convinced. "I'm telling you, your woman wakes up and you're not there, she'll never forgive you." After a few more seconds of silence, he added, "Trust me. I know about these things. How do you think I manage to still be married?"

Lynch finally nodded.

The detour only took a few minutes. When Sorensen got on Highway 101, he saw that the traffic was still horrible. He drummed at the steering wheel with his fingers for the entire thirty minutes it took to get to Blake Higgins's office. The parking lot was still pretty full, but the building was closed, and there was no receptionist to open the doors for him. He called Blake's number, but he didn't answer.

"There's not even a call box," he said out loud, frustrated.

He turned to get back to his car when the sound of the door unlocking made him stop. A young Indian man was exiting. Sorensen backtracked and caught the door right before it closed.

The man looked at him and, with a low voice and slight accent, asked, "Do you work here?"

Sorensen opened his jacket and showed his badge. "Police business."

"Oh," the man said, adjusting his backpack. "The receptionist is gone." He looked at the empty desk.

"I'll figure it out. Thank you," Sorensen said, moving inside the premises already.

"You won't be able to get in. There's another security door inside. You can only get in with a badge after business hours." Before the detective said anything, he added, "Maybe I can page somebody for you?"

They both walked inside the reception area. It was well lit—maybe a little too bright for the contrast with the dark night outside. Sorensen gave him Blake's name, and the man took out his phone and started typing in the search box.

"We have a full directory of everybody in the company," he explained. "We're all on call until . . ." He stopped himself.

Sorensen nodded. He knew he was going to say "the sale" of the company but cut himself short, as that was still confidential. Sorensen knew only because Jon was brilliant.

He went in a different direction. "What do you do here?" he asked.

"I'm the lead researcher for the quantum computing team."

"What's that?" Sorensen wasn't sure that was relevant for the investigation, but he had a soft spot for the crazy ideas these geniuses came up with in Silicon Valley.

"It's the use of quantum effects to perform computations."

"That sounds like spooky science to me," Sorensen joked.

"It's the coolest thing. You need to use supercooled atoms. Anyway, it's in its infancy, but that's what makes it so exciting," the Indian man said, many lines framing his eyes as his smile reached them. "My name is Mohinder Mishra, by the way."

He extended his hand, and Sorensen shook it. He was a bone crusher. Sorensen liked him even more.

"I found Blake's number. Let me call him."

"I just tried his cell. He didn't pick up. You have his office number?"

"Yep," he said, and tapped his phone.

They both waited in silence while the phone rang. After a couple rings it went to voice mail.

"You want to leave a message?" Mohinder asked.

Sorensen took the phone and said, "Mr. Higgins, this is Detective Sorensen. I'm at your office and would like to talk to you tonight."

He left his contact information before he hung up, wrote Blake's desk number in his notepad and handed the phone back.

"Sorry we couldn't reach him. What's going on?"

"Thank you for trying. Routine questions on an active investigation. Nothing serious."

"Right," the engineer said, adjusting his backpack again.

"I catch a hint of sarcasm," the detective said.

Mohinder seemed to ponder what to say.

"Blake's an interesting character. One of the smartest engineers I know, but he comes from really old money, so he thinks he can do whatever he wants. Like he's entitled, you know? I wouldn't be surprised if that attitude eventually caught up with him."

"Have you seen him get into trouble before?"

"Not trouble trouble. But he's rowdy. One time, when we celebrated our Series B funding a few years back, we all went to a strip club. It was all guys back then," he added, as if he needed to explain.

Sorensen nodded for him to go on.

"He got fairly drunk and started getting really grabby. They had security kick him out, and he fought the entire way. It was pretty funny. And awkward. He showed up with a black eye the next day."

"He does this often?"

"Things like that. He brags about having a pro at his beck and call. I don't know, he's one of those guys that if you hadn't seen it with your own eyes, you wouldn't believe half the shit he boasts about."

Mohinder stopped by a polished, dark blue Prius.

"Nice meeting you, Detective. I hope you reach him." He shook hands again, but before he got into the car he said, smiling, "If you're going to arrest him, don't do it for a couple days. We don't want the bad news to screw up something big we got coming, okay?"

"Deal," Sorensen said, already halfway to his car. "Good luck with that kooky science of yours."

Mohinder saluted him by tapping his forehead with his index finger, and got into his car.

Sorensen called Lynch. "No luck. He wasn't in the office. I'm going to head out to his house, but I don't think he'll be there. I'll keep trying his cell. Any news?"

"Still in surgery. Anything I can do from here?"

"No."

CHAPTER 69

Darcy got more coffee in the visitor's lounge and headed to Jon's room. The bitter taste of the old burnt coffee almost made him throw it in the trash. He thought about Seattle, where even bad coffee was better than most of the stuff he found here. He didn't really miss the rain and the constant dampness, but he still remembered the gorgeous emerald city on the few sunny days.

Then he thought about that warehouse on Harbor Island. About Stepan Kozlov and Gigi. He felt the knife puncturing his eye again. The blood seeping out of his eye socket and Gigi's life expiring just a few feet away from him. He massaged his temple harder than usual, but the cold feeling didn't go away.

"Detective, I was about to call you," Jon said as soon as Darcy walked in.

"You've found something?"

Jon looked behind him as if he was expecting Sorensen to also walk in.

"He's not here. He's trying to find Higgins."

"That's what I was going to call you about."

Darcy sat on the chair by Jon's bed. He felt tired.

"Higgins and Mitchell did boot camp at the Marines together."

"Seriously?" Darcy straightened up on the chair, suddenly not tired anymore.

"Yep, but Higgins washed out, and Mitchell went on to have a stellar career. Two tours in Afghanistan. Plenty of commendations. He earned the Silver Star rescuing a fellow Marine under fire."

"So Ethan Mitchell's a hero?"

"It looks that way."

"I didn't find out much else about Higgins while he was in boot camp. Maybe we can get Detective Sorensen to call his friend in the Marines."

Darcy called Sorensen and brought him up to speed.

"Okay, I'll call Loren. I'll let you know what I find," Sorensen said.

This was the link they'd been waiting for. All the cases were connected through Blake Higgins and Ethan Mitchell.

"Can I get you anything?" Darcy asked Jon.

"Nah. Waiting for my mom's pie." He smiled, but his eyes never left the laptop.

Darcy refilled his cup and went back to Jon's room. The phone rang. It was Sorensen.

"He didn't have a lot of info but promised to find out more. On its face it looks like Higgins was dismissed because he was unable to do what it takes to be a Marine."

"What does that mean?" Darcy looked at Jon. The intern's puzzled expression was probably a reflection of his own.

"That's Marine-speak for coward. Loren figures this was your typical rich kid wanting to stiff it to his parents, and when he realized what it really meant to be a Marine, he freaked out and went running back to mommy."

"Nice. So we have a coward who now hires the muscle somewhere else," Darcy said.

"Yep."

"We need to find this guy," Darcy said.

"Can we track his phone?" Jon asked.

"Do you have a warrant?" Sorensen asked.

Darcy looked at his watch. "Any judges you can buy dessert for?"

"Ping Virago. I'm on my way to pick you up." He paused for a few seconds. "Unless you want to stay there. I would totally understand if you do."

Darcy checked his watch, then looked at Jon, who shrugged.

"No, I'll go with you." He headed toward the emergency room reception desk. "I'll check on Saffron's status and meet you downstairs."

CHAPTER 70

"Detective Sorensen, I think you cashed out all of your favors a while ago," Judge Martinez said when he opened the door.

The Victorian house was well lit. He lived alone with a big German shepherd, which was sitting by his side.

"I know, Judge. Trust me, there are many other things I would rather be doing right now," Sorensen said.

Darcy let the dog smell his hand and then scratched him behind the ears. The dog lifted his head and closed his eyes.

Judge Martinez read the order and signed it. "You think this guy's good for the Los Altos homicide and the bank?"

"He's connected. Doubtful he did the job himself, but he was there."

"Okay, here it is." He handed the paper back to Sorensen. "You owe me a good bottle of scotch."

"It'll be my next Christmas present."

As soon as they got back in the car, Darcy called Jon. "We got it. You can start the trace."

"Give me a few minutes."

Sorensen kept the car idling but still parked.

"I got him. He's in Santana Row," Jon said with his mouth full.

"Are you eating pie already?" Darcy asked.

"Sorry." Jon swallowed.

"I could have told you he would be there," Sorensen said.

"Then why did we waste our time with the warrant?"

"Just to be sure." Sorensen put the car in gear and sped out of the cul-de-sac. "I'm taking the highway."

"It's past eight. It should be fine."

It was the right call. Traffic had finally died down, but it seemed that everybody had decided to go to Santana Row, which was bustling with people.

"I don't recall seeing so many families here before," Darcy said.

"Nah, today's special. They had the Christmas tree–lighting event, and a lot of kids come here for that."

Darcy nodded and walked the rest of the way in silence. People looked happy, hopeful, as if they didn't know there was a terrible world out there. He pulled his phone and checked for updates from the hospital, but there weren't any. Saffron's surgery was taking a long time.

Jon had texted them Blake's DMV photo. They reached Braseiro and searched for him. Sorensen spotted him first. He was sitting by himself at the bar, nursing a tall cocktail glass, half-empty. The detectives stood behind him, forming a triangle, so if he wanted to make a run for it, he would find a body blocking him in either direction.

"Blake Higgins?" Sorensen asked.

"Yeah?"

"We would like to talk to you." Sorensen opened his jacket so Blake could see his badge.

"You're flashing yourself to me?" Blake started laughing.

Sorensen looked at Darcy. "This guy's so funny."

Blake turned around and took a long sip of his drink. "I'm busy right now. Can't this wait?"

"No, it can't wait, dickhead," Sorensen said, grabbing the drink from his hand and placing it on the counter. "You need to come with us right now."

"Are you going to arrest me?" he asked, still snickering.

Darcy watched Sorensen switch his weight from one foot to the other. It was too dark for him to see his partner's jugular, but he was sure it was pulsing.

He stepped in. "We just need to ask you a few questions. We can do this outside or at the station, but better not to do it right here."

Blake finished his drink and, grabbing two twenties from his wallet, he put them under the glass.

"You win, Detectives." He got off of the stool. "And I was going to get laid tonight too," he said, eyeing a petite blond as he passed by her.

Darcy saw her return Blake's smile and wondered why women could not spot douche bags a mile away.

CHAPTER 71

Higgins must have texted his lawyer, because by the time the three of them got to the station, a man in a crisp suit and a gorgeous tie was already waiting for them. Darcy reached the counter first but didn't introduce himself.

Sorensen cursed under his breath and leaned close to Darcy. "It's either going to be a long night or a very short one," he said.

"Why?" Darcy asked.

"Blake, have you said anything?" was the first thing the lawyer asked.

"Of course not, Dad."

"Oh," Darcy said, looking at Sorensen, whose expression said, I told you.

"Blake Higgins Sr. I'm representing my son." When nobody bothered to acknowledge him, he asked, "Why are you bringing him in for questioning?"

Neither detective answered. Darcy logged both the attorney and suspect in, and led them to the elevator without saying a word.

The bullpen was deserted. Even Virago was gone.

"The coffee is probably cold and stale. Do you want some?" Darcy asked as soon as they'd entered the interview room to wait for Sorensen.

"We're not going to stay long enough to taste it. Detective, you have to tell me what's going on right now."

Only Darcy sat down.

Sorensen came in carrying a couple files. He leafed through some photos. Settling on one, he put it on the table. Blake looked. A couple seconds later, he jumped out of the chair.

"That's gross. Why are you showing me this?" he asked, pushing the photo away. He couldn't stop looking at it, so he turned it over.

"The leg belonged to Suresh Malik," Sorensen said. "He was a patent reviewer at McKenzie & Shaw. But you knew that already."

"Don't say anything, Blake," his father told him.

"Dad, I'm not stupid."

Sorensen opened another file and took out nine different pictures. Spreading them over the table, he said, "These are all the people who were killed in Lost Altos two days ago."

Each photo was more gruesome than the previous one. Blake started looking a little green.

"Can I have some water?" he asked.

Neither detective moved.

"I would like some too," the lawyer said.

Sorensen got up and left the room.

Darcy owned the Los Altos case, so he took over. "Blake, we know you were there."

"He was not." His father's voice sounded indignant but genuine.

Darcy realized that the lawyer didn't really know his son.

"We know you contacted a Madam X and asked to be invited to the party. We know he provided you with the companionship of a call girl."

"Detective, none of this is true." Blake's father pounded on the table and stood up.

Sorensen walked into the room with a couple glasses and a pitcher of water. He sat next to Darcy and didn't serve anybody.

"You have no proof." Higgins Sr. ignored the water, even though his voice was now raspy.

"Blake knows it's true." Darcy took the pitcher and poured himself a glass. He looked over the rim at Blake while he drank half of it.

He thought very carefully about his options. If he accused him of anything that wasn't true, he would lose his credibility, and Blake would know they had nothing concrete on him yet. He really wanted to tell him they'd found evidence but decided against it.

"Madam X confirmed this."

"Who's that?" Without waiting for the answer, the lawyer said, "That sounds like a pimp's name. You're going to believe the word of a pimp over that of an outstanding citizen?"

Sorensen scoffed. The lawyer looked at him.

There was a knock. There hadn't been anybody at work, so the interruption was more than unexpected. Sorensen got up to open the door.

Darcy heard whispers but couldn't make out the actual conversation. After a couple back-and-forth sentences, Sorensen said, "Lynch," and motioned for him to leave the interview room with him. Once outside, he said, "Your sister's downstairs."

"What? Why?" Darcy asked.

"Apparently she needs to talk to you right now."

"Did she say what about?"

"No," the officer looked embarrassed. "She was very insistent that she needed to talk to you right now, though."

"Can you bring her up?" Darcy asked the officer.

He nodded and left.

"What do you think that's all about?" Sorensen asked.

"With my sister, you never know."

She walked into the bullpen escorted by the same uni who'd been there just moments ago. She was tall and thin, and her shoulder-length hair had been styled with soft curls. She was wearing an evening gown and a fur coat.

"Pretty risky wearing that in California," Darcy said, pointing at the coat.

"It's cold out," she said, and leaned in to kiss Darcy on the cheek. Shenodded at Sorensen. "Detective."

"To what do we owe the pleasure?" Darcy asked.

"Do you know who Blake Higgins Sr. is?"

"Oh boy," Sorensen said, looking away.

"You do," she said to Sorensen.

"I don't," Darcy cut in.

"He was the best man at the mayor's wedding."

"And?" Darcy asked.

"Don't be obtuse."

"I don't care who he is. His son is a person of interest in the multiple homicide in Los Altos, in which, may I remind you, several of your friends were murdered. And this guy is connected to Jon's shooting."

"I'm sure there's a misunderstanding somewhere."

Darcy looked at Sorensen, who seemed to be enjoying the exchange.

"You're sure there's a misunderstanding? Are you kidding me?" Darcy squared his stance in front of his sister.

She sighed. "All I'm saying is to tread carefully. He's a very powerful man and can make your life miserable."

"Thanks for stopping by. Tell your husband we'll make sure to do our jobs."

She locked eyes with him, turned and started walking toward the door. She stopped and walked back. When she was really close to Darcy, she winked and said just loud enough for Sorensen to hear it too, "He's a scumbag. The apple doesn't fall far from the tree, so nail him if you can. Just be careful. He has a lot of friends."

Kate hugged her little brother and gave him another kiss on the cheek, leaving a crimson mark on it. Then she left.

"Didn't see that one coming," Sorensen said.

"She's funny that way." Moving back to the interview room, he said, "Let's get this guy."

The moment they opened the door, father and son stood.

"It's late, Detectives. We're going home."

"Not so fast. We're not done here." Sorensen's bulk filled the door frame.

Darcy noticed that all of the photos had been turned upside down. He wasn't sure if Blake was feeling guilty, ashamed, or was just squeamish. Darcy took one of the photos and turned it over. It was the close-up of the black call girl, Sandra Howell. Her eyes were open but lifeless. They'd been ebony dark. There was a bullet hole in her forehead.

"You were here, Blake. You either saw this happen, or you did this," he said, waving the photo close to Blake's face.

"That's ridiculous," his father said. "Come on, let's go."

Blake met his dad close to the door, which was still blocked by Sorensen.

"Stop wasting your time with my son, and figure out who did this to those poor people."

"We just want his help," Sorensen said. "If he knows something, he should tell us, or we'll arrest him for obstruction."

"You try that," the lawyer said, challenging Sorensen until he moved over.

After the two men left, Sorensen sat facing Darcy in the interview room. Neither said a word for a few minutes.

Sorensen picked up the photos and put them back in the appropriate files. "Do you think he's good for this?" he asked.

"No. Did you see his face when he was looking at the photos? But I think he knows a lot more than he's letting on."

"We can probably get a warrant."

Darcy checked his watch. It was almost eleven o'clock. "You'll get a new enemy if you knock on any judge's door right now. Let's do it tomorrow. I don't think he's going anywhere, and I need to go back to the hospital."

CHAPTER 72

His dad wouldn't stop talking, but Blake tuned him out immediately. He insisted on taking him back to the house, but that would have only led to more preaching. So when Blake Higgins Sr. dropped him off at the front door of the Omega tower in downtown San Jose, Blake was relieved.

"Thanks for coming to the station," he said, getting out of the car.

"Blake, really. Please think about what I just told you."

"I will, Dad," he said but had no idea what his old man had yapped about. "Say hi to Mom. I'll be there for Thanksgiving, okay?"

In the middle of his dad's reply, he closed the car door and walked up to his building. As he entered, a sudden rush of heat engulfed him. He hadn't realized until that moment how cold it was outside.

"Good evening, Mr. Higgins," the security guard said.

"Hi," he responded, mostly dismissing him.

Blake waved the fob over the reader, then pressed the button with the number sixteen. When he reached his floor, he walked the long corridor to his condo. The only sound in the quiet hallway was the rattling of his keys. The walls were burgundy, and the doors a light shade of sage. Those colors always made him feel as if he lived in a high-end hotel rather than a tower in San Jose.

His door was the very last one. When he was still several feet away, something caught his attention, and he almost tripped on his own foot. Regaining his step, he walked faster to see what was leaning against his door.

The yellow envelope was about two and a quarter by three and a half inches. The words "Watch Me" were printed in black letters. He took it, opened his door and set the keys on the kitchen table. He looked at the envelope, not wanting to open it. His mouth felt dry. He tapped his tongue against the roof of his mouth to generate some saliva and noticed that he had started to sweat even though his condo was not warm.

He felt the envelope. Turned it around a few times. There was something small and rectangular inside. A thumb drive? He didn't know what it could be about, or who could have left it there. He thought about his regular encounters with the call girl, but nowadays, who really cared about that? He doubted that was material for blackmail anyway.

Blake pulled his Mac out of his workbag and fired it up. As soon as it booted, he ripped the envelope open and dropped the contents onto the counter. It was a thumb drive. He plugged it in.

A video file opened. He immediately recognized the setting and froze.

CHAPTER 73

"Sorensen, in my office," the captain yelled through her open door.

Lynch had just left, and the bullpen was a ghost town, so there was no need to yell. He put down the marker he was using on the board and walked in, but didn't sit. Virago took one more bite of her Chinese salad and threw the rest in the garbage.

"I thought you were already gone," Sorensen said, recalling the empty office when he and Lynch came with Blake Higgins.

"How is it going, Detective?" She chewed and ignored his comment.

"Not so good. It must be a full moon or something, because we got too much stuff going on these past couple of days."

"Want to talk about it?" she offered.

Sorensen checked his watch. It was past 11:00 p.m. "Maybe tomorrow. I'm wiped. So what's up?"

"I was wondering if you've thought more about the proposition of going over to SJPD."

Sorensen breathed in and then exhaled for a long time while he looked down at his hands. "I don't know, Captain."

"I'm trying to see if I can transfer your pension or make a similar arrangement."

He didn't say anything. He knew how close to impossible that was, but he appreciated her trying.

"I'm glad Jon's doing well," she said.

"Me too. You really think you can bring him on with you?"

"They won't let me hire him here. And I want to get him on the payroll before he graduates, or we'll lose him to the next hot start-up. I already put that in as a condition for the transfer."

"Wow, you feel that strongly about it?"

"Absolutely. It's total bullshit that they won't let me bring him in full-time."

"What about Lynch?" He didn't really want to ask. He felt conflicted.

"What about Lynch?" She eyed him.

"You're really taking him with you too?"

"That's what I said."

There was a dare in her eyes. He decided to take the bait.

"If I may speak freely, I think he's a liability," he shared before he could convince himself that it was better not to.

She interlaced her fingers on top of her desk.

"I don't know how they do things in Seattle, but the shit he pulled chasing the van and getting Jon almost killed should have got him suspended, if not fired." There was more bitterness in his voice than he cared to show, but he wanted Virago to know how he felt about the fact that she hadn't disciplined him.

"Do you think I'm giving him special treatment?"

"You said it. Not me."

"Do you really?" Her right eyebrow arched, her voice showing surprise for the first time.

"Come on, Captain. Anybody else would have been buried with interviews, paperwork, and Internal Affairs. But this guy gets to go back into the field and work as if nothing had happened? What the fuck's that about?"

"He is going to talk to IA. But we need to get these cases solved."

"We were doing just fine before he came on board."

"He saved your life."

"So what? He almost got Jon killed because he had to prove how macho he is. Honestly, he shouldn't even be in the field with only one eye." His voice was rising. He looked out into the bullpen and was glad to see that it was still empty.

"He passed the qualification. He's good police." Virago removed her reading glasses from the top of her head and set them on top of a pile of files. "I thought you guys were getting along."

"We were. We are. Whatever. You partnered us, so we have to work together. We're learning to get along better, and we complement each other sometimes. But this is not about that. He has a chip on his shoulder. He has a need to prove that he's like the rest of us, or better. He'll put himself and others at risk to show how fearless he is. That's a walking liability if I ever saw one."

She looked at him. Sorensen knew she was gauging him. He felt he needed to explain himself.

"Yes, I think he's receiving special treatment. I don't know if that's because of his sister being married to the sheriff, or because you feel pity for him—"

"Don't be ridiculous," she interrupted.

Sorensen put his hand up, stopping her, and went on: "I know you feel bad for him. What happened to his eye is fucked up, but we've all had close encounters. You do whatever you want. I won't question your motives. I'm just telling you what I think."

CHAPTER 74

Blake was staring at Carlos de la Rosa's living room on his computer screen. The angle was close, so it must have been shot by somebody who was in the house.

Blake hit Play. The video was raggedy, amateurish, and definitely shot from a phone. The frames moved from one person to the next, showing the fear that turned their faces white and wet with tears. The women covered themselves as best they could. The men looked as if they wished they still had their robes on.

Mouths moved, pleading for their lives, but there was no sound on the video. Blake saw himself. He was the only one who wasn't tied up. Or crying.

The video had been edited to not show any of Ethan's men, just the victims and every once in a while, him. There were a couple instances in which he actually saw himself smile. His face showed a certain air of excitement mixed with anxiety.

He felt weird watching the events, while his brain filled in the blanks with the memories. The video showed the group of people staring in the same direction off-camera. Blake remembered one of Ethan's men bringing de la Rosa and Belle into the room. He remembered the buffed black man pushing the hooker and telling Ethan that he'd found her talking on a phone. They exchanged a couple more sentences, but their voices had been too hushed for Blake to hear what they were saying. He hadn't been totally surprised when they took Belle with them later.

The camera focused on the victims again, showing the terrified glares of eleven people who had no idea what was going to happen next. All eyes followed the action off-camera: one of the other goons was taking the black pro to another room. A few moments later the camera showed them jumping backward, as if hit by an invisible blow.

Blake knew it had been the shot from the Sig P226 that caused them to retreat. He watched them whimper and read their lips as they started pleading for their lives. They tried to move away, but duct tape prevented everybody from moving very far from each other. Then the video showed the tip of a Beretta pointing at one of the attorneys, and the subsequent bullet entering his head.

The man's eyes bulged in surprise, but he was dead before he fell on the white leather sofa behind him, almost dragging the woman by his side down with him. The rest retreated as far as they could, as if trying to avoid getting soiled with the blood spatter. The actress look-alike, who was taped to the deceased, knelt over him and cried over his naked torso. She looked up and her lips asked, "Why?," and she continued to sob for her dead husband.

Blake remembered covering his mouth with both hands when Ethan had shot the man. He hadn't expected this. A simple kidnapping—that was the plan. Then he was suddenly sucked into the rabbit hole, and his world completely changed.

Before he could say, "What the fuck, man?," which was what he was thinking, Ethan handed him a latex glove and the gun. Blake didn't move. None of this was on the video. The image he was staring at showed the woman wailing over the dead man, and the others probably fearing the worst for themselves.

"Take it," Ethan had said to him.

"No. Why?" Blake had asked. He took a step back, as if trying to prevent contamination from some virus.

"Put on this glove and take the gun," Ethan said, shoving the items closer to him.

Blake looked at the other men, seeking help, but got no eye contact, no response. He then looked back at Ethan, who still held the gun and the glove.

He took another step back but stopped when he heard one of Ethan's men move behind him, blocking his escape route in case he dared trying.

He looked at the glove. It was black. He looked at the Beretta. It was also black. He'd had firearms training when he was at the Marines boot camp and was no stranger to guns. He took a deep breath and grabbed the glove. After he put it on, he took the gun.

Ethan pointed at the woman who was on the floor, still mourning her husband's death, and said, "Shoot her."

"What, a woman?" Blake asked. "No way. Not a woman."

His eyes darted toward the men. Carlos was hyperventilating. There was another fat man, who looked as if he was about to pass out.

"Okay then. You choose," Ethan said.

"This is not necessary," Blake said, still pointing the gun to the ground.

Ethan nodded very slowly. "Unless you know how you can prevent them from talking, there is no other way."

"Right."

"You don't have to kill us for that. We won't talk," Belle, his date, pled.

Ethan looked at her. Blake did too. Her eyes moved from one to the other.

"Come on, I'm no genius, but I bet we've seen enough to understand that we need to keep our mouths shut forever, or we'll end up dead anyway." She looked around. Several people nodded in agreement. "I wouldn't risk it." Her baby-doll barely covered her breasts and pubic area.

"She's pretty smart, this one," Ethan said to Blake, ignoring Belle. "Come on, we don't have all night."

Blake aimed the gun at the man's chest and wrapped his finger around the trigger. He started to squeeze. He knew his brain was sending contradictory commands and wondered which one would win. Before he was able to fire, Ethan's index finger moved the barrel up to aim at the head.

"Consistency," he said.

Blake felt the kick lift the Beretta and shut his eyes. When he opened them a split second later, he saw the man gasping for air on the sofa, unharmed. The sound of the shot was still ringing in his ears when Ethan spoke again.

"You're going to have to do it a second time." His voice was cold as black ice.

Blake reaimed the gun and saw it shake at the end of his hand. Then he heard a shot. The man fell backward with a clean hole in the middle of his forehead.

He remembered looking back at Ethan. He felt an exhilaration he'd never felt before. He had just ended a man's life. He remembered smiling, feeling a bit like God, and then he turned and puked his guts out.

Of course, that wasn't on the video. Ethan's men had wiped the entire house to ensure they were leaving absolutely no trace evidence. What wasn't on the video either was that he hadn't been the one killing the man. He never fired the second shot. One of Ethan's men did. The video, however, ended with the man dying on the sofa and a close-up of Blake's smile, with a crazy look in his eyes.

He was fucked. Ethan had framed him, and he didn't really understand why. Was this his insurance policy, or was he trying to get more money out of him?

CHAPTER 75

Friday

Ethan talked to Carlos de la Rosa while he removed the ligatures that held him to the bed. As he undid each one, he explained what he was doing, like a surgeon describing a medical procedure.

"This one's the last one holding your torso. After this, I'm going to move to your right leg," Ethan said.

De la Rosa was still gagged, and only whimpered and nodded here and there. His body was covered in a myriad of wounds, and his chest was a large blister. Ethan paused when he got to the ankle strap. He focused on the toes. They were red and inflamed where the nails had been, but at least he wasn't bleeding anymore. He had taken care of that with the torch.

"When you stand up, you will feel weak, and you may need to support yourself. You will also have a hard time planting your feet on the floor, and you won't be able to walk very well." Ethan had moved to the other side of the table and was removing the left leg's ligatures.

"I want you to hold on to me, okay? I will help you." Ethan only derived pleasure from the actual torture, not the aftermath.

When de la Rosa was finally free, Ethan helped him sit and then handed him some clothes. "They should fit. My dad was about your size."

De la Rosa nodded; he still had the gag in his mouth. It was a simple piece of cloth secured in place by duct tape. After de la Rosa had put on the T-shirt, Ethan went to his side and helped him slide off the table so he could pull his sweatpants up. As soon as the man planted his feet on the ground, a shriek of pain reverberated in the soundproof room, and de la Rosa almost collapsed onto the floor.

"Carlos, I warned you about this." Ethan held him and made sure he was steady. When he was ready, they began to walk. De la Rosa whimpered with each step.

"You should be happy. I'm taking you home."

De la Rosa's eyes bulged, and he looked at Ethan. His face was a mixture of disbelief and hope, contorted by the terry-cloth fabric stuffing his mouth. But his face turned ashen, and he almost pulled himself away from Ethan when he caught the ghastly stare in his captor's eyes.

A shriek from the other side of the room made Ethan look back. The woman tied to the ceiling by the metallic restraints pled with him to let her go home too. The shackles rattled, and Ethan smiled, knowing that fresh blood would soon be sliding off her wrists down her ivory skin.

Almost by the door, Ethan looked over his shoulder and said, "Babe, I'll come back later and let you down again. Then you can have some more of your favorite smoothie."

The last thing Ethan heard before he shut the door to his playroom was a faint moan that sounded more defeated than sad.

CHAPTER 76

Ethan didn't hide de la Rosa in the backseat. They'd had too many close calls with random police stops to risk it. So he sedated him enough to make sure he wouldn't be making any noise and put him in the truck bed. It was cold out, so Ethan covered him with a blanket and secured the cover that hinged around the borders.

Carmel wasn't that far away, and they went against traffic. Most of the way was uneventful, until they got to the last leg of Highway 1, which had only one lane each way. For some reason it was bumper-to-bumper traffic, and the last twenty miles took longer than the previous sixty.

They finally reached their destination. As soon as he pulled into the driveway, he saw Curtis come out of a brand-new Acura parked on the other side of the street.

Ethan unlocked the front door and walked inside, disarming the alarm by entering the code de la Rosa had given him. He walked to the garage and hit the button to open the door. As soon as it was high enough Curtis ducked in.

"Nice car," Ethan said when he joined him.

"I figured it was better to use something that blended a little in this neighborhood." Curtis looked at the Bentley to his right and added, "I guess I should have aimed higher."

"Yep," Ethan flashed him a smile. He got into the truck and parked it next to the Bentley. Curtis closed the garage door.

"He can't walk very well, so help him out," Ethan instructed Curtis. "All he has to do is call his gofer to dismiss the case. Make sure he's always on speaker and that you have a full view of his computer screen at all times."

Both men helped Carlos into the living room. Ethan followed the directions his host had given him earlier and went looking for the office. A few minutes later he came back carrying a laptop.

"Call me when it's done," Ethan said to Curtis. Addressing Carlos, he added, "Remember what we've talked about. Your toenails will grow back, but if you ever say anything to anybody, I'll find you and do the same thing again. But next time, I won't stop there."

Carlos's cheeks jiggled as he nodded, demonstrating his full understanding.

"Very well," Ethan said, as if he were training a puppy to shake.

CHAPTER 77

Darcy had spent the whole night with Saffron. She'd come out of surgery right after he got to the hospital. He'd sat by her, holding her hand, stroking it until dawn. She hadn't woken up yet. The doctor said that she was in a very critical condition and they would have to see how the next twenty-four to forty-eight hours went. It didn't sound very reassuring, but it was all he had.

At seven thirty they'd let him take a shower in the staff quarters, but he had put on the same clothes he had worn the day before. He went back to the room after getting a coffee refill. Saffron was still sleeping. She had a gash on her cheek that was already healing and a nasty black eye. But she was still so beautiful.

His cell phone vibrated on the bed. He checked it but didn't recognize the number.

"Detective Lynch."

"Leon Brantley here. You told me to let you know if I heard from Carlos de la Rosa . . ."

"Yeah. Is he at the office?"

"No. But I just got a call from him. He said he'd been at his brother's house in Carmel this whole time."

"What was he doing there?"

"Working. But that's the thing. He asked me to redraft the paperwork of the latest lawsuit we were about to file.

He wanted to remove several patents we were going to contest."

"Is that odd?"

"Yeah. Off the record, de la Rosa is like a rabid dog. He always pushes us to overreach. I've worked with him for almost fifteen years, and I've never seen him remove a patent from any potential lawsuits before. In fact, he always asks us what else can we add, as if he's sure we've missed something."

"Do you know the address?"

"No. Sorry."

"Did he say anything else?" Darcy asked.

"No. Just told me to call him as soon as the paperwork was redrafted."

"How long does it take?"

"A few hours," Brantley said.

"Stall until you hear back from me." Before Brantley could protest, Darcy added, "This is very helpful. Thank you."

He immediately called Sorensen and asked him to pick him up at the hospital and bring the last shirt he still had in his drawer.

Ten minutes later Darcy met him downstairs. "At least I would have brought you coffee," Darcy said, getting into the car. "You're a shitty partner."

"I brought you your shirt," Sorensen said, pointing to the backseat. "And fed your fish and let your dog out. Man, she really needed to go."

Darcy grabbed it and took off the old one. "Thank you."

"Hey, hey. No striptease in my car."

"Where do you want me to change? At a rest area?"

"Good point. Okay, I won't look," Sorensen said, blocking the view with his open palm. "You have the address?"

"Yeah, Jon texted it to me right before you came. Once you hit Carmel, I'll give you directions."

"Have you tried calling him?"

"His cell is in Evidence," Darcy said. "We found it at his house. Apparently the brother doesn't have a landline. De la Rosa called Brantley from a blocked number."

"Of course he did." Sorensen shook his head. "I don't think it's a coincidence."

"Neither do I."

"He's been coerced, blackmailed, or paid off to drop the case," Sorensen said, as if thinking out loud.

"Why the killings, though? If all they wanted was this guy, why kill all of those people?" Darcy looked out the window.

"Leave no witnesses?" Sorensen took the exit for Highway 85 south.

"A little extreme, don't you think?"

"One of the first lessons my TO taught me after the academy was that a hit to kill is much cheaper than an assault. Witnesses talk, and corpses don't."

"Good point," Darcy said. "That's why they left the guns at the scene. That way we won't find one on a schmuck and connect the dots to the crime."

When he could, Sorensen sped up to 80 mph, reaching CA-156 in less than an hour. Later they merged onto Highway 1, and Darcy navigated for another twenty-five minutes until they reached de la Rosa's brother's house. They parked half a block away and watched it for a few minutes. There was nothing especially suspicious.

"Okay, let's do it." Darcy double-checked that his extra magazine was full and got out of the car.

"The vests are in the trunk," Sorensen said.

Darcy stopped. "We're just going to talk to the guy."

Sorensen cursed and put his on. "That's why you checked your magazine?" He left the back door open. Once they both had their vests on, they walked to the house.

Darcy went to the front door but just stood to the side, while Sorensen went around the perimeter.

A minute later he was back. "I can't see anything. All the blinds are drawn. I couldn't hear anything either."

"Okay, let's find out," Darcy said, knocking on the door.

There was no response. He pounded harder.

Darcy tightened his fingers around the grip of his Glock as footsteps got closer to the entrance. They moved to opposite sides of the frame. Darcy fanned his fingers around the grip one more time, making sure he had a strong hold on it.

The door opened, and a short linebacker with long sideburns peeked his head out.

"Mr. de la Rosa?" Sorensen asked, knowing it wasn't him.

"No. I'm his nephew."

The two detectives exchanged glances. They were both Hispanic, but otherwise they looked nothing alike.

The man eyed the drawn guns. "What's this about?"

"Detectives Lynch and Sorensen. We need to speak with him right now," Darcy said.

"I'm sorry, he's not here."

"We have information to the contrary." Sorensen inched toward the open sliver.

"He's not feeling well. I think it's better if you come back another time." He started to close the door.

Sorensen pushed his foot in before the "nephew" could close it. "I think it's better if we talk to him right now."

"Okay," he said, reopening the door. "But please put your guns away. You won't be needing them." He moved away from the door and led them to the living room.

Neither detective holstered his weapon.

The man they met sitting on the sofa was a shadow of his DMV photo. Carlos de la Rosa was very white, and his eyes were bloodshot and wide open, showing the terror he felt. A three-day salt-and-pepper beard covered his face, and he seemed ten or fifteen years older than his age. He was wearing baggy sweats with a gray T-shirt, and he looked as if he hadn't showered in several days.

"Mr. Carlos de la Rosa?"

Sorensen walked toward him. Darcy stayed behind, his back to the wall, eyeing the "nephew," who stood only a couple feet from him right by the door.

"Yes." His response sounded more like a question than a statement. His voice quivered, and he kept looking back at the young man.

"Is everything okay?" Sorensen asked him.

"Yes." He paused, looking back at the "nephew" again. "Why are you here?"

"Are you aware of what happened at your house on Tuesday night?"

De la Rosa looked past Sorensen, who followed his gaze. Darcy did too.

"Can you move over there, sir," Darcy said to the "nephew," pointing at the sofa where de la Rosa was sitting.

The man met Darcy's eyes. In a split second, he dropped his shoulder and closed the distance between them, driving his entire weight into Darcy's solar plexus. Before Darcy could regain his breath, the "nephew" scurried through the door, and the sound of two muffled shots made Darcy focus back to the room.

He yelled to Sorensen. "Are you okay?" .

"Yes, but de la Rosa's hit."

"I'm going after him. You got this?" Darcy was already in the hallway to the front door.

"Yeah, catch that asshole."

Darcy hurried out of the house and looked down the street. He saw the man running west. He was surprisingly fast for someone so short. At the cross street, the "nephew" took a left on Carmelo. Darcy ran faster. As he reached the intersection, he saw the perp taking a right on Thirteenth. He was going to lose him. Darcy took the corner and, looking up the street, he saw him almost two blocks away, taking a left on Scenic Road.

Maybe Darcy had just caught a break. Unless the man got onto the beach, he would have to run straight for a while. Darcy raced forward, trying to get to him before he had a chance to hide.

Darcy reached Scenic Route but didn't see him.

"Shit," he said, wheezing, and stopped running. The perp must have gone into a house or hidden in a backyard.

As he approached each residence, he stopped to clear it, checking the lush front yards and the long driveways. He didn't see anything in the first few homes.

He pulled his phone and called Sorensen to let him know where he was.

"De la Rosa didn't make it."

"Call for backup. I don't know where this guy is."

"Already done. I'll wait here until somebody comes, then I'll head over your way."

"Okay," Darcy said, and hung up.

The next house was the largest on the block. The door was open. Darcy walked up to it and announced himself: "Detective Lynch with the Santa Clara Sheriff's Office. Everything okay in there?"

There was no response. He walked into the foyer, then took a step toward the next room and heard a whimper. It was low but undeniably human.

He knew he had to wait for reinforcements, but he had no idea how long they would take. By the time they showed up whoever was in there might already be dead. He closed his eyes and remembered the cold warehouse in Seattle, running around the building, trying to find Gigi. He'd gone in and seen his CI bleeding on the floor. He hadn't waited for reinforcements and he'd still been too late.

He would never be too late again.

He pushed forward, his gun close to his chest, pointing in front of him. Another faint moan followed by a distinct "Hush." He took a few steps closer to the doorway leading to the next room. Darcy wished he had a search mirror so he could look inside without showing half his face. He then looked up toward the window and saw the faint reflection of the man he was after, holding a woman hostage.

"I know you're there," Darcy said.

There was no response.

"Come on, you have to let her go. Let's just do this man-to-man," Darcy said.

"Throw your weapon into the room and walk in here very slowly," the man replied.

"You know I can't do that."

"Then I don't think we have much to talk about."

Darcy called Sorensen. "Mute your phone," he whispered. He then put the phone away and focused back on the perp.

"Let the woman go."

"This is how it's going to work: you render your weapon and come in with your hands behind your head. Then I'll tell you what my demands are."

"Okay, I'm coming in." Darcy took a deep breath, readjusted his vest and inched his way in.

"The gun first."

"I told you, I can't do that," Darcy said, entering the room, holding the Glock high over his head.

The guy had the woman in a chokehold. She was pregnant; probably in the last trimester. A Sig P226 with a suppressor pointed directly at her belly. Tears flowed down her face, but she wasn't making a sound. Her feet barely touched the floor and her right hand gripped the perp's muscled arm while the left one protected her baby.

"Come on, let her go. She's pregnant." Darcy didn't dare look around. "What's your name?"

"Don't pull that shit on me, man. I've done it a million times," he scoffed.

"Are you police?" When he didn't say anything, Darcy added, "Military? A Marine?"

The perp pulled the woman closer to him and moved a few steps backwards. "Who's coming?" he asked.

"Local law enforcement," Darcy said, and saw the man look down the hallway to his right. "SWAT is on its way too, but they'll take a little longer."

The man looked composed. There was a thin sheen of sweat covering his face and sweat stains under his armpits, but that was probably from the run.

"You know things will go much better if you stop this now," Darcy urged.

The perp kept silent and glanced into the hallway again. Darcy knew he was weighing his options.

"There's no escaping this." He hoped Sorensen was listening. "We know Bishop and Mitchell are involved. If you help us, we can help you."

The mention of the names caught the man's attention. He eyed Darcy as if he was trying to figure out how much he knew. A second later he pushed the pregnant woman hard against Darcy, who grabbed her before she fell on the floor.

"Are you okay?" he asked over the sound of glass breaking.

She nodded, still not making a peep. He helped the woman to her feet and ran after him.

"He's jumped through the window, south side of the house," Darcy said, trusting that Sorensen could hear him.

Darcy was tempted to jump but decided to look outside first. Before he could spot the perp, a bullet hit the windowsill. Darcy returned fire and heard steps moving away. "Stop shooting. You're making things worse," he shouted.

He cleared the shreds of glass from the window frame with the barrel of his gun and heaved himself through. Darcy landed on the ground and saw the perp running the long driveway toward Scenic Road. He pulled the Glock. "Stop or I'll shoot you," he yelled.

The "nephew" accelerated.

Darcy cupped his right hand and fired. A dead click made his heart stop. "Misfire. A fucking misfire," he whispered between gritted teeth, hoping that Sorensen was close.

The perp must have heard the muffled click with no bang because he stopped running and, faster than Darcy was able to rack the slide back, turned to face him and fired his own weapon. Darcy rolled toward the wall as Sorensen screeched to a stop at the beginning of the path, closing the perp's exit route.

The "nephew" never took his eyes off Darcy. A shot hit his back, pushing him forward. The next four shots exploded his rib cage. The perp fell on the ground, lifeless.

Sorensen got out of his car and ran to them, yelling, "What the fuck?"

CHAPTER 78

It took them a few hours to clear things with the local police, but finally they were able to get the bodies up to the San Jose morgue. Virago had to come personally to smooth things out with the Carmel PD captain. Her jaw seemed temporarily clenched, and she looked more pissed than Darcy had ever seen her.

Before she left to drive back up to the station, she summoned both of her detectives and said, "I want to talk to both of you as soon as you get back. I suggest you start driving now."

Sorensen refused to talk to Darcy the entire ride. Every time he tried saying something, Sorensen cupped his ear and yelled, "I can't hear you. I'm deaf after having to shoot my gun inside of my car."

Darcy wasn't in a talking mood either. His head was spinning. He kept replaying the events, trying to figure out if there was anything he could have done differently.

Still in silence, Sorensen parked and locked the car. When they reached the elevator, he shoved his hand close to Darcy's face and said, "You need to go up the stairs. I can't stand being in a closed space with you any longer."

"Man, it happens. You tell me you've never had a misfire?" Darcy said, not understanding why Sorensen was being such an asshole.

"Nope." The elevator started beeping because Darcy was holding the door open. "I had to kill a man because you couldn't wait for backup. I don't give a shit whether you had a misfire or not."

"I couldn't wait for backup? What the hell are you talking about? He would have been long gone if I hadn't gone after him."

"That's procedure. You need to wait for backup, because when you don't, bad things happen. You should've never gone into the house without backup. You should have waited."

"Wait for what? For him to escape through the back door? He was a trained killer. Our only option was to go after him if we wanted to have a slim chance of catching him."

"You put a pregnant woman in danger like you put Jon in danger. You're out of control," Sorensen yelled at him, and kicked Darcy's foot out of the way.

The doors of the elevator closed, and the noise stopped.

Darcy ran up the stairs and met him when the doors were opening. "You told me to get him after he shot de la Rosa. He's a killer. I couldn't let him escape."

Uncharacteristically, Sorensen walked by him without having the last word. Darcy stood in place for a second and then decided he didn't want to stay in the bullpen. He headed back to the stairs, but before he reached the door, Virago stepped out of the other elevator right in front of him.

"In my office. Now," she said, not looking at either as she walked past them. "Both of you," she added.

Sorensen pushed his way through the door first, and Darcy closed it behind him.

"I have to waste some of my detectives' time to investigate both of your officer-involved shootings before I send the reports to IA and the DA." She took off her glasses and massaged the bridge of her nose. "What the hell happened?"

"We got a call that de la Rosa was in Carmel," Sorensen yelled.

"Detective, we're right here," Virago said, signaling with her hand to bring the volume down.

"Sorry, boss. I'll be hearing-impaired for a few days from shooting my weapon inside the car."

"Oh, please," Darcy said under his breath. Yeah, he knew the ringing in the ears wasn't pleasant, but Sorensen was being pathetic.

Sorensen stared down at Darcy for a few seconds. "We went to ask him a few questions. When we got there, there was a suspicious character in his house who turned out to be the perp. He took off running after shooting and killing de la Rosa, and Lynch went after him."

Darcy continued: "He went into a house, where he took a pregnant woman hostage, but then he tried to escape through a side window. I went after him. I told him to stop. He didn't. My weapon misfired. The perp shot back at me as Sorensen arrived and shot him. It was a good shoot. He saved my life."

"I don't doubt that," she said. "What I wonder is, why did he have to?"

"You too?" Darcy asked, now genuinely surprised. He saw Virago lock eyes with Sorensen. Darcy got out of his chair and started pacing. He wanted to leave but knew he had to stay.

"Sorensen, give us a minute, but don't go anywhere. Yee will take you statement." Before he left, she added, "If you have any concerns at all, wait for your lawyer."

"I don't."

She nodded, and he left. Once the door was closed, she looked at Darcy, but waited for him to sit back down before she started talking. He knew she wouldn't say a word until he had, so he took the same seat as before.

"I don't know what's happened to you," she said.

Darcy had no idea where this was going. He started rubbing his left temple but stopped almost immediately.

"A month ago you only wanted shitty cases nobody else would touch, all the boring stuff that would keep you as a desk jockey. Now you're going rogue, getting into shootings at the first opportunity you get, putting yourself and others in danger."

"It's the nature of the job." He fixed his eyes on hers.

She eyed him back and sucked her cheeks in. "No, it's not, and you know it." She squeeze the arm rest on her chair, then let go and leaned forward. "I get what you did for Saffron. That was legit. However, you put Jon in danger unnecessarily—"

"That was—"

She put a hand up, and he stopped talking.

"I know you were trying to get them. The moment they started shooting you should've stopped the pursuit and called in the location. You know that. Jon could be dead right now. Hell, you could be dead right now." Before he tried to interrupt her again, she shoved the hand closer to his face and continued: "The same thing today in Carmel. The moment the perp went into the house, you should have waited for back-up."

Darcy fought an overwhelming urge to walk out of Virago's office. He didn't owe her or the Sheriff's Office anything. He didn't need the job either.

She continued the lecture: "I've worked with Sorensen a very long time, and he's never killed anybody before. I'm sure it was a good shooting, but I wonder why it had to be done at all. You're the only one who can answer that question."

"The perp would've escaped. I made a judgment call and went in to make sure he didn't. My weapon misfired. It happens."

She wringed her fingers. Her eyes remained locked on his. They were hard and dark. "That's not procedure, and you know it. You should've waited for backup or for SWAT instead of running into an unknowable situation." Taking a long moment to proceed, she finally said, "I don't need any dead heroes on my squad."

"I don't have a death wish, Captain."

"You better sound a lot more convincing than that when you talk to IA," she said, and pointed at the door, indicating that she was done with him.

CHAPTER 79

Ethan was amazed that the police hadn't figured out how to block their communications from being picked up by scanners. He'd just heard that Carlos de la Rosa was dead and that Curtis had been killed. His crew was getting smaller by the day. He had to wrap this mess up.

He needed time to think. Maybe go to the gym and lift some weights. He always felt better after sweating a little. But he had something else much more soothing than working out.

He double-checked that his front door was closed and headed for the playroom. It had been originally built as a safe room by the previous owner. They must have been a rich, paranoid couple. The moment he saw the condo and the real estate agent told him about the panic room, he knew he had to buy it. The foot-thick walls and steel door that only opened with his fingerprint were perfect to keep his toys secret.

He removed the four books on the second shelf and kneeled to see the keypad. He entered his pass code, and the fingerprint reader appeared. He pressed his right index finger against the pad, the light turned from red to green, and the big door unlatched.

There was dry blood on the floor from de la Rosa that he needed to wash soon. Beautiful Belle looked up at him, her eyes only half-open and semifocused, her lips blue. Then, as if the last couple days came rushing back to her brain, she recoiled, and her body tensed.

"Babe, don't be afraid."

Ethan walked toward her, his eyes wandering over her naked body. He got close enough to touch her and passed a finger over one of the blisters from the welding torch.

She winced but couldn't move back any farther. She was as far away from him as the shackles would allow.

"Please don't," she whispered.

"Please don't what?" His fingers traced her collarbone and moved down to her breast. He circled the nipple with his index finger and then cupped the whole breast in his hand. It fit perfectly.

"Please don't hurt me anymore," she begged.

"Of course not. I'm going to take care of you," Ethan said, and watched as her skin rippled with goose bumps.

He reached up to the left handcuff and unlocked it. Her arm fell to her side and shook the rest of her body. She was still hanging from the other one. He went to the table and grabbed a dog collar that looked as if it could subdue a rabid pit bull. Before Ethan walked back to her, he heard his phone ringing in the other room. He hadn't bothered closing the door, because he knew her voice wouldn't carry very far anymore.

"Hold that thought, babe," he said, wondering if that was the call he'd been waiting for.

He left the safe room, locking the door behind him. He threw the collar on the sofa and answered the phone.

"You got my gift?" Ethan asked.

"What the fuck's wrong with you?" Blake said. "Why did you do that? You don't trust me?"

"What do you techie guys always say? Trust but verify. This is the same thing. In case you get the itch to talk to the wrong people, or your high-powered daddy convinces you to give your friends up, we have proof that you single-handedly killed everybody in that house."

"You have more video?"

"I don't need more video. I got you shooting an innocent man. The police have the guns and matching casings. I also have the glove with your fingerprints and gunpowder residue. What more do you want?"

The silence at the other end went on for what seemed like a minute.

"I didn't touch the Sig," Blake said.

"Remember that target practice we did about a month ago?" Ethan reminded him.

Another minute passed. Ethan could hear Blake pace back and forth.

"You didn't have to do this to me," Blake finally said.

"Oh, I know. I just did it for fun," Ethan responded, and hung up.

CHAPTER 80

Sorensen looked at his hands. They were trembling just a little. He pushed on the soap sanitizer pump and spread the transparent dollop all over them. The intense smell of alcohol almost made him sneeze. Once there was nothing left to rub, he looked at his hands again. They still felt dirty, so he got another squirt and rubbed them some more.

He felt Lynch watching him. "What?" he asked, more defiant than inquisitive, and stopped smearing the sanitizer.

Lynch shook his head.

Sorensen had a huge urge to get more cleanser, but didn't. "They just feel dirty," he said to himself, as if he needed to explain it.

He'd only shot somebody once before. That perp lived but was now in a wheelchair. It had been a long time ago, when he was still on patrol. He'd walked into a domestic disturbance and found a man beating the crap out of his elderly mother with a wrench. The man would not stop hitting the woman, so Sorensen tried to pull him off her. But the offender was stronger than he looked and shook Sorensen off. After taking a couple steps back, Sorensen told the man to stop or he would shoot him. The man turned around and charged at him with the wrench. Sorensen shot once. The bullet went through the stomach, somehow missing all the vital organs, and lodged in his spine, paralyzing him forever.

Sorensen didn't feel bad about that. He had no choice. The perp's mother was seventy-two and frail, and he'd done a number on her. She eventually recovered from a few broken bones, a concussion, and multiple lacerations all over her upper body.

Sorensen knew deep inside that he had to shoot the man he killed this morning too. But he still felt as if he'd done something wrong, or could have done something different. Sorensen eyed the hand sanitizer. Before he could grab it, Lynch took it from his desk and moved it just far enough to be out of reach.

"What are you doing?" he asked, but felt somehow relieved.

"I'm taking your self-pity away."

"Fuck you. I saved your life today. Asshole."

"I know. And I appreciate that. A lot. But you need to stop disinfecting your hands, and help me close this case."

Sorensen got out of his chair and left the bullpen. He wanted to hit Lynch. Go at it until the man had pulp for a face. Instead, he went up to the vending machine, which was almost empty. He hit D5 and got the last Red Bull.

"How many guys do you think are in this?" Lynch asked as soon as he walked through the door.

Silence.

Sorensen sat back down and pecked at the keyboard. He saw Lynch walk toward his desk and stand on the other side, until he looked up.

"Four went into the bank. Possibly one more sitting in the getaway car," Sorensen finally said.

Darcy looked at the boards. "Samuel Barr died after running over Saffron and crashing his car into the bank. Curtis Gutierrez died in Carmel."

Sorensen leaned over the table and grabbed the Purell bottle. He got a good pump out and rubbed his hands.

"Rory Bishop and Ethan Mitchell are still out there. Maybe one more . . . The brains?" Darcy continued.

"I think the brains were at the scene," Sorensen said.

"Risking getting caught?"

"These guys are military. They're in the middle of the action. They make the action. I don't think you get somebody to orchestrate this from the safety of their own home."

"What about Blake Higgins?" Darcy chewed on his pen. "I don't think he was the driver, or that he's the brains. But I think he started the whole thing."

"We need a subpoena for his bank records," Sorensen said.

"I think he's smart enough to not leave a trail that easy to follow."

"Or," Sorensen added, "he may have thought that his little plan was going to work much better than it did, and he wouldn't have to worry about covering his tracks."

Darcy got up and faced the boards again. Pointing to the bank kidnapping, he said, "Okay, I buy that. He hires a group of goons to kidnap Suresh Malik, the patent controller, to make the case go away. Malik dies before he can make the changes, so now he either needs to let it be and face the consequences of the lawsuit, possibly losing the buy offer and maybe even the company, or he needs a plan B."

"So he lets the goons into the party somehow, and they kidnap the big boss of the lawsuit and kill all the witnesses except Saffron's sister. Why?"

"She's involved?" Darcy's voice quaked at the end of the question.

"How's Saffron? Can we ask her?" Sorensen asked.

A dark shadow covered Lynch's face. "I've bartered a year's supply of Starbucks with the head nurse in exchange for hourly updates." He checked his phone. "She's still sedated."

"You should be with her," Sorensen said, looking at Darcy for the first time since they'd got back to the station after Carmel.

"I need to find out who did this to her," he said.

Sorensen didn't push.

"Okay, so let's say her sister's involved. We need to go through her records, see if there's anything funky going on."

Sorensen finished his drink and started typing on his computer to put together the paperwork to get the legal order.

"If she's not involved, she's either dead or in a really bad place," Lynch said.

"Let's find out one way or another."

Less than an hour later they had the subpoena, and Jon had already done a preliminary assessment. On the speakerphone, he said, "I didn't find anything out of the ordinary. She has considerable amounts of cash coming in, but that seems to be consistent more with call girl–type work than anything else."

Sorensen looked at Lynch. "And you would know that how?" he asked, wishing the intern was there and he could see him blush.

"Well, yeah, I mean, based on, you know, what—"

"We got it. Just giving you a hard time, kid," Sorensen said.

"Is there anything at all that seems out of the ordinary?" Lynch asked.

"Not that I can see, but I'll keep looking."

"No. It's better that you focus back on Blake Higgins. Anything new there?"

"Not on him, but I just saw a tweet that the acquisition is going forward, and they expect to close the deal by tomorrow."

"I wonder if they're trying to rush this through, given the circumstances. I thought Blake had told us the merger was happening in a few days, and that it was secret," Sorensen said.

"So the whole issue about the patent infringement lawsuit never came to light?" Darcy asked.

"Not that I've been able to find," Jon said.

"Should we . . . maybe place an anonymous call to the buyers?" Sorensen asked with a smirk on his face.

"Can I do it?" Jon asked.

"Whoa, getting shot has changed you." Sorensen looked at Darcy, surprised.

"Even if it doesn't make them reconsider the buy, at least they may delay it a few days," Jon pushed.

"No. We shouldn't. It would affect many people who have nothing to do with Higgins's criminal activities," Sorensen said, thinking about Mohinder Mishra, the man who tried contacting Blake when Sorensen went to NanoQ after hours.

"We just need to get Higgins arrested for multiple homicides," Lynch said.

"But we have no solid evidence."

"We have enough for that search warrant we talked about yesterday," Lynch insisted.

Sorensen checked his watch. "Okay, let's go bother the judge again, but if this is the last favor he does for me, you're going to owe me big."

CHAPTER 81

Lynch, Sorensen, and four uniforms walked into NanoQ's reception area and showed the warrant to the receptionist, who immediately made a call.

A few seconds later a young man appeared and said, "I'm Martin Dunn, the CEO. How can I help you?"

The man's face was reddish with acne, and he probably had to stretch to reach five foot eight. His hair was in desperate need of a haircut, and the black T-shirt with the logo of the company was too tight around his waist.

Sorensen pulled the paperwork from his pocket and handed it to Dunn. "We have a warrant to search and seize the specified items from Blake Higgins's office, or anywhere else where he may have them."

The CEO opened the order and scanned it. Then said, "Please wait here while I call our lawyer."

Darcy started walking toward the glass doors that separated the reception area from the actual offices and said, "Mr. Dunn, we don't have to wait. The order is legit, and we're going to start the work. You can meet us when your lawyer arrives."

The door remained locked. Darcy turned and looked at the two receptionists, who were staring back, their eyes as big as plates.

"If you don't open this door immediately, I will arrest you both for obstruction," Sorensen said.

The petite one with the blond hair pushed something, and a buzz indicated that the door was now open.

Once they were inside, Darcy said, "You like saying that, don't you?"

"What?" Sorensen teased.

"Have you ever followed up on the threat?"

"Once."

"How did it go?"

"I cuffed her and walked toward the exit. Before I got there, her tone changed, and I've never had a more cooperative receptionist in my life."

Darcy smiled. He wasn't sure Sorensen was telling the truth, but it was a good story.

Once they got to Higgins's office, they started going through his things. The laptop was gone. He didn't have anything in the first drawer besides a toothbrush and a nearly-empty toothpaste tube. The middle one was empty.

"Look at that. I thought I was the only one who did this," Darcy said, pointing at the bottom drawer. Higgins had a couple new shirts tucked in there.

"Oh dear."

"What? I'm serious. I've never known of anybody else who did that."

"I thought your thing with Saffron was going well . . ."

"What is that supposed to mean?"

"The only douche bags I know who need clean shirts in their drawers are assholes like Higgins who hope to get laid at a moment's notice. I figured you and Saffron were serious and you didn't need clean shirts to hit the town." Before Darcy could protest, Sorensen changed the subject. "I've never had a search and seizure be this short. This guy has nothing in his office."

At that moment Martin Dunn appeared with another man—a little older than him, but not by much.

"This is our general counsel, Jae Cho."

Both detectives shook his hand.

"What exactly are you looking for?" Mr. Cho asked.

"Everything is detailed in the paperwork," Sorensen said.

"I saw that. I guess the question I'm really asking is, why are you looking at Higgins? What do you think he's done?"

"We're investigating him in connection to a multiple homicide."

"What? That's ridiculous," Dunn protested.

The attorney looked at him, and Dunn stopped talking. At the end of the day, both Martin Dunn and Jae Cho probably cared a lot more about NanoQ than about Blake Higgins.

Darcy did a 360, hoping to find something he'd previously missed. But there was nothing. He wondered if Higgins was just a minimalist, or he simply didn't like stuff.

On the way out to the parking lot, Darcy said, "Now we have to go to his house. I hope nobody warned him."

"I sent a couple uniforms to watch his place. If he leaves, they'll call me."

They sent what little evidence they had back to the station with one of the officers and jumped back into Sorensen's car.

Before starting the engine, Sorensen checked his phone to retrieve the address. "I guess we're going back to San Jose."

"Since we are already babysitting him, I think we need to do a little detour before," Darcy said.

"Where?"

"Ethan Mitchell lives in Mountain View."

CHAPTER 82

Blake was pacing the living room in PJ bottoms and the white T-shirt he'd been wearing the day before, even though it was late afternoon. He hadn't slept all night. He had tried. The double dose of sleeping pills didn't do anything, and he'd been scared of taking more. He didn't want to commit suicide inadvertently.

He rubbed his chin. Day-old stubble shaded his face. He walked to the fridge and took out the nearly empty gallon of apple juice. Straight from the jug he finished it, and left the container on the counter.

When Sally called him from the front desk to tell him that the police were there to take his stuff, he panicked. He didn't know what to do or whom to turn to. He almost called his dad, but the "I told you so" was almost worse than facing fate by himself.

Before he left the kitchen, the thumb drive still inserted in his Mac caught his eye. He felt sick to his stomach and puked the juice into the kitchen sink. On the way to the bathroom to brush his teeth, he looked out the window and saw the patrol car parked outside. There was no way out. He needed to figure out if he was going to fight this or turn himself in.

Blake decided to get cleaned up. The hot water always helped him think. He scrubbed his body hard until it was raw. But it didn't make him feel cleaner. He hadn't killed that man, but everybody would think he had. He had no way to prove he hadn't, and his word probably wouldn't carry much weight.

After he was dry, he called his dad. Reticence aside, Blake was smart enough to know that his father was the only one who cared enough about him to help him.

CHAPTER 83

Ethan lived in one of the few sky rises in Mountain View. The building was new, lavish, had tiny balconies and tall windows that reflected the valley outside. Sorensen parked in the only visitor spot that was open and walked inside with Lynch.

"Good morning, gentlemen, what can I do for you?" the security guard asked.

The detectives identified themselves, showing their badges.

"We don't see police come here very often," he said, shaking their hands, and added, "Jamal Johnson at your service."

"Ethan Mitchell—what can you tell us about him?" Sorensen asked.

The man leaned against the front desk and looked away. His elbow rested on the shiny surface and slid a couple inches before he pulled himself upright again.

Sorensen looked at Lynch but didn't say anything. This can be good or bad, he thought.

After another moment the security guard shifted his weight and shoved both hands in his pockets. "I don't like talking smack about my tenants, you know. It starts that way, and then you become the fountain of gossip."

Sorensen didn't really care about this guy's moral code toward his residents, but before he could tell him that, Jamal continued.

"But yeah, I understand this is different." The guard's eyes focused on the holstered gun on Lynch's waist.

"Yes, it is. Tell us about Mitchell," Sorensen asked, and saw his partner cringe a little. Lynch always wanted things to follow an organic pace, and sometimes you didn't have all the frigging time in the world to let that happen, so he nudged things along.

After another pause, the security guard went on: "He's a real piece of work."

"What do you mean?" Lynch asked.

"He's one of those guys who thinks the world should be grateful because he walks in it, you know?"

"No, I really don't know." Sorensen brushed his blond curls away from his forehead and leaned against the front desk just a few inches from where the guard had just been.

"He's always asking me to pick up things for him, or sends me on stupid errands. Like I work for the guy or something."

Sorensen nodded for him to go on.

"Like the other day—Tuesday I think it was—he comes from the garage and tells me that he has a box he needs help carrying up. I bring down the dolly, and when I get to his car I see the box is frigging huge and weighs like three dead bodies or something."

Sorensen looked at Lynch, who met his eyes, a little sparkle in them for the first time in days.

"How late was this?"

"It was late. Probably close to midnight."

"What was in it?" Lynch asked.

"I don't know. But the point is that he's standing there and didn't even help me take the box out of the truck. I think I even twisted something, because it still hurts." He started massaging his lower back.

"And you have no idea what was in it?" Sorensen pushed.

"No. I asked him jokingly if he had rocks in it, but he just waved me to keep moving. Then, when we finally reached his place, he gave me a hundred dollars. So the guy's generous— he's always giving money away—but he's just a real dick about it."

"Anything else kind of weird or different happening in the last couple days?" Sorensen asked.

The massive man thought about it for another few moments. "No, not really. He brought a woman up the same night, but she was pretty messed up. He likes the ladies."

"What do you mean 'messed up'?" Lynch asked while he pulled a photo of Aislin. "Is this the woman?"

He shoved the picture so close to him that Jamal almost crossed his eyes.

"I couldn't tell. Her hair covered her face. It could have been, but I can't be sure."

"Did you see her leaving?"

"No, but I didn't work Wednesday and Thursday. Today is my first day back since then."

"We'll need the names and contact info of all of the other security guards who work here."

"Of course," he said, walking around the desk. He started writing the information down on a piece of paper. When he was done, he handed it to Sorensen.

"Is Mitchell here now?" Lynch asked.

"Yeah, actually I just saw him going up after his run."

"Number 2306, right?" Lynch asked.

"Yep. The nicest two-bedroom condo in the entire building."

"Oh yeah? Why is that?" Sorensen asked, already halfway to the elevator.

"The top floor has a totally different layout than the rest of the building. His is very spacey and has a great view of what used to be Moffett Field. I bet he saw a few shuttles land back in the day."

As the elevator doors opened, Sorensen said, "They never landed shuttles at Moffett. Maybe a blimp or two."

CHAPTER 84

The security guard promised them he wouldn't announce their arrival. When they reached the twenty-third floor, the doors opened to a hallway splitting to the left and to the right. They took a left.

"How do you think this guy can afford this on a Marine's salary?" Sorensen asked.

"Lottery?" Lynch joked.

"You think?" Sorensen matched Lynch's sarcastic tone.

Sorensen pressed the doorbell. Asian chimes echoed through the quiet hallway. "How manly," he said right before the door opened.

"I don't normally get unannounced visitors," Mitchell said. "Please come in." He was wearing only boxer shorts. Mitchell's body probably had less than 3 percent body fat, and he was hairless.

Sorensen tucked his loose shirt and sucked in his stomach. When he realized what he was doing, he hated himself a little. He wondered how this guy had time to work out with the many clandestine activities he had going on. Without being invited to do so, he carried his bulk across the room and sat down on the black leather sofa.

"Can I get you a beer? I only have Redhook."

"We heard you brought in a hefty package the other night," Sorensen said, ignoring the offer.

"I didn't know that was illegal."

"What was it?" he pressed.

"None of your business, Detective. I hope you didn't come all the way to ask me about my deliveries. So, either get to the point, or I'll have to ask you to leave, as I have a very busy evening."

"How do you afford a place like this with a Marine's salary?" Lynch asked. He didn't sit. Instead, he kept moving about the living room and open kitchen.

"Again, none of your business. But since you're here being nosy, I will tell you that I have a trust fund and spend the money as I please. I'm in the Marines because I enjoy the challenge. As soon as I get bored, I'll do something else."

"Of course you will," Sorensen said under his breath.

"Have you ever seen this man or this woman?" Lynch pulled the pictures of Carlos de la Rosa and Aislin.

"They don't ring a bell."

"Funny, because your guard downstairs said he saw you coming in with this woman a few days ago," Lynch bluffed.

Sorensen knew they were risking it, so he added, "She was pretty out of it. What is it, they'll only come home with you if you get them drunk?"

"Ah, very funny, Detective Sorensen. I guess you would know all about that from Sarah," Mitchell said, standing by the kitchen counter.

Sorensen felt as if somebody had punched him in the gut. "How the fuck do you know my daughter's name?"

"The Internet is an amazing thing. You have no idea the kinds of things she posts online."

Sorensen launched himself off the sofa and got in Mitchell's face. He was about twice his size, but he knew he would lose in a fight with Mitchell.

"Can I use your bathroom?" Lynch asked, and wandered off down the hallway without waiting for a response.

Sorensen didn't move an inch. He stood still, tensing his body, staring at Mitchell, breathing on him and hoping that he would make a peep so he could punch him.

After a few seconds, Mitchell slid away from under Sorensen. He walked to the fridge and took a beer.

"If I catch you less than a hundred yards away from my daughter, I will arrest you."

"For what?"

"I'm a very resourceful man. Don't push me."

"You have to understand, Detective, I have nothing against you, nor do I want anything with your daughter. But you come into my home, you don't tell me what you want, and instead you accuse me of lying when I tell you I've never met any of those people . . ."

Lynch returned before Sorensen could say anything back. "The prank—whose idea was it?"

Mitchell shifted his attention to Lynch. "I'm not sure. I think a group of us came up with it over beers one day."

The silence became almost uncomfortable.

"But why?" Lynch asked.

"Our gunny is a dick, and we thought it would be great to teach him a lesson. We knew we couldn't do it ourselves, so we talked to the other guys." He finished his beer but didn't take another one. "It was supposed to be harmless really. In hindsight, of course, I can see that it was stupid and short-sighted to think the police wouldn't get involved."

"You think?" Sorensen snorted. A small bubble of spittle flew from his mouth, landing on an orange.

"As I said. We should have known better."

"You'll face disciplinary action," Sorensen promised.

317

"I'm sure."

"You don't care?"

"Not really." Ethan shrugged his shoulders, each muscle flexing, each tendon stretched.

"How do you know Blake Higgins?"

"That name doesn't ring a bell either." His face didn't show any indication that he was lying.

"You guys did boot camp together. I thought you were all brothers once you went through boot camp."

"Apparently not." Mitchell turned around and, checking the time on the microwave, said, "Now if you excuse me, I have somewhere to be."

"You need to come to the station with us," Sorensen said. "We have more questions."

"Are you arresting me?" When neither detective said anything, he continued: "Exactly what I thought." He moved toward the door and held it open. "When you have probable cause, come back, and I'll meet you with my lawyer."

CHAPTER 85

Darcy and Sorensen got a report that things were quiet at Higgins's place, so they decided to stop by the station before going to visit him. They didn't talk much on the ride back to San Jose, except when Darcy shared the news that they were going to keep Saffron sedated for at least another twenty-four to forty-eight hours. Once they were in the bullpen, they both stood in front of the boards, which were filled with a growing amount of information leading nowhere.

"I don't know what it is about this guy—"

"He's a dick." Sorensen spat. "What the hell was that about my daughter? He was bluffing, right? How can he know anything?"

"Social media."

"Shit. Yes, of course." Sorensen's face suddenly drained of color.

"Anybody can know everything about everybody nowadays. You know that—you're the one from Silicon Valley." Darcy was tapping on his keyboard. After a few strokes, he said, "Mitchell doesn't have a trust fund."

"He lied." Sorensen threw an empty Red Bull across the room into Detective Ramirez's trash can, missing it. "Crap, I never make that shot." He got up, picked up the can and let it fall into the trash.

"And he lied about knowing Higgins. I mean, even if the coward didn't make it past boot camp, Mitchell would remember everybody he did it with."

Sorensen plopped back in his chair.

"He possibly lied about the girl too, but when I took a peek, I didn't see a sign of her," Darcy said. "The problem is the evidence we have is at best circumstantial, and not strong enough to really tie him to any of this."

Sorensen shifted. "We need to follow the money."

"I wish we could. There's nothing on this guy. I mean, not even a basic checking account."

"How does he get paid?"

"He probably cashes the checks."

Sorensen looked through his notes, and after putting the phone on speaker, he punched in a number.

"Sergeant Major Williams, I have a quick question for you. Are all Marines required to have a bank account for payroll purposes?"

"It didn't use to be. But it is now."

"Can you find out if Ethan Mitchell used to get paid via check, and how he's getting paid now?"

There was silence on the other end.

"Please."

"I can't access that information. Give me a second to reach out to Personnel."

Darcy could hear the sergeant major tapping on a keyboard, and then there was silence. She'd put them on mute.

After a few minutes she got back on, "Most of his old checks haven't been cashed. And since we went to direct deposit, he hasn't been paid, because we've had no account to send it to."

Sorensen thanked her and hung up.

"Great, we now have even less," Darcy said, and sighed.

"Is there anything at all we can use to bring him in?" Sorensen asked, thinking out loud.

At that moment Darcy's phone rang.

"Detective, you asked us to notify you if we saw any air traffic activity for Mr. Higgins's plane."

"Yes, what's up?" Darcy urged.

"A flight plan was just filed. Destination Belize."

CHAPTER 86

The Gulfstream G650 was supposed to leave San Jose International Airport at 2000 hours. Darcy and Sorensen hurried there, but Sergeant Marra and a few of his men got there much faster. The pilot hadn't started the preflight check yet, so they didn't have to rush into the runway with the spinners and full sirens blowing, which Marra confessed had been disappointing.

The first thing Darcy saw was Blake in handcuffs with a couple unis by his side. His mouth was moving but Darcy couldn't hear the words. When they finally reached him, Blake was demanding a phone call to his lawyer.

"Oh, don't worry about that. You'll see him soon enough. We're going to arrest him for aiding and abetting you," Sorensen told him.

Blake stared at him, his expression a mixture of defiance and fear.

Sorensen wasn't kidding, though. "You may want to call your sister to give her a heads-up," he told Darcy.

"I'm sure she already knows."

"Let's all go back to the station, where we have bad coffee and very uncomfortable seats," Sorensen said, turning away from everybody and dragging Blake by the arm, hands handcuffed behind his back.

"The pilot is over there. I'll bring him in too," Marra said.

Sorensen looked over his shoulder and said, "Thanks, man. That was some fast work. I appreciate it." Then he pushed Blake into the car, not caring if he hit his head on the way in.

"You got it." Marra headed in the opposite direction toward the pilot, who was in a corner, biting his thumbnail.

When the detectives got to the station, Virago was waiting for them.

"Trying to escape. How cute," she said, redoing her ponytail.

"Yeah, not sure who advised him to do such a stupid-ass thing," Sorensen said, shoving Blake into the first interview room.

Virago went next door to watch him in action. Darcy followed her.

Once Blake was sitting, his cuffs still on, Sorensen left the room and came to see them.

"I'm going to go all the way."

"As you should," Virago agreed.

He went to the kitchen and grabbed two cups of coffee. The stale smell made his nose wrinkle.

"This," Sorensen said, placing one cup in front of Blake, "is the best coffee you're going to have for the rest of your life."

He pushed the cup closer to him and watched as Blake looked at it but couldn't drink it, since his hands were still cuffed behind him.

"Oh, right, you're going to want to savor it. Let me remove those for you."

As soon as he did, Blake rubbed his wrists. The metal had left red marks on the skin.

"Go on, enjoy it," Sorensen pushed.

"Where's my father? I asked for my lawyer," Blake said, looking at the steaming cup but not taking it.

"I bet he's being arrested right now. If I were you, I would start looking for a replacement in your contact list. But in the meanwhile, I'm not here to make you talk. I'm not even going to ask you any questions. I'm going to tell you what we have on you and how you're going to rot in prison."

Blake leaned against the chair and crossed his arms. A smirk grew on his face, and his eyes dared Sorensen to entertain him.

Darcy watched through the one-sided mirror, rage building inside him until he spotted a sheen on Blake's temple that beaded into a single drop of sweat. The room was not hot. That was when he knew they had him.

"But first," Sorensen continued, "Let's make sure you understand your Miranda rights." Sorensen recited them and Blake wrote his initials by each one and finally signed on the dotted line.

The smirk was gone.

"We know McKenzie & Shaw filed a lawsuit against your company for patent infringement. The company you've built from the ground up with your buddies. The same company that Karsum Conglomerate is about to pay you a hundred sixty-eight million dollars for. Of course you couldn't let the suit go forward. So you went to your buddy Mitchell to kidnap Malik, but the poor bastard died of a heart attack before you could coerce him to drop the suit."

Sorensen took his own cup of coffee and brought it close enough to sniff. The smell was so bitter he almost gagged. He hated coffee, so he put it back on the table without tasting it.

"Now, I'm curious. He was just a reviewer—what did you think he could do for you?"

As soon as Blake started to talk, Sorensen stopped him: "Oh no, wait. You invoked your lawyer privilege. You can't say anything."

Blake protested, but the detective talked louder until Blake shut up. "Anyway, whatever you hoped to get from this Malik, he couldn't do, because he died. By the way, this is the first felony murder I'm charging you with."

Sorensen brought the cup to his lips as if he was going to finally take a sip and watched the suspect over the rim of the paper cup. Blake's eyes looked more red than white, and sweat beaded his forehead, wet hair falling in limp bangs.

This is just the beginning, Darcy thought, always impressed by Sorensen's skill.

"With Malik dead, you needed a plan B: to get the big fish—de la Rosa—and persuade him to change his mind about the lawsuit. It would have been simpler to get some compromising pictures at that party, but no, you had a different idea. You wanted to terrorize him so badly that he would do anything for you. That's why you killed eleven people."

"That's not what happened!" Blake yelled, and stood, pushing the table into Sorensen.

The detective pushed the table back. "Mr. Higgins, sit down right now. You've invoked your right to a lawyer, and I cannot allow you to say a word until your attorney is present. So shut the hell up."

"No, you don't understand, I revoke it. I don't care. You need to listen to me." He managed to sit but bounced in his chair as he said each word.

"Let me get this straight: Are you agreeing to talk to me without your attorney present?"

"Yes, yes, whatever. I just need to tell you I didn't kill those people. I shot the gun but it didn't hit anyone. He made it look like I did. I know what the video shows, but it's manipulated. It's not true."

Darcy looked at Virago. He had no idea what video Blake was talking about. He knew Sorensen was thinking the same thing but couldn't let Blake know he didn't know about it. Darcy called Mauricio and asked him to get the evidence they'd just collected at Higgins's place ASAP.

"Well, you're right. It doesn't look like that at all. Why don't you explain it to me."

The door opened, banging against the wall. Blake's father walked in and didn't bother to close the door behind him.

"I'm going to sue you. This is unacceptable behavior for law enforcement. You should know better than this, Detective."

Virago walked into the room. Darcy watched the show from the other side of the one-way mirror.

"And you should too, Captain." Higgins Sr. stabbed his finger too close to her face.

"Unfortunately, you should have taken a refresher in criminal law, because aiding a criminal to escape is a felony," she said, putting both hand on her hips, blocking the exit route.

"What are you talking about? I did no such thing."

He was much taller, so she had to look up a good foot to meet his eyes.

"Your plane, your son, for God's sakes. We very clearly said yesterday that we needed him available and to not leave town. A flight plan to Belize? Unless there's a city with that name I'm not aware of within a few miles from here, this is not looking too good."

"Yeah, you try to prove that," he said. "I need a minute with my client. I will appreciate it if you leave us now."

They left father and son in the room.

Once outside, Virago said, "There's a huge conflict of interest here, but let's see what happens next before we worry about that, okay?"

They both nodded and turned to watch them talk. They were facing each other, so even if they wanted to, they wouldn't have been able to read their lips.

"You know what video this moron's talking about?" Sorensen asked Darcy.

"No clue, but Mauricio is going to send us the files in his computer right away."

"Have Mauricio send them to Jon," Virago said.

Darcy called Mauricio and asked him to have the computer and any data-related equipment transferred to the hospital immediately. Then he talked to Jon and instructed him to look for any video of the party first.

Before they had time to get back to the kitchen for a freshly brewed cup of coffee, Blake's father came out of the room.

"We have some information, but we want to talk to the DA first."

CHAPTER 87

"Ethan, we have a problem," Mac said on the phone.

"Give me a sec." Ethan looked at the worn body of Aislin in the panic room. He put the phone on mute and instead of going back into the room to rinse the new blood off the floor, he shook his head and closed the door. When he got to the kitchen, he asked, "What's up?"

"Your boy's singing."

Ethan wasn't surprised, but he still punched the polished countertop. He ignored the pain, which reached his shoulder. He shook his arm and then pressed his palm against the cool surface.

"What do you know?"

"Not much, but my buddy at the station told me they brought your boy in handcuffs, and then his dad came. A little later the DA showed up. I don't think we can assume anything else."

"Okay. Is your uncle's warehouse available?"

"Probably, but I'll confirm."

"Do that. Make sure he stays away tomorrow. We'll meet there at 0900 hours."

"I'll see you there."

Ethan looked back at the fake wall hiding his playroom. He really hated it when he had to leave the room dirty, but duty called, and he needed to take care of the mess they were in. He made a mental note of what he needed and headed out.

In the elevator, Ethan pressed the button for the garage but then decided to make a quick stop on the main floor. The doors opened, and he saw the security guard who ratted on him to the police at the end of the short hallway.

"Hey, Jamal," Ethan called out still a few feet away. The large man looked up and recoiled. Ethan despised men who had no balls.

"Mr. Mitchell. What can I do for you?"

"I'm waiting for a package. Can you let me know the moment it arrives? It's very important."

"Absolutely. I'll call your cell." Jamal checked his watch. "Tonight?"

"No, it should be here sometime tomorrow morning. You working then?"

"Yes. Sure, no problem. I'll call you as soon as it gets here."

Ethan pulled out a hundred-dollar bill and slipped it into his hand with a handshake, then turned and headed for the elevators. We do have great service in this building, he thought.

CHAPTER 88

Carlotta Cece, the DA, spent almost two hours talking with the Higginses. Darcy, Sorensen, and Virago watched the entire time from the other side of the one-sided mirror. Darcy wondered how somebody like Blake could sink so low. He had it all. He was smart, good looking, had a lot of money, a great education, and yet . . . here he was.

"It really pisses me off when we have to compromise," Virago said when Higgins Sr. managed to work a deal where he would serve no jail time. He would have to give up his law license, but he could happily retire and spend the rest of his days playing golf.

"At least we got what we needed to go after Mitchell and Bishop," Darcy said.

"On that note, what are you guys still doing here?" she asked, checking her watch. "If you're going to catch them, you won't be doing it from here." She arched her right eyebrow and stared at them until they moved.

"Mitchell first?" Sorensen asked, grabbing his jacket from the back of the chair.

"He's the big fish, yeah. He should be home. It's almost 10:00 p.m."

"Man, I can't remember the last time I was home for dinner."

As if on cue, his stomach rumbled, and Darcy laughed.

"Let's grab some food on the way there. In-N-Out?" Darcy suggested.

"You got it."

The line was short at the In-N-Out drive-through off of Coleman Avenue. Darcy felt more like a venti coffee from the Starbucks next door but went for a Protein Style with fries. Sorensen got two 4x4s.

While they ate, Sorensen took Taylor to Highway 87 and then merged into Highway 101. When they got to Mitchell's place, they parked in the visitor area and found the security guard they'd met before eating a pepperoni pizza.

"Late dinner?" Sorensen asked, not feeling so bad for having just finished his.

"No, these are leftovers." Jamal wiped his greasy mouth with a wrinkled paper napkin and, putting both hands on his stomach, said, "You have to work hard to look this way." He laughed, jiggling his fat belly.

"That's what I keep telling this guy," Sorensen said, patting Darcy's shoulder.

"You here to talk to Mr. Mitchell again?"

He threw the rest of the pizza into the garbage can below the reception desk.

Sorensen nodded.

"You just missed him."

"You know where to?" Sorensen asked.

"No. But he told me he's expecting a package and that I should call him the minute it gets here."

"Tonight?" Darcy asked.

"No. Tomorrow."

"Okay. Would you let us know when Mitchell gets back? And when the package arrives?"

"You got it."

Both detectives shook hands with Jamal and left.

Darcy zipped his jacket while he walked to the car. "I have no idea where to go looking for this dude."

"I'm beat, man. Let's call it a night. We have an APB out and all eyes on him. I don't feel like going on a wild-goose chase for nothing." He opened the car. "I miss my wife." Sorensen sighed.

"Can you drop me off at the hospital?" Darcy asked.

"Yep."

CHAPTER 89

Saturday

Ethan was the first to arrive at the warehouse. Mac had given him the lock code, so he let himself in and brought inside all the supplies he'd bought the night before. He cleared a space on the tiny office's desk and got to work. When he finished the package, he called the messenger to come and pick it up.

Just as the messenger van pulled up in front of the warehouse, Mac's car appeared on the other side of the street. Ethan gave the young kid specific instructions for the delivery and watched him leave before he opened the loading gate. Mac drove in and parked next to Ethan's M3.

Mac was alone. Ethan looked at his friend and tilted his head slightly while he waited for an explanation.

"Bishop's not coming," Mac said as soon as he was out of the car.

"Why not?" Ethan kept his voice level.

"Man, you're really asking?"

Mac walked up and down the loading area. His hands seemed sweaty, because he kept rubbing them against his thighs.

"This has gotten out of control. I'm not even sure why I came."

"Really?" Ethan's tongue rolled out the word.

Mac stopped pacing and leveled his eyes with Ethan's. Then, he said, "No. Well, you know what I mean. It's just that I don't know how things have gotten this fucked up."

"Actually, no, I don't know what you mean. In fact, I think we're quite okay. We have full knowledge of what the rich asshole's doing, we have the two million wired already into the account, and now that Bishop's out, we only have to divide it in two parts." When Mac didn't look fully convinced, Ethan added, "What's he gonna do? Tell the police?"

Nothing came out of his mouth, but Mac's expression said, He can do that.

"Mac, if he talks, by the time he tells the police anything, we'll be long gone." Ethan could see his reassuring tone wasn't working as well as he expected.

He walked up to Mac and made him stop pacing. Taking him by the shoulders, he waited until he had his full attention, then said, "Staff Sergeant MacAlister, I have never failed you. I have in fact saved your life a couple times."

"Yeah, but that was in Afghanistan. This is here." Mac looked down at his feet. "I can't go to prison, man."

"As I said, I've never failed you. I will not let you go to prison. Do you understand me?" Ethan said, drilling into Mac's soul with his black, piercing eyes.

When the man's tense body seemed to ease a little, Ethan punched his shoulder just hard enough to let him know he was playing with him.

Mac shared a forced smile and finally relaxed enough to take a full breath.

"Okay," he said.

"Now I want to discuss the plan with you," Ethan said.

Mac nodded but didn't move.

"Can you get the duffel bag from my trunk?" he asked, as if it was easier for him because he was closer.

Mac turned and started walking toward it.

Ethan pulled his Sig P226 with the suppressor and shot his long-time friend. He eased his index finger off the trigger as the bullet entered Mac's skull.

"You're not going to prison. You'll never be as miserable as Gomez is," Ethan apologized.

Just as the blood started pooling on the concrete floor, his cell rang.

"Mr. Mitchell, your package has arrived. You wanted me to call, right?"

"That was fast. Can you tell me who it is from?"

"It says Detective Sorensen, from the Santa Clara Sheriff's Office."

"Yep, that's the one," Ethan said, pulling the burner phone out of his bomber jacket.

He dialed a number he'd memorized a while back and held the cell he was talking on a foot or so away from his ear. Then he heard a split second of the explosion before the line went dead.

"Tying up loose ends," he said, wiping his prints from the burner cell and cupping Mac's fingers around it.

Ethan popped open the trunk of his car and took out two cans of gasoline. He walked into the office and started pouring it over the open file cabinets. While he did that he wondered what he would do to Detective Sorensen now that he'd had to use his little present on the security guard at his building.

CHAPTER 90

Darcy spent the night in the hospital with Saffron even though it didn't make sense, since she was still sedated. He'd asked every doctor in the ICU about what they might expect, but the consistent message he got was, "We have to wait and see." Not very reassuring.

He leaned in and kissed her cheek. It was warm, almost feverish. He moved a strand of hair away and tucked it behind her ear, as she often did herself. Then he left the room to meet Sorensen downstairs.

"This chauffeuring around is getting pretty old. Any news on your car?" Sorensen asked as soon as Darcy got inside.

"No. Maybe a couple more days. How's Shelby?"

"Your dog's fine. I'm this close to taking her to my house, though." Getting back to the car conversation, Sorensen added, "As soon as you get the Cobra back, I'm going to the shop with mine, so you'll have to drive me around."

Darcy nodded. Sorensen had a point. He should have rented a car.

A few minutes later they both walked into the bullpen. Virago saw them and raised both eyebrows.

"What on earth are you guys doing here empty-handed?" she asked, marching in their direction.

"We need to regroup. Mitchell's not home. Instead of driving around a city of one million people hoping to run into him, we decided to come here and be strategic about it," Sorensen said.

Virago started responding, but her cell rang. She held up a finger, as if she were asking two little kids to hold tight to be reprimanded, and answered. Darcy watched her expression go blank. She turned sideways, nodded a few times and finally said, "On our way."

She hung up and faced her detectives.

"Didn't you say Ethan Mitchell lives in a high-rise in Mountain View?" she asked them.

"Yep, at the High Sights. Why?" Darcy asked.

"There was an explosion there."

"That can't be a coincidence," Sorensen said. "You think he blew up his own building?"

"Any casualties?" Darcy asked, fishing through his drawer for the extra magazine. It was full, and he slid it in his pocket.

"Too early to tell, but the security guard is unaccounted for."

"Yeah, that's no coincidence," Darcy said. "Mitchell killed him."

"You're reaching." Virago looked to Sorensen for confirmation.

"I'm one hundred percent sure," Darcy said, already heading out the door.

"Mountain View PD has this," Virago yelled after him.

"I'm sure. I'm just going to see if I can help."

Darcy noticed that Sorensen wasn't following him. That was okay with him. He needed some time alone.

"Can I take your car?" he asked over his shoulder.

"Take mine," Virago said when Sorensen didn't reply. "The keys are on my desk."

"Thanks. I'll bring it back in one piece."

"You better."

Darcy retraced his steps, grabbed the keys and left the bullpen alone.

Darcy found Virago's Chevy Malibu parked close to the parking entrance. It was black and in dire need of a wash. He started the car and was not totally surprised when the radio was tuned in to NPR.

He checked the map app on his phone and saw that Highway 101 traffic was red in more spots than it was green, so he decided to go via Central Expressway. As he drove close to where he and Jon had been shot, he started hearing sirens. There was a big tower of black smoke rising over the low buildings. He killed the radio and turned on the police scanner. The fire had started a few minutes ago, and it was growing rapidly. They expected foul play.

He left the smoke behind and concentrated on speeding all the way to his destination. When he finally got there, he also found numerous fire trucks. The area was already cordoned off, and several Mountain View Police cars surrounded the building. Darcy double-parked a block away and walked over to the officer controlling the entrance.

"Detective Darcy Lynch." He flashed his badge.

The uni looked at his list and, not finding his name, he said, "I'm sorry, but I can't let you in."

"Can you call your supervisor? I think I know who did this. He's under investigation on another case."

"Give me a sec." The uni turned his back to Darcy and spoke into his radio. A second later he said, "My sergeant is coming over. Please wait here."

A man in his late fifties with piercing blue eyes and short salt-and-pepper hair introduced himself as Sergeant Cowan. His handshake was firm, and he wasted no time.

"Detective Lynch, you have something for me?"

He lifted the tape and invited Darcy to step inside with him. They walked toward the entrance of the building.

"This was a bomb, right?" Darcy asked.

"I thought you had information for me." Cowan gave him a sideways look, sizing him up.

Darcy nodded. It was only fair to share before asking.

"We're investigating a tenant in this building. We think he's connected to the multiple homicide in Los Altos as well as a couple other things. My partner and I came yesterday to talk to him and got some valuable information from the security guard. We think the guard might have been killed so he wouldn't talk to us anymore."

"That's a bit extreme, don't you think?"

"Maybe. But we think this guy whacked eleven people at the party, and probably a couple more since then. He may be covering his tracks."

The entrance of the building was covered in soot and water from the sprinklers. The reception area looked like a war zone. Darcy had never seen anything like this before. The desk was blown to pieces. The artwork had dropped from the wall and fallen on top of what was left of the desk. The chair had been propelled to the opposite side of the room, and multiple body parts were peppered with the flowers that had previously sat on top of the reception desk.

"We're waiting on the SJPD Bomb Squad to do the thorough assessment, but yeah, it's obviously a bomb," Cowan said, answering Darcy's original question.

"Do you know the identity of the victim?"

"We'll need to confirm DNA, but . . ." He looked around and then said, "Gonzalez, can you show me again what you found a minute ago?"

A young uniform, looking as if he was about to puke, came over, almost relieved to not have to look for evidence on the floor anymore. When he reached them, he handed over the sealed bag.

Darcy grabbed it and read the name tag: "J. Johnston." Handing the evidence back to Cowan, he said, "The guy we talked to yesterday was Jamal Johnston. Let me know when you confirm his identity."

"Will do."

"When do you think I can come back and search our suspect's place?"

"Give me an hour. That should give you enough time to get a warrant, unless you have one already."

Cowan gave the evidence back to Gonzalez.

"Processing right now. See you then."

Darcy shook Cowan's hand and walked back to the car to call Virago. He wanted to make sure the paperwork was ready by the time he got to the station.

CHAPTER 91

Virago told Sorensen the latest news from Darcy as he double-checked the warrant. He got one covering Ethan Mitchell's condo and the Marines barracks. While he waited for Lynch to show up, he called Sergeant Major Williams at the 23rd Marine Regiment.

"Sorensen here. Have you seen Mitchell or Bishop around today?"

"No. They've been AWOL the last couple days. We'll have to initiate disciplinary action as soon as they get back."

Sorensen whistled.

"Things must be loosening up at the Marines." When the sergeant major didn't respond, he added, "I would have imagined the Marines would summon a court-martial if somebody was late more than ten minutes."

"Things are changing, Detective."

"If you see or hear from them, you have to call me right away. They're our prime suspects in several murders, including the Los Altos massacre." There was silence again. "You're not surprised . . . ?"

"When I saw the news about the murders, it never even crossed my mind." She paused. "I'm stunned to hear that about Bishop, but Mitchell . . . I have to confess I'm not surprised. I don't know if he did it, but is he capable of something like this? Maybe."

Now it was Sorensen's turn to be quiet. He thought about her statement and how much he wished she had told him this a couple days earlier.

"Why didn't you say anything before?"

"As I said, until you mentioned it, I didn't really make the connection. I probably didn't really want to make the connection."

Sorensen shook his head. He couldn't blame her, but he was angry. They could have gone harder after him if he'd known this, and probably saved a life or two. Instead, now they had to launch a full manhunt to try to find the bastard.

"Sergeant Major, I'm confused. Don't the Marines do psych tests and provide honorable or dishonorable discharges for people who have mental issues?"

"We do."

"But I thought I just heard you say that you are not surprised to hear he's my prime suspect . . ."

"I'm sure you can understand that we need a certain type of person to take care of things in war zones. You expect that person to do the right things for the right reasons. Sometimes that same person confuses what those might be." Before Sorensen could drill her further, she added, "And some are just very good at masking who they really are."

Sorensen knew that was true.

Before the silence became uncomfortable, she said, "One more thing, Detective . . ."

He waited.

"I double-checked, and neither Mitchell nor Bishop were actually in the barracks on Tuesday, the day your guy got shot."

"You lied to me?" He stood and planted a massive hand on the desk, making sure the noise carried through the phone. "You told me they both were—"

Before he could continue yelling, she cut him off. "I didn't lie to you. I just trusted what my staff told me. They've been appropriately dealt with." Without letting him get another word in, she said, "I'll let you know if I hear from either one, Detective."

She hung up.

Sorensen stood and walked to the vending machine. He put in a dollar bill, but the machine wouldn't take it. It was too old and wrinkly. He flattened it and tried again. The machine spat the bill out. Sorensen grabbed a newer one and put it in. There were no more Red Bulls, so he pressed D2, settling for a bag of chips.

He thought about Sergeant Major Williams. He wanted to call her back and accuse her of reckless endangerment. Or threaten her with obstruction. Sorensen headed toward Virago's office, but before he walked in, his phone rang. From the corner of his eye, he saw Lynch coming in, and then Virago waving them into her office.

"We have a situation," she said when Sorensen closed the door after they were both inside.

CHAPTER 92

Ethan had a plan. He always had a plan. Or a few, in fact. He always had several contingencies for everything he did. That's why he was the best at what he did.

Yes, of course this last mission had turned out to be a major cluster fuck. Part of the problem was that he had overestimated Blake. He thought Blake really wanted his issue to go away. But he should have known better. Blake was the typical rich boy who wanted to play tough but when the shit hit the fan went running back to daddy.

And that was exactly what Blake had done at boot camp. When it got rough, he chickened out, and daddy pulled strings to get him out. Ethan should have realized people like Blake don't change.

But he'd believed him. When Blake called him out of the blue with the proposition, Ethan was skeptical. But Blake swore to him that he was serious, that he needed the lawsuit to go away quietly and he was willing to do whatever it took to get it done. And to prove it, he'd wired Ethan one million dollars just for him—a small enticement, he'd called it. And again, Ethan should have seen through that. For Blake, everything was about money.

The white Jeep Compass he was following stopped suddenly at a yellow light. The noise of the screech on the asphalt pulled him out of his thoughts and made him slam on the brakes as well. His car stopped a mere inch from the bumper of the car in between them. He cursed under his breath. He had a better plan than to crash into her. The light turned green, and she pulled forward. He followed her, this time focusing his full attention on the road.

She took a left on Alum Rock Avenue and headed toward the hills. There were fewer and fewer cars the farther east they got. A few miles later she took a right on White Road. At the next stop light, he pulled up next to her and rolled down his window, then signaled for her to do the same. She finally saw him but only lowered it halfway, as if she feared he would be able to reach her all the way from his car.

"I think your left rear tire is flat," he said.

"Oh, you think?" she asked, looking behind her as if she could see it.

"Yeah, it looks pretty flat to me," he urged.

"I guess I should stop and check it out then," she said, but it sounded more like a question than a statement.

When the light turned green, she went through the intersection and pulled over by the curb. He stopped in front of her.

Getting out of the car, he met her by the flat tire.

"I'm a mechanic," he said, pointing at his left breast, where the Mike's Cars & Parts logo was prominently displayed. He saw her check it out and relax a little. "I can help you."

"That's so kind of you. I'm sure you have somewhere else to go, though. I would not want to inconvenience you."

"No, it's okay. I just finished my shift. Do you have a car jack?" he asked, walking with her toward the trunk.

"Yes, I think I have everything here." She opened it and pulled up the rug. There was a huge hole where the spare tire should have been. "Oh no. That's weird," she said. She pointed at the hole. "Isn't that where the tire is supposed to be?"

"I'm afraid so." He took a few steps away from the car. "Let me go and check mine. Maybe my spare will work."

He left her there, still confused about why her tire was gone.

He looked and saw that the open trunk door blocked her view. He ducked into the car and grabbed her cell phone from the seat. Then he opened his trunk and closed it a couple seconds later.

CHAPTER 93

Sorensen was tempted to ignore the call, but it was weird for his wife to phone him in the morning, so he answered.

"Honey, I'm super-busy. What's up?"

"Detective Sorensen, Ethan Mitchell here."

Sorensen checked the caller ID. "What the hell have you done to my wife?" he yelled into the phone.

"The question, Detective, is what am I going to do with her."

The phone went dead.

When Sorensen turned, his face was white.

"He has my wife," he said, locking eyes with Virago. His voice was barely audible.

"What happened?" Virago asked as Lynch walked into her office.

Sorensen told them exactly what Mitchell had said.

"Call her."

Sorensen dialed, but the call went to voice mail.

"Can you track her phone?" she asked.

Sorensen tapped into the tracking app and saw that his wife's phone was off the grid.

"He must have pulled out the battery."

"When was the last time you spoke with her?"

"This morning." Sorensen felt his temperature rising. He wiped the sweat forming on his neck with his hand.

"I'm getting a couple unis to go to your house and to your kids' schools," Virago said. "I'll have them pick them up and bring them here."

She called and gave very specific instructions.

Sorensen nodded as a thank-you. "I need go to look for her."

"Detective, I know what you're thinking, but the best thing you can do is concentrate on finding Mitchell."

Sorensen stopped pacing. He looked at Lynch, who nodded, agreeing with Virago.

When Sorensen gave in, Virago said, "Here's the warrant. Take it with you, but the bomb squad has to do a floor-to-floor sweep, because we received a threat of another bomb in the building."

"We all know Mitchell's not at his condo, anyway," Darcy said.

Virago continued: "The reason why I called you in here is because there was a fire at one of the warehouses close to where Jon's shooting took place. The preliminary information indicates that it was probably intentional, as there was an intense smell of gasoline emanating from the place. The hazmat unit is there. SJFD managed to put the fire out already. They found a body on the premises. No ID yet."

"You think it's related?" Darcy asked.

"Too close for comfort." She pushed her glasses onto her head. "I would like you guys to stop there for a second and sniff around."

Sorensen started to complain, but she cut him off: "You don't have to stay long. Just go and check it out personally."

"Are you sure that's the best place we can be at?" Sorensen pushed.

"Do you have a better one, Detective?"

CHAPTER 94

Darcy loaded his additional extra magazine and put it in his jacket pocket. He checked that he still had the other one. Three were always better than two. He watched Sorensen grab another mag too.

On the way down to the parking lot, his partner pointed toward the accessories room, and Darcy followed him.

"Do you still have the vest in my trunk?" he asked Darcy.

"I don't know."

"Yeah, that's what I thought. I don't remember if mine is there either. Let's make sure we go prepared. This guy's sick."

They got the vests and headed for Sorensen's car.

"I should drive," Darcy said.

"No way in hell you're driving my car when I'm in it."

"I thought you may want to have a free hand if your phone rings or something."

"I can drive with one hand."

They got in the car, and Sorensen drove out of the parking lot, tires screeching with each turn.

"What would you do if you were me?" Sorensen asked Darcy when they were en route to the fire scene.

Darcy was quiet for a second. He looked out the side window and watched as they passed the parked cars much faster than they should. He rubbed his temple. The motion made him realize how dry his eye felt. He blinked a few times and exhaled for a long time. When he felt his lungs completely empty, he took in a deep breath and said, "I don't know."

"That's helpful."

Darcy didn't say anything. He actually didn't know. He closed his eyes and willed himself to stop rubbing his temple.

"I would do whatever it took to find my wife."

Sorensen looked at him, as if surprised that Darcy would fight in his corner.

Darcy continued: "But I think Virago's right. If he took her, your best bet to find her is to find Mitchell."

"Why do you say 'if' he has her? Of course the asshole has her. How else could he have her phone?"

"Technology is crazy these days. If nothing else, that's one of the things you keep reminding me since I moved to Silicon Valley."

"You're saying he hacked into her phone somehow?"

"I don't know. All I'm saying is that this guy's very smart. Kidnapping somebody in broad daylight is hard. Maybe it's easier to make you think he has than to do it for real."

"Like he hasn't kidnapped enough people in broad daylight already," Sorensen scoffed.

"True, but the execution was extremely elaborate."

Sorensen drove in silence for a while. Darcy was about to say something else when they got to the fire scene.

Sergeant Marra was waiting for them.

After shaking hands he said, "I know you guys are thinking about coming on board at the SJPD, but frankly I haven't been this busy in years, so I think you bring bad luck. Can you please stay at the Sheriff's?"

Darcy laughed and saw Sorensen smile a little.

"Don't worry, we just want to make a grand entrance," Sorensen said. "Things will slow way down after that."

"Well, we like it when crime goes down, so just keep that in mind."

Marra started walking toward the entrance of the warehouse.

"Why do you think this is related?" Darcy asked.

"Well, maybe it's too early to tell, but we found another crispy. The preliminary cause of death is gunshot wound to the back of the head. A Sig P226 was found at the scene just like the one from the mess in Los Altos."

Madison was by the ambulance, a body bag next to him.

"Show them what you found," Marra said to him.

The ME looked through a few of the evidence bags he'd already collected and pulled two. One contained an ID. It was somewhat burnt, but the picture of an African American man in his early thirties, angular face and black eyes, was almost intact. His name was Alex MacAlister. The other bag had a partially melted Trident pin.

"We found this in his wallet," the ME said.

Darcy took the evidence bags. "Could it be fake, just something to throw us off?" he said, waving the bag with the pin.

"Maybe, but I was a SEAL, and it looks pretty real to me," Marra said.

"Neither Curtis Gutierrez nor Samuel Barr were Marines. But we didn't check other branches," Sorensen shared.

Madison offered to call his office and see if they had found something. He put the phone on speaker. After the second ring, a female voice answered.

"Medical examiner's office, Giovanna speaking," she said.

"Can you get the Barr file—the man who ran over Miss Meadows?"

"Give me a sec."

They could hear steps moving away from the phone, then coming back.

"Got it."

"Do you have anything in the notes about him having served?"

"For our country?"

"Yes." Madison sighed. "Not the sharpest tool," he whispered after covering the phone.

Darcy almost smiled. He'd never heard Madison say anything non-PC before.

"I'm going through the notes . . . Wait, maybe this counts," she said, but stopped talking, as if she needed permission to continue.

"What is it, Giovanna?"

"He was a Navy SEAL up to 2009. He left to work for a security company called Blue Ghost and should still be on their payroll."

"Thank you. Anything else?"

"No. You want me to email you the file?"

"Yes, please." Madison hung up. "Better you check it out for yourselves," he said to the three men, forwarding the email on. "Now if you don't mind, I'll take the body to the morgue."

"That," Sorensen said, pointing at the leaving ambulance, "cannot be a coincidence."

CHAPTER 95

Darcy inspected the warehouse crime scene and sighed. It was ugly, but he didn't think they added any value being there. He nodded to Sorensen to get going. They both said good-bye to Marra and headed to the car.

As Sorensen was getting in, his phone rang. Darcy watched him fumble with the phone and almost drop it.

Sorensen just listened and nodded. After a few moments, he said, "Can I speak to her?"

"They found my wife," he mouthed to Darcy in a low whisper, then turned around to talk to her.

Darcy stepped out of the car, giving his partner some privacy.

When Sorensen was done, he waved Darcy back into the car and said, "The asshole took her spare, then slashed her rear tire and posed as a good Samaritan wanting to help. When she wasn't looking, he stole her phone, leaving her stranded. One of the unis stopped to assist and then realized she was my wife."

"I'm glad she's okay," Darcy said. "Do you want to be with her? I can catch a ride with someone else."

"No. She's fine. I told her to take the kids and go to my sister's."

"Are you sure?"

Sorensen nodded, then asked, "What now?"

He put the keys in the ignition, but the engine remained dead.

"I need coffee," Darcy said.

"I need pie. Anything we need to do around Saratoga?"

"You want to go all the way to Big Basin for pie?" Darcy turned, staring Sorensen straight in the face.

"We can always ask the pimp if he knows Mitchell. Good Sam is close."

"Your sense of direction is as horrible as your sense of style," Darcy said, already tapping on his phone. "Greenlee's Bakery. Does that measure up?"

"Ah, that's good. They have the best cinnamon bread in town. Let's go."

It didn't take them long to get there on surface streets. They spotted the brown building with the green awnings a few blocks away and parked in the first available spot.

Darcy could smell the cinnamon even before he opened the door to the store. He was surprised when he realized his mouth was watering. He ordered a cup of coffee and got cinnamon bread.

"You should get two orders."

"I'm fine," Darcy said.

"You'll come back, I guarantee it."

Darcy ignored him and walked to the farthest table. He chose the chair with the back against the wall. Sorensen came a moment later, moving the chair that faced Darcy to the side so he could also view the front door.

"We got a warrant we can't use until Virago tells us the sweep is done." Darcy sipped his coffee. It was black and steaming. His stomach rumbled. He should have ordered a sandwich instead.

"We have no idea where this guy is, and he's really good. Even if we can search his place, I don't think he would have left us any gifts . . . Unless he wanted us to find them."

Darcy took his fork and cut off a piece of the gooey bread. The moment he put it in his mouth, it melted.

"Holy crap, you were not kidding. This is amazing," he said with his mouth full.

"I told you, you should have gotten two pieces."

"You were right."

Darcy bowed his head. Before he took another bite, he went to the counter and got a second serving. Sitting back, he said, "We need to go after Bishop."

Sorensen nodded. "He's the weakest link."

CHAPTER 96

Ethan sat inside the car, about a block away from the entrance to the park. The car he'd stolen was indistinct, and he was sure it wouldn't call any attention. He sipped his perfect cappuccino. He savored it and then swallowed before taking another sip. He did this until he was done. The ham and cheese sandwich remained untouched on the passenger seat.

He was pleased with himself. He figured they'd found the detective's wife already, unharmed. He felt smug. All he'd wanted to do was to mess with them. Because he could. He knew they would have dedicated a bunch of resources to finding "one of their own." He also wanted to send a message. A very loud and clear message that said, "I can do whatever I want, and you can't do anything to stop me."

He checked his watch. It was almost 1300 hours. He wondered if he had enough time to say good-bye to his mother but figured he shouldn't. He was sure they were watching her place just in case he showed up. He would send for her when things cooled down a little.

There was only one more loose end he needed to take care of. There was nothing glamorous about doing what needed to be done, but somebody had to do it.

He picked up the prepaid cell he'd just bought and called Bishop. He thought he would have to work hard to convince him to meet up, but Bishop wanted to get the hell out of CA and needed the money Ethan was offering to do so. After giving him instructions on where to meet, he got out of the car and fetched the big duffel bag from the trunk. He only had thirty minutes to get ready.

CHAPTER 97

Darcy pulled out his phone and scrolled a couple screens until he found the tracker app he was looking for. He tapped on it, and a map opened. There was a green dot, flashing.

"It looks like he's home."

He showed Sorensen the screen.

"You know that's illegal, right?" Sorensen took the last piece of his cinnamon bread and washed it down with soda.

"Nope. I have a warrant."

"When did you get that?"

"Earlier today. I asked Virago to get me one for Bishop and one for Mitchell."

"Sometimes you surprise me." Sorensen got up and started heading to the door. "Very rarely in a good way," Sorensen added, and opened the door to let Darcy go out first.

As he did, Darcy locked eyes with his partner. They were framed with crow's-feet, and they were smiling. Maybe we've turned a corner, Darcy thought.

"He's moving," Darcy said when he sat in the car and checked his phone again.

"Where to?"

"I don't know yet. He's heading south. Keep going down The Alameda. We may run into him."

"But I don't want to stop him. Better we see where's he's going first."

"That's what I'm thinking."

Darcy continued to update Sorensen with Bishop's position. At least he was hoping it was Bishop and not somebody else using his phone.

"Turn right on First. He's still going south."

First Street became Monterey Highway, and they continued on. As Bishop turned, Darcy updated Sorensen.

"Where the hell's he going?"

"No idea, but he's slowing down." A second later he added, "He took a right on Cedar Road."

"Oh shit, he's going to the park."

Sorensen accelerated.

"You think we'll lose him there?"

"No, the Dot Tracker app should be okay even with the trees, but Bishop may spot us."

Sorensen passed a couple cars on the right.

"The park has been closed a few months for renovations or something."

As Sorensen had predicted, Darcy watched Bishop's green flashing dot take a left into the parking lot at Honey Park and then stop for less than a minute. The Jeep followed him there but didn't enter the lot until the dot started moving again. The detectives left the car behind. Darcy put on his vest and brushed his hand over his extra magazines just to check they were still there.

When they entered the park, they noticed the gate was open, but there was no one in sight. They passed the swings on their left and continued walking north toward the puppet theater. The dot stopped, and they did too for a second, then began to search for a visual of Bishop through the trees.

"Let's make sure it's him first," Sorensen said, grabbing Darcy by the arm, making him slow down.

"But if it's not him, then it won't matter," Darcy said, wanting to push on.

The dot remained stationary. They walked by another building, passed some trees and spotted Bishop standing by a dry fountain.

Darcy watched Bishop pace. His hands were in his pockets. He didn't seem to be hiding anything bulky, but his gaze was strained, as if he was trying to see something and the trees weren't letting him.

"He's here to meet somebody. I'm going to check around," Darcy said. "You got this?"

Sorensen waved him off and accelerated toward Bishop.

Darcy took a right and headed to a run-down building. He looked over his shoulder and saw Bishop react when Sorensen reached him. That's when the dot appeared on Bishop's chest. It was red, small, and very bright.

Time seemed to slow down. Darcy's call to take cover was buried by a shot. Sorensen's body fell on top of the target beside the fountain.

"Are you hit?" Darcy yelled, making a 180 and running back toward his partner.

Silence. Sorensen wasn't moving, and Darcy couldn't see Bishop underneath his partner's mass.

CHAPTER 98

"Are you hurt?" Darcy shouted again as three more shots shattered the fountain, spraying cement shrapnel several feet away.

Before he reached them, Sorensen rolled onto his side and dragged Bishop behind the base for cover. Another two shots hit the structure, blowing off the side where Sorensen had just been.

"You okay?" Darcy asked, taking cover behind a tree.

"Yes, yes," Sorensen said under his breath, but loud enough for Darcy to hear.

"I'm going after him."

Darcy started running toward where the shots had come from. The only sounds he could hear were his shoes hitting the ground and his heart pounding. The path ended, and he slowed down through the trees. There were no more shots. He now heard nothing but a few birds and the distant sound of traffic growing closer. Finally, he reached the end of the park and faced a long parking lot with only two cars in it.

It was much larger than the one they'd parked at, and as he walked, he felt completely exposed. He scanned the empty place and pulled his Glock to his chest as he closed in on the first car. It was an old Datsun, rusty and overflowing with dirty clothes and garbage. He looked over the hood and then ran to the other car, finding it also empty.

After Darcy cleared the parking lot, he walked back to the fountain and found Sorensen and Bishop gone. He saw them a few yards ahead, heading toward where they had parked. Sorensen was dragging Bishop by the arm.

"Holy shit, I'm amazed how hard the bullet hits you, even with the vest," Sorensen said as soon as Darcy caught up with them.

When they reached the car, Sorensen shoved Bishop into the backseat. Darcy rode next to him to the station and called the captain with the update.

"Put him in Room 4. I want all of us to watch," Virago told Sorensen as soon as they walked into the bullpen.

Even though her face was stern, the right side of her mouth was tilted slightly upwards.

Darcy was starting to recognize her unintentional cues. She was probably relieved that they'd been able to contain the situation without additional casualties.

The two of them watched Sorensen place a can of Red Bull on the table close to where he was sitting. Bishop looked at it with indifference but didn't say anything.

"You want something to drink?" Sorensen asked.

Silence.

"Listen, dude, I just saved your life."

Bishop's lips puckered.

"I got the frigging hole in the vest to prove it."

"You guys probably staged it," Bishop finally said.

"Are you fucking kidding me? Why would we do that?"

Bishop didn't answer.

"Okay. Play it that way. But Mitchell, the guy you're protecting, just tried to kill you. Whether you want to believe it or not, you're screwed. You're going to jail, and if this guy really wants you dead, there's no easier place to get that done than there."

"Why would he want me dead? Uh? He saved my life. There's no way he would shoot at me."

"So who then? One of the other guys?" Bishop looked at Sorensen, challenging him. "I'm fairly certain it wasn't . . . since they're all dead."

For the first time since the shooting, Bishop showed surprise. Sorensen realized he finally had an in.

"Ah, you didn't know, did you?"

The Marine looked away. He tucked his smaller foot behind the other one and crossed his arms.

"Samuel Barr was killed after he ran over a woman right outside our station. Curtis Gutierrez was killed after he assassinated Carlos de la Rosa. Alex MacAlister was killed by a shot in the head and burned in his uncle's warehouse this morning. So it's only you and Mitchell left."

Before Bishop could protest, Sorensen continued: "It's either you trying to clean up this mess, or it's Mitchell." He let the statement settle for a few seconds. "You tell me."

Sorensen got up and left the room. He came back a minute later with a cup of coffee. He set it by Bishop, sat back down and crossed his arms over his ample stomach.

"You have to be lying," Bishop said. There was no conviction in his voice anymore. He watched the steam rising from the black liquid.

Sorensen left again. Darcy met him right outside with the case files for each suspect. Sorensen walked back in and closed the door behind him. He placed the folders on the table and squared each corner, forming a neat stack. He opened the first one and pulled out a close-up shot of a burnt head with a very visible exit wound in the forehead.

Bishop pushed the coffee mug away but glanced at the photo. Sorensen pulled a print from each file and placed them on the table so that they faced Bishop.

The Marine rubbed the bridge of his nose and then this eyes. He finally took a very long sigh and, leaning against the chair, said, "What do you want?"

"We want to know where we can find Mitchell."

"I don't know where he is. Try his condo."

"He blew up the lobby this morning."

Bishop didn't say anything.

"Apparently he decided he didn't like his security guard anymore."

There was still a hint of disbelief in Bishop's face, so Sorensen pulled out a photo of the lobby peppered with Jamal Johnston's body parts.

"Bishop, you're a Marine. I understand your loyalty, but Mitchell is getting rid of everybody who can tie him to Malik and de la Rosa. That means he won't stop until you are the next picture on this table."

Bishop covered his face with his hands and let a long breath out.

"I don't know where he is. Really. He talked about going to the beach, somewhere far away, once this job was over."

"He hasn't left the country yet. Do you know if he was going to drive?"

"Well, obviously that wasn't the original plan," he scoffed.

"What else can you tell me? Does he have a girlfriend? Is he close to anybody?"

Bishop started wringing his hands.

"Come on, you got to give me something."

"He's close to his mom."

CHAPTER 99

Sorensen sprinted out of the room. Darcy and Virago met him outside. They all moved away from the door so Bishop wouldn't hear them.

"Go back in there and try to get more," Virago said to Sorensen.

He nodded but didn't move.

"Lynch, I want you to get whatever you can on the mother so we can arrest her. You better do it in less than thirty seconds. We need to act before Mitchell gets too far."

Darcy went to his desk and called Jon. While he typed, he shared all the information with the intern so they could both work different angles at the same time.

A few moments later Virago poked her head out of the view room. "What do you have?"

"Nothing. This woman's clean. There's a parking ticket, but she actually paid it."

"Then make something up. We don't have time."

Darcy looked up at her. Jon was still on speaker.

"What do you mean, 'Make something up'?"

"Exactly what it sounds like. Call your reporter buddies and tell them you are about to arrest the mother of our number-one suspect in the Los Altos homicide for aiding and abetting a dangerous criminal and now fugitive."

Darcy felt his jaw actually drop.

Virago must have seen it, because she said, "You can close your mouth, Detective. I want this done now. Get to it."

Darcy hung up the phone with Jon and dialed Janet Hagen, his contact at Channel 6. He whispered the news story as if it were a secret and confirmed that the newscaster would be at Mitchell's mom's house in twenty minutes.

"We got fifteen to get there," he yelled at Virago as soon as he was off the phone.

"You head out there. Sorensen and I will stay here. There will be ten cars, full spinners and sirens, as soon as you give them the go."

Darcy nodded.

"And Detective," she said, grabbing his attention again before he left the bullpen. "I don't want a single shot fired."

"You got it."

Before he got to the elevator, he realized he still didn't have a car. Man, this is getting old, he thought, and went back to get Virago's. She threw him the keys as soon as she saw him coming back.

While he sped through the streets, Darcy had Jon call the mother to ensure she was home. The house was a modest rambler in East San Jose, with a chain-link fence, a tall dead tree, and a few rosebushes, which stood in the middle of the yard.

As soon as he parked, he called the unis. He was still in his car when he heard the first sirens. The first patrol car pulled into the street and stopped. An officer got out and ran toward him as backup. Darcy waited.

A second later there were about seven police cars rushing in and still a few more arriving. As the unis came, they killed the sirens but left the spinners on. Once the last car arrived, an eerie silence engulfed the entire street.

Another glance behind him. The first news van had arrived. Now the show could start.

CHAPTER 100

Ethan's plan to go to a beach after the job was done hadn't involved getting there by car. He knew it was now the only way to get out of the country. So Ethan drove south. When he was close to Carmel, he heard the news on the radio. He slammed on the brakes harder than he intended, then pulled over on the side of the road.

He activated his phone and swiped the screen until he found the news app. The blond newscaster appeared. Ethan fumbled with the phone and almost dropped it on the floor before he was able to get it on speaker and turn the volume up.

". . . as you can see behind me, the police are now arresting Mrs. Dolores Mitchell, on charges of felony murder and aiding and abetting her son to escape. Could Dolores Mitchell be the Ma Barker of the twenty-first century?" The shine in the anchor's eyes made Ethan's gut churn.

"She's been arrested and will be transported to the Santa Clara Sheriff's Office for questioning. Mrs. Mitchell is fifty-three years old and suffers from MS . . ."

Ethan stopped listening. Behind the anchor he could see the deputies surrounding his mother's house. The door was off the hinges. His mother was being escorted by the fat detective's partner, Lynch, and an officer.

He noticed that his left hand was grasping the steering wheel so hard that circulation to the tips of his fingers had stopped. He let go and opened and closed his fist a few times until he felt the blood flow again.

Still watching, Ethan put the car back in gear and drove until he found an exit. He took it and stopped at the first gas station he found, parked but didn't get out. He was still watching the blond woman behind the big microphone with the Channel 6 News logo talk about his mother. The camera finally left the anchor and followed a car disappearing down the street, with his mother inside.

"This is bullshit!" he shouted inside the car at no one in particular.

He threw the phone onto the passenger seat and put the car in gear. He got back on Highway 101—but now he was heading north.

CHAPTER 101

Darcy followed the patrol car, but he was only half paying attention. He kept looking at his phone. He knew it would ring. He was just hoping it would be sooner rather than later. After about fifteen minutes, he entered the station's garage and caught up with the officer processing Mrs. Mitchell.

Darcy removed the cuffs, then escorted her into one of the nicer interview rooms. They hadn't exchanged a word since he arrested her.

"Can I get some water please?" the woman asked once she took a seat. She was shaking like a leaf.

Darcy nodded, but before he could leave to get it, the door opened and Virago walked in with a pitcher.

"Hello, Mrs. Mitchell," she said, setting a paper cup near the woman. "I'm Captain Virago."

She poured some water and nodded for Darcy to leave.

As he walked toward the door, he checked his phone. Still nothing. He met Sorensen outside, and they both walked into the observation room.

"Do you think it's going to work?" Sorensen asked.

"I really hope so. Have you been checking your phone? He may call you."

"Yep, nothing here. Maybe he calls the station. Who knows?"

As if on cue, Darcy's phone rang. The number was blocked. He nodded to the technician to start the trace. "Detective Lynch," he answered, and put it on speaker. He glanced at the door to check if it was closed. It was.

"You think you're very smart," Mitchell said.

"Not as much as you are, apparently," Darcy said.

"You know you have nothing on my mother."

"You need to turn yourself in, or your mother's going to prison for a long time."

"You have nothing on her. Charges won't stick."

"We can be very resourceful when needed." Darcy looked at Sorensen, who shrugged his shoulders as if saying, It might work.

Silence.

"Turn yourself in," Darcy said. "We have Bishop and Higgins. When we find you, it'll be much worse for you."

Mitchell scoffed. Darcy watched Sorensen wipe the sweat off his forehead, then dry his hand on his pants.

"I have the pro from the party—do you care at all about her?" Mitchell asked.

"Is she dead?" Darcy asked, and looked at Sorensen. The seconds of silence felt like minutes. He suspected Mitchell was probably sweating as much as his partner was.

"Let my mother go, and I will tell you where she is."

"Is she still alive?"

"Maybe. I will call you in exactly one hour. I want my Mom happily home by then. If she is, I'll tell you where you can find the hooker."

"You know that won't work. I can only let your mother go after you've turned yourself in."

The laugh at the other end of the line was loud and almost sounded genuine. There was something sinister about it.

"Detective, you care a whole lot more about the hooker than I care about my mother."

CHAPTER 102

"Can you buy more time?" Virago asked as soon as Darcy told her what had happened.

"I don't have a way to reach him," Darcy said.

She rubbed her eyes and paced the length of the room. Darcy wondered how she managed to not run into anything while she did that.

"Anything from the trace?" she asked.

Darcy shook his head.

"Do we really think Aislin's still alive?" Sorensen asked.

"It's the only body that hasn't turned up yet."

Darcy looked at the case boards on the other side of the bullpen. He suddenly thought of something, and walked out of the room. He reached his desk and rummaged through the case files until he found the one he wanted. Grabbed it and walked back to Virago's office. They both waited until he spoke.

Darcy flipped page after page of his notes until he found what he was looking for.

"Here. I think I have something," he said, stabbing a word nobody else could see.

"What, for Christ's sakes?" Sorensen asked.

"Well, remember when we went to Mitchell's condo? We were talking to Jamal Johnston, and he told us that Mitchell has the best two-bedroom in the entire building."

"Yeah, so what?" Sorensen's voice had that annoyed tone he got when Darcy was starting to piss him off.

"When we went to talk to Mitchell, I went snooping. I only saw one bedroom." Darcy looked from one to the other, his eye shining, but found no reciprocity. "Don't you get it?"

"No. So Johnston had it wrong. So what?"

"Or," Darcy offered, "Johnston got it right." Without further explanation, he left Virago and Sorensen as clueless as they had been before and ran to his desk to call Jon.

"I need you to find who sold Mitchell his condo. The security guard said he'd bought it a couple years ago."

"Okay, let me see."

Darcy could hear the intern typing on the keyboard.

"How are you doing, by the way?" Darcy asked.

"Better every day. I think they said they might release me next weekend."

"Early enough for Thanksgiving?"

"Maybe." Before Darcy could say anything, he added, "I found it. Lily Folsom."

Jon gave him her contact info. Darcy thanked him, and as soon as he hung up he dialed her number. A woman answered after the second ring. Her voice was assertive, clear, and sophisticated. She probably catered only to the rich. Darcy wondered again about how much money Mitchell really had.

He introduced himself and gave her enough information for context, then said, "I need to know if the condo you sold him was a one- or two-bedroom."

"It was a one-bedroom," she said.

He felt as if a brick wall had just fallen on him. "Are you sure? The security guard in the building seemed to think it had two."

"Well, technically it did." She paused. When he didn't say anything else, she went on: "Originally the condo had two bedrooms, but the previous owners had converted one into a safe room."

"Yes." Darcy punched the table and smiled. Then, realizing he had Virago and Sorensen's attention, he waved them over. He put the phone on speaker.

"What can you tell me about the safe room?" he asked, checking that the other two were now on the same page.

"Pretty standard. Disguised by a bookcase. Biometrics to get in. Full video and comm system."

"Can the manufacturer get in?"

"Well, I believe they always have a way to override the system."

"Who was the manufacturer?"

"I don't know offhand. I'll look it up in my files."

"Okay, we'll wait," Darcy said.

After a brief moment, she said, "I'm showing a mansion in ten minutes. I can call you in about an hour and half."

"Miss Folsom, this is a matter of life and death. I need this information in the next thirty seconds. Call your assistant." Darcy looked at Sorensen.

"She doesn't have access."

"Well, you better give it to her then," Darcy pushed.

Miss Folsom smacked her lips so hard it almost sounded as if she'd hung up the phone. "Give me five minutes."

They hung up and waited. Sorensen went to the vending machine for another cold drink. Darcy went to get coffee for himself and Virago.

The phone didn't ring. They all stared at it as they sipped their drinks.

"We only have forty-three minutes left," Virago said.

"Let me head over there. When she calls, patch me in so I can listen," Darcy said.

"You go too," she told Sorensen.

Darcy still had her keys, so they ran downstairs to Virago's car. As soon as they got in, Sorensen's phone rang. He put it on speaker.

"She just called. The manufacturer is Barusch and Sons. I'll give them a call and get a patrol to go pick them up and take them to Mitchell's."

CHAPTER 103

The entrance of the High Sights building was an eyesore. It was still black with soot, and the smell of ash assaulted Darcy's nostrils the moment they walked inside.

They met with the Mountain View Police officer who was guarding the area. "Everybody was evacuated, and the bomb squad finished the sweep about a half hour ago. There's nobody inside," the officer said after they introduced themselves.

"We need to go into one of the units," Darcy said.

"The elevators don't work." The officer looked apologetic.

"Oh, you've got to be kidding me. There's no way to get one working for a little bit?" Sorensen asked.

"I'm afraid not." He shook his head for emphasis.

"I think you'll be climbing the twenty-three flights by yourself, my friend," Sorensen said to Darcy.

"See, I told you you needed to get in shape. You never know when you'll need to sprint in hot pursuit, or climb some stairs." He started walking toward the emergency exit door. "Call me as soon as the guy shows up from the Barusch company."

"You better pray he's fit, or you'll be doing this remotely."

Darcy stopped walking for a moment. That thought hadn't occurred to him.

The first five flights weren't a problem. Darcy was actually almost enjoying getting his heart rate up. The next five were not as pleasant, and by the time he reached the fifteenth floor he no longer had a spring in his step. When he was about to step on the landing for the twentieth floor, his phone rang.

"Yeah?" He was hoping to hide it, but he was out of breath, and it showed.

"Enjoying it much?"

"I hope you didn't call to mock me. At least I'm doing it."

He kept climbing.

"Yeah, yeah. I'll tell Virago to give you a commendation or something. Anyway, the guy's here. He's like you, so he'll be meeting you up there in a couple minutes."

"Great."

Darcy hung up.

Nothing on the twenty-third floor would indicate that the building had been vacated. It looked normal. Quiet, but not spookily quiet. He was about to walk down the hallway but then decided to wait for the guy. He checked his watch. They had less than twenty minutes before Mitchell would call again. If he was punctual.

A few minutes later a tall, lanky guy in his late twenties opened the emergency exit door and met him on the landing.

"Darcy Lynch." He extended his hand.

The man looked at it for a second, as if he wasn't sure what to do with it, then took it. His shake was surprisingly strong.

"Roberto Gonzalez," he said.

Maybe not all the "sons" were actual sons of Barusch, Darcy thought.

"You installed this one?" Darcy asked, already rushing down the hallway.

Roberto, still a bit out of breath, followed suit.

"Yes," he said. "It was one of my first jobs. Well, I assisted. I didn't do the installation myself, but Mr. Barusch couldn't make it because he's in a wheelchair."

They reached the door, and Darcy picked the lock. The place looked exactly as it had when he was there with Sorensen. He didn't really know where to go, so he took step aside and let Roberto lead.

The kid took a piece of paper from his jacket pocket, unfolded and studied it for a few seconds.

"I remember now," he said, looking up. "It's behind the bookshelf."

Darcy followed his stare and saw the floor-to-ceiling bookshelf that he didn't even think twice about when he was here last time.

"You can open it?" Darcy asked.

Roberto had managed to figure out what books were hiding the keypad to gain access.

"Yeah. Every single one of these things has an override."

"Doesn't that defeat the purpose?"

"Uh? No," Roberto said, and looked at Darcy, pausing what he was doing.

Darcy urged him to continue, pointing at the keypad with his hand, and explained, "If somebody can gain access to the override, the safe room is not that safe."

Roberto didn't say anything for a few moments. Darcy wondered if he was thinking about his comment, or the kid was concentrating on what he was doing.

Then he stopped again and, pushing his glasses up on the top of his nose, he said, "Well, I guess it depends on what you want the room for. I guess it is possible that somebody could get the override code and then do a home invasion, but we keep the codes pretty well safeguarded, so I don't know."

Darcy looked at his watch. Nine minutes to go.

"Please go on. We don't have a lot of time."

"Right, right."

Roberto flipped over the paper and looked at some scribbles. He punched in a few numbered sequences and waited. There was no green light flashing; there was no sound of a door opening.

"Hummm," Roberto said.

"What? What's going on?"

"Well, that should have worked."

"What does that mean? You can't open it?"

Seven minutes.

"This should have opened it." He looked at the paper again, then at the keypad. "Let me try again. Maybe I mistyped something."

Roberto tapped the keys a bit more slowly this time. At the end of the sequence, nothing happened.

"What?" Darcy asked, wanting to pace up and down the living room, but he remained where he was.

"I don't understand."

"Well, fix it. We have five minutes left." Darcy raised his voice.

"I have to call my boss. Maybe he wrote it down wrong."

Roberto pulled his cell out of his pocket and made the call. Darcy watched his every move, listened to each word, only breaking his stare to check the time. He was starting to hope that Mitchell wasn't a punctual man. But he was sure he was.

"We have three minutes," Darcy said as the kid listened to what his boss was saying on the receiver.

Roberto moved back to the keypad. He held the phone between his ear and his shoulder, and while he listened he started pressing keys again.

CHAPTER 104

Ethan knew he wouldn't be able to make it all the way to San Jose in one hour. But he would be close. Besides, he had to be really careful about how he moved through the city. There were webcams and cops that could spot him. Then the game would be over.

He had one more hand to play. It would either work and his mom would be left alone, or it wouldn't. The charges were bogus, and he doubted they would actually fabricate evidence against her, but he couldn't be a hundred percent sure they wouldn't. What worried him most was her health. They could make her life miserable for a while, and she didn't deserve that. So the best thing that could happen was for them to release his mom in exchange for the hooker.

Ethan checked the clock on the dashboard and saw there were only five minutes until the detective's time was up. He saw the E Dunne Ave exit and took it. Morgan Hill was a good town to stop in and make a call. He took a left on Murphy Avenue and then a right on James Court. He parked under a tree. He wasn't too paranoid about satellites, but one couldn't be too careful.

He looked at the dashboard. The time showed 4:43 p.m. He checked his watch to confirm and then dialed from his throwaway. It rang. After the third ring, he started to wonder if the detective wasn't going to pick up. He checked the number. He had it memorized. It was correct. The phone rang one more time. Ethan stared at his watch as the time changed to 4:44 p.m.

After the fifth ring, the voice mail kicked in. He couldn't believe it. He hung up. Still holding the phone, Ethan looked up through the windshield. There was a huge house at the end of the courtyard. The phone lay inert, resting in his hand. This was the first time he'd been genuinely surprised since this operation started. Not even when Malik died of a heart attack had he been as stunned as he was now.

"Maybe the dick has the ringer off," he wondered out loud, and decided to call again.

The phone rang. And rang. But this time it only rang three times. Then the voice mail started again. For a second, Ethan considered leaving a message, but he decided against it. He wasn't sure he would be able to mask the surprise he felt. He hung up.

"What the fuck?" he yelled as he smashed the phone against the dashboard until it broke into pieces. One edge dug into his palm, making him bleed. He didn't even feel the pain, but the stickiness of the blood made him stop. "Fuck!" he yelled again, and hurled the remaining bits of the phone on the floor.

Ethan grabbed his duffel bag from the backseat and searched inside until he found his emergency kit. He inspected the gash. It was about two inches long and probably a quarter-inch deep. He poured disinfectant on and sewed a few stitches, then covered it with antiseptic tape. He put both hands on the steering wheel but didn't start the car. He stared out in front of him at the huge house and thought about what had just happened.

Either the asshole missed the call—doubtful—or they'd decided they were going to play hard to get.

A third option was lurking, but he wasn't ready to consider it yet.

CHAPTER 105

"I need the paramedics right now!" Darcy shouted into the phone before he let it drop on the floor.

Aislin was unconscious, propped against the wall with one arm raised by a chain hooked to the ceiling. Both wrists were crusted with dry blood, and the one holding her up was raw almost to the bone.

"Go to the emergency exit where you came in and wait for the paramedics, then run back here with them," he told Roberto.

The kid didn't move. He seemed in shock, as if he couldn't believe what he was seeing.

"Now." Darcy snapped his fingers in front of his face.

"Right. Sorry," he apologized, and ran out of the safe room.

Darcy managed to get the chain unhooked from the ceiling. He picked her up and carried her out of the room. The clanking behind them was deafening. He laid her down on the sofa and checked her pulse. It was faint, and her lips and nails were surprisingly blue.

He grabbed a blanket from Ethan's bedroom and covered her. He then went back to the torture chamber to pick up his phone. That's when he saw that he had two missed calls. The number was blocked.

He'd missed Mitchell's calls.

While he waited for the paramedics, he thought about Mitchell. Two calls. That was significant. Mitchell wanted to talk to Darcy more than Darcy had imagined. Nobody calls twice when they have the upper hand.

Interesting.

"Hey, Mitchell called. Twice," he told Sorensen on the phone.

"Twice? What did he say?"

"I missed them."

Silence.

"Okay, the paramedics are here. As soon as they reach you, come back down. We got a lot of shit to do," Sorensen said.

Darcy looked at Aislin, now covered all the way up to her neck. She looked like a little girl sleeping, except for the blue lips. There were no other sign on her face of what she'd just gone through.

A few minutes later the paramedics burst into the room. Darcy wondered how they were able to climb twenty-three floors with all their equipment and the gurney in such a short amount of time. He felt old.

"What can you tell me, Detective?" a burly guy with a healthy mustache asked him while the other two started working on Aislin. His name tag said "Gowan."

"She's probably been here since Tuesday night. She's suffered numerous bouts of torture. Some of the injuries look fresher than others. She might have been poisoned."

Gowan looked at Aislin, then nodded when he saw her blue lips. Darcy shared as many details as he could about her, the investigation, and Mitchell.

"Can you take her to O'Connor in San Jose?" Darcy asked.

"Why? That's pretty far." The paramedic sounded annoyed.

"Her sister's there. She was in a hit-and-run Thursday and is slowly recuperating."

"Some bad luck."

"Related case."

"Okay, we'll assess on the way." Gowan eyed Aislin, then added, "But we may have to go to Stanford."

"I understand. Thanks."

Darcy shook Gowan's hand before heading out.

The hallway seemed shorter than when he had come in, and he ran down the stairs. Even though it was much easier going down than climbing them, Darcy was out of breath by the time he reached Sorensen.

"You drive," Darcy said, handing him Virago's keys.

"Finally."

CHAPTER 106

"So, you missed two calls?" Sorensen asked once they were in the car driving on Highway 101 back to the station.

"Yeah, back to back. No voice mail."

"You know for sure it was him?"

"Well, it was a blocked number, but the first one was exactly at 4:43 p.m."

"And you didn't answer?"

Darcy eyed him and felt a burning sensation building up in his gut. Sorensen didn't meet his stare.

"You didn't see what this bastard did to Saffron's sister. He's an animal."

"Just busting your chops." The side of Sorensen's mouth turned slightly upwards.

Darcy shook his head. He should have known better than to fall for it.

"How is she?"

"Alive. Barely."

Darcy described what he found when they opened the safe room.

"That guy's a real psycho," Sorensen said after hearing the full description. "He can't possibly know that we got the girl."

Darcy thought about this. That was probably true.

"Okay, so let's say he doesn't know," Darcy started speculating. "And let's say he calls back. What do we tell him?"

Sorensen smiled. "That you were in the bathroom."

Darcy ignored him. "We need to get Mitchell to come in." He rubbed his left temple. It felt sore. "We need to tell him we've found the girl so he knows he's got no leverage left."

"The question is, does he really care about his mother enough to turn himself in?" Sorensen turned the car into the station's parking lot.

"I doubt it." Darcy saw his partner close his eyes and nod in agreement.

CHAPTER 107

"Okay," Ethan told himself, "I'm going to have to call back." He was heading north on Highway 101, driving just a few miles per hour faster than the limit so as to not raise suspicion. He would reach San Jose in about thirty minutes. He needed to seriously think about what he was going to do next.

Calling the detective again would make him appear even weaker. He was upset with himself for having called the second time. He hadn't made a rookie mistake in a long time, and it seemed that in the past twenty-four hours he'd forgotten all his years of experience. What he needed to do was to cool his head.

Traffic was light in this direction. The sun was gone. It would have been another gorgeous evening in Northern California if not for the fact that he was a hair away from being arrested and put away for life, if not killed. He needed to seriously consider whether freeing his mother was the most important thing he could do at the moment.

CHAPTER 108

The station was bursting with people. It was after six, but nobody was going home. Darcy grabbed two cups of coffee on the way in and met Sorensen in Virago's office. Placing one on the captain's desk, he gave her the play-by-play.

"Will she make it?" she asked when he was done.

"Gowan just called me. They didn't take Aislin to O'Connor to be with Saffron," Darcy updated them. "Even though the burns and lacerations don't seem to be life threatening, they believe she's been severely poisoned."

"She'll need major therapy if she makes it," Virago said.

"And a change of lifestyle," Sorensen added.

"Whoa," Darcy said.

"Hey, I know she's your girl's sister and all, but she's a prostitute. Nothing good comes from that."

"Okay, enough." Virago put a hand up to stop the bickering. "How are we going to catch this guy?"

"No way to trace the call," Darcy said, still staring at Sorensen, who was ignoring him.

"Do you think he'll call back?"

"If he does, what do we say?" Sorensen asked.

"Maybe we need to give another news update." Darcy met some arching eyebrows in response. "I'm serious. This guy thinks he has some leverage, right? He has the girl, she's hidden, and we have his mother. He wants the mom in exchange for the girl. If we have the girl and the mom, what does he have?"

"He may run. He's already told you he doesn't care a whole lot about anything, including his mother." Before anybody could say anything, Sorensen added, "Asshole."

"He cared enough to try to negotiate and then make two phone calls. He may be saying he doesn't care, but I think his actions tell a different story," Virago said. "You okay with this?" she asked Sorensen.

"I've got no better plan."

"Okay, go for it, but this time . . . answer the phone when he calls," she said to Darcy.

"Jesus." Darcy stood. When he reached his desk, he called the news anchor.

CHAPTER 109

Ethan passed the "Welcome to Santa Clara County" sign. After a few miles, he took the Curtner exit and drove east until he saw the entrance for the Oak Hill Funeral Home and Memorial Park. He pulled into the parking lot and backed into the last spot. He locked the car and walked into the graveyard.

There was something unique about cemeteries. They were always green, well kept, and in a sorrowful way they were pretty. He got off the main path and started walking on the grass between the gravestones toward the fountain. The moon was shining through the trees. He was listening to the local news through his earbuds. The weather, the traffic. Nothing interesting. BART was on strike again.

"We have breaking news," the anchor said, a bit of excitement in his voice.

Ethan stopped walking, his neck suddenly moist with cold sweat. While he listened, he pulled his phone out of this pocket and tapped the app for Channel 6 News, switching to the coverage on TV.

"The Santa Clara Sheriff's Office has made an incredible rescue today. A woman, the only surviving victim of the Los Altos massacre, was found barely alive."

Ethan stopped walking. He felt a bead of sweat trickle down his back. He passed the first set of low walls and finally reached the fountain. Sitting by Saint Thomas, he watched as the good-looking anchor shattered his world with each word.

"The police believe that she was kidnapped by the main suspect in the case, Ethan Mitchell, and subsequently tortured in his condo. She's in critical condition, but there's hope that she'll be able to give a statement before the end of the day. The hospital she is being treated at is being kept confidential at this time."

When she finished the update and they moved on to traffic again, Ethan set the phone down next to him and looked up at the gravestones. He rested covered his face with both hands. The game was over. He needed to leave. He needed to escape. Ethan stood, pulled the earbuds out and shut the app in the middle of another BART update.

He started walking toward his brother's grave but stopped a few yards short, knowing that he wouldn't be able to face him. He had failed.

Ethan turned and walked back to his car, every footstep heavy on the pavement. There was not much he could do for his mother now.

Before he got back in his car, he looked over his shoulder in the direction of his brother's grave. He was a lot of things, but a coward wasn't one of them. He wasn't going to run like a fucking dog with his tail between his legs. If he had to go down, he was going to take somebody down with him.

CHAPTER 110

Sorensen had left to fetch some dinner. Darcy clicked his mouse, browsing through the crime scene photos, hoping to find something that would indicate where Mitchell might be. So far he had nothing.

"Lynch, can you come here a sec?" Captain Virago waved him in from her office.

Darcy welcomed the distraction. He locked his computer, walked in and sat on the chair closest to the door.

"What's up?"

She didn't answer right away. Virago leaned back in her chair and pushed her reading glasses up onto her head.

Darcy watched her. She was taking too long to speak. Something was up. Did IA finish their report yet? He rubbed his temple and looked at her.

"I talked to SJPD," she finally said.

He stopped rubbing.

"They approved the transfer. Should happen in the next two to four weeks."

Her eyes looked dull. He wondered if it was just fatigue.

"Okay . . ." Darcy scooted back.

"I haven't told the others yet."

He felt removed, almost as if they were in a teleconference rather than a face-to-face meeting.

"SJPD red-lighted your transfer."

He took a long time to exhale, then combed his short hair back with one hand.

"Given the recent shootings—"

"I'm going to be cleared—you know that," he cut her off.

She nodded. "They want the investigations to be closed and found in your favor. Then they want to see what happens in the next few months."

"How will they know what happens if you're not going to be here to give them a report?" he spat, before he stood and walked toward the door.

"Lynch, sit down. I'm not done."

He leaned against the closed door.

She went on: "I told them I don't want anybody else." She let her words settle in. "So they agreed to hold the position open, but on stand-by, until it's time to reevaluate your application."

"Don't bother. I like it here." He turned to leave but waited to open the door. "Is that it?"

"Yes." Her voice was coarse. She sounded more defeated than tired.

CHAPTER 111

It was almost ten o'clock, and Mitchell hadn't called. Darcy had felt like leaving after his little chat with Virago, but on his way out of the bullpen, he saw the photos of Saffron, Jon, and Aislin. He stopped and looked at the boards. De la Rosa and the other victims stared back at him, pleading. He went back to his desk and continued working.

Sorensen showed up a few minutes later with a couple pizzas, and they ate, mostly in silence. Then they spent the next few hours doing paperwork, updating the case boards and coming up with theories and courses of action, depending on what they imagined Mitchell might do.

Darcy continued to check the phone constantly, as if he was worried that it might ring and he wouldn't hear it. Sorensen also checked his with the same result.

Now they both sat at their desks. Darcy was playing with a pen, twirling it between his fingers. Sorensen was gnawing on the end of his.

"Go home, you two," Virago said on her way to the exit. "If he hasn't called by now, he may never." Before they could protest, she added, "And if he does, you both have each other on speed dial, so nothing's lost."

Neither moved.

Virago stopped walking. "Detectives, this was not an ask. It's an order. Go home. We have a lot of shit to do tomorrow, and I'm not even talking about closing the loop with Internal Affairs. So go home, get a good night's sleep and come up with some brilliant idea on how to get this son of a bitch tomorrow."

Sorensen took the tip of the pen out of his mouth and puffed.

Darcy got up and put his jacket on. "Fine," he said. He felt tired and was not terribly upset about being ordered home.

"Keep your phone on. Keep it charged," Sorensen told him.

"Yes, Dad," Darcy said, and waited for him on his way out.

"No stairs today?" Sorensen asked, pressing the elevator button.

"I think I did enough stairs for a while," Darcy said.

"Oh right. I forgot," Sorensen said, almost laughing.

When they got to the garage, Darcy stopped, realizing he didn't have a car. Man, this is getting really old, he thought.

Sorensen must have remembered the same thing, because he said, "I'll give you a ride."

"Sure?"

"Why not. Hospital or home?"

Darcy thought about it for a minute. He checked his watch. "Home. I don't think I can spend another night on the visitor's chair."

They rode mostly in silence. Darcy was sure they were both thinking about the case— where they were, what they had. There was no way to know what Mitchell would do next.

Right as Sorensen was pulling into Darcy's driveway, he said, "I hope to God we find him."

"Me too. He's bad news."

Darcy nodded good-bye and left the car. When he got to his front door, he was surprised that the porch light didn't come on. Really? he thought. "I'll deal with it tomorrow," he muttered.

CHAPTER 112

When Darcy opened his front door, the only thing he heard was rattling, as if a fox was trapped inside a cage and trying to escape. Then he heard Shelby whimper, more rattling, and a few yelps so loud that an ice-cold shiver ran through Darcy's body.

"Shelby?" he called after her.

The dog responded with barks that ended in cries for help.

Darcy pulled out his gun. He flipped the light switch on, but nothing happened. He strained his eye and took a step, then another, trying to listen for anything that wasn't his own breathing or his dog's yelps.

Shelby cried for him again. He wished he could tell her he was coming for her, but he knew he had to remain quiet.

Darcy finally reached the living room; the open kitchen was to his right. A quick glance confirmed all the knives were in their place. Good, he thought. He checked the other side of the room, where the fireplace was. Nothing. It looked undisturbed. Lola swam in her tank on the mantel, oblivious to Shelby's suffering.

Darcy still couldn't see his dog, but he could hear her. He figured she was getting more distressed as he was getting closer, making her yelp with each move.

With his back to the wall, he kept walking until he finally saw that his coffee table had been replaced by the most macabre thing he'd ever seen. Shelby was enclosed in a metal cage. The edges were thick, and metal hinges held the frame together. The sides were made of barbed and razor wire. An electrical current shocked the dog every time she moved and touched the metal. Darcy moved closer.

When Shelby saw him, she wagged her tail, getting shocked again. She yelped. Darcy's heart sunk. He showed her his palm and made a downward motion instructing her to lie down. The bottom of the cage wasn't electrified. The dog obeyed, and for the first time since he'd walked in, she stopped crying.

He continued walking by the wall until he could see the other side of the box. There was no cord plugged to the wall. Darcy couldn't understand how the awful box worked. He took a look around the room, his Glock close to his chest. He tightened his grip. Metal mesh and barbwire covered the sides. He touched a corner with the sole of his shoe, pushed on it. The frame didn't budge a hair. It was solid. Well made.

"I'll be right back," he mouthed to Shelby. He needed to get his tools from the garage.

He could see she didn't understand, her eyes dark with sadness when she saw him move away from her. His heart broke in a thousand pieces, and a ball of anger burnt his chest when she started whimpering again.

He knew he had to secure the premises before doing anything else, but he didn't know how long Shelby would last. As he reached the hallway, Mitchell appeared aiming a Beretta at him.Darcy raised his Glock.

"Don't even think about it," Mitchell said, aiming between Darcy's eyes.

"What do you want?" Darcy asked.

"Drop the Glock on the floor."

"I'm not going to do that."

Mitchell took a step closer and cupped the hand holding the gun. "And when you do, also remove your ankle weapon."

Darcy didn't move.

Mitchell fired. The bullet passed barely an inch away from Darcy's left ear and lodged in the wall.

Darcy fought the urge to shake his head to stop the ringing in his ear. He acquiesced and raised his arms over his head, then knelt down. He set the Glock on the floor and removed his concealed weapon, placing it next to the other one. Once he was upright, Mitchell walked toward him and pushed Darcy back into the living room.

Shelby started barking, moving and yelping again.

"What the hell do you want?" Darcy asked, wondering why Mitchell didn't shoot him dead.

As soon as Darcy was side by side with the torture box, Mitchell stopped walking.

"You're in too deep, but I can get your mother out of this mess," Darcy said, trying to reason with Mitchell.

He scoffed. "It's amazing that after everything that's happened, you still believe I'm that stupid."

Darcy looked past the Berretta, making eye contact with Ethan and keeping it.

"You know the charges against my mother are bogus. I doubt very much the DA will move forward, but even if he does it'll be dismissed before it goes to trial. I'm not worried."

"Why are you here then?" Darcy tried to sound less worried than he felt.

"You really are dense." Mitchell moved toward the kitchen island and leaned against it without losing his aim at Darcy's head. "I wonder if your partner, the big guy, is smarter than you." He shook his head, mocking him.

Darcy needed to get an angle on this guy fast or things would end really badly—and maybe not just for him and Shelby.

"So humor me. If it's not to get your mother out, why are you here? Why hurt my dog?"

"I actually like dogs. I felt kind of bad about doing this to her." He lowered his gun, secure in the distance that separated them. "I built the cage for a person. It was my latest creation, but I never got a chance to use it, since you pushed me out of my condo before I could try it on the hooker."

Darcy felt his body tense up. He wanted to charge at him but knew he didn't have a chance.

"But why do it at all? You had us, you had escaped. I bet you were probably on your way to Mexico when you saw the news about the call girl."

"Very good, Detective."

Before Mitchell could continue, Darcy's cell rang.

He didn't make a move to retrieve it. Mitchell didn't give him instructions either way, so they both stared at each other without saying a word. After the fifth ring, it stopped.

"You have a bad habit of not answering your phone," Mitchell said.

"Only when I'm busy with something important."

Mitchell nodded almost imperceptibly. Darcy was amazed at how used to the darkness his eye had gotten. He could see the man's face clearly, his microexpressions, his nascent crow's-feet. His eyes were cold. He'd seen those eyes before in Stepan Kozlov. Darcy lifted his hand to rub his temple, but before he was able to soothe his itching eye, Mitchell shook his head.

"Keep your hands away from your body."

Darcy was sure Mitchell was going to kill him. What he didn't know was if he would torture him first. As soon as he was done with whatever he'd come to do, he would end his life. There was no doubt.

His phone started ringing again. Mitchel shook his head. There was a hint of annoyance in his expression.

"So tell me what you want," Darcy said over the noise of the phone.

He watched the man's face. The moment he blinked, Darcy made a quick lateral move and charged against him. Mitchell fired. The bang masked Shelby's whimpers. The bullet shattered the window that led to the backyard and got lost somewhere in the night.

The phone started ringing again.

Darcy pushed his body against Mitchell's, hoping to crack his back against the edge of the kitchen island. He grabbed the arm that held the gun, keeping it from pointing at his head again.

Mitchell's body bent backward against the flat surface, but there was no expression of pain. With sheer force, Mitchell managed to lift his torso back to a straight position, and headbutted Darcy. The pain was so intense, Darcy saw a flash of white. It took everything he had to not let go of the hand with the gun.

Then Mitchell threw a left hook straight to his right temple, and the white he'd seen before turned into a hundred flashing stars. Darcy rotated and slammed Mitchell's arm on top of the island, then landed his right elbow on Ethan's forearm with the entire weight of his body. As soon as the arm gave a little, Darcy slammed it against the edge, trying to break it. Mitchell cried out, and the Beretta flopped onto the floor.

Before Darcy could go for it, Mitchell punched him in the ribs. Darcy felt one or two crack. He was short of breath but continued to scramble to get loose.

As he turned, a flash of outside light reflected on the blade of a six-inch knife in Mitchell's hand.

Darcy's first reaction was to move away, but he was too slow. Mitchell pushed the knife into his side, just below where he had punched him a second earlier. Darcy felt the thrust of the blade, breaking skin, then going deep. Mitchell pulled the knife out. Before Darcy could cover the wound, Mitchell stabbed him in the stomach. Darcy doubled over, trying to shield the lacerations, feeling the warm blood seeping through his fingers.

"Man, what the hell are you doing with the door open?" Sorensen's voice came through from the front door. "Why aren't you answering your phone?"

Darcy wanted to yell, but nothing came out. He looked up, still holding his side, and slowly sliding to the floor. He saw Mitchell weighing his odds. A split second later, Mitchell dropped the knife on the floor and sprinted out of the house through the broken window.

In a low voice he wasn't even sure left his mouth, Darcy called for his partner as everything went black.

CHAPTER 113

Six days later—Black Friday

Saffron looked around the room. The flowers that had filled it for days were starting to fade. They had been gorgeous, colorful. They'd brightened the room, especially when it was sunny outside and the light made them shine. But now some petals had fallen, and the previously cheerful colors were a dull brown that matched the darkness she felt inside.

Trying to push her sorrow away, she reached for her Kindle. The broken ribs and the stitches in her torso screamed for her to stop. I know better than this, she scolded herself. Instead of moving her entire upper body to get the e-reader, she reached for it with her arm. Feeling it, she grabbed it and turned it on. She browsed through the books she already had but decided to get something new.

"Busy?" Darcy asked from the door.

She set the Kindle on her lap and looked up. He was smiling.

"I've missed you," she said.

He nodded.

"They let you get up?" she asked him.

"No. I had to work my charm with the head nurse." He rolled himself slowly into the room, pushing in front of him a tall IV drip connected to his arm by a long tube and a thick needle.

"Should I be jealous?" She reached out to touch his arm.

"Absolutely." He kissed her palm. "I need to get a black marker and write something on your cast." He tapped her leg.

"You do."

She touched his face. His stubble tickled her hand.

"Do you guys brag about the wounds acquired in the line of duty?" Saffron asked.

Darcy smiled. "Sometimes. More early on. It's like stripes: the more you have, the tougher you are." He paused for a few moments. "Then you realize it's actually better to have fewer than many, and you stop bragging."

"Bummer." She pouted.

"Why?"

He pulled himself off the wheelchair and was trying to sit on the bed, but it was a little high, so he was having a hard time. He winced but finally managed.

"No reason."

"Oh come on." He tapped her leg again.

A shadow passed over her face.

"I'm sorry I couldn't save your sister," he said, squeezing her hand.

"I'm sorry I couldn't save my sister," she said, a feeling of guilt swelling up in her throat. "He made her drink antifreeze . . ."

Saffron wiped her eyes, feeling more rage than sadness.

There was a knock on the door.

"I had to pull in a lot of favors to get her in here," Sorensen said, still outside the room, holding Shelby by a short leash. The dog's tail was wagging so hard, her entire body swayed from side to side.

"Oh my God." Saffron tapped the side of the bed to get Shelby to come to her. Sorensen let the leash go, and the dog ran toward the bed. They both petted her, trying to move their bodies as little as possible, to not pull any stitches. The dog moved from his hand to hers, licking both.

"So you came to get rid of the dog, or you really missed me?" Darcy joked.

"Melissa offered me a choice: I could go shopping with her and my mother-in-law, or I could come visit you." Sorensen made a weighing gesture with his hands. "It really was a hard choice."

"She hates you that much?"

"Apparently." Lifting two large paper bags, he added, "I brought turkey and cranberry sandwiches. Leftovers from yesterday."

"And Jon promised to bring his mom's famous pecan pie later," Darcy said.

"I'll go and get drinks," Sorensen said, leaving the room.

Darcy looked at Saffron. Tiny lines framed his eyes. She hadn't seen him this surprised in a while.

"Are you okay?" he asked.

She nodded and caressed the hand that was now brushing her cheek.

Sorensen coughed as he walked back in, then set the drinks on the table and started handing out sandwiches.

Saffron took the first bite. "Yum. I've never had anything better in my life."

Before Darcy took a bite, he asked, "Any news on Mitchell?"

"Nope. He's gone."

"For now."

THE END

ACKNOWLEDGMENTS

Thank you for reading my book! Thank you, thank you for taking the time to read it, and for sharing a bit of your life with me. I hope you loved it. I hope it entertained you, and you had a good time while you were immersed in it!

B F—Thank you for sharing some incredible experiences with me that helped spark a couple great scenes in the book. Thank you also for giving me ideas I would have never come up with on my own.

Chris Grall—Thank you for reading my book with fresh eyes, and for working relentlessly on all the pieces that weren't quite working. Thank you for creating such awesome scenarios on PowerPoint (I'm very visual, and those helped so much!). Thank you for brainstorming with me and for not giving up, even when I was whiny and stubborn! Your weapons, police-procedure and military-procedure knowledge has been incredibly valuable in making my book much more realistic than it would have been. You are definitely an incredible asset for any author working in mysteries or thrillers.

Dan—Thank you for reading my rough draft and for providing insights that made it better.

Sergeant Dave Gutierrez—Thank you so much for taking the time to meet with me and for giving me such an in-depth view of the life of a homicide detective in SJPD. I learned a lot, and you definitely helped make my book much more realistic.

Don Lee—Thank you for reading an early draft, providing feedback, and for keeping me honest about how far Carmel really is.

Ely—Thank you for sharing your connections with me. Finding Jorge was absolutely invaluable.

Grant Blackwood—Thank you for being my teacher at the Master CraftFest. I cannot express how much I learned in that class. You are such a great teacher, and I am a better writer because of your class and your feedback on my first three thousand words.

JF—Thank you for brainstorming with me until our brain cells were dry. Thank you for all the insight into the Marine Corps, for all the nuances and the gems only somebody who loves the Marines and has been a part of them for so long would really know.

J. Valdes, 4138—Thank you for taking me on such a great ride-along, and for helping me gather so much information I will be able to use in the future. Also, thank you for letting me in on the code for fire.

Jack Zowin—Thank you for wanting to help me again on my second book. Thank you for sharing your experience and expertise, for reading an early draft, and for providing the insight and feedback I needed. I really appreciate that you relentlessly question things that don't make sense, and because of that, my work is always improves after you've read it.

Jemmy—Thank you for reading one of my earlier drafts and taking the time to provide comments and fixes. Thank you for being honest. I truly believe the story is better because of you.

Joe Torre - Thank you for sharing with me your vast knowledge of firearms, for recommending cool, believable guns for my characters to use, and for walking through some scenarios with me, to ensure I wasn't making a fool of myself. Thank you for reading the relevant excerpts and for pointing out where I could make things more credible.

Sergeant John Marfia—Thank you so much for setting me up on ride-alongs and for answering my crazy questions at all hours of the day or night. Thank you for sharing information and for giving me such an incredible insight into SJPD.

Jorge—Thank you so much for reviewing the book with me and for the great suggestions. I feel much happier knowing that you've taken a look at my final draft.

Kevin Metcalf—Thank you for telling me my first chapter was awful and that if you didn't know me, you would have stopped reading right then. I fixed it, and I think it is much better because of you. And no, my intention was not to start a new genre!

Lisa Fitzpatrick—Thank you for the amazing cover. Thank you for making it so easy to work with you, for having such deep sensitivities about book design, for being so much fun to work with, and for taking on the work of my website and my dad's project! Thank you for all of the extra stuff you do to help me. I love working with you!

Mos—Thank you for being the best mom in the world! Thank you for being with me every step of the way. Thank you for brainstorming with me, for telling me when plot points work or don't work, and for always being supportive. Thank you for the endless hours of editing, for not letting me give up, and for always pushing me to never settle, to always make the book better. There is no way I could have written a second book without your daily help. I love you.

Marcus Trower—Thank you so much for being my copy editor again. I cannot express how grateful I am that you decided to work with me on my second novel. If you don't watch out, the third one will be on your lap before you know it! (If there are any typos at all, they are all my fault for changing something at the last minute without running it by you. I'm sorry!)

Marge—Thank you so much for working on my back-cover copy. It is probably the most stressful thing in the entire process of writing the book, and you made it so easy and fun!

Mariella—Thank your for all of your help with the back-cover copy too! Your contributions made it perfect. Thank you for creating the fun FB group, and thank you for always being supportive and encouraging. I'm so lucky to be your friend!

Mark Nelson—Thank you for reading my roughest draft. Thank you for helping me so much with the wordsmithing, for hearing me vent, for not allowing me to give up, for helping me with the bio and the back-cover copy. Thank you for being at SUAW, and for cheering me on. And when are you going to get your book out? It's time!

The Marine Corps and all the other branches of the military—Thank you for being brave and honorable and going out there in the world to do things most of us don't have the guts to do. I apologize for not putting the military in a good light in this book, but that does not reflect my opinion in any way. I admire what you do, and I am very grateful for your hard work and dedication.

Matt Croucher—Thank you so much for taking me on such interesting ride-alongs. I learned a lot about San Jose, its crime community, gangs, police procedure, and so many other things I never would have learned on my own.

Mickey—Thank you for working out some medical scenarios with me and figuring out what were the right recovery times for specific injuries.

Miguel Angel Lopez—Thank you for describing in so much detail several medical procedures, for helping me with research, and for being so awesome!

Panera Bread—Thank you for allowing us to crash in your café for hours on end while we write and write and write. Thank you for not kicking us out, ever! But please change the music—it really is horrible.

Papos—Thank you for loving me, supporting me and always encouraging me to go as far as possible. You are an incredible inspiration and I love you so much!

Ted Smits—Thank you for reading my rough draft, for being honest, for always cheering me on, and for being so supportive!

ThrillerFest—Thank you for another incredible conference this year. Every year it is better; every time I learn so much! Thank you for supporting thriller authors, and for making the experience so valuable and so much fun!

Writers' Police Academy and Andy Russell—Thank you for the incredible four days in NC learning hands-on so much about police procedure and emergency response. I cannot describe how incredibly valuable this conference was (and it was so much fun!). Also, the workshop on the felony murder investigation was incredible! I learned so many things I needed to know for my books. Thank you, Andy!